ASHER'S FALL

ASHER'S FALL

THE DESCENDING WORLDS BOOK 1

JUSTIN S. LESLIE

Podium

Published in 2023 by Podium Publishing, ULC
www.podiumaudio.com

ASHER'S FALL

*"The battlefield is a scene of constant chaos.
The winner will be the one who controls that chaos, both
his own and the enemies'."*

—Napoleon Bonaparte

JUICE

Alarms screamed like a hungry newborn child in step with strobing red lights around the cockpit as angry blast shields slammed shut. Footsteps hammered on the grated floor as the ship's commander and the main pilot thumped into their seats.

"*Asher-5*, report!" Captain Rick Bearing, better known as Juice, barked at the flashing monitor.

"Sir?" Laura, also known as Mac, a newly minted copilot, asked without purpose, staring at her screen.

The ship's AI system dinged, replying under the commanding direction of its senior officer. "*All systems have been diverted to preservation protocol.*"

"Sir?" the young pilot again asked in desperation.

Juice leaned back in his padded seat like a man knowing the stars above had decided their fate, giving him no choice but to accept it with open arms. "We're no longer this ship's priority. Plus, you can drop the *sir* bullshit; that game just left the station."

The man's often stoic yet mild Southern accent was no longer having its usual charming effect. Captain Bearing now sounded at peace with whatever situation they were now in.

"What… Sir? What the hell does that mean?"

Smacking the screen in front of him, Juice silenced the alarms. Red strobing lights continued dancing off the dull, shadowed metal walls as the blast shields slowly started to reopen. "Meaning whatever is in the cargo bay of this ship is more important than us."

The ship's uncaring automated warning system sprang to life. "*Please vacate the main sectors and proceed to your designated evacuation pod. The life-support system will go offline in five minutes.*"

"I don't understand." Laura replied, confused, standing up as Juice continued to relax in his seat, his firm jaw jutting forward. "Sir, we have to go."

"You go. Use the crew pod. It's still accessible. There's only room for one in there. I'll be fine. A captain goes down with his ship and all that jazz. Plus, I want to see what the hell just attacked the ship and try to report back."

"Attacked the ship?"

The two paused as Juice looked back with bloodshot yet calculating eyes, again reinforcing his previous command. "Go to the crew pod. Report that we have been attacked and ping our location. Hell, we're so far out, I doubt they'll even get the initial alert for months."

"We have fighters in the bay always on standby. Can't we scramble them?" Laura asked.

Juice pressed another button as a sizeable monolithic screen quickly lurched out of the industrial metal floor in front of them. There, staring back at the two, was a diagram of the ship. Unlike any prior representation of the *Asher-5*, this one only showed the cockpit and storage hold in a slowly decaying green. The rest of the ship was a violent red.

"How is this possible?"

Before the alarms went off, the two had been in the primary crew rest area, separate from the rest of the ship. Steaming cups of coffee sat in front of them while the crew prepared to disembark on an uncharted planet simply called OB-3, standing for *outer bands* plus the correlating planet number in their assigned sector. The issue was this was an unexplored sector. At least they assumed as much.

"About to find out. Lieutenant, tell you what," Juice started in a fatherly tone. "You go prepare the escape pod, and I'll be along shortly. There's another one still in the green area."

Laura shook her head, hesitating as she turned, finally running out of the cockpit. Juice, sensing her out of harm's way, pressed the bridge-lock override, slamming it shut. The woman froze, only to have the chaotic noise of the bridge go silent.

"Sir! Dammit! Sir!" she screamed to an uncaring blast door. Realizing the shit storm Laura, also known as Lieutenant McAlister, Mac for short, was now in, the young woman sprinted to the yellow hatch she had trained to use while in the Fleet Academy.

This wasn't supposed to happen, Laura thought, slowly twisting the sealed release catch, only to have a sucking hiss make her stomach flip. The seal was disintegrating between the small pod and the ship. Whatever damage had occurred likely destroyed the other escape pods, sealing the fate of the rest of the crew.

She knew what the violet-red on the status monitor meant. The rest of the crew and attached fighter wing would not be joining her on the planet's surface. A tear streaked the young lieutenant's face out of frustration more than sadness. She quickly closed the main pod door, screaming in rage, her soft, pale skin turning colors in time with the flashing warning lights.

Ignoring all the safety checks from her academy training, the young woman slammed the restraining straps over her shoulders as a helmet slowly lowered over her head. Within seconds, a full suit of space armor had also joined the chorus, setting in place around its host.

Without further thought, Lieutenant McAlister hammered the red button clearly labeled to keep low-rating new recruits from pushing it. With a lurching *whoosh*, the thrusters screamed to life, shooting the pod away from the ship at eye-blurring speeds.

Juice reached into his flight suit, pulling out a small flask. While he never drank on the job, it was a tradition in the Void to carry a small shot-sized liquor flask from home. For the captain of the *Asher-5*, home was Tennessee, and the flask held whiskey.

Continuing his planned ritual for situations like this, the man pulled out his small personal tablet. After a few quick jabs, a family materialized on the screen from happier days.

A woman with sun-kissed skin beamed a thousand-watt smile while Juice himself wrapped one of his arms around her waist. Green grass and inviting trees surrounded the group in a loving embrace supporting the weight of their happy lives.

In front of them were two golden retrievers. One was almost reddish brown, resembling an old glass of sherry. The other was close to cloud-white, both grinning at the camera, clearly wanting to turn back to their owners.

"Sorry, guys. I let you down, but I'll be around," Juice told the glowing tablet. He followed this by kissing the screen, only to be met by the biting sting of whiskey. He knew this would be his last taste of home. Thoughts of good times long past skipped off his tastebuds as a slight grin perked his lips, reminding him how drunk he had gotten off the stuff the night he had met his future wife.

A comet-like streak jetted out of the ship to his right as an escape pod shot toward the planet, leaving a trail of glowing sparks. Seeing this, the doomed ship's commander focused on the chaos unfolding before him.

Remnants of the back of the ship floated in front of his accepting yet angry eyes as light flickers of electricity danced from the still-active parts of the ship's guts now drifting in front of him. Juice slid his fingers over the weapon controls, knowing they wouldn't work.

Leaning forward, he pressed a red button, followed by entering a code. Screens flickered as several silent alarms started sounding. The man was effectively hitting the ship's delete button for all systems. This also included a recently installed and activated one-of-a-kind artificial intelligence system.

Before a glowing light enveloped his vision, Juice's eyes widened as he homed in on the indescribable attacker. "Station one, this is Captain Bearing…" Silence followed as a focused beam of light evaporated the bridge's sole inhabitant.

CHAPTER 1

TERRA MINOR THREE

Overly loud rock music echoed off the walls of the small temporary Viper Company command pod sitting on the edge of a temporary camp overlooking the sparkling blue ocean of Terra Minor Three. Two men in half-soldier, half-leisure wear lay sprawled out in retractable lounge chairs sitting on orange-tinted grass, finally forced to move after several hours of napping contemplation.

"Sir, First Sergeant," Specialist Kline huffed out, looking at his feet as the more grizzled of the two men grunted, pushing himself up. The one thing about deep-space quadrant missions the two experienced men hated was the requirement for a captain and a first sergeant to be in charge of not only their company but the ship's command as well.

"Specialist Kline, I take it the universe is ending, or we're finally getting the new AI system activated?" First Sergeant Tim Becket growled like an old V8 of years long since passed. Hard lines and a perpetually stubbled chin sounded like sandpaper as the man rubbed his face.

The much younger yet also battle-worn man sitting beside him started the same process of sitting up as Kline began to talk, only to have Becket hold up a finger.

"Sir, Specialist Kline here thinks something's really important." The two men snorted lightly as Kline's radio barked to life.

"Kline, you better be by the camp. It's General Ran," a stern woman's voice commanded. It was Pearl, their Solarian navigational and executive officer. This got the two men's attention, as they immediately shifted into soldier mode.

"Music off," Captain Ben Dailey instructed the small box sitting on the ground. "What's up? We finally get slotted to get the AI activated?" Dailey followed in a conversational tone echoing Becket's, running a hand through his chin-length wavy blond hair. While the man was tall, he wasn't overbearing. Dailey kept an air of confidence swirling around him, often compared to a tornado in a trailer park.

Being from Florida, Captain Dailey had ensured his sun-kissed skin remained an acceptable shade of tan. As for the rest of him, from the aviator sunglasses to the light smell of rum from Earth, rarely had anyone ever had to ask him where home was. On the other hand, Becket held those cards close to his chest.

"Sir. General Ran has requested a conference. Still no word on the AI."

Becket glanced at Captain Dailey. "Boss, did we send in a sitrep for the month?" He clearly assumed they hadn't.

Dailey cleared his throat as the scar tracing Becket's face from his hairline to his jaw twitched. "For once. Yes."

Both men grunted as the radio again erupted. "He's waiting."

The sheer effort needed to conduct a live conversation, not to mention live or holo-projected video feed this far out was enough to draw anyone's attention. This meant that every relay station between their current location and that on the other end had to be coordinated, synched, secured, and managed.

This doubled the immediate pucker factor, pushing the two men to take off briskly. Overhead, a shuttle hummed away from the mid-sized space frigate known as the USF *Murphy*, dwarfing the landscape. USF stood for United Space Federation, a naval designation that had been tweaked and applied to spaceships over the decades.

The one positive note about deep-space quadrant missions was the use of interstellar frigates capable of landing on the surface of a planet. Most space-fleet ships' extra capabilities were steered toward offensive capabilities instead of orbital thrusters.

The USF *Murphy* was one of the more versatile and fastest new ships in the Fleet, capable of additional suborbital stationary operations several miles or even feet off the ground. If the frigate couldn't stand and fight, it could put on a pair of running shoes and disappear into what was known as the Void.

The Void was a term used for mostly unexplored space on the outer reaches of the galaxy, its origin coming from the blind spot on the opposite side of the Milky Way's galactic core. To put it into perspective, Earth was roughly twenty-five thousand light-years, give or take, from the center of the Milky Way galaxy, on the edge of a spiral arm called Orion's Spur, meaning Earth was located halfway between the center of the galaxy and its outer edge.

Double that and add another twenty thousand light-years in the opposite direction, and you found the opposing edge of the galaxy, also considered the Void. The term was now used when referring to any area not fully charted and explored. As of the dawn of true interstellar space flight, most of the outer spirals, often called bands, had been explored on Earth's side of the galaxy.

The aforementioned AI system was a new protocol recently approved for installation in Fleet military ships to help navigate such vast distances. All the *Murphy* needed was one final upload to activate the protocol. This would allow for smoother operation onboard and, as a plus, the ability to go long distances with a smaller crew.

Many of the galaxy's mining corporations already had AI installed on their ships, as well as private civilian ships. It had taken a literal act of congress, or in this case, the Federation Senate, to get the approval to use AI systems in a military capacity.

For every inch of unexplored space covered, the Void grew smaller. Soldiers, Fleet crewmembers, and aviators alike on the USF *Murphy* had undergone the Void ceremony twelve months prior. This included getting hammered off cheap fleet rum, not the real Earth stuff, and getting a tattoo of a black triangle on their forearms. The gesture added to the other symbolic tattoos adorning most of Viper Company's members as well as the attached attack-fighter wing.

Not caring about his flowery open short-sleeved shirt, Captain Dailey jumped in the front seat of the vert rover. "Sir, you need me to drive?"

Kline asked with no response as he was quickly slung into the seat by the aggressive acceleration of the combat rover.

Whirling electric motors and jingling loose items clanked as the vehicle shot toward the lowered cargo bay of the ship. The USF *Murphy*, compared to the alien landscape, sat like an angled metal beast of war. Massive thrusters adorned the long hull of the ship as it sat a couple of stories off the ground on extended compression jumpers.

Its belly looked bloated, full of attack-wing fighters poised to rain death on anyone that dared call the machine fat. The impression of a large belly was short-lived as one looked up at the peaking topsides adorned in antennas and god only knew what type of weapon systems. Large turrets for photon, plasma cannons, and various other armaments sat ready at a moment's notice to protect the vessel's precious cargo as well as dishing out a volley of pain.

Sitting afront the forward hull, resembling a sleek tower surrounded by two large skeletal-style braces, was the bridge adorned in glass and blast-shield bays. Above the bridge and slightly behind, the ship's main communications array and several super turrets stretched along its spine like an all-you-can-eat buffet of kiss my ass, served directly by the USF *Murphy*. The ship sheltered well over one hundred Army soldiers, Space Force pilots, and Space Naval Fleet support crew on loan from Fleet Command.

Viper Company consisted of four platoons of highly capable, often problematic Space Nova Rangers considered to be amongst some of the most elite fighters in the Fleet. The attached attack-fighter wing was just as prominent. The metamorphic armor the Rangers wore allowed them to function in almost any environment, including being coupled to the side of the specialized attack fighters assigned to the group.

This lethal combination had created some of the most storied adventures the Fleet often tried to bury as *unrecommendable risky behavior,* meaning Viper Company was currently running exploration missions after being put in the time-out corner.

The once mighty company, a group of Space Nova Rangers from the famed Pathfinder Battalion, had been effectively sidelined to exploratory missions on the opposite side of the Central Systems, away from the rest of the Fleet. They had earned this light punishment after some questionable tactics during the Scourge Rebellion two years prior.

After destroying an uninhabited moon, less the bad guys, in the Wren sector, including their own ship, the Company had been symbolically reprimanded in public and praised in private, including the attached attack wing.

Luckily for the group, this was only a mild necessary slap on the hand, as they had also prevented the Scourge, a nasty group of anti-Federation off-world terrorists, from taking over one of the Fleet's prized space destroyers.

When the final report was sent in, all Captain Dailey stated was, "*The entire Scourge Rebellion is effectively over.*" Asked to clarify, the man simply replied, "*They go boom in my ship. I need a new ship…*"

No longer concerned with anything else, the two men marched through the ship, catching any watching eyes' attention, finally making it to the briefing room. A holographic older man, with more rank than Dailey or Becket would ever obtain, shifted.

"Sir," Dailey spoke up quickly, realizing what he was wearing. "Shit," he huffed as the general cleared his throat.

"I see you are setting a good example as always, Dailey. Becket, can't you keep him at least looking presentable?"

The use of names and not formal rank caught both men off guard. While it seemed informal, this meant something to the men. They were about to be asked to do something incredibly dangerous, under the radar, or a combination of both.

"Sir," Becket replied gruffly, smirking at Dailey. "I'm lucky he has pants on today."

With the bullshit-cutting banter out of the way, solidifying that this was likely under the radar, General Ran started. "We received a message from Captain Bearing and a subsequent report that his ship was either lost or…"

"Or what?" Dailey interjected, not liking the mention of his friend Juice being in harm's way.

"Listen, in case you two have forgotten, I was put in charge of the Outer Perimeter Colonizing Command. Sounds boring, but I can assure you it's anything but."

Becket walked over to the holo-table, handing Dailey a cup of go juice. "Sounds like a flower name to cover up a covert operation."

Ran nodded. "Yes."

"Why are you reaching out to us? You have the entire Saturn fleet at your disposal for the most part," Dailey asked as Kline nodded, crossing his arms over his chest, garnering a stare from even the hologram. "Kline, get Lieutenant Brax in here. She needs to get any strays back onboard."

The ship's commander was referring to the attack wing's leader, a lead squadron pilot that had joined the crew immediately after her predecessor had bowed out due to what was referred to as a *lack of intestinal fortitude* after the Scourge Rebellion incident.

While the combination of branches wasn't out of the ordinary, the space frontier Rangers were a different breed, their blend of space-infantry fighting and all-out capability for ground assault leading to the odd mix. Most traditional ships and commands hated the autonomy afforded the Pathfinders, an even more specialized group of Nova Space Rangers.

"I'm not going to sugarcoat it. The *Asher-5* was last reported half a parsec from your current location."

This forced what coffee Dailey had in his mouth to shoot out violently, including a quick dribble now escaping his nose. After regaining his composure, Becket stepped forward.

"Sir, that's almost a light-year from our location, and we are as far out as it gets. There are no reports of anyone or anything this far out," the gruff first sergeant noted as the flat look on General Ran's face answered the assumption.

"It's always something," Dailey mumbled. "General, send the coordinates. If Juice is in trouble, that means he needs help. Hell, we all might need help."

Dailey and Juice had not only attended the academy together but had been bitter rivals in climbing to the top of Pathfinder selection. It was a rivalry that started with disdain and ended in utter respect for each other.

Either knew all they needed to do was reach out, and the other would be there. Seeing the expression on Dailey's face, General Ran knew he had the right team on the job.

Ran paused, not cutting the feed. "Be safe. And let's keep this off the front pages. Captain Dailey, I'll send what I can on Captain Bearing's mission."

"What precisely is that mission?" Dailey asked, not using the past tense.

"It's classified, but I'll send what I can on the secured red line."

With that, the figure winked out of existence as stale silence filled the humming void of the holoprojector.

"How long will it take to get the attack wings in?" Dailey asked, calculating as Lieutenant Jenny Brax shuffled into the room. Jen, as her counterparts called her, was middle height, blonde, and full of wire-tight youthful strength.

"Nice shirt," she teased as Becket rolled his eyes. The captain's Hawaiian-style shirt had not gone unnoticed while making his way to the briefing deck. "Oh, shit, this is serious."

The look on Dailey's face was all the leader of the fighter attack wing needed to see. "I'll get them here and docked in thirty minutes. We only have three fighters out today. They were only going three sectors away to drop off a supply pod to one of the habitations."

Habitations were small scientific and pioneering teams that had become the USF *Murphy*'s recent assignment. While Terra Minor Three's surface was flush with plants and semi-friendly wildlife, it lacked any sentient life, from what the group could tell. They had, of course, also not explored the entire planet, opting to take a little break on the pristine shores of the nerve-calming ocean, a habit the crew was not complaining about as long as the rations of rum stayed intact.

Science Officer Bellman had figured out a way to synthesize the Nova Rangers' beverage of choice from a sweet fruit on the planet's shoreline resembling a coconut. He had been given an unofficial award for bravery in the line of duty for this accomplishment in forwarding science in the name of the crew's sanity.

The truth of the matter was the crew, even though taking a break, was training on drop tactics and marksmanship. The creed of Viper Company had spilled over to the attack wing as well: *Play hard and fight even harder.*

CHAPTER 2

THROUGH THE FIRE AND THE FLAME

Skeletal trees, still naked from the initial landing, snapped as the massive thrusters of the USF *Murphy* joined the initial shock of the compression jumpers activating, giving the enormous space bull a much-needed push. Dailey tapped several buttons on the console in front of him as the rest of the crew worked like a well-oiled machine in completing their assigned ground launch protocols.

The bridge was set up for tactical efficiency. Captain Dailey sat in a sizeable pod-like throne in the back of the cockpit. Two fleet navigators sat in oversized chairs connected to consoles and controls, both being manipulated as dull lights allowed them to focus on the data fed through their monitors. A ground launch was one of the more technical maneuvers the space frigate undertook.

In front of this group were two weapon specialists surrounded by targeting screens. To Dailey's left and right was the engineering team consisting of two officers with one simple job: ensure all the blinky lights on the ship layout panels continued blinking green. In the event they turned red, well, that was how they earned their paycheck.

This crew had been with Captain Dailey and First Sergeant Becket during the Scourge Rebellion and followed their fearless leader's orders without reservation. They would have nothing less. This included some rather odd selections for members of the bridge crew.

First Sergeant Becket stayed in the launch bay with the attack wing leadership. Part of the launch protocol was for the pilots to be in their fighters, ready to evacuate or protect the ship at its most vulnerable.

"Jamison, thruster report?" Dailey requested as the young, skinny, one-eared man jabbed several buttons, already knowing the answer but giving one last confirmation before the order to go into orbital thruster overload.

"Forty percent, sir. Ready for thrust-off."

Satisfied with the report and row of green indicators on his screen, Captain Dailey signaled the lead navigation officer, known as Pearl for her snow-white skin.

"Engaged," Pearl replied as gravity mushed the crew's asses as far down in their seats as physically possible.

Pearl was an off-worlder from Solaria, also known as ASP-1, or Active Society Planet Number One. This was the first known friendly civilization to make contact with Earth, and its most trusted ally.

The Solarian had joined the Fleet after her planet had been selected for inclusion. To date, ten worlds had earned this distinction. On the other hand, only Solarians were allowed to join the Fleet, with others wanting to follow.

Roaring thrusters, combined with the sound of stressed reinforced-metal structural supports flexing, converged in a droning hum, putting a smile on Dailey's face. However, this grin was short-lived as he started pondering what had pushed Juice this far out of the Central Systems, having not yet reviewed the mission files.

Within twenty minutes of concluding General Ran's meeting, the USF *Murphy* was starting its ascent into the heavens.

The main front still being watched from the Alurian Wars was an area of the Beta quadrant far from the Central Systems dubbed the Outer Spiral. The Central Systems were an oddball cluster of stars that kept revealing habitable planets, often populated with various levels of civilization, some already with space travel capabilities. On the other side of the Outer Spiral was the deep ocean of space between the two galaxies also referred to as the Void.

Terra Minor Three, the planet they had just vacated, was void of native sentient life, much like the majority of worlds the Fleet encountered farther away from the Central System they explored. The main front, on the other hand, had on several occasions also produced less than hospitable discoveries and planets.

As of 2075, the development of inverted reverse fusion had finally allowed the inhabitants of Earth to reach for the distant stars. Thermal fusion-thruster technology had been the tool that allowed ships to leave orbit and continue on at unimaginable speeds. This was, over time, improved through the use of thermomagnetic fields around starships, allowing what was lovingly called hyperdrives to slingshot whatever vessel they powered at mind-melting, faster-than-light speeds.

This, in turn, created a power struggle on the planet's surface, leading to several short, violent wars in an effort to avert total global domination by what was once upon a time called the West. From this, the United Federation was formed to prevent such acts of war from happening again.

Soon after the Federation's creation, the first of several alien races came seeking a supposed peace. This peace was short-lived. The will of the human race proved too much to control as the inhabitants of Earth came together in a time of great need.

What was known as the Tectonic Wars lasted twenty destructively grueling years, mainly against the Alurians. The race of moderately humanoid aliens was pushed back to whatever hole they had come from, with the help of the Solarians.

An off-putting shade of greyish green, the Alurians looked like the mix between an oversized human and a lizard of some random pissed-off type. They leaned more toward the human end of the spectrum, ensuring their lizard-like features only gave them a nightmarish appearance.

While also known as the Alurian War, the shift, created not only from the physical scars of war on the planet but of humankind itself, was compared to the shift in Earth's tectonic plates, forever changing the planet.

It wasn't lost on anyone that the Alurians' home world or worlds had never truly been identified. The Federation's best guess was the near side of a neighboring galaxy. Random encounters, while rare, still occurred as the Federation continued to expand. During this time, as with any war-driven society, technology and the will to develop grew at an unmatched rate with the inclusion of captured alien technology.

While it wasn't stated in the open, the worlds the United Federation had signed a treaty of inclusion with were shocked at the level of resolve and power the human race now possessed.

"Sir, we have reached stable orbit; powering down main lift thrusters," Pearl announced as Dailey nodded.

"I want us clear of the planet in an hour. Here." Dailey started plugging in a set of coordinates given to him by the general. "Put us on the following heading. Also, radio the habitation team and let them know we have relayed their coordinates to the closest Fleet outpost if needed."

With the crew not having been fully briefed before leaving, this caught the rest of the bridge's attention.

"Sir?" One of the young navigators, named Brick, for his massive size, spoke up.

"I need a few hours to get everything situated. I'll get a briefing together for twenty-two hundred," Dailey paused, knowing he needed to give his team the trust he expected in return. "Captain Bearing has been reported missing, and his ship is not responding."

Satisfied with this brief explanation—the crew knew the professional relationship between the two captains—asses shifted in seats.

Pearl unbuckled her harness, standing up. "There are no known reports of any mission farther out than ours in the Void. A few wandering mining companies, sure, but it would stand to reason that Captain Bearing was out here on a mission."

Dailey grunted. "Game faces, guys. This may be nothing, but it's no different than any other mission."

Dailey also unbuckled from his seat, running his fingers through his longer-than-regulation-permitted hair. "Twenty-two hundred, briefing room."

The door slid shut behind the man as Becket stood in the hallway. "The mission package just came through. We also have a small problem."

"There's no such thing as small problems in our world. Spill it."

Becket pointed at the small arms closet as a whimper followed by the smash of flesh against metal echoed in the dimly lit hall. He quickly scanned his handprint and the door slid open, revealing a medium-sized dog, a smooth-coated, jet-black animal.

Rule number one on an exploratory vessel was to not harbor any un-approved or unidentified creatures onboard without following protocol. "Great, a stowaway," Dailey noted, leaning down.

The creature had round, dark black eyes sitting further apart than a dog's from Earth. It also had an oddly shaped body with a catlike frame mixing with the stance and demeanor of a dog. A pink-scaled tongue darted in and out of a round mouth. Dailey finally figured out what was different about the creature. It had a short snout, taking on an almost humanlike appearance.

When Becket reached down, the doglike creature bowed its head, allowing the man to lightly pet it. A light spark popped as he touched the smooth, sleek fur. "Good boy, or… You promise to be good?"

The creature blinked, licking Dailey's hand. "Deal. For now, we'll call you Sparky," he responded. "Set Sparky up in the freight bay. One of the engineers down there will take care of him," Dailey noted as Becket nodded, punching out a note on his tablet for someone to take the creature. Most crews would simply eject the creature into space. Not this team, and sure as hell not in front of the other crewmembers.

Dailey had always judged people on how they treated animals. This was carried over into his own philosophy. Kline quickly appeared, having received the message, as if he had been looking after the creature the entire time.

"At least somebody likes you," Becket chuckled as the two men headed toward the briefing room.

"Secure the room," Dailey instructed the ART system. Standing for Artificial Reliance Terminal, the system was capable of not only following instructions but also suggesting them in certain nonmilitary-related circumstances. This included things such as *I recommend flushing the toilet* or *Please close the window.*

A red halo traced the door, telling not only the two men standing inside but others walking by that important, possibly classified information was being reviewed inside.

Becket walked up to the main briefing table in the center of the room, punching several buttons as an interstellar map appeared in the air. The tinkle of ice caught the man's attention as Dailey walked from the far wall with two glasses of brown liquor.

The two stared at the map as Dailey held his hand out, shrinking the view, trying to get an idea of how far they were from the location noted. "Let's get Lieutenant Brax up here. She may see something *we* don't."

"We?" Becket asked as Dailey shook his head.

"You at a loss for words? If you knew, you would already be bragging about how back in the day, you used to take moon farm girls out there for dust-offs."

Becket grinned at the accuracy of his statement. The older the man got, the more he missed his misguided youth prior to joining the Fleet. The unfortunate part of both men's past that tied them forever together was an attack on a Fleet outpost five years prior, where Dailey's unbeknownst-to-him pregnant wife and Becket's son both died in an attack by off-worlders.

They were there for a military ceremony, and both men blamed themselves. Nothing would change that burden; truth be told, they didn't want to. Some called their cavalier actions a direct result of this.

Both men sipped their drinks in reflection as the door clicked open, allowing Jen to join the private meeting. "Drinking on the job, I see."

"Help yourself," Dailey directed as Jen grinned, still wearing her flight suit, quickly making her way to the hovering space chart.

"Hmmm," she let out, shaking her glass more than sipping from it. After a few short seconds, she shifted the chart, shrinking it into a basketball-sized sphere. "So, why do they call him Juice?"

Both men grinned. Dailey walked up to Jen and clinked her lowered glass. "Because if you're brave enough to squeeze the man, you get the Juice, all of it, every last damn drop."

Becket chimed in. "What he meant to say is, you mess with Captain Bearing, you're likely to regret it. He was either outmatched or would still be fighting if something bad happened."

"Sounds familiar. Blow your own ship up to take out the enemy…" Jen noted, setting down her glass. "I've seen some of this area on projected star charts, but what the hell is he doing out there? There's nothing but a handful of uncharted planets. I don't even think we are chartered to go out that far."

She pointed at the USF *Murphy*, highlighting the majestic beast of war. "We are here. Looks to me like we are going into uncharted territory. The area hasn't even been truly scanned yet."

Jen was referring to the process of sending several probes to and around identified planets for several months, if not years, to report back data. Terra Minor Three had been probed the year prior and had only recently been cleared for contact. In the event a sentient civilization was found to be present, additional assets would be deployed. This was, of course, a hit-or-miss process.

One team had reported encountering what was only described as dragon-like creatures on a surface landing several months before. In many ways, while exploration duty was considered less than favorable, it had its perks when something interesting was encountered.

Jen traced a path between the last reported location of the *Asher* and a hazy belt of debris in between. "That's the Shade Belt. It stretches for… hell, almost ever. It will add some time to our trip, but I suggest we avoid it."

Dailey contemplated the statement. Becket pressed another button, dropping the map, as a video feed snapped to life. Captain Bearing and a young Lieutenant McAlister appeared to be running into the cockpit of the smaller vessel.

"Audio?" Dailey asked as Becket shrugged, finding the override protocol on the sent files. They had been encrypted. Once again, thanks to Science Officer Bellman, things like this were not a roadblock. General Ran was well aware of this.

The doomed conversation between the two pilots sprang to life as they relived the *Asher*'s final minutes. Dailey stared blankly as the cameras shut off just as Juice pulled out his flask.

"All right, so they were attacked," Dailey noted as Jen cocked her head.

"Were they? I mean, they may have hit debris or something along those lines."

"No," Becket replied, zooming in on the status screen Juice and Laura had been looking at. "The power plant, weapons hold, and fighter bay were all taken out. That's not a coincidence."

"What I'm saying is nobody's supposed to be out there," Jen replied slowly as if talking to a kindergartener about weapons thrust compensation in space.

The two men again glanced at each other, talking without saying a word. While it was annoying to Lieutenant Brax, she had grown used to it.

"Not everything you read or hear about is true. There's a reason we're out here, exploring the unknown. We're so far out if our jump thrusters went out, it would take years, if not decades, to get to an outpost. There are things in the Void that haven't been found yet," Dailey replied in a more level tone as Becket leaned forward to throw in his thoughts.

"Or found us yet…" Becket trailed off as Dailey stood up, taking a lung-busting breath.

"For now, we need to get moving. Once we clear the sector, I want to stop for a function check on the crew. Full drop gear and all," Dailey ordered.

Becket and Jen stood up, both saluting Dailey. "Sir," Becket started. "We need to brief the rest of the crew. We still good for later? You didn't mention anything."

Dailey paused reflectively. It wasn't that he was being indecisive. Something was not sitting right with the commander. "Yeah, let's still debrief the crew, but let's keep it to platoon and attack wing leaders. I need to talk with General Ran one more time first. I have a few questions."

"You think we need to let Colonel Freeman know?" Becket followed up.

"I'm pretty sure he already knows through General Ran. Hell, the way it looks, he will take Ran's spot when the day comes. Anyway, I tried to reach him earlier, with no response. Once we stop, I'll try again."

Clearing the closest system would allow the ship more leverage to practice in the event others were watching from a distant moon or planet. Here, the crew of the USF *Murphy* would do what was known as a functions check.

This included the Nova Rangers donning their ODA, meaning orbital drop armor and generally referred to simply as armor. They were massive yet maneuverable suits, made to allow their occupants to not only fight in space but also drop from orbit.

Every platoon had its own color and style when it came to the armor setup. Most units of the Space Infantry, officially called the Outer Orbital Infantry, tied to the still-functioning regular planetary Army had set armor. The Rangers of Viper Company did not. Not all military units were built to support fully offensive operations. Viper Company was offense focused, all while keeping diplomatic considerations in place.

While not large and automated enough to qualify as mechanized space Marines, these suits allowed the Pathfinders to fight and train on any and all battlefields they might encounter.

Viper Company consisted of four main platoons.

First Platoon, also known as First Foot, took pride in their lighter-styled armor broken down into its basic form, also allowing for additional thrusters. This meant the platoon prided itself in being first to the fight.

Their symbol was that of a golden foot adorned with a wing symbolizing Hermes, the Greek god of speed. They had taken the god's mantle of being the messenger of the gods to another level, meaning they were there to personally send a message care of the Rangers. This message often included justified violence on the receiver's end.

In typical fashion, this led to Second Platoon, lovingly known as Second Foot, to do just the opposite. Less thrusters and more armor, meaning more firepower. Each suit of armor was able to stow two primary weapons as well as limited rocket capabilities.

Second Foot also carried what was known as Bertha, a fully automatic laser Gatling gun. The weapon was developed from alien technology seized by the group during the Scourge Rebellion. Second Platoon's signature pride and joy were the classic pinup-style drawings of classic calendar girls on their armor from World War II. A distant memory, but still a memory.

The only exception was Dawn, the female targeting specialist. She had overlaid an odd pinup version of a man in tighty-whities that the rest of the team took great pride in drawing on. In many ways, Dawn felt slighted if an attempt wasn't made to disturb what she considered classic art.

Third Platoon was, of course, named Third Foot, being a mix of its predecessors. This was the platoon the team used when they needed to grind through a situation. Nothing overly fancy or specific, but the members of Third Foot where the best at what they did, and do it they could. They prided themselves on the lore of the Spartans, all having their face visors painted like ancient warriors.

They also liked to call themselves "the devil's rejects." This was from several of them being released from the Space Marines for various reasons. This also lent to the blood-red accents on their suits. Usually, this meant they were hotheaded or tended to be too aggressive in combat, a much-needed commodity within the Pathfinders.

Fourth Platoon was, as guessed, called Fourth Foot and was considered the scouts and marksmen of the Company. Their armor was different than the others and more suited for defensive action while still being able to carry out the mission. This included plasma shields that were often used to protect not only the other Rangers but the fighter wing they were attached to.

They used a simple yet widely known symbol for their section. A grim reaper with a skeletal finger held up to its shadowed face in a *shut the hell up* manner was widely feared. Rumor had it that if you ever saw this symbol, it was too late. Their armor was muted black, as dark as space itself.

As for the fighter attack wing under Lieutenant Jenny Brax, each platoon was supported by four light infantry space fighters, officially called X-80 Raptors. Three additional support Raptors, including the LT's, rounded out the group. Each fighter was specially designed to allow Nova Rangers to attach themselves to the hull in several locations to either fight, protect, or be transported as needed.

The rest of the Fleet generally relied on larger, heavily armored ships. The main purpose of the Raptor was for interplanetary patrolling and offensive use if needed. This meant they mainly protected the main prize… Earth.

With the need to conserve room on ships such as the USF *Murphy*, plus their ability to independently go toe-to-toe with alien tech, the Raptors were the perfect choice for missions away from the large supporting armaments of the Fleet itself.

CHAPTER 3

THE VOID

"Sir?" First Foot's platoon sergeant, Don Grantham, blurted out after the initial situational brief was completed.

Captain Dailey nodded the go-ahead as the dozen other senior non-commissioned and commissioned officers turned toward Grantham. The man also happened to be the Company's orbital drop leader and one of the team's longest-standing members.

Peppered grey hair and a five o'clock shadow that showed up immediately after shaving gave the man an overall vibe of knowing what the hell he was doing. This was also likely due to him living as long as he had as an orbital drop leader for the Pathfinders.

"Yeah… sir, so… what you're saying is Juice is likely dead, and we need to figure out what did it, and then what?" Master Sergeant Grantham asked dramatically, pausing as if still working on computing the fact that another Federation ship was that much farther out into the Void than the *Murphy*.

"Return pleasantries, I'm sure," Dailey replied in the same drawled-out manner, garnering a light snicker from the assembled leaders. "All kidding aside, from what I can tell, we're on our own here. We're going to have to adjust fire as things progress and hope we still have reliable, timely comms that far out."

This time, Second Foot's lieutenant spoke up before the platoon's master sergeant. The man had been enlisted prior and was not given a choice, gaining his commission by attrition. No one had questioned it, as attrition often meant stacks of the dead or wounded. "We could drop a comms outpost before crossing the Shade Belt," Lieutenant Brian Cardinali interjected. His team simply called him Card. The short man carried what he lovingly referred to as the "freshman fifteen" around his waist, only to be offset by slabs of raw, naturally gifted muscle.

Science Officer Bellman stepped forward, clearly already having the same concern. "I talked with Operations Officer Chip and Lieutenant Brax about that. They both stated it wouldn't be safe unattended. We would have to leave a detail to secure the comms post."

Captain Dailey nodded, already having been briefed on this. "We're going to need everything we got." The look on his face was more telling than he intended, setting a light haze of thick unease around the briefing room. "I wanted to digest everything before reconnecting with General Ran. I'll ask Outpost Thirteen to send a comms-relay team as far out as they feel comfortable. They should be heading this way."

"Since when do you care about other people's feelings?" Master Sergeant Janix asked matter-of-factly. The de facto leader of Third Foot had decided to chime in as the Company often did in order. Before boarding the *Murphy*, the platoon's lead officer, Lieutenant Nathanial Adams, had been sidelined for reclassing in the Fleet. The man was going to get promoted, much to his disapproval.

Janix was a Solarian, same as Navigation Officer Pearl. Both had joined the Fleet at the same time. The difference between the two was Janix being raised as a warrior on their home world of Solaria. A planet twice Earth's size meant twice the number of problems to solve and things to fight.

Unlike Pearl's pale white complexion, Janix had pitch-black skin, the color of space itself. It was nearly impossible to tell the difference between humans and Solarians from a distance. Their pupils were twice the size of a regular human's, also accompanied by the fact that none of them could grow an inch of hair anywhere on their bodies.

Solarian ears were also slightly different, lying closer to their skulls as well as being slightly smaller. Topping it off was a marginally broader and larger frame than a human's. From twenty feet away, it was hard to tell the difference unless you were awkwardly gazing. One key takeaway was their horrible sense of timing when telling a joke about things they didn't have back on Solaria.

"We're too far out to call for help. If none of you have already noticed, we are the help. Lieutenant Dasher, before you ask, we're not sending out a scouting party," Dailey added.

Lieutenant Dasher, the leader of Fourth Foot and, as an additional duty, intel officer, generally only wanted to do one thing: grab his team and his assigned attack wing fighters and head off in front of the ship like a bunch of rogue cowboys looking for cattle rustlers. The young, thin man grinned, popping a toothpick in his mouth.

The young man's voice was calm, cool, and collected, coming from somewhere Dailey assumed was the Midwest.

Janix stood up. "Sir," he started, making it official. "I think I can speak for the rest of the crew, Viper Company at least. The team is ready."

This reaped a grin from Dailey and First Sergeant Becket. "We understand that. Captain Dailey and I want to make sure everyone's in order. Hell, it's been months since we've done any formalized all-hands checks. We don't know what we are about to get into, and I agree with the boss. I would rather have every single one of you underpaid and overprivileged soldiers together.

"Going further into the Void than anyone has ever recorded is something not to be taken lightly. We are moving as a unit. No scouts or trail parties are keeping watch over a damn comms relay station. Not to mention if we did need help, whatever shit storm had taken place would likely be over by the time they arrived," Becket relayed to the group of approving nods.

Dailey motioned for Senior Navigation Officer Pearl as she stepped forward. "I've asked Navigation Officer Pearl to talk about the Void and what we might expect going into the Shade Belt."

"Oh, shit. This is really happening." Grantham grinned. "I thought for a second this might be a training exercise." Another round of grunts followed in support of Grantham's statement.

A holographic star chart erupted from the flat table in front of the team. Lines and various other symbols started populating the graphic like a kid's drawing gone wrong. This included a large streak clearly labeled the Shade Belt. Beyond that, a defined red star annotated the last known location of the *Asher*.

What was mildly disconcerting was the massive gap in space between the *Murphy* and its supposed destination. Tick marks lining the side of the table now being projected into the air indicated parsecs, garnering a few whistles.

"As everyone is hopefully aware," Pearl started, letting any village idiot in the room know this wouldn't be a star chart class, something she had damn near bored the leadership team to death with several months prior during ODP, also known as Officer Development Program. The same old crusty requirement for soldiers and other Fleet members alike to better themselves through often useless knowledge, all for the greater good.

"The Shade Belt in this sector has not been charted or, from what we have reviewed, been explored. Meaning we are unsure of any sentient life in the region. Worst-case scenario, we may run into a few automated scout miners or scavengers likely up to no good."

Scavengers, for lack of a reasonable name, was the title given to straight-up space pirates, a term still used by most Fleet members that garnered stares from the Solarians. This was one of those word things that always got to the two species having different meanings for it. Luckily for the crew of the USF *Murphy*, no scavenger would dare take on an out-of-sector Fleet frigate with Pathfinder markings.

That was unless they had a death wish or were simply that stupid, which had occurred on a few occasions. The main exception being the Durg, who leaned on the latter of that equation. A race of short, impish creatures that had somehow managed space flight. It was eventually found out that the Alurians had given them the tech to do so in an attempt at getting the Durg on their side to be used as cannon fodder during the Tectonic Wars.

Much like the overzealous kid on the playground that would rather get in a fight than move out of the way, the Durg had the temperament of grade-school children all jockeying for status. Sure, they could be dangerous, but more times than not, they would fire at Fleet ships, not understanding how powerful the shields were, only to overheat their weapon systems and, in most cases, destroy themselves. It was literally SOP, *standard operating procedure,* to raise shields and wait for them to self-implode.

Dasher raised his hand, being the ever-present scout in the room. "How long are we talking in open space?"

"At least two months under full hyperdrive," Pearl noted as a few whistles let loose.

After that, more hands shot up, forcing Dailey to step forward. "We are going to push her to her limits. This is what this ship is made for. We'll take a break a few sectors away from this system and do our functions check. After that, we don't stop unless we are shifting courses until we reach the *Asher.*"

Becket stepped forward. "The engineering team will be busy. We will keep an eye on the ship. You all just need to get your head back in the game. Vacation's over. Pearl, please continue."

"My, well… our main concern is what is beyond the belt. I looked for any scan reports of the Void beyond, with no results. Before anyone asks, I understand the *Asher* would likely have all the scan data we could want, but that isn't an option till we find the ship. The Captain has made it clear that we don't know why they were out there." Pearl walked over to a stack of tablets and handed them out.

"This is a star chart of the area up to the Shade Belt and the coordinates of the *Asher*. We have three separate route shifts planned while on course and have loaded them in your mission tablets." The room knew what this meant. In case something went wrong, as it always did while on a mission, the mothership had redundant backup plans if a platoon was lost.

"Ma'am?" Grantham asked out loud, raising a hand as if asking for permission to go to the bathroom. "Are we planning to leave the ship during these shifts?"

Pearl glanced at Captain Dailey. "I got this," Dailey noted, walking in front of his team. "I don't want anybody straying off. We got three planned route shifts. The intent is not to take any longer than a few hours to do so. Meaning, everyone's to stay on board unless it's absolutely necessary."

In most instances, when the *Murphy* traveled through open space, it wasn't uncommon for one of the attack wings and a few soldiers from Viper Company to scout the immediate area as soon as the vessel disengaged its hyperdrive. It wasn't that any of the platoons were trying to poke holes in the plan. They were simply trying to determine their left and right limits during the mission. There was no such thing as a dumb question during a mission briefing.

With the plans uploaded in the platoon's tablets, and the main guts of the briefing complete, First Sergeant Becket dismissed the group. The soldiers, pilots, and accompanying Fleet members would have a day to get their shit together. While sounding unassuming, Captain Dailey's functions checks often involved a few surprises.

CHAPTER 4

STELLA

The door slid shut as the flowing yellow haze of Captain Dailey's quarters greeted him like an old friend. Pictures of friends past and present sat on various surfaces in no real order. As with the other offices, the captain of the ship had a viewport allowing him to overlook the side of the ship.

Being located a few levels below the bridge afforded the room's inhabitants a reflective view of space and their responsibilities. This was often addressed by the handful of Earth whiskeys sitting on a small table under the blank monitor that Dailey had yet to turn on since taking over the living quarters.

Grabbing a small remote off a dresser by the door, Dailey quickly gave Miles Davis control of the room as "Stella by Starlight" started to soulfully seep into every corner of the room. It didn't take much to see that Dailey was a complex man driven by the simplicity of things.

Good whiskey and even better music were all he needed to get his shit together. All the violence and worry would come in due time. It always did.

Gazing out the viewport, Dailey let out a lifetime's worth of sighs. The void of space was his new home, a fate he had accepted years before as personal penance for the loss of his family. With that thought, he glanced down at the picture of him during much happier times. A young officer full of piss and vinegar with his loving wife, Stella.

They were the future of a recovering Earth. Dailey remembered sitting on the beach in Florida, listening to Miles Davis while he and his future wife talked about the adventure they were about to undertake. A starry sky and cheap whiskey, including an even-cheaper bottle of wine, were all it took to drive the conversation into dawn's light. He missed her. Even worse, he missed everything that made Earth his home after losing her. He also despised it for haunting him.

Warm sand underfoot, a fireplace raging as feet of snow covered the ground in the mountains, the sound of birds, all things that he missed and, in many ways, also now hated. He had lost the love of his life to protect his future family and Mother Earth.

If never stepping foot back on Earth meant he could at least still accomplish one of those things, he would fight till every last fiber of his being was gone. Having recentered himself, Dailey walked over to the comms center in the corner of his cozy yet working quarters.

After a few taps of the keypad, Communications Officer King appeared on the monitor. "Sir?"

"I got your message. It looks like we have an active link with the *Brightstar*. Patch me through to General Ran. He's expecting me. Use the following comms protocol," Dailey noted, punching in a set of numbers only he, Colonel Freeman, and General Ran used.

Dailey stared at the screen as a familiar bark echoed from the speaker. King glanced down, mumbling, "Not now, Sparky."

"Problem?"

"No, no, sir. The ah… Sparky keeps getting out of his room. Can't figure it out. He just pops out of nowhere and starts licking everything."

Holding back a grin, Captain Dailey turned off his view monitor. He liked animals, and anyone that didn't treat them right didn't sit well with him. King was clearly entertaining the doglike creature.

After a few minutes, General Ran appeared on the screen. While the link took time to establish, once connected, they would be able to communicate with little to no delay. This would change the farther out the *Murphy* made it into the Void. "Dailey, how are things?" Ran asked, also looking to be in his quarters.

"Good for the most part. The team's ready to go. I have more questions than answers for them."

Ran nodded. "What's at the top of that list?"

"I've been trying to reach Colonel Freeman. I'm sure you've briefed him, but we need to check in. I want to go over this with him."

General Ran paused long enough to get Dailey's attention. "Dailey, I need you to listen very closely to me on this. I don't have any easy way to put this, but Colonel Freeman was also on board the *Asher*."

Dailey let the statement marinate in his brain like a cheap taco that had been left out overnight. "Sir?" It was a simple ask for clarification.

"I want to tell you more, but now isn't the time. He was escorting a team with a very specific mission."

"You do know I'm usually the guy that gets called, right?" Dailey replied, his pride cutting through like a knife. The statement told Dailey that Ran didn't trust the comm link they were using.

"Dailey," General Ran stated, using his name to cut through the typical military bullshit. "I'm heading to the Shade Belt first thing in the morning. It will take too long for us to get there to intervene. I… Hell, we need you to find what's left of the *Asher* and carry on with its mission."

"Intervene in what? What aren't you telling me?"

"It will have to wait for now. There is a lot I don't even know. Hell, Freeman wanted to pull you in, but he still feels guilty about everything."

"I don't need anyone's sympathy, sir. This just stinks of Federation bureaucrats. Wait, guilty about what?"

Ran took a deep breath, staring directly into the monitor. "I don't know. This came from the top. Freeman and I were briefed on a few things, but he ended up getting the full package after the *Asher* made way."

Dailey sipped his glass in full view of the general, who let out an approving huff. "Mind if I join you?"

As both men sipped their drinks, no words were spoken for the next few minutes.

"Sir, Colonel Freeman, hell, Juice wouldn't do something like this without letting me know. Plus, they knew damn well where we stand," Dailey finally added.

"They knew you were there if they needed you. I also have—well, had orders to contact you once their mission was completed. Listen, I'm not a Federation senator, just a general." Both men took the statement in stride, chuckling lightly.

It still bothered Dailey that Ran hadn't confided in him what was happening. Truth be told, he and the rest of the crew had been slacking off, for lack of a better term, avoiding the Federation for some time. Not enough to get them in trouble, but enough to keep them out of the loop.

This was different, however, as it included one of his peers and his damn commander. "You have our flight plans. Will you catch up by the time we reach the Shade Belt?" Dailey asked hesitantly.

"No. It will be weeks even traveling on the *Brightstar*."

The *Brightstar* was the latest in propulsion and military technology. Rumor had it the ship had a new propulsion system on board they were testing, allowing it to travel twice as fast, if not more, than the USF *Murphy*, which by all accounts was one of the faster ships in the Fleet.

"I'll report in when we hit the belt." Dailey closed out the conversation as Ran nodded.

"Be safe and stay out of trouble."

Dailey stared at the black screen for what felt like an eternity. They seemed to be sending a lot of expensive, if not powerful, people and vessels into the Void. The thought didn't settle well as motives started swimming around the man's thoughts.

Something danced out of Dailey's mind's eye as a knuckle-busting rap at the door made him almost spill out of his seat, watered-down whiskey sloshing onto his lap.

"For the love of all that is holy, there is a ringer," Dailey exclaimed as Lieutenant Jenny Brax's voice responded.

"I guess I'll just leave you at it, then, and whatever it was you were doing," she replied as the man scrambled to pull himself together.

"Give me a minute," Dailey replied, wiping off his unauthorized century-old Guns N' Roses T-shirt. Being that he was the captain, it really didn't matter. He had put in place a rather popular casual Friday, the day the Scourge Rebellion was laid to rest. It was always legendary when one defeated an aggressive enemy while wearing vintage band logo T-shirts and flip-flops. Today just happened to be Tuesday.

After a quick scan of the room, he was surprised by the actual organization he kept in his own quarters. A quick breath check later, Dailey opened the door to a grinning Jen. "'Sup?" was all the man could muster between the load of utter shit that had just been dropped on him and the oddity of LT Brax showing up at his door also wearing civies.

"Something must have you in a tizzy," she noted, walking in without a proper invitation. "The crew's meeting in the cantina for a send-off toast. Becket asked me to come get you, since King said you were on the comm with General Ran."

Dailey felt odd not talking with Becket first, but Jen had gained the man's trust in a short period of time. Trustworthy, fun, and lethal all at the same time. There was tension between the two. A cat and mouse of slightly flirtatious comments, never enough to cross the line or make a solid go at the other, but there nonetheless.

This contrasted with her ball-busting demeanor within her own fighter wing. It was necessary, though, to carry that level of respect from one's new team. For Dailey, that train had left the station years before. The members of Viper Company respected and never questioned the man.

"Guess there's no honor among thieves these days," Dailey joked, making fun of the small-town vibe deep-space ships often attained. Everyone knew everyone's business or was doing a damn good job of trying. For the most part, the three separate groups on board kept most of their dirty laundry to themselves.

"Spill it. You look like a mix of someone killing your dog and seeing a ghost."

Dailey cataloged the observation for his own personal use later. She was spot-on. "Looks like we got a new dog, and as for the ghost, that's yet to be seen. Close the door for a minute." Jenny paused, raising an eyebrow. "It's something I don't want getting out yet." The captain huffed, shaking his head.

"Shame" was all she replied, leaning on his dresser as she scanned all the pictures staring at her. She had never been in his quarters. To date, Becket was the only other soul on board that had.

"Let me ask you something. What if I told you Colonel Freeman was also on the *Asher*, and no one let me—hell, any of us know?"

The statement caught her by surprise and she stood back up. "That would mean somebody knows something is happening on the other side of the Shade Belt, something bad."

"My thoughts as well. The fleet's big. It's not lost on me that we're just one bird in a flock. But having this many Pathfinders on the opposite side of the Central Systems, it doesn't add up."

"You're worried," Jen noted as Dailey shrugged.

"Perhaps; you knew the deal when you got assigned. We do the things that the Federation doesn't want plastered on the front page. I'm going to push everyone when we stop to perform a functions check. Just have your team ready."

Jen grinned. "Of course. We will always follow our fearless leader. Tell you what: let's go join the crew for that toast, then go from there. Oh, and, ah, that dog thingy, Sparky, showed up in my quarters. No clue how."

The two smirked as Dailey cleared his throat. Jen had been a welcome distraction. "Let me get cleaned up. I'll be down in five."

CHAPTER 5

FUNCTIONS CHECK

First Foot, this is Red One. We are cleared for launch," Devin, the lead pilot for First Platoon, notified as the roaring sound of thrusters barked to life, erupting from the underbelly of the *Murphy* like an angry bee leaving its hive.

The *Murphy* had left the newly charted system, making it into cold, lonely open space. After the navigation controls were set, the ship and its crew were ready.

Grantham walked in front of his platoon, signaling the team to step into their suit mounts. During normal, everyday business, the Rangers' space armor was set in a three-piece transportable ensemble. A helmet, one metallic briefcase, and a large backpack, all thanks to a combination of Solarian and Alurian technology. Not to mention a slight dash of human-kind ingenuity, all melded into a mix of nano-armor and what was called symbiotic magnetic plates.

Tony Stark would have been proud of the eye-blurring speed at which the armor enveloped its wearer. As soon as the briefcase was set on the ground, all the soldier had to do was place it on the floor and step on it. The pack and magnetic nano-plates did the rest. After a brief minute of clinking and clanking, the soldier was ready.

When on high alert, the suits were left in what they liked to call half-baked configuration in standup bays. All the soldiers had to do was simply step into the shell and allow it to close around them. This was the standard for Viper Company. However, as Captain Dailey was aware, the team needed a little pep in their step, and he was just the asshole to supply it.

The drill was simple. Master Sergeant Grantham would lead the platoon outside the ship's electromagnetic field and perform a series of exercises, including the attack wing. Lieutenant Ponce, the platoon's once-upon-a-time Fleet Academy dropout—primarily due to fighting—would then send a swarm of drones set to various levels of competitiveness to fire back impulse rounds, identifying critical hits and immobilizing the soldier.

The data would be collected and then sent to Dailey for an after-action review, better known as an AAR. For this training exercise, however, Captain Dailey had something else planned. Known when on mission by his call sign Viper Six, Captain Dailey had a very distinct set of armor and his own modified fighter flown by the one and only Lieutenant Jenny Brax.

The fighters themselves paid homage to anything and everything humankind could smack together from centuries of sci-fi movies. The funny thing about it was that the moviemakers of old hadn't been too far off the mark. When the Alurians first attacked, everyone thought the rebellion from *Star Wars* was attacking the Earth, as if it was an Imperial stronghold, in X-wing-styled starfighters.

Sleek and agile, the fighter of choice for most of the forward-deployed Fleet was the AX-13. The cockpit of each fighter held two pilots. When attached to a Pathfinder company, that second seat was for one of the soldiers from the company if needed. In most cases, the Nova Ranger would attach themselves under the wing like a missile while in space. Two large pulse engines sat tucked under the body, sloping into the wings, as three maneuvering-thruster flaps shot out from the vehicle's ass end.

From there, several weapon systems sat nestled beside the engine intake ports as interchangeable armaments slid into the wings before they thinned out like old-style video game cartridges. In the mood for thermal rockets? *Sure thing; let me get those loaded for you.* Oh, wait, want a thousand tiny seeker rockets to celebrate the fourth of July, a holiday that didn't hold as much meaning as it used to in deep space? *No problem; I got you covered.*

"Viper Six, this is Viper One. We are set and deploying. Link up at marker one," Grantham proclaimed while the platoon activated their boost jets as if dancing in step, launching out of the open bay.

Thanks to the electromagnetic field, space truly didn't smack you in the face till about twenty feet away from the hull. This allowed for the massive increase in speed and open-air feel of the launch bay.

Linkup was a fairly routine event. The platoon was broken into four squads, with two fire teams each. From there, they separated to their assigned fighters and would attach to the outer body in one of two designated areas behind the cockpit.

If needed, the armor's magnetic boots would allow the soldier to walk on the skin of the fighter while in combat, joining the shit show likely taking place. This was generally considered dangerous, taking years of certification and boring schools to be considered for the qualification.

Several figures darted from the ship with laser-like precision as if swarming the smaller ships awaiting their arrival. Before the linkup could fully occur, not only did Lieutenant Ponce, known simply as Ponce, release the drones, but a fired-up combination of Captain Dailey and Jen pressed down as if from the heavens themselves, firing a slurry of down-phased plasma bursts into the unsuspecting platoon.

What they didn't expect was the explosion that followed, sending several of the Rangers scrambling and causing one of the ships to lose its booster jets, sending it drifting from the blast.

Dailey paused, checking the weapons panel, ensuring his setting was correct. Had he just fired several fully charged plasma rounds into his own people? Panicked, Jen spoke up just as several of the USF *Murphy*'s eat-shit-and-die cannons opened fire in front of the ship, opposite the group.

"That wasn't us," Jen barked over the radio as a scramble of chatter erupted over the comms.

Dailey didn't say a word, not one peep, as he smacked the override controls of the fighter.

"No, no, give my controls back," Jen demanded as the fighter ripped at full underthrust into the rain of flak cannons firing into the void of space. Captain Dailey, being the commander, had an override code to all systems aboard not only the frigate but the fighter he was assigned to as well. After this, if there was an after, she would find the circuit and fry it straight to hell.

Squinting, Dailey finally spoke. "Viper One, report."

"All units accounted for. Bates is shaken up, and we have one fighter down. They're still breathing."

Grantham paused, awaiting the inevitable order about to come. "All Viper elements are to stand down and scan the ship's aft section. There may be more. I got these assholes."

No response or clarification was needed as the platoon regrouped immediately, darting toward the back of the ship. The entire length of all this was less than a minute, and another smaller ship shot out of the bay, grabbing the out-of-commission fighter from its floating nap.

"Sir!" Jen shouted as Dailey again pushed the fighter to its limits, and she finally saw the target he was so desperately chasing.

Like a tiny firefly in an ocean of stars, the blueish-red glow of a thruster pulsed as if being turned off and on in rapid succession. Lasers from the forward batteries sliced through the dark void surrounding the ship as Jen clenched every muscle in her body.

Dailey was flying under the electromagnetic field, meaning that when he hit the reverse thrusters, yoking the fighter directly up and out of the protective embrace of the ship's field, everything that had entered Jen's stomach evacuated into her throat, only to be forced back down before finding its way back into her shut mouth.

"Hmmph," she gagged as Dailey pressed down the main thrusters, chasing their target toward the unsuspecting crew aft of the ship. "I didn't think you were a pilot," she gasped.

"Yeah, me neither," Dailey grinned, refocusing on the small red dot that had winked out of existence.

"Viper One, report," Dailey asked again as the ass end of the ship came into view.

"Set; nothing on our scan or on visual."

Just as the words left Grantham's mouth, the red dot again came to life, bearing down on the group. "You have a shot!" Jen barked as Dailey surprisingly turned toward the platoon.

"Sir?" Viper One asked as both Dailey's fighter and the other started peppering the group.

The member of First Foot had switched their systems to lethal. While not fully armored, they never left the ship without live ammo.

For good measure, Captain Dailey launched a plasma pulse into First Platoon's Alpha Team, forcing them to shoot above the ship to take the fight into space away from the *Murphy*.

"What the hell," Jen yelled, confused as Becket's voice came over the comms just as the secondary attacker sliced through the group, only to have one of the Rangers grab the wing.

"Sir, think they had enough?" Becket asked before following up with, "Oh, shit, one's on my wing."

Dailey switched to internal comms. "Calm down; just getting their juices flowing."

"You blew them up?" This isn't—" Dailey cut her off.

"It was a plasma pulse. Completely harmless." He paused, spiraling the fighter through the group at about the same time First Foot's soldiers realized what was finally going on.

It wasn't an attack. It was Captain Dailey putting them through their paces. A few smacks bounced off the vehicle's hardened exterior just as they switched their weapons to training mode.

"Those weren't," Jen noted as the team finally started getting in their groove as a flurry of practice rounds bounced off the cockpit.

"Seems like they figured it out," Dailey replied as Becket's fighter spiraled away from the group, finally dropping its excess baggage. "Ponce, hit 'em with the drones. Aft above the engines."

"Yes, sir," Ponce replied, very glad he hadn't been at the receiving end of the ass-kicking the soldiers of his platoon had received. He would get that later during the AAR.

"Never take control of my fighter again," Jen insisted, almost pushing the lines of command.

"Fair enough."

"That's it?"

"Yeah, next time we do a functions check, you got it, right?"

Jen paused. "Are you always like this?"

"Yup," Dailey grinned.

Becket cut the conversation short, having heard the back-and-forth. "What do you think, sir?"

"A little rusty, but I think it got their blood flowing. You a little rusty on the stick, sir?" You could hear Becket and Jen's muffled chuckles at the light jabs of a close-knit team.

"Let's keep it professional," Dailey replied as Becket cut back in.

"You mean like that time on Wejar-Nine—" Dailey cut the radio off before Becket could get to the point. He was having fun after hearing the two talking.

Truth be told, getting out and stretching their legs was doing them some good. Now they just had to figure out how to surprise the three other platoons.

After word was out about the game of cat and mouse, the team got in synch. Jen even joined in, instructing her pilots to get involved by the time

Fourth Foot came around. On the last iteration, the fighters all turned on the Rangers.

By then, Dailey and Becket had set themselves up in the radar array above the bridge, taking notes. First Foot was given some slack, having received the initial surprise slap in the face. The rest of the platoons had a heads-up.

The expected results came to fruition. Second Foot, through brute strength, pushed through the exercise, eventually superheating the space around the rigged drones enough to melt them. Third Foot operated like surgical bees protecting the hive, outmaneuvering and then overpowering through extreme violence. Jen volunteered to send a remote fighter as well as herself out of sector on a chase, trying to lure them away from the *Murphy*.

Fourth Foot, in typical fashion, figured out a way to disable Jen's ship and the drones before the show even started. On a whim, Captain Dailey sent Grantham and the rest of First Foot out for a good old-fashioned game of laser tag. With real lasers…

When all was said and done, only one minor injury was reported, and that was the soldier that had latched on to Becket's ship during the first functions check. When Becket had gone into the ship's electromagnetic field, the rapid spinning and subsequent jerk of exiting the field had decompressed a portion of their suit.

Not only would this weakness be corrected, but the soldier would be back to duty by morning. Medical Officer Casey Franklin always insisted on a good night's rest after any part of one's body went through a rapid decompression. That and plenty of water and Motrin, the US military's tried-and-true cure for everything. Even decades later, with medical advances far beyond what the mind could comprehend, humans were still, after all, human. Tradition still meant something.

Headache? Motrin. Scratch? Motrin. Loss of limb? Motrin. Being tied to the front of a hypercannon and it fired? No Motrin needed; not even a body bag.

In conclusion, the suits would be calibrated to handle extreme interspace electromagnetic shifts while spiraling out of control.

"At ease!" Grantham barked as Captain Dailey entered the room. Becket followed with a steaming mug of coffee.

"Carry on," Dailey replied as a silent mumble fluttered around the room.

With that, the leaders of both the attack fighter wing and Viper Company all settled in for the AAR. The rest of the Fleet and noncommissioned officers stood against the back wall, also joining in. They had, after all, fired the forward batteries directly up the good captain's posterior.

After a few quick taps of his tablet, a holographic 3D copy of the ship appeared in all its glory. Behind this was a live video feed from Becket's fighter.

"All right, first of all, I can see by the way everyone's dressed, including myself, we all have our game faces on now," Dailey started to a round of self-deprecating chuckles. Everyone was in their full duty uniforms from head to toe, including the attached Space Force pilots and Naval Fleet personnel.

"Next, I want to talk about how we exit the ship no matter what from this second forward. Always alert and always with your head, or whatever the Solarians call it these days, on a swivel," Dailey stated again, getting a light chuckle.

It was his style. While he could be the hardest-ass prick the Fleet had ever cut a paycheck to, he was also protective of his team and knew the value of trust.

"Ponce, what do you think I mean by that?"

Standing up, Lieutenant Ponce stepped forward. "Be combat ready at all times. Even while exiting the ship."

"That's right." Dailey shifted, looking at Grantham. "You get those instructions."

Grantham kept his mouth shut for a few telling seconds. "It's part of our SOP, sir, so that's on me."

"It's on both of you. It's on all of us. It starts at the top and trickles down like a bad shot of whiskey. I'm going to save everyone the hassle of hearing the same thing, but this was the most glaring thing I think we now have under control. Card, remember that time you had that one specialist think Ralphie was a bad guy?"

Veterans of the crew damn nearly lost their shit laughing. "Sir…" Card replied, grinning.

"For those that don't know, we had a private. I'll leave his name out for reasons. The other person involved, Ralphie, however, was a Fleet engineer outside the ship, repairing a relay hub we had been asked to check on Christmas Day. The rockstar vaporized the damn thing in an attempt to take out Ralphie."

One of the Fleet engineers from deep in the backwoods of Alabama in the back of the room raised his hand. "Sir, what happened to Ralphie?"

"You ever heard the nickname Red Rider before, Red, or whatever they call him these days?"

"That's Ralphie? The Lieutenant Commander with the eye patch?" the young engineer stammered, visibly knowing of the man.

"Yup."

The young engineer again raised his hand. "Why do they call him the Red Rider, sir? I don't think we heard why at the academy."

"Because Ralphie about—well, *did* get his eye shot out. You know… Red Rider BB gun? The old Christmas movie? It just seemed to fit for some reason. Ralphie… the engineer Ralphie lost an eye, even though it wasn't his fault. For clarification, Ralphie attached one of his booster rockets to his plasma torch and shot it at the young soldier. Things got messy. Long story short, be on alert, but don't be stupid."

The old classic *A Christmas Story* had been replaced by several other holiday classics over the years. This included *Elf IV–VIII.* They didn't talk about *Elf II* or *III.* Those were off the table as disasters almost as bad as the initial Alurian attack.

Some people were nostalgic like that, especially in the military. Dailey was an old soul in this manner. He was likely one of the few persons present to get it. People even forgot he never shot his eye out, making matters worse. Like Captain Dailey said. It just fit.

The story was absorbed, and the point was made. "Dasher, A for effort, but you got to pay the piper. Engineering is still cleaning up whatever the hell it was you did."

Dasher popped a toothpick into his mouth. The once-upon-a-time British commando and team knew what they were getting into. "Sir, I got the team helping."

"Well, as a bonus, Fourth Foot gets to be on route-shift standby," Becket spoke up as Dasher nodded.

"Fair enough" was his only response. This meant that while the other platoons were doing whatever the hell they were up to, Fourth Foot would be in the hangar bay in full armor, acting as a quick reaction force.

After another thirty minutes of detailed comments, including feedback from Jenny, it was time to get underway. Pearl stepped forward.

"We will be engaging the hyperdrive in thirty minutes. After that, it's a week at max power," Pearl again noted for the team. What that translated to was something along the lines of *We are going to slam the accelerator all the way to and through the floorboard. The ship's not made to be nor has in the least been tested at max hyperdrive for more than thirty-six hours straight.* The course shifts would only be momentary slowdowns to adjust course.

Dailey cleared his throat. "We are going to push her till the wheels damn near fall off. Just be ready and aware. She's a good ship. But a ship nonetheless. I'm not going to sugarcoat it. The manual simply says *don't* when referenced. That means all power will be diverted to the engines and electromagnetic field."

Ships like the *Brightstar* had a new tech that was only now being discussed behind closed doors that, from all reports, could travel in some undisclosed manner and speed. Only the best for General Ran.

CHAPTER 6

GHOST WHISPERS

On Earth, today was known as Memorial Day. The one day of the year that everyone stopped and reflected on the dead lost in battle, making the ultimate sacrifice. Mostly an American holiday, after the US took the lead during the Tectonic Wars, the country also brought this tradition to the eventual Federation.

Entire generations of families had been wiped off the face of the Earth. In many ways, it had turned into a celebration of the old ways of life and those who didn't get to bear witness to the surprising onslaught or prosperity that followed. Today was Memorial Day for the crew of the *Murphy*.

The galley was full from the promised surf-and-turf combinations accompanying the celebrated day. Solarian bran steaks and lobster from home sat in hydration containers seasoned to perfection and ready to be devoured.

Senior Chief Thron, the assigned Solarian head of the *Murphy*'s galley, was a star amongst the stars. Along with his human counterparts, he was one of the ship's hidden secrets. One that First Sergeant Becket had ensured stayed within arm's length throughout the past several deployments.

Dailey had even gone as far as shifting a hefty chunk of the team's budget over to Thron, allowing the mess crew personal access to whatever made their life and jobs easier. There were times when the galley was sealed shut with odd noises coming from inside, and no questions were asked. This was, of course, them blowing off steam through libations.

"Senior Chief, another feast, I see." Becket smiled, walking behind the current line of pilots being served and checking out the bountiful meal. As was tradition, the commander and senior noncommissioned officer ate last; there, however, due to Solarian customs, that wasn't precisely the deal.

"Only the best. Your tables are ready" Thron's gravelly V-8 of a voice growled back.

The Space Fleet was nothing more than a fancy replacement name for the Navy on Earth. Ships were managed, minus the Pathfinders, same as the Navy. Solarians, much to everyone's surprise, held a very similar train of thought. One difference was the chow situation.

Instead of waiting on the last military able body, no matter the branch, the Solarians not only insisted but required their senior leadership to dine and be separated from the rest of the crew. A Chief's mess on steroids. To-night was special, while the rest of the time, it was simply a separate room for the senior leadership to eat.

Dailey and Becket, being what would be considered Army in the old days, still insisted on walking the line during celebratory meals, inspecting the goods. In reality, it was also to boost whatever ego the cooks almost certainly always had.

A door at the far end of the mess hall separated the peasants from the ruling class. All joking aside, it was a new hybrid tradition that was some-thing to look forward to for the younger crew members. Stories of fortune and glory on the other side of the ever-so-secret senior leadership mess were quickly becoming things of lore.

Upon entrance, it was obvious the difference between on- and off-worlders, in the choice of decor. Thron at least allowed for some traditional entrees from the two British cooks on his team.

Wood panels imported from both worlds were a mix of rich, dark ma-hogany and Solarian char wood, covering the walls and ceiling. The smell of honest-to-god real wood almost always added to the mouthwatering scents already present. Dailey even stated other meals just weren't the same without the tang.

A handful of booths, covered in puffy red leather with patterned table-cloths, also added to the vibe. Topping it off were several pieces of military art on the walls, as well as a few random military artifacts.

Hand-painted pictures of old Spanish and British galleons from a more civilized age in a white-capped ocean flowed into a Solarian water general standing atop a massive cylinder-shaped ship, clearly being pre-tech era.

As Dailey and Becket sat down, Jen and Pearl smiled from the next table. Dasher and Card sat opposite them as a fully dressed chef walked out with a bottle of wine from Earth. Science Officer Bellman, who in reality was the ranking officer on board, coming in at a cool lieutenant commander with the Fleet, sat in their assigned seat, followed by Ponce.

Dailey liked life as a captain, not to be confused with a Naval or Fleet captain. Being a company leader from the Pathfinders afforded him all the clout and authority he needed. One of the few overriding positions. In reality, he was addressed as commander outside the mighty walls of the USF *Murphy*.

The rest of the Viper platoon's senior leadership shuffled in, as well as two other officers from the attack wing. Once the last Fleet officer was in the room, the door was officially closed.

On the far end of the room, a one-way viewport overlooked the galley where the rest of the crew smiled, smacked backs, and told half-cocked stories about catching the biggest fish. Dawn, Second Foot's one and only female heavy-weapons targeting specialist, threw what looked like a biscuit directly in the face of Barnes, sitting across from her. Rumor had it they had been caught rolling in the proverbial hay.

The group all laughed as Barnes joined in. He had earned the vicious biscuit of doom being thrown at him. Captain Dailey and Becket shook their heads, preferring not to know.

Wine was poured as the first course was served. Warm bread wrapped in an even warmer napkin was quickly molested as Bellman damn near destroyed the entire basket.

"I don't think I'll ever get used to this. My last ship didn't have food like this," Dailey started as Bellman replied, spitting out bread flakes.

"It'fth traditiothun," he spat, finally sipping some water. "I know this is your first Fleet ship command, but I think it's more of a motivator than anything."

"To get fat?" Becket joked.

Bellman shrugged. "You had an old Fleet interceptor. Big ship, but not new enough or, hell, large enough for the supporting crew. You're in the bigs now."

The comment hit Dailey in the gut like a bowl of beans. "Sir?" Becket asked, by now knowing the story about Colonel Freeman, the Pathfinders battalion commander.

"Bellman, you're a smart guy. Hell, one of the smartest Fleet science officers I've had the pleasure or displeasure of meeting," Dailey declared.

"Thanks?"

"Part of being a Pathfinder is avoiding the bigs. Working in the shadows. Not being served wine and lobster in the middle of deep space. I'm starting to think that slap on the wrist I got for blowing up my old ship, you know… being assigned this frigate is turning out to be something more."

The gentle hum of the hyperdrive on max power filled the gap in the conversation as Bellman paused. Dailey glanced at the viewport on the far end of the mess hall. While the hyperdrive was activated, it wasn't like in the movies. The stars didn't create streaking lines, moving by more like the night sky on a slight fast-forward. To the naked eye, one could see the nearest stars moving by. In deep space, the Void… nothing was close enough to make the view exciting.

"That was my assumption. Someone like you." Bellman looked at Becket. "And you, on a new frigate, with a full-on fighter attack wing and a full complement of Fleet crew, plus officers. Oh, yeah, you got someone's attention. If you ask me, you"—he corrected himself—"we're at the exact place, at the exact time, someone wanted us to be. LT? What do you think?"

Ponce turned, having stayed mostly out of the conversation. "It's not my place, but the crew's been talking. Mostly the Company. By the sounds of it, you already may have it figured out. We all think it's no coincidence we're out here, either. It passes the initial smell test. A company of Rangers from the Pathfinders being punished in deep space, pushing the boundaries of exploration for blowing up a Fleet ship while also stopping a rebellion." Ponce sniffed the air, acting out the statement.

"Then you start thinking about it. At first, we all bought the bullshit. No offense, sir," Ponce noted to Dailey, not Bellman, who had asked the question. This was an airing of grievances and a confirmation of what the Company was gossiping about.

"Then we started digging around the armory and all the weapons and shit we got. There's a damn container of Solarian Sauder rifles. The fancy ones and more ammo than there are bolts on this ship. From there, it just keeps going down the rabbit hole. Not to mention the Fleet crew on board, for all it's worth, is top-notch."

"We have Solarian Sauder rifles?" This got Dailey's attention. "I didn't see them on the manifest."

"We found them a few days ago, after we hit hyperspace. I was meaning to get with you, sir."

"Well, that's not a mistake," Becket added.

Solarian Sauder rifles were the cream of the crop when it came to handheld weapons. Usable on and off planet, the rifles' magazines held five hundred mini titanium rods. Once fired, the small rods were then superheated by a small onboard fusion core and launched out the tube so damn fast, it looked like an old-style minigun firing.

The thing was, the rounds could cut through damn near anything and had absolutely no kick and very little noise. As for range, that was up for debate. The kicker of it all, the weapons' compact fusion reactor, tucked away in the stock, could power a small vehicle or building if needed.

Titanium was at a premium due to it being used to make starships. It was no mistake they were there. The weapons Viper Company used were some of the best in their own right, but these were a prize.

"Am I signed for them?" Dailey asked Becket as he scratched his stubble.

"Not that I remember, sir. Maybe one of the Fleet crew members. But not you."

This meant one thing and one thing only: they were going to use the hell out of them.

"Well, shit. I mean, good shit." Dailey added, "Listen, tell the others what I said here. Don't sugarcoat it. Tell the truth. I didn't know about those weapons and have figured out the same thing. We are lined up for something more than finding the *Asher* and Juice. What that is, I don't know. We will need to trust each other this far out. We are pioneers in a foreign land. I know a little more, but it's not ready for dissemination yet."

Just as he finished his sentence, several communicators beeped in the opulent room. "That didn't last long," Becket growled as Dailey slammed his glass of wine.

"Never does," the ship's commander stated, standing up while also grabbing a roll off the table. "Listen up. Top and I are going to head to the bridge. I want you all to finish up."

That garnered a few hooahs. "Not the alcohol." This then earned a few boos, most likely from his own soldiers. "I'll let everyone know what's going on."

Communications Officer King, a lieutenant, stood up, hiding in a back corner. The guy was smoking a vapulizer, the future's version of vaping. A mix of nicotine, vapor, and what the Solarians called fetch. It was shocking to most folks from Earth that the Solarians, as advanced as they were, hadn't invented vaping. It was like a miracle had occurred when the first Solarian tried nicotine.

Fetch, on the other hand, to humans had an energy-producing effect. It didn't matter; the habit was still gross to most folks, but to military folk, it was a gift from whatever gods had been discovered in the universe.

Sparky the wonder dog harrumphed, shuffling out from underneath the table, surprising the communications officer and his tablemates. Ever since Sparky had been on board, he'd had the uncanny ability to show up basically anywhere at any time. This included the day Captain Dailey walked out of the shower to have Sparky sitting there, licking what he assumed was his ass.

While King was one of the lower-ranking officers in the room, he still counted as part of the ship's core officer staff. "Sir, it's a message coming from the other side of the Shade Belt."

Everyone stared at him blankly. "From close to the *Asher*'s last reported location."

This news not only got Dailey and Becket's asses in gear but that of several others. Pearl, King, Jen, Grantham, and Dasher also joined the parade to the main bridge, Dasher because he was on standby duty, as mentioned before, as well as the ship's intel officer, and Grantham because that was simply what the man did. All things being what they were, Pearl was the Fleet crew's de facto leader and, as the navigator, would work with King to triangulate the signal.

"King," Dailey barked as everyone stood around the main helm. Pearl continued pulling up a star chart on the main holo-monitor.

The bridge was compact and set up for maximum efficiency. Ambient lighting allowed the pronounced glow of various monitors to lightly reflect off the muted metal dullness of the room.

Individual cockpit-like workstations allowed maximum use of the space as well as an intimate feel for the crew. In the back of the bridge, an open area led into several alcoves occupied by various staff sections when needed, including engineering when they weren't in the power-module room, keeping an eye on the hyperdrive.

Becket walked up, handing Dailey a cup of steaming hot coffee. The two men didn't even look at each other or exchange pleasantries. In all fairness, from a distance, it looked like Dailey was psychic. Truth be told, the two men had spent that much time together. It was considered SOP for Becket to hand his commander a cup of hopefully fresh go juice when they both needed to be on the bridge.

The first sergeant preferred to stay with the troops.

King continued smacking buttons, adjusting his headset. "One minute, sir. I'm trying to see if we can ping it."

This meant that while they were still actively receiving the signal, there was a chance of getting an extremely precise location ping.

"Sir," Pearl interrupted. "I suggest taking the ship out of hyperspace.

Dailey nodded as the growling hum of the hyperdrive went silent. The odd shift in constant noise to the day-to-day beeps and whirls of regular operation created an awkward silence. Dailey was fairly certain if he talked, he would be talking way louder than needed.

"There we go," King barked. Dailey was right. "And..." the man said, licking his lips and smacking the keyboard as if it had insulted his mother. "Got it!"

Pearl bent over her panel. "I also have usable geo-metadata." She grinned, looking back at Dailey.

Geo-metadata was a type of radar imprint included in audio signals. The technology had come from the Solarians and was the equivalent of attaching a bat's sonar senses to a radio message.

"I have the audio," King huffed, finally letting out a breath he had been holding for the last three minutes.

Static, followed by a scratchy feminine voice, faintly came through the bridge's intercom. "This... Laura McAl... Ash... Attac... Near... planet... Survivors..."

The message cut off as everybody held their collective breaths. "One more time, King," Becket growled, squinting his eyes as if it was going to help his already-atrocious hearing.

After the message was played twice more, Dailey walked over to Pearl. "Let's see the geo-metadata."

At first, there was only one planet, then another, followed by a third. By the looks of the holographic representation, they could easily have been considered moons. Pearl minimized the small system, relating it to the last known location of the *Asher*. Once that was complete, she zoomed out further in relation to the Shade Belt.

Every piece of information helped shape the battlefield. Not only were the crew of the *Murphy* getting a better picture of what they were about to encounter, but they also had another target. Possible survivors. How many and in what shape was another question.

Without asking for guidance, Becket picked up his communicator. "Senior Chief," he started, talking to Thron. "Go into the chief's mess and tell everyone to stand down. Something big has come up, but it shouldn't take precedence over a full stomach."

"Roger" was all the Solarian chef replied.

Dailey glanced at Becket. "It's the right thing to do. I need to talk with General Ran, and I say we go ahead and do one of those route shifts. Pearl, load that chart on my tablet. Dasher, once you secure the area around the ship and we're ready to reactivate the hyperdrive, I need to talk to you. Might be an opportunity for you to do some of that cav-scout bullshit you all love to do."

He was referring to the fact that the scout platoon still wore what he considered damn annoying cowboy-like cavalry hats and what was now called space spurs. The Solarians loved the godforsaken things more than human cav scouts. Solarian military tradition would take weeks, if not years, to explain and often got sidetracked.

This was of course the opposite for humans actively serving in their primary military. As mentioned before, Earth, through sheer willpower or attention-drawing stupidity, had quickly out developed their IPF or Interplanetary Force.

It still baffled the hell out of everyone how both planets had a firm understanding of English, the now-international, not to mention interplanetary, language of both worlds. Cue the conspiracy theorist. Who came first? The chicken or the egg? Or more like the Solarians or humans?

While the Federation had basically overlaid the United States military structure, the Solarians did it differently. They created a branch for damn near every job. From there, the branch would support the other branches. Fat, bloated, and confusing as hell, the Solarians had also started taking on what humans considered a more streamlined self-supporting force structure.

Dasher grinned, putting on an unnecessary pair of blocky sunglasses. Wearing his ARBs—armor-prep boots—already, he clanked out of the bridge, heading toward the fighter bay as the sound of him barking orders into his communicator went silent from the internal blast shield hissing shut.

—

CHAPTER 7

THE CALM BEFORE THE STORM

"Sir," Pearl spoke up. "We are coming out of hyperdrive."

Captain Dailey squinted as if it helped him. Once again, the droning of the hyperdrive thrusters faded, bringing the sounds of everyday operations into focus. "Lieutenant Hontz. Status report on the hyperdrive."

Fleet Engineering Officer Junior Lieutenant Barry Hontz, spent most of his time in the engine room. A tried-and-true generational mechanic, Hontz was not only a chip off the old block, he was also Irish. Having joined the Federation at a young age, he was carrying on an age-old family tradition of working on surface-navy ships which eventually translated into space.

Back in the day, a ship like the *Murphy* would have dozens, if not hundreds, of able-bodied individuals keeping the vessel running. With the drastic technological shift, the fleet had the engineering team down to roughly ten able-bodied persons.

What the Federation had absolutely taken from the Solarians was their cartridge-like use of technical systems. If an engine or a central reactor were to go down, they would simply jettison the damaged or old part into space, then neatly and effectively slide in a replacement. In many cases, it was just that simple.

Back on Earth, this technology changed not only how on-worlders lived but how they purchased things. Much to everyone's surprise, cars, both fossil fuel and electrically driven, still peppered Earth's surface. While flight-capable personal vehicles were absolutely part of everyday life, they were only available in most cases to the middle to middle-upper class of society.

The best way to put it was in relation to a car. These days, when you went down to the dealership, you were there to purchase a frame. The engine, dashboard, transmission, and just about everything else was easily swapped out. And before you ask, it could be done in the luxury of your very own garage or home.

Instead of the guys coming over and drinking beer, staring at an engine, with a few quick snaps and pushes of various buttons, the motor housing merely unlocked, able to be pulled out on a pallet jack. Instead of extended warranties, the dealerships offered parts pickup and drop-off, not to mention car cartridge replacements.

The same styling went for houses. While there were still thousands, if not millions of stick-built houses still on Earth's surface, homes were purchased similarly. You bought a lot and put whatever modules you deemed necessary for your family on it. This included a very coveted Louis Vuitton bar module. Yes, that's still a shit-ass thing in the future.

"Sir, all systems are showing ninety percent. Once the hyperdrive thrusters fully de-phase, we should be at one hundred percent in roughly five minutes. I think it's safe to say she could be pushed a little more," Hontz's thick Irish voice replied from the small engineering station positioned in the rear of the bridge, tucked out of the way in a small cubby-styled station.

Dailey grinned. There would be time for a celebratory drink later. "Great news. This means we can turn on the deep-space transponder and check in with General Ran."

Glancing down, Dailey saw a small red light blink as a video feed of Fourth Foot launching out of the hangar bay flashed. A full two weeks of uneventful traveling had come to an end. On the books, this was the farthest any manned ship had ever traveled into the Void. Off the books, Dailey was starting to highly doubt the notion.

"I'll put a report together. Weapon systems and shields are now at one hundred percent," Hontz finished as the group turned back to the front viewport.

In front of the ship was a minefield of asteroids, many large enough to be moons as far as the viewports allowed. Dailey walked in front of the bridge, crossing his arms. While it was mostly stationary, random shifts interrupted the massive field, like a small ripple of water on a large lake.

Besides the engineering team, the heavy-weapons armaments section also sat in the back of the bridge beside Specialist Kline. Sitting front row was usually a specialist manning the weapons-control station.

After more begging than First Sergeant Becket could handle, he caved, giving Specialist Kline, the prior artilleryman, his chance to actually target and coordinate fires with the *Murphy*'s main weapon systems. There were six other weapon stations scattered throughout the ship allowing for an occupant to control one of a myriad of armaments.

This included plasma cannons, missiles, and automated laser turrets. Monitored by someone from the armament team, the reloading and energizing of the pods and weapon systems were down to the simple push of a button.

Dailey finally spoke again. "Kline, anything on the targeting radar?"

"No, sir. It's a little splotchy with all the meteors floating around," Specialist Kline replied as several armored Rangers streaked by the ship's bow.

"Fourth Foot is fully deployed," Dasher erupted over the comm. This was followed by him hovering in front of the bridge in his armor before shooting forward.

The well-oiled crew was in rhythm after Captain Dailey's wake-up call before getting underway. Pearl cleared her throat. "I am scanning a nav route through the belt to see if we can identify any anomalies."

"Good idea," Dailey grinned, walking back to Hontz as the twenty-something turned around. "So, you think all that bullshit about pushing the hyperdrive thrusters is just that? Bullshit?"

Hontz shrugged. "Total shite, sir. She had more in her. I don't even think we needed to deactivate anything, either. Typical Fleet nonsense." The man told it straight, how things were, and Dailey respected that in him. "I wouldn't doubt it if this ship could actually go a wee bit faster."

"Well, the Fleet is filled with all kinds of surprises these days. Get a report together for me. If we have a capability that will help us, I want to know it."

"Yes, sir. I will say there are several subsystems that seem to be locked. I would assume those are the overrides for the hyperdrive."

"Get with Bellman. The guy is a living, breathing problem-solver. There's a high probability he might have even helped design the damn system locking you out."

After a few more reflective minutes staring at the overbearing mine-field in front of them, Dailey keyed his communicator. "Meet me in the briefing room."

"Be there in five," Becket replied as Dailey motioned for Pearl to join him.

Becket sat in one of the plush command chairs on the other side of the holo-table.

"Sir," the first sergeant noted as Pearl also slumped in one of the large seats. Prepping to come out of hyperdrive had kept the crew on their toes, and it was showing, as everyone was taking a much-needed breath. Dailey knew that breath would be short-lived.

"I'm going to get right to it. Dasher went through the signal and all the geo-metadata from it over the past couple of days. He believes the message came from a live signal. He worked with King, and they were able to finally ping the transponder earlier today. Meaning it's still active."

Pearl pulled out her navigation tablet and punched a few instructions, finally turning it around. It was clear she had been computing possible routes. "Sounds like we are going through the Shade Belt, aren't we?"

Dailey nodded as she continued. "It would take another two weeks to navigate around the belt."

Becket leaned forward, tapping his fingers. "I miss the old force some days. You just got told what to do and how to do it. This… well, we're on our own… again," Becket drawled out, his slight Texan accent making an appearance.

"You see any issues cutting through?" Dailey inquired as Pearl ran her palm over her smooth head.

"Besides the massive meteors and the fact they're moving in some areas?" she joked, already knowing the challenge ahead. "We can make it, sir. Just don't quote me on it. Glad the Fleet has insurance."

That lightened the mood just as Dailey's communicator chimed. When it dinged instead of chimed, it meant a message only meant for his ears was coming through.

The readout displayed General Ran. "Sir," Dailey replied, placing the communicator on speaker. At this point, this far out in the Void, there would be no secrets.

"Thank God. I tried reaching you, but you must have still been in hyper-drive," Ran started. When traveling at high speeds with the electromagnetic field activated, comms were known to be hit-or-miss. Not to mention how far out they now were. "I wanted to tell you as soon as possible. There's been an attack back home."

You could taste the tension in the briefing room as the three glanced at each other. "Sir… on the surface?"

Ran sighed. "It's bad, Ben," he continued, using Dailey's first name. "An unidentified craft broke orbit and obliterated the spaceport outside Orlando."

Another pause. "What does unidentified craft mean?" Dailey asked skeptically.

"They know but don't want us to know."

Dailey glanced at the ship's updated feed on the monitor. The news would come through soon and be broadcast throughout the ship. This system also updated sports scores, major headlines, and the ship's dinner menu all in the same place.

"You should have the package I sent from Dasher. What's your ETA?" Dailey inquired.

"About two weeks. We had to make a stop. Listen, Ben, I know you're about to haul ass and find their transponder. I know how you think. I'd prefer you secure the *Asher* and wait on us."

"Roger, sir," Dailey replied as Ran grunted in approval. Truth be told, the captain hadn't agreed to anything.

"Keep in touch. Ran out."

Dailey and Becket looked into each other's eyes as if trying to see their very souls. Pearl spoke up first. "I take it this is what you like to call bullshit?"

"Yeah, bransaz, as you like to call it on Solaria," Dailey replied, no humor in his voice.

"Boss," Becket started, pointing at the teleprompter as *eighty-five thousand dead* flashed on the screen. The message was delayed by a few weeks, but when out in the Void, that was to be expected. There was likely more to the story by now, being that it had just uploaded while the two ships were linked during the prior conversation.

"Why do I feel this is all connected? I mean, we could be talking about a new threat. It's clear it's not an on-worlder, or they would have plastered that shit everywhere," Becket correctly suggested.

"Or an old one," Pearl piled on.

"Let's not get in front of the ion cannons here. I've had that same feeling the whole time. The *Asher* in an uncharted sector, hell, system by the looks of it with those planets; this attack just seems too convenient."

"Convenient, sir?" Pearl asked.

"Just saying, us being where we are now, with a company of Nova Rangers and a fighter attack wing, in this beast of a ship. It's not that far-fetched that whoever or whatever intercepted the *Asher* had already figured out where home is. Might even be why they were out here."

"You're saying there have likely been other attacks?"

"I would bet a bottle of Solarian Moog juice on it. Space is a big place, and the Federation is spread out. Solaria, if you think about it, is shockingly far away from Earth. The hyperdrives help, but without them, it would take lifetimes to get there. Just remember, there's always someone bigger, meaner, and faster out there. Let just hope…" Dailey trailed off, not wanting to say Alurian.

Communicators started chiming in rhythm. "Sir, might I recommend we get underway? Keep the crew focused."

"I can be ready in a few hours with a route solution," Pearl noted as the main screen flashed several scrolling updates.

The Federation has not commented if this is a new threat or the work of terrorist. As of this morning, it is projected ninety thousand on- and off-worlders have been killed. All space traffic has been halted until further notice. Fleet representatives have activated all surface and orbital units.

A puff of ozone wafted through the room as Sparky strutted out from behind the back row of seats. "Barsh! Barsh!"

"Yeah, something like that," Dailey noted as the doglike creature walked up to the group, planting its butt firmly on the ground.

"What is it, boy?" Pearl asked, petting the smooth, sleek fur on his head.

Again, Sparky let off another round of barks, followed by a growl, "Barsh!"

"The dog doesn't like something or is giving us a warning. Smartest damn soul on the ship," Becket admired, joining in with a light back scratch. A pop of static snapped between his hand and the fur as a knock on the door interrupted the moment.

Dailey pressed the door open button as another pop of ozone snapped. Looking down, Sparky had done his famous disappearing act.

Lieutenant Jenny Brax briskly walked forward. "You all see this?" she began, pointing at the screen they had clearly been watching. "Are we heading home?"

"There's plenty of Fleet vessels back home to handle it. No, we're pressing forward. We just talked with General Ran. He didn't seem to have any additional information," Dailey replied, putting an emphasis on the word *seem*.

"I get that, sir, but we have team members with family that work at that spaceport. We have a detachment stationed there, sir."

The concern was cutting through in her voice by way of her use of the word *sir*. The two had quickly established a first-name-basis relationship when the others weren't around.

This didn't bother Dailey for some reason, and it was starting to eat away at him. Ever since the loss of Stella, thinking about another woman, let alone actively flirting, wasn't even a notion. Being lazy on a planet far, far away while drinking Moog juice, sure; looking for love, no.

"Jen," the commander started, even catching Pearl off guard by the casual use of her first name. "We all know someone that either worked or lived around the spaceport. Here, now, we need to focus to make sure we get back. We were just in here talking about it. Something's up; we're not sure what, but it's something."

She immediately shifted gears after hearing that. "You think this is connected?"

"Connect the dots" was all Dailey replied as Pearl stood up. The look on her face was flat as she walked by Jen, not pausing for the usual pleasantries.

"I'll get the course data together," Pearl stated, a slight tension appearing out of thin air.

"You better get the attack wing ready. You might be on meteor target-practice duty if things get tight, Lieutenant," Becket stated as Jen also left, leaving the two men alone.

The two men looked at each other without saying a word as the door slid shut. Becket couldn't hold it in any longer. "You old dog, you."

Dailey turned fifty shades of red, shaking his head. "What?"

"First-name basis with the LT? You see the way Pearl reacted? If I'm not mistaken, I would think one of those two has a little crush on you."

Pausing, Dailey's face gave it away. "It's not the time and place for that. I just want to get to know my crew."

This was, of course, the wrong choice of words. "I bet you do."

At this, both men let out a much-needed chuckle before Dailey finally came to terms with the truth. "She's a good pilot. Hell, you heard her over the comms during functions check. I do like her, maybe not in any particular way. Hell… I'm the one that needs to get focused. Not sure about Pearl."

"Well, I trust you, sir. You know that. I also know the chances of us losing a few souls on this mission, or whatever the hell it is, are highly probable."

"Yeah, let's try to avoid that, Top," Dailey noted, using the old Army term of endearment for top-ranking senior noncommissioned officers. "Maybe it's time we take a break after this."

"I'm not saying no, boss," he followed as the two men sat in silence, watching the news feed as it updated.

CHAPTER 8

THE SHADE BELT BLUES

I on cannons, smaller than their bigger plasma brothers, thumped as car-sized space boulders sparked into dust. Several soldiers from First Foot were walking on the bow attached to the ship's hull through heavily charged magnets.

Dailey stood once again with his arms crossed, overlooking the front of the ship, as was his new habit. Asteroids the size of, if not actual moons, slowly allowed passage of the USF *Murphy* with only a few minor close calls. Again, the ion cannons thumped, followed by the spatter of fire from the forward plasma turrets.

"Pearl, what's the good word?" the commander asked without turning.

Whatever weird vibe had happened in the briefing room had since disappeared, at least to the best of the man's knowledge. First Sergeant Becket was still goading his friend, as friends often did and should. In many ways, Becket was happy to see his friend interested in something other than the mission or ways not to report back to the Fleet promptly.

Once upon a time, back on Earth, when Dailey was a young butter-bar lieutenant and Becket was a staff sergeant, the two had made a bond that was on many levels. Not only were their significant others friends, but they considered each other family. This mostly stemmed from neither of them having any true relatives, a common theme among Nova Space Rangers.

"Good timing. Specialist Kline just sent over targeting data for what appears to be a large object ahead that looks to be a ship."

This perked everyone's ears as she followed up. "Whatever it is, scans show no forms of life, and if it is a ship, it's likely a ghost ship."

"Ponce, Grantham," Dailey called over the communicator.

"Sir," Ponce responded first as Grantham grunted.

"Looks like we might have a ghost ship ahead. That's all we know. I'm going to suit up and join you."

This garnered a round of stares. The man needed to get out and stretch his legs. Walking over to Communications Officer King, Dailey picked up the intercom.

"All hands. This is Commander Dailey. We have reports of a ghost ship a few grids ahead. I need Third Foot to report to the drop hangar and their assigned attack wing. Assume battle stations at this time."

He followed this by pressing the squawking all-hands alert. Red lights flashed as the sound of boots shuffling erupted around the ship.

"Pearl, the ship is yours in my absence," Daley instructed, getting a slight smile from the Solarian woman.

In the drop bay, Dailey pressed a couple of buttons on his assigned trifold A-series space armor. It wasn't like the armor the others wore. It was scarred, pitted, and no less than two generations older than the current suits the rest of his company wore.

He leaned back, and a round flexing metal strap slapped around the man's waist, pulling him into a cuddle-like embrace. Like the rest of Viper Company, his armor was also on standby, only needing a few quick clinks and clanks. While taking slightly longer by only a few seconds, Dailey had learned that the newer armor wasn't nearly as flexible. Still, what it lacked in newer nanotechnology gusto it made up for in its unrelenting amount of armaments. This included a built-in Moshan fire blade that could erupt from the suit's right arm on command.

While the inhabitants of Mosha were a smaller, less industrialized civilization, they had a material often translated as the chosen rock. Moshans were small, furry, animal-like creatures that look like more refined raccoons.

Their planet had a steampunk vibe, and its inhabitants were in the initial phases of spaceflight. It surprised Dailey how advanced the civilization was to have not attempted space travel. When asked, they simply responded with another question: Why?

Two pods of compact plasma mini rockets, much like the ammo in the fancy Solarian rifles but with an explosive tip, sat in hidden cartridges on his shoulders. As for the left arm, a retractable thrust-buster, as it was called, could take over his hand.

This weapon packed one hell of a kinetic punch, even able to degrade lighter-gauge ship hull armor if needed. Dailey called it his asskicker. He tended to use it more often than not to either knock down walls and doors or, his personal favorite, ensure whoever it was pointed at would be on their ass.

A few other tricks adorned the armor that had been more of a prototype than anything, combining tech from several different groups. It had been shelved, only to have an overly intoxicated Dailey requisition it, sort of officially, as he liked to say. In reality, it was one of those feel-good projects that allowed all the different worlds to work together. It had been deemed impractical and costly.

One of Third Platoon's squad leaders, a newer buck sergeant they simply called Stix, still had his visor up, seeing the armor for the first time. Dailey had also grabbed one of the Solarian Sauder rifles.

"Does this armor make me look fat, Sergeant?" Dailey asked as Stix froze in place.

"Sir… no, sir," he stammered, regaining control of his bearings.

"Here," Dailey huffed, throwing the rifle toward Stix, who eagerly caught it like a fat kid getting candy thrown directly at their open mouth.

"Stix!" Master Sergeant Janix barked as the thump of his boots smacked the deck. The Solarian leader of Third Platoon walked over, staring a hole in the buck sergeant. "When you have your nose out of the good commander's third point of contact, line up."

After a short jog to the forming platoon, Janix turned to Dailey with a shit-eating grin across his face. "He'll be talking about that for weeks, sir. How do you want to play this?"

"Bellman's coming. Pearl just sent over the scan data from the ship. Looks like it's an honest-to-god UUO."

"UUO sir?"

"Unidentified unflying object," Dailey joked as Janix again grinned. "All joking aside, she can't make out what type of ship it is or, more importantly, who it belonged to."

"Guess that's why the ship's stopped," Janix followed up.

Dailey glanced over at the platoon now in formation facing out into the void of space. "I want one squad to go in with us. One fire team can secure the entrance and the other go in. I want you with us. Bellman often needs adult supervision, as you know."

"I heard he sleeps with a teddy bear."

Dailey grimaced. "I heard the same thing. Anyway, I want the rest of you checking out the exterior. Once inside, we'll find the cargo bay, if it has one, and get it open. Get inside and see what you find."

"ROE, sir?" Janix asked, which stood for rules of engagement. It was basically used to gauge at what point you shot versus vaporizing the asshole causing you problems.

"Only fire if fired upon. Let's get in and get out," Dailey confirmed as Bellman walked in, noshing on a bag of potato chips, wiping his hands on the awkwardly standard skintight flight suit he was wearing. Following behind him was Sparky, lightly drooling.

Bellman didn't have a set of full space armor and instead wore what was simply called a space tac suit, or STC for short. With limited armor and more scanning and other capabilities, the suit wasn't designed for front-line combat operations.

"Thing is shrinking," Bellman exclaimed, walking over to his STC.

The two suited-up warriors glanced at each other in a fight for first smart-ass comment dominance. Dailey won, as Solarian humor was always poorly timed.

"Want me to hold those chips for you? You know, I heard they cause uniform shrinkage."

Bellman looked down, realizing he likely looked ridiculous. Sparky let out a chuff, walking up to Dailey. The captain and others had started wondering if the doglike creature could actually understand what was being said around him.

"Omph… ahg," Bellman groaned as he finally pulled the suit on.

"So, what are you gonna bring?" Janix asked as Sparky sat down beside Dailey.

"A few things. A material graft scanner to see how old this thing is."
Dailey added, "Why?"

"According to Pearl, this thing looks to be old. Like, real old."

"Okay, what else?" Dailey followed up quickly as an arc of electricity snapped between Sparky and his leg.

"Air analyzer and a few comm-link kits, in case we can find a working computer and try to power it up," Bellman responded as Dailey and Janix started to haze over.

The three men walked to the rest of the platoon, having gone over a few other details. Looking down, Dailey looked at the small scorch marks from what the Rangers called a hopper.

There are two ways to jump out of a drop bay with an electromagnetic field activated around the ship. The most common was simply stepping off and then activating one's armor boost thrusters, launching them several hundred feet away from the ship.

After that, there was what was called the bunny hop. The soldier would do a quick burst from their thrusters while standing on the bay's edge, then launch forward. The effect was a more-controlled launch that led to a faster exfil of the bay. Only a handful of experienced Nova Space Rangers used the bunny hop. Dailey was one such soldier.

Dailey stood on the front of the ship's bow as the platoon cleared the ship in formation. Looking down, the man smiled at a stenciled smiling hot dog with a face, hands, and feet looking up at him, giving a thumbs-up.

This was a prank that his first operations team had pulled on him. More specifically, First Sergeant Becket, then staff sergeant. The team had been stenciling the unit's crest on the back of the gauntlet-style gloves. Dailey just happened to be what was determined to be rolling in the bushes with Stella, missing the event.

Paying penance as soldiers often did, he left the homage to the disgusting meat tubes of yesteryear. This also gave Dailey a veritable cornucopia of catchphrases to use against bad guys.

To put it in context, the last time he used a catchphrase, it went something like this, after cornering a space pirate from Earth:

"Want to see my wiener?" This was followed by a confused look from the pirate.

"What the hell, man?" This would then be followed by a full-on backhanded slap across the pirate's now Frankenstein-like flat skull.

Dailey even gave it a nickname at one point: Harvey the Wonder Wiener. After a few years of being in the force, stories were often told about Dailey and his wonder wiener. It used to drive Stella crazy when another woman asked about Dailey's wiener and if the rumors were true. All fake, and of course spread by the other Nova Rangers.

At one point, someone had filmed Dailey in action firing a weapon. Other soldiers quickly noticed he was pulling the trigger with his right hand as Harvey the Wonder Wiener shook violently. This video was eventually removed by the Federation.

"Second platoon set," Janix proclaimed as Bellman, having to walk to the front of the ship, finally made it to Dailey.

"Report," Dailey asked.

"We've identified an entrance point. The outer hull is secure. You're good to head this way with Bellman," Janix reported.

"So, are we going to…" Bellman trailed off as Dailey grabbed the man by the pull handle on the back of his suit's pack, springing forward.

Thrusters barked to life as several previously unheard-of curse words spattered through the radio.

Janix looked over at Stix, smiling. They knew what Dailey was doing.

"All right, they'll be here in a few minutes. Let's get this airlock open," Janix instructed a pair of soldiers holding plasma cutters.

Within a few minutes, the airlock was open. The two soldiers pulled a folded door from one of the fighters, holding it in front of the butchered opening. After the press of a few buttons, four sheets of shiny, thin Solarian aluminoid foil shot out, hugging the opening around the airlock like a wet first kiss. The edges flashed white, fusing to the ship's hull. After another few seconds, a green light blinked, telling the group they had resealed the airlock.

Bellman floated as light dusters, a smaller version of a thruster, hissed, keeping the man in place while he pulled out a thin, flat monitor and attached it to the hull. Two fighters hovered overhead, in conjunction with one squadron atop the vessel and the other underneath, all waiting on the thumbs-up to activate their mag boots, effectively attaching them to the hull.

The meter on the flat plate blinked green. Bellman gave the thumbs-up as several things happened all at once. The two squads latched on to the hull of the ship. One fighter hovered on each side of the vessel. They would either blast the ship out of the black heavens or push it into one of the hundreds of meteors.

That was something that hadn't gone unnoticed. One of the points Bellman had made prior to leaving was the question as to why the ship hadn't been crushed like pepper in a grinder over the years.

Dailey, Bellman, Janix, and one fire team of two soldiers stood in the airlock, looking at the interior door. While unfamiliar in design, the general operation of the door was easy enough for Bellman to figure out. Odd or not, the man was loved by all for a reason. This was reinforced when he pulled out a set of power jumpers from the square pack on his back, activating a clearly magnetic locking mechanism.

"What are you doing?" Janix asked before Bellman turned and winked. His face shield was clear, unlike that of the Solarian armored suits, which had HUD displays.

"Going to pour some juice into this thing, then reverse the magnetic polarization with this." Bellman followed this by pulling out a long, solid metal stick. This was magnetil from Mosha, the same planet his blade originated from. Moshans were always compared to the dwarves from *The Lord of the Rings*. Furry and more advanced, of course.

Bellman held the stick against the door, and the two halves slowly parted, allowing one of the soldiers to jam a retractor brace in the gap, a compact tube that, when activated, sprang out to be several feet long.

Haze greeted the team as particles floated in front of the bluish-white lights activated on their helmets. The ring around the clear shield on Bellman's helmet lit up in a halo. It annoyed the hell out of the others when he turned to talk to them while the damn thing was on.

Tarnished metal sat dormant in the round hallway, stretching into the dark void. A few containers sat stacked randomly on the flat section. While the others took in the scene, Bellman pulled out a small silver sphere and chucked it down the hallway. The team had done this before, and the two men trusted his methodology. After all, he was the rum guy.

A quick green flash popped down the hall as a hazy green line traced from the device down the hall, finishing on the group. Pulling out a tablet, Bellman held it up to the wall, attaching it with a magnetic click.

He was in full nerd mode. A full, all-you-can-eat dork buffet, and Dailey wouldn't have it any other way. The man was a genius in his own right. Quirky for sure, but he had saved the team's asses on more than one occasion.

A 3D map of the hall manifested on the screen detailing the passageway. This was followed by a flashing red light on the tablet. He was clearly going to map out the ship.

"Well, I guess that's that," Bellman huffed as Janix and the two soldiers, not seeing any warning, took a step into the corridor.

"'Sup?" Dailey asked as Bellman pulled out a microphone-looking device. Dailey knew this one. It was an atmosphere meter, a device that could determine if the air was safe to breathe, and if not, why.

"I ran the corridor layout against all known ship design records. See that red blinky light?"

"You mean the one blinking red? Yeah," Dailey prodded back.

"That means there are no records of this design registered or mapped. Meaning we are likely on a totally alien ship."

"Figured that much. How about the air?"

Bellman clicked his tongue. "Huh."

"I don't like that shit, Bellman, you know… *Huh* is not one of my favorite words," Janix chimed in.

"The air is showing as breathable. I wouldn't recommend it, but the meter is green. There are a few sub notes on here, but for the most part, we could theoretically breathe in here."

"Hard pass from me," Dailey added, walking forward as Bellman pulled out another small device.

This time, the device glowed an ominous, almost evil red. Bellman pulled out his tablet, rapidly firing away several commands to the small device. As he held it in front of him one more time, the vicious red light again sprang to life.

"Okay. Good news or bad news?" Bellman asked, staring at his tablet, not looking up.

"Always bad; you know bad news always comes first," Dailey noted. The two soldiers accompanying the group were already setting up small round lights in the hallway, illuminating the entire space.

"Well, it appears that our prior scans were incorrect. There is a dormant but still-active power source on board. The sketchy part is, according to this meter, there is also organic material on board. What kind, I couldn't tell you."

"The good news?" Janix asked, turning to check on the fire team down the hall.

"I'm not hungry anymore," Bellman replied, having lost his appetite not only due to the excitement of the discovery but the fact that he was on board an extremely old abandoned ship in uncharted territory smack-dab in the middle of the Shade Belt. For some reason, it was at that moment that Bellman finally realized the gravity of the situation.

"Where's the organic material and the power source in relation to where we are at?" Dailey asked quickly.

"From the looks of it, on the other side of that far blast door seems to be where the power signal's coming from. The organic material signal is further out. Since I don't have a map of the ship to overlay this on, all I can tell you is general proximity. Sir, there's something about the signal that doesn't make any sense to me."

Dailey walked closer to the tablet, glaring at the display. Bellman was right. All the readout said was Organic Unidentified. This also concerned the captain, as he had literally seen the same device explain exactly what kind of creature was two hundred feet ahead of them one time in the woods.

The device had also explained that the creature had been dead for twenty years. It had something to do with particles in the air and what Captain Dailey considered to be witchcraft at times.

"*Murphy* One, this is Viper Six, over." Dailey was feeling the need to report back to the crew of the *Murphy*.

"Sir," Pearl replied. Solarians had never truly figured out the whole radio-etiquette thing. It was something close to their horrible attempt at timing jokes.

"Bellman's going to send over some data. In the meantime, I want you to keep an open channel with us. I'd rather you hear us as we go," Dailey instructed.

"Affirmative. We are already watching Lieutenant Commander Bellman's live video feed."

Becket stood beside Pearl as he squinted at the video feed. Without having to look at any fancy readouts, Becket knew the ship wasn't anything they had ever encountered, from the odd airlock design.

"Sir," Becket started back up, almost in a whine at this point. "I think we may have activated something. It could be as simple as a small remaining energy cell reporting the ship's likely dead. Or something else."

"What do you mean, 'something else'?" Janix countered, getting impatient.

"A transponder beacon? Some type of odd security system? We just need to be careful. I'll get behind you guys and make sure I didn't miss anything on my scans."

"There it is," Dailey blurted out. "The ghost ship and Mr. Chicken. I missed you, man."

The commander didn't have to turn around to know that he was being flipped off. A momentary break in the wire-tight tension already floating through everything involving military banter was welcome.

CHAPTER 9

WHISPERS

The large, round, complicated room sat resolute as if waiting for a lover that it knew would never appear. Dull ambient yellow lighting came from round tracks overhead. This was the source of the power showing on Bellman's scan.

Part of the fire team consisting of Private James Atwood and Specialist Jenna Jones had taken position on the far end of the room, next to what appeared to be other offshoot passages. Bellman had thrown what was called a night star at the center of the compartment. A night star was a Solarian-designed flashlight grenade.

Once thrown, it would pop and snap, slinging what looked like glowing fluid all over the surrounding area, lighting it instantly. This was one of those things that Dailey jokingly considered to be witchcraft. The material from the grenade literally lit whatever surface it touched as if it had a light beaming directly on it, shining on the surrounding area.

Bellman's throw had lit up the entire center section, as well as dotted the rest of the far end of the room.

"No time like the present," Bellman grumbled to himself, holding out a small metal pen-shaped scanner playing a game of hot or cold with the console.

Within a few short seconds, several rapid beeps froze the man in place, coming from a small set of wall-mounted controls. Without hesitation, he lightly pressed it, activating the panel as it flipped around, exposing a small screen.

Several small icons dimly appeared on the pad as Bellman scratched the outside of his helmet, clearly needing to rub his head. This was a habit the man had at times when he was really, truly thinking.

"Wait a minute," Janix said, stepping forward. "Those look like old Solarian symbols. I think they would compare to what you Earthers call hieroglyphics."

Stepping out of the way, Janix walked up to the monitor, tracing his fingers over the carbon-encrusted corners.

"This one means energy or to be powerful. This one"—Janix pointed toward the bottom left hand of the screen—"stands for releasing, or something like that. You know, to let go. And this one," he said, pointing to the last symbol, which had a light red haze to it, "translates into something like emergency."

The group was slightly stunned at the simplicity of the controls, but also impressed with the lack of bullshit most Fleet vessels had. After quick deliberations, the three amigos decided on pressing the power button.

Pearl and Becket voiced their displeasure with the decision but knew it wouldn't matter.

"You press it yet, sir?" Becket asked.

"Oh, yeah, I pressed it way before asking you if it was a good idea," Dailey responded.

The room slowly filled with light, still keeping a muted contrast to everything. Buttons and other random controls started glowing to life, adding to the feel of a waking ship. After a quick check with the teams outside, nothing had changed.

Several other square panels flipped around, displaying designs and layouts of what they could only assume was the rest of the ship. Janix was writing on the walls with a luminary pen, for everyone to know what they were looking at.

Pearl had made several corrections to Janix's less-than-accurate interpretation of the historical symbols. One thing, however, that was still a mystery to Bellman was the presence of oxygen in the air. What Janix translated initially as a toilet symbol was corrected by Pearl as a life-support button, as well as some type of filtration nodes shown beside it.

What stopped the show was another panel appearing to show Latin. Bellman, after scanning the phrases, got the tablet to quickly translate them. It was a separate panel relating to supporting some type of cargo. There was another identical panel with the Solarian symbols on it, as well as a third, which contained an alien language neither they nor the scanner understood.

"Bellman, get that age-scanner thingy out," Dailey ordered, not fully remembering its name.

"The material graft scanner?" was all the humor Bellman had left. It was pure work at this point as he set his pack down, pulling out several suction-cup monitors and quickly hooking them up to his tablet, same as the other instruments.

A groaning sound reverberated as metal that had not moved in a very long time once again found its rhythm. Bellman again spoke up. "If anyone is wondering, that's likely the air-filtration system changing the air scrubber. See the blinking light that just stopped by the filter symbols? I think another few minutes, and we should at least be able to lower our masks and go off our oxygenators," Bellman noted, getting to work.

Dailey looked down at the air meter, seeing the readout now steadily glowing green. Bellman attached the suction cup to the metal hull with a squirt of magno gel. The material made a weird mix of the material being tested and that of the cup itself. The gel was the medium. Once absorbed, it would send back all pertinent data, creating a listing of not only the material used but even by who and when.

The Federation Tracking Office and their need to digitize everything had paid off through the development of the PAL. The Population Automated Library was loaded with maps, charts, construction plans, material profiles, and even what material was manufactured by whom. The DNA portion of the system went as far back as old FBI files from before the war. The full system was only available on an as-needed basis, and, well, the crew of the *Murphy* needed it.

The point was, if the human race was ever destroyed, there would be a record of it all tied up in one neat bow. This did create a security risk at the same time, lending to certain aspects of the PAL to be cold-stored on physical drives in undisclosed locations.

For the third time since arriving, which was going into the hour range by now, Bellman looked confused. "Something has to be messing with these readings," he grumbled as several pops emanated from behind one of the doors they had yet to explore.

"Lay it out," Dailey instructed as Bellman retracted the visor of his helmet, taking a deep breath prior. The man also tapped the side of his ear as he pressed the comm-link button on his tablet. He needed to talk in private.

Once he was comfortable with everyone around doing the same with their communicators, he let out his breath, sucking in a gasping lungful of air. Everyone froze, waiting for him to either keel over dead or turn several shades of blue. He did neither.

Dailey quickly followed, and both men looked as if they could smell something unpleasant. Janix did not, however, join the party. He and his men were there in case something went wrong.

"I don't know what I'm looking at, but the one thing I know about this damn Moshan tech is it's never wrong. Like, never. Like, I'm never going to get a girlfriend, never," Bellman began, confusion in his voice.

It was a fair statement that Dailey took to mean the man was confident in what the tablet was telling him. Bellman was always in the zone; here and now, the man looked as if he was staring at a ghost.

"Okay, so, what do all these numbers mean?" Dailey asked. Some of the data he understood, but the jumble of numbers and letters outside of the base data wasn't something he was used to seeing.

"This ship is roughly one thousand years old. Give or take a few hundred." Bellman paused, tapping his finger on his lip. "That means that…"

"What? Means what?" Dailey prodded.

"It's really old."

"Yeah, we get that, Sherlock. What's got you spooked?"

Bellman looked down at the tablet. "This would mean this ship is the oldest known space vessel we have ever encountered; I believe that includes the Solarians. They only developed a true space program five hundred years ago, a few hundred before us. Earth first landed on the moon roughly three hundred years ago. The Alurians around a thousand, from what we can tell, maybe longer."

Dailey's brain was working like an energetic cocaine-snorting hamster in an exercise wheel to sort this news out.

Seeing his expression, Bellman gave the hamster wheel an extra push. "This ship predates everything we know. It has three different panels, one in old Latin, one in even-older Solarian, and one in some unrecognizable doodles. Meaning…" The man trailed off again, clearly about to jump in the hamster wheel with Dailey.

This time, a clank banged outside the far door. Janix looked over, looking for direction as Dailey finally focused. "Hang tight. We're going to check this place out."

Giving the signal to turn communications back on, Dailey reported to the *Murphy*. "We're going to inspect the rest of the ship. Bellman was able to get the power source working, and there are signs of organic matter on board."

Back on board the *Murphy*, glances were exchanged as Becket hit the intercom. "Fourth Foot, I need you to suit up and be on standby."

After a few brief confirmations, Becket returned what he knew the good captain was waiting on. "The QRF is stood up, sir."

QRF stood for *quick reaction force*, the oh-shit factor in case things went sideways. The old adage *waiting for the cavalry to arrive* always came to mind.

With that, Dailey pulled the group in. "Bellman, which one of those hatches leads us to the organic reading you're picking up?"

"The one to the left. Are you thinking there may be hibernation pods on board?"

Dailey hadn't even given that a thought. "Yeah, sure. The one where all the sounds are coming from," the man emphasized. "Drone first, then we follow. Don't touch anything until we have figured out what we are looking at. Home base will be monitoring to help if needed."

The team of five all nodded as Janix started barking orders over the radio. "Second squad, I need you to rally at the entrance point. Once inside, follow my beacon; you'll find us at the end of the long corridor."

"Sir," Janix asserted. "Once second squad is here, we can go."

"I'll take door number one, Alex," Dailey joked. His love for vintage TV was often lost on others.

After several minutes of getting set, the additional soldiers showed up in what they were now calling the main control room. It wasn't a bridge but rather a central hub for all the systems running the ship's environment.

With the main control room secure, the team opened the door. The violent rush of stale air swept through the opening as if a thousand deep breaths were being exhaled at one time.

Janix tossed several more light grenades down the corridor as the fire team slid two light canisters in conjunction as far as they could. The hallway in front of them was significantly different from the one leading into the control room: fifty yards long and wide enough to drive a small transport vehicle through, with large bulky doors adorning both sides, giving the space a cargo-hold vibe.

The only sound present was armored boots lightly clicking as the team pushed forward. Bellman stayed several steps back, waving around a sensor rod as if he was about to perform a magic trick.

There it was, about halfway down the corridor to the right, the clicking noise they had been hearing. After a few short-held breaths, Dailey could tell there was no rhythm to the noise, meaning they could have a problem.

Janix signaled the team to take position on either side of the hall as they moved forward. Upon closer inspection of the doors, they started to take on a more ominous feel. Large round magnetic drums started from the top of the large opening, tracing all the way to the bottom.

In space, keeping things secure oftentimes meant ensuring the ship overall would never be captured or taken over. By the looks of the doors, including what appeared to be several different entry protocols, the entrances looked to keep something behind them neatly tucked away and out of the main crew's way. Dailey was starting to assume this was a prisoner ship.

The fire team took position on either side of the door with their backs pressing against the far wall, while Janix and the others all situated themselves closer to the door.

Private Atwood stepped forward, immediately noticing a slight shuffle in the door as it vibrated back and forth at random intervals. Even though it was only a few centimeters, it was enough to cause an unnerving racket that was echoing in all directions.

Turning, Atwood—also known as Woody—lowered his weapon, letting the tension out of his body. "Master Sergeant, looks like the door is having some kind of mechanical issue."

"I've got an active signal!" Bellman barked a few seconds too late.

The door violently lurched as an eight-foot-long metal spike shot out of the small gap at blurring speeds. Whatever material the spike was made of ripped straight through Private Atwood's back armor plates like a serial killer's knife through the bare skin of an unsuspecting victim.

Before Atwood's rifle dropped to the ground, Janix and Specialist Jones were already pouring the hypercharged titanium rounds into the foot-wide crack in the entrance. The spike retracted as quickly as it shot out after being peppered with several of the stinging rounds. While it wasn't time to reflect on the new weapons, they were firing so many rounds per second, it looked like a continuous stream of bullets from an old-school minigun being fired at night.

Dailey activated his armor's blade, launching himself forward enough to avoid the gunfire. Blood spread in all directions from Private Atwood as the weight of the armor started to bear down on his flinching body. He was no longer in control of his armor, and whatever the spike had done, it had clearly damaged several of the suit's systems. In most cases, the armor would go into protection mode and even remove its occupant from the battlefield if need be.

Gore trailed back to the gap where the spike had retracted. The door was still chattering like cold teeth. Bellman had backed up several feet as an additional fire team on the secondary squad ran into the corridor. There would be no need for heroics today. Atwood would likely never enjoy another warm meal aboard the *Murphy*. He would possibly die here, in the dark void of deep space.

"Everyone, stay back!" Dailey shouted, keeping not only his extended blade activated but a pod of rockets also directly targeted on the small chattering gap. "Janix, get to the other side. No one steps in front of the door."

"What the hell was that!" Jones exhaled, breathing hard into her communicator.

"What the hell that is is what we need to worry about right now," Dailey replied, reminding her that whatever had just shredded Private Atwood was still very much alive on the other side of the door.

The other fire team was set next to Dailey, with every bit of firepower they had on hand pointing directly into that small gap. Even if they ended up blowing a hole out the backside of the ship, they would have their revenge. Bellman tried to speak again before Captain Dailey cut him off.

"Janix and I are going to pry the doors open enough for all of you to sling whatever you can into that room," Dailey announced to a nodding, eager team.

Jones wasn't having any of it. She had gotten a good glimpse of the spike and Atwood's face. Whatever was on the other side of the door was massive, and it knew exactly what to do in order to kill one of her team members. She remained steady, working to focus.

There was no need to pull Atwood out of the way, as the streak of gore tracking to the opening was quickly ensuring the man would likely not be rejoining the fight. They used to have a saying that in space, no one could hear you scream. This was a lie, as Atwood let out his final gasping grunt of frustration.

Just as Dailey was about to give the nod, the door slammed open as several projectile spikes rained out through the doorway. One landed in Jones's leg, implanting itself in the outer layer of her armor.

Diving out of the way, the rest of the team opened fire as they shifted to the near wall, out of the line of fire. In a moment of clarity, Dailey leaned forward just as a nightmare-inducing spike slammed into the hallway, looking as if it belonged to a massive mechanoid spider, launching two small light explosive-tipped rockets around the corner.

With another quick pop, the spike retracted, allowing the door to slam closed once again.

"Is everyone good?" Janix asked as everyone gave a thumbs-up. A light haze of smoke filled the corridor from the weapons as Jen looked down at the spike, yanking it free before sliding it down the hallway to Bellman. It hadn't penetrated the outside shell of her suit. This was the only positive news out of the short-lived encounter.

The object was mirror-reflective metal with several barbs on it to rip through either flesh or metal. When the woman looked inside, organic red material greeted her like a nightmare.

"Sir, I say we get out of here and turn this ship into a cooked space brick," Janix recommended, his snappy term coming out wrong. Soldiers from Earth were used to the Solarian take on human humor, often getting a kick out of that alone.

Dailey glanced at Bellman as he hovered another sensor over the spike. There was something about the vessel that wasn't sitting right with Dailey. It wasn't how old it was but rather the implications of the different types of languages and/or planets/civilizations that may have been involved.

It took at least a dozen years after the Tectonic Wars for most of human society to learn that much of the history they learned in school was only half the story and, in many ways, none of it. This was something that Dailey couldn't sort out, and even more concerning was Bellman struggling with the situation. The thought fluttered out of his mind just as quickly as it had landed. That and the snap of ozone that had just slapped the air beside him.

There, with its tongue hanging out the side of its mouth, was Sparky. A light layer of electricity arced over his black fur as he sat down as if wanting a treat. "I don't have time for this," Dailey mumbled as Pearl came over the radio.

"Is that Sparky?"

"Yeah, it's Sparky..." He trailed off, then spoke to the alien dog. "Stop. Bad boy. Sit, don't go out there."

Dailey's words were lost on the creature as it walked in front of the large, still-stuttering door, looking down at the pool of blood. Lifting his head, Sparky sniffed the air. This was followed by a rumbling growl and damn near laserlight show of blue electricity dancing off his back. Spikes of fur shot up as Sparky faced the door, letting out several growling barks.

Same as before, the door shot open, only this time, Sparky rushed the small gap like an out-of-control torpedo. "Sparky, no!" Dailey barked. The truth of the matter was they had grown attached to the creature.

One thing Dailey had picked up on was whatever was inside that room was thinking. It had changed its attack or method every time it opened the door.

Without much thought, Dailey swung around the small lip he was behind and slammed his now-energized blade into the door's controls. This put an immediate end to whatever had been holding the door shut, as it slammed open.

What lay before him as he turned the corner with a full armor-piercing rocket pack ready to unleash hell was a web of electricity dancing around the room coming from Sparky. On the far end was a thing of hellish dreams.

The room was roughly the size of a basketball court, and at the far end was something that Dailey could have gone a lifetime without seeing. A massive ten-foot-tall hairy ball surrounded by several spiked legs covered in gleaming metal sat frozen as electricity danced around the metal sections of the creature. This included a metal plate under its belly and an odd head full of deep dark rows of pitch-black eyes.

This was an honest-to-god biomechanical space spider. While previously not a real thing to Dailey and the crew, as of two minutes ago, it now was. Quickly realizing that the electricity had somehow shorted out the beast's systems or at least was paralyzing it, Janix and the rest of the team poured into the room. They made sure to not wander in front of Sparky, the wonder dog. If this worked out, Sparky would be getting all the dehydrated ham he could stomach.

Taking the lead, Dailey launched several small rockets into the fleshy part of what would now be known as the super scary space spider. Smacks of clear goop erupted from the now-shattered hairy skull as the others joined in. Pings and pangs of superheated rounds melted into the room and spider, taking hold of the lack of radio chatter.

This was Third Foot. The platoon you called when you needed textbook, precise fighting. No specialties, just pure Nova Space Rangers doing what they did best. Sparky shut down the light show just as the massive creature faltered, the tension leaving its frame.

It was over. A lingering haze hovered overhead, being pulled into the vents as the two squads split the room in half. Two soldiers peeled off, securing the empty corridor, calling in help to secure Woody's body. They would mourn later, swearing he was looking at them.

This time, they had taken the creature by surprise, all thanks to Sparky, which led to Dailey's next point of order. "Sparky, what the hell was that?" he asked as if the dog could understand him.

Sparky simply plopped his butt on the ground with a resounding thud, his goofy grin taking back over. Realizing how stupid he looked, Dailey shook it off, petting the dog. "Good boy. I don't know how or why… Jesus, I'm talking to a space dog that came out of nowhere to take on a space spider."

Becket chimed in over the radio. "Looks like you have a guardian angel. The platoon control shows everyone green minus one. What's going on, sir?"

Becket had called him *sir,* something that was as telling as the silence they often shared. "Don't know yet."

Refocusing on the scene in front of him, Dailey looked around the room, seeing what appeared to be ages of scratching and scraping on the walls and, more importantly, the door. The creature was digging its way out and had made a big-enough rut to catch one of its legs in the door. From there, it was a mystery.

It took several minutes to remove Woody's body from the entrance, including cleaning up the mess. Upon further inspection, he was still some-how alive. Something wasn't right about the entire situation, but Dailey and the others would take it. Jones chalked it up to his meat-and-potatoes upbringing in the Midwest, while Janix, after seeing him still alive, blamed it on his being too stupid to figure out how to die. This was all in jest to calm the group's nerves.

"Bellman, get in here!" Dailey yelled as the man froze in place after seeing the creature now sprawled out on the far end of what was deemed a holding cell.

Upon entering the room, the science officer also stared at Sparky sitting on his butt with his tongue hanging out, panting lightly as if waiting on a treat for doing something good. He had indeed done something good, something that Dailey and the others were still baffled by, let alone figuring out how the hell he got onto the ship.

"I'm going to need you to see if that thing is still alive and if there's any more of them. If there's a chance that any more of these are on board, and I mean even a fleeting chance, I need to know about it," Dailey instructed.

Bellman set his pack down, pulling out a small tripod and extending what looked like a metal rod almost to the ceiling. After the quick push of a button, the top sprang open to an umbrella-styled mesh cap. The man quickly shifted gears, moving to one of the sprawled-out shiny metal spider legs of death.

"Hey, hero," Specialist Jones offered. "Sir, use the spike I gave you. It's the same material."

"Yes, of course," Bellman stammered, finally realizing that the immediate threat was over. It wasn't that the man was a coward. He just wasn't built for combat. What the man lacked in intestinal fortitude, he made up in smarts. Dailey understood his value and knew the power of the pen, so to speak.

"What are you doing, and how long is it going to take you?" Janix asked as Dailey turned, both looking at the man.

"I want to use the Moshan material analyzer, then plug it into the spectral frequency array. If there's anything else identical to this in the ship, that'll find it."

"That means you're gonna need some of this," Dailey proclaimed as he quickly scooped up a handful of the clear gooey material still attached to a chunk of whatever skull the creature had once had.

Luckily for Bellman and the others, they had raised their face shields. Not only the sound of the splattering goo at his feet but the nauseating smell of death and sulfur made its way to his nostrils, throwing the man into a fit of retching gags.

Curling his fist in a ball and placing it in front of his mouth, Bellman finally regained his composure. Dailey grinned. "Let me guess: you didn't snap an odor capsule in the main room. Those damn black-hole-flavored Doritos you keep eating must have fried all your senses."

One thing the future didn't ignore, as well as the mega food companies back on Earth, was the significant increase in flavor possibilities for their products. Solarian-flavored momo potato chips scooped into what was called moon dust dip were starting to become a nostalgic flavor combination. People like Dailey, on the other hand, enjoyed the classic, old-school, nacho-seasoned Doritos, and just plain-ass boring potato chips, preferably kettle-style.

The Nova Space Rangers were trained to always carry at least two of the small capsules on them for situations just like this. It was SOP for them to crack one as soon as something less than appetizing was in the air.

While smelling was one thing, the sounds and macabre visions alone were enough to put anyone off balance. Bellman went to work as the team continued examining the room.

CHAPTER 10

IT'S NOT THE HOW BUT THE WHY

Sir," Janix called from the entranceway. Dailey, closely followed by Sparky, walked into the small huddle surrounding the opening mechanism. "Besides where your blade cut through all the servos, it looks like somebody tried to weld the actual door lock shut. Each of those three locking mechanisms looked at various set openings for the entrance. That thing in there had been clawing away at the inside of the door and had broken two of the locks. I'm guessing the gunfire destroyed the last one, and your blade wrecked the mechanism opening the entrance."

"So, you're saying somebody locked that thing in there?" Dailey asked as Janix nodded in affirmation.

"It looks like it. Once we're done here, we can shut the door back. It won't lock, but we can close the door and seal it shut. Just my two cents' worth, sir," Janix suggested.

Dailey pondered the recommendation, looking down the empty corridor door. "That's fine. I want to clear the rest of the ship before we look behind any more of these doors."

Nods were given and orders doled out as Bellman finally walked out of the room. His report was straight and to the point. He had logged the creature's signature and rescanned the entire ship. They would not be finding any more monsters hiding in a closet.

On the other side of the blast doors leading away was a space he suspected to be the ship's bridge. Of particular interest to the science officer was naming the creatures. This went through a few iterations, including the Bellman Bug, Octo-Bell Arachnid—after its eight spike appendages—and Dailey's personal favorite, the Space Arachman Bellifica.

The spider motif was fitting for the ship. It was already giving everyone the proverbial creeps. Between the ambient lighting and light-speckled haze throughout the ship, the team was surprised a vampire, or even a ghost, hadn't jumped out yet. It wasn't like they believed in any of that, but what they had witnessed of the ship so far was enough to keep the team on their toes.

After thirty minutes of back-and-forth chatter with the *Murphy* and the final sparking weld of the door, the space spider was now buried in its eternal tomb. The team had chosen to move forward with two full squads: one to stay in the main corridor and the other moving forward. Fourth Platoon had been dispatched to the ship as soon as things went sideways.

Sparky, on a good note, was sitting in front of the blast doors, wagging his tail. Dailey took this as a good sign. That was confirmed when the commander walked up and simply pressed the green-tinted button, opening the large doors.

Unlike the rest of the vessel's sterile appearance, the feel of the ship changed. This was the crew area. While still dank and dark in contrast to a ship that hadn't been floating through the void for hundreds if not thousands of years, the forward area of the ship was more inviting. Ambient lighting flickered on, likely connected to the door mechanism's being activated.

Sparky whooped and then ran into the main room. This was followed by a curt sniff and light jog down a section of hallway into what appeared to be a small galley and sitting area.

"I doubt whoever locked that thing up made it off this ship," Dailey reassured the group as well as himself. "Just be careful. Don't touch anything."

His words were interrupted by Sparky rummaging in something out of sight. "That means you, too, Sparky!" Dailey added. The crew watching on board the *Murphy* grinned at the interaction. It was funny to watch the hardened Captain Ben Dailey unsuccessfully reprimand an alien dog.

"Sir," Specialist Jones spoke up, looking at a panel on the wall facing down the corridor. "It's a locking panel. It controls all the doors."

"How do you know that?" Janix asked as she pointed to the symbol shaped like on a door-open-and-close button in an elevator back home. "We can get to that later. Sergeant Tucker, stay here and secure this area. Pick someone to stay."

The rest of the main entrance room was fairly uneventful. The interesting part was the small mess hall that Sparky ran into. Alien food-service equipment sat in a neat row. In the center of the room, a waist-high table had several large benches.

By all accounts, it was larger than an average Solarian chair, which was considered SXXL. That stood for Solarian double extra-large size or, as most of the other soldiers dubbed it, SWL, standing for Solarian wide load. A term of endearment that was loosely translated into the old saying: *Baby got back.*

Human military types and their acronyms were enough to drive the other alien races insane. It was something that people from Earth primarily did, much like playing golf and enjoying what was really a G-rated adult entertainment industry at best. Alien porn was something that could not only change a person but likely keep them up at night due to it usually being a significant emotional event.

"Looks like this place was used well after the ship stopped whatever it was doing," Bellman stated, looking down at a stack of guck-covered plates.

"Sparky, get your nose out of that," Dailey scolded, only to get a glare from the dog.

Ignoring the command, Sparky turned around, picking up an honest-to-god device resembling a dog collar. When Dailey stepped forward, his light hovered over a pile of dusty bones. The dog looked up, then back at the bones, before dropping the collar at his feet.

"I don't have time for this." Dailey chuckled, picking up the device as Sparky let out a yip. "Okay, I hear you, boy. Bellman, scan this and secure it to take back. It seems our friend here might know something we don't."

"You see the skull?" Bellman asked.

"Yeah. Looks like Sparky's overgrown dome. Space spiders, space lightning dogs…" He trailed off, aware of how absurd it sounded.

Absurd and worrying. Terra Minor Three, Sparky's home planet, was the closest system to the Shade Belt following their course. They had assumed it was void of sentient life. Sparky alone had proven that to be wrong. The fact that he knew tech and hopefully didn't just want a new chew toy opened up an entire flurry of questions that Dailey didn't have answers for. The dog was being too specific about the device.

"All clear, sir," Janix said, getting a report from one of the privates standing at the door. "The bridge appears to be on the other side of the secondary blast shield down the hall. There's living quarters across the hall. It's going to take some time to sort through it. Appears the crew were in here for a long time."

"I'm betting whatever is left of them is on the bridge. Same as any ship, it's a priority for the life-support systems, but those seem to be working."

Picking up on this, Janix nodded, motioning Specialist Dion Belts, known as Buckle, and Private Jake Jenna, known as Private Parts, over. "Secure the bridge door."

With a few quick nods, the group ran down the dimly lit hall. There was a feel about the ship. Something that was off. It wasn't a mining ship, but something else. The lack of weapon racks and security monitors had convinced the group this wasn't a prisoner transport.

What lay before their eyes when the bridge doors shuffled open was something that defied explanation. A nightmare that was trying to tell a message of better days.

Taking the first step in, Dailey immediately noticed the pile of skeletons that had been leaning on the door, causing the slow opening. They now understood what all the popping and snapping was.

Light blankets fluttered in the newly introduced air, hanging on the walls, making small sectioned-off sleeping areas. Pillows, trinkets, and other personal items such as combs lay in each area, as well as random sets of bones.

What caught Dailey in the gut was a family of people no taller than four feet. One had its arms wrapped around the other as lovingly as a skeleton could. Beside them lay a smaller set of children's bones. It was a family that had perished together.

The Nova Space Rangers had a high level of intestinal fortitude and had seen unimaginable things, but this made the entire group pause as they huddled around the family. Clanking pans interrupted the reflective silence as Specialist Jones stepped over several pots and pans before talking.

"Sir, the skeletons over here are humanoid. Not Solarian, either."

This raised eyebrows, as the piles of bones at the entrance had been jumbled and smashed. Shifting their attention, the group walked closer to the front viewport. Happy drawings of clouds and smiling stick figures were plastered over half the viewport, covering the dark backdrop of space.

Upon closer inspection, the pictures in some areas, presumably the tail end of the fairy-tale drawing, while still from a child's hand and mind, grew darker. Smiles turned into frowns as several barely recognizable final sketches were simply of the bridge's blast door. Even more concerning was the presence of several Egyptian-styled hieroglyphics also randomly included.

"Look," Dailey pointed out. One of the drawings had a spider-like monster with spiked legs. Under the spider, a red crayon had been scribbled at a feverish pace, likely portraying blood. The commander traced his finger to another drawing. This one, Mom or Dad had likely helped with.

The one the adult had likely helped with showed a ship in front of the bridge window. The next showed a group of stick figures running through the bridge's main entrance. Behind them was a massive figure in a black space suit.

He stopped following the pictures as he got close to the floor. A smaller human skeleton sat partially leaning up against the wall. Several half-done drawings lay strewn around, as well as a bowl. No one dared breathe when the flashlight beamed on the body. A small dress and what appeared to be tiny handmade bracelets were all Dailey needed to see as he turned inward, taking in the entirety of the bridge.

On top of that, Sparky hadn't entered the room. It was a grave. As tough as Dailey was, the thought that someone so young had suffered so much punched him right in the gut, right in the very core of what allowed the man to be capable of unyielding violence.

"Goddamn looks like they came in here and starved to death or something," Dailey huffed out to no one in particular.

The familiar ding of Bellman's DNA monitor garnered a whistle from the man.

"I don't think these were the crew. Look at the clothes," Bellman stated, making a good point. "They're all the same... and bland. None of this makes sense."

"Spill it," Dailey insisted, motioning to cut off the comms.

"I just checked some of the bones by the door. They're a mix of human and... well, Earth humans, to be precise, Moshan and likely Solarian as well. I got a trace signal."

"Time to rewrite the history books," Jones grunted. She had been uncharacteristically vocal the entire time they had been on board.

"Becket, change of plans?"

"Yes, sir. What are you thinking?"

"This place is, from what we can tell, a graveyard. There's more to it. Get Comms Officer King suited up and over here. I want him to try and extract what data he can from the ship. We're going to clear what looks like storage or holding bays, then I'm heading back."

"Well, looks like your sidekick beat you to it." Becket shrugged, looking over to see Sparky sitting on the helm.

Becket and Dailey had been trying to work out just how gifted Sparky was. For starters, they were quickly realizing the hound could apparently teleport or fly through space. He was intelligent, arguably more so than Moshan Dragonian dogs, and he had taken a liking to the good commander.

Over the next several hours, the team carefully inspected the bridge of the alien ship. Or was it alien? The shock came when they started opening the rest of the bay doors dotting the long corridor. Inside were even worse visions of horrible fates. Unlike the still-intact remains found on the bridge, the ones they found were not only separated by race but in piles of charred rubble.

Between the blast marks on the walls and blackened bones, it appeared as if someone had simply opened the door and unleashed a flurry of blaster fire. They were right: this was a grave.

From what the team pieced together, a group of the passengers had escaped to the forward section of the ship, only to be stuck. It was clear from the overall vibe of the survivors' area that they had been trapped. When and how the space spider had been sealed into the one bay was a mystery they were not likely to solve.

Janix suggested the actual crew had probably figured a way off the ship, accounting for the lack of additional bodies with guns and spacesuits. Whatever had happened had been contained, swift, and violent. Even more interestingly—the ship was a small piece of a much larger vessel.

Dailey and Janix stood in the central control room as people shuffled in and out, almost done going through everything found. King had been successful in pulling a sector off the data drives. While the equipment was something they had yet to see, it was reasonably straightforward with the technology now afforded the inhabitants of Earth.

Captain Dailey rubbed his thumbs on a sleek metal box, trying to figure out why it was not only warm but lightly vibrating. His best guess was its being some type of storage device. The device would be coming back, as well as several other small pieces from the ship.

"It feels like these people were being transported like cattle," Janix noted, looking at several containers of random junk in the corner.

"Perhaps. All I do know is this is something the Fleet will want to keep under wraps until we figure out more. I mean, according to Bellman, whom

I trust with all that shit he uses, those are humans. Jesus, or whatever flavor of the month, was walking the Earth after this ship was likely operational."

"I'm struggling as well here, trying to figure out what happened," Janix breathed out.

"It's not always the what that's important but the why. We're going to leave the ship the way we found it. Power down this system and leave these souls alone," Dailey replied. This was a Solarian comment about not messing with souls. A word that was for all intents and purposes universal.

CHAPTER 11

PROGRESS REPORT

’m glad you’re out of the Shade Belt. We can finally talk,” Ran said as Dailey sat in the briefing room with Becket and Jen. “I received your report.”

“Yes, sir. Since you’re heading this way, I’ll fill you in on the rest when I see you.” Dailey had held back several vital pieces of important information.

“For it to be that sensitive, I’ll make sure we have no more delays,” Ran followed up.

One week after leaving the ghost ship, the crew of the *Murphy* had finally made it to the outer bands of the Shade Belt. Most importantly, they had done so with relative ease. The maneuverability of the frigate-class starship and the soft touch of Navigation Officer Pearl had likely kept them from being smashed into stardust.

As soon as they could get a secure signal, the crew contacted General Ran aboard the *Brightstar*. They had stopped at Terra Minor Three for an undisclosed reason.

“Yes, sir. Some things are better communicated face-to-face. We paused on the outskirts of the Shade Belt to stay out of sight for now,” Dailey expressed cautiously.

“That sounds like a good segue into a recent recommendation.”

Dailey seized the opportunity that had just been teed up for his smart-ass comment. "You mean the one where we get to go off to another uncharted planet for a good three- to four-month snooze?"

"You do understand everyone knows what you're up to, or lack thereof, when you're out on a mission and not sticking to the bad guys, right?" Ran lamented jokingly.

"I wouldn't have it any other way, sir," Dailey coolly replied.

"Fleet reached out a couple of days ago, asking about you. They are fully aware Colonel Freeman is likely missing in action. With that, they have recommended you be promoted, taking his billet as commander of the Pathfinder Battalion."

Both men breathed into the communicators.

"Sir, I'm not sure that's a good idea. That would mean I have to report back to Fleet command or figure out what the rest of the battalion is doing, at the least. All the companies are extremely independent. They could be spread all over the cosmos. I haven't talked to one of the other companies in at least seven months."

"About that. Alpha Company has been assigned permanent on-world duty back home. Charlie Company is on a mission heading toward the Outer Spiral. As for Delta Company, I really don't know," General Ran stated bluntly.

"That doesn't make any sense. So, why promote me if I'm not needed?" Dailey scoffed.

"You're a lot of things, Captain Dailey. One of those happens to be that you're dependable and, most importantly, know when and how to keep your mouth shut."

"I don't know about that," Dailey said, trying to reassure him.

There was more to Dailey's statement than a smart reply. News of his battalion commander being farther out than any other reported human was already a big-enough gut punch. Finding out that Fleet and operational headquarters had no clue the location of one of its prized possessions was a whole other can of Solarian slime worms to open.

Ben Dailey knew something wasn't right about the entire situation, so much so that he was starting to question General Ran's intentions and the reason Juice and the others were on the other side of the Shade Belt.

"The promotion would have to wait until we were together, either way. Meaning you can take a deep breath for now. We're both still hoping to find Colonel Freeman still breathing. I would like you to stay put until we link up. Any questions?"

The entire thing about words was that they actually meant something. Lawyers and generals alike were usually good at making ambiguous statements during meaningful conversations. By Captain Dailey's interpretation of the likely off-the-cuff closing statement, General Ran hadn't ordered the *Murphy* to stay put. He simply stated that he would like everyone to stay where they were. A fact that was bothering Dailey, knowing lives were likely on the line.

"Yes, sir," Dailey replied quickly, wanting to close the conversation. General Ran obliged as both screens went blank.

"Odd," Becket grunted.

"You think he's messing with us?" Dailey asked.

"I don't even really know any of you, and I can tell he was feeding you a line of half-cocked bullshit," Jen agreed.

"I'd give anything to talk with Juice for even two seconds. Even if that means he's haunting me. Which I think he threatened to do at one point," Dailey joked as Becket shook his head.

"Hopefully, he's not. Before you say it," Becket emphasized, "I'm already figuring we aren't sticking around here."

"Oh, hell no," Dailey replied as Jen looked confused. "We're totally going to the *Asher*. Remember that thing I always say about words meaning something?"

Becket grinned, while Jen continued to look confused by the entire interaction. "Lieutenant Brax, what the good captain is saying is sometimes it's better to play dumb, even though they know you're not."

"I prefer the term *ask for forgiveness*," Dailey cut in as Becket finished.

"The general is not being forthright with us, and for lack of a better way to put it, he didn't order us to do anything."

Jen's face shifted to light amusement. "Thus the reputation."

"Yup, and don't think about ever doing that to either of us." Dailey smiled as Bellman came over the communicator.

"Sir, we just finished the data review, and you might want to come down to the science bay to check that thing Sparky grabbed."

Bellman stood at the far end of a room resembling Frankenstein's cyberpunk castle. Meters, computers, and monitors all sat in the man's version of organized chaos. Sparky sat on his butt, panting in his usual fashion. After returning to the ship, the dog had spent most of his time in the science bay. It was a clear message to check out the collar.

"What's the good word?" Dailey asked as Becket walked over to the old-style Mr. Coffee. Bellman, Lieutenant Dasher, and the two men appreciated vintage things such as the Mr. Coffee machine, which were mainly from the pre-war days.

The yellowed plastic husk had been white at one point. The heating plate had been replaced along the way, but the pièce de résistance was the original glass bowl complete with the brown plastic handle. The men all swore by the smell of hours-old burnt coffee.

"Well, all that data was right. The humanoids were at some point from Earth. The Solarians as well are from their home world. As for the data, there are two main takeaways. Dasher," Bellman started, handing it off to Lieutenant Dasher. The young man was not only a platoon leader but also moonlighted as the intelligence officer, being that he was in charge of the scouts.

Becket walked the line, filling up cups of steaming hot go juice. Dasher smiled, pulling the toothpick out of his mouth for once. Something any other respectable man from Texas would never do.

"Sir, First Sergeant. I'll start on the easy-to-digest part. The ship's name was the Terminus. Those people on board were enslaved."

"So, that's the easy-to-digest portion? It was a slave ship?" Dailey asked, working through the details.

"If you want to put it that way… yes. They were being transported to a location close to the final reported coordinates of the *Asher*."

"Thousands of years ago," Bellman added for dramatic effect. Sparky shuffled his butt on the floor in agreement.

"All right, hit me with it," Dailey caved, trying to save some mental processing for the foot that was likely about to drop.

"The ship is likely Alurian," Dasher spit out.

It was simple math. The Alurians' planet was considered to be outside the galaxy on Earth's side of the Milky Way. The Outer Spiral was located outside of the charted galaxy in the general direction the Alurians had come from. No one ever found their planet or where they were truly from other than speculation and triangulation on the outer system the ships were originating from.

"Shit," Dailey exhaled. "No wonder everyone's tight-lipped about this area. Our only saving grace is how old that ship is and the fact that it may have drifted over the years this way. The Space Stream is more than capable of moving something extremely far over a few hundred years."

While Dailey was trying to delude himself into not wanting to think about the Alurians, Bellman pulled out his tablet, punching in a few numbers.

"It would take hundreds or even thousands of years to drift here from Earth through the Space Stream," Bellman announced, bursting Dailey's bubble.

The Space Stream was named after the concept of the jet stream back on Earth. It was a fast-flowing section of space that, while denser than actual space, seemed to be in a constant state of movement. Like a sailboat, once inside the stream, a ship could be transported several parsecs with little to no energy used.

Still mostly a mystery and in much need of further exploration, the Space Stream was often unexplained. The closest the Federation had come to understanding it was as a partial temporal distortion field without all the time nonsense. Or, as several genius-level scholars once described it, a river filled with dense, flowing black hole–like materials instead of water.

After years of political infighting, the mining corporations were given the rights to the Stream, allowing them to mine moons and other derelict planets faster. All for the greater good, not to mention obscene profits.

Mining companies, in many ways, had turned into their own entities. Overpowered and harsh, the corporations seemed more like the mafia than a reputable business. They owned planets, not caring what happened to them.

Dailey and Becket both knew as soon as you pulled the curtain back on a pirate or raider ship, there was likely a mining corporation lurking in the shadows.

"All right, we can shelve this for later. For now, we're going to activate the hyperdrive as soon as we clear the outer belt and head toward the *Asher*."

"Still a few days before reaching the *Asher*?" Bellman asked. The man usually didn't pay much attention during briefings, having his thoughts elsewhere.

"One week," Becket spoke up, refilling everyone's coffee.

"That cluster of planets isn't too far. We should be able to see them," Dailey started. "We'll be close to the *Asher*. The signal came from the nearest planet. Once we clear the field, we should be able to get a good scan of the system. Pearl sent out a probe already."

Sparky, seeing the conversation coming to an end, chuffed, standing up. "Oh, I almost forgot," Bellman added. "Two things. First, that weird computer box thing I couldn't get working or open, it's not explosive or sending any signals. Good news is, I got this collar working, and it seems to be some type of translator. That's about as far as I got."

Sparky nudged Bellman as he leaned over, snapping it on the dog's thick neck. Everyone waited as Sparky strolled up to Dailey and subsequently bit his leg, followed by several light snaps of electricity.

"Bad dog!" Dailey yelled as the others started laughing.

"No bad dog, want ham," a voice floated through Dailey's thoughts at the same time that Sparky barked.

"What?" Dailey asked as Becket shook his head.

"What?" Becket countered.

"What did one of you say about ham?"

The group looked around at each other, finally staring at a smiling Sparky. After a light growling chuff, Sparky plopped back down on his butt.

"I like ham," the rather well-fed, clearly ham-loving intergalactic electricity pooch quickly responded.

"I'm going crazy," Dailey stated to thin air as the others looked confused. "You do hear that, right?"

"Hear what?" Jen asked as Bellman cleared his throat.

"Translators are often one-way streets. You can hear Sparky?"

"I think so. Sparky, say something," Dailey instructed.

"Ham, I watch ham, and to go to the big chair to want lights." The chunky yet fitting voice echoed in Dailey's thoughts, going along with the light bark he had rolled out. The system was clearly calibrating itself to Sparky.

"What did he say?" Bellman asked as Becket and Jen continued to stare at the interaction.

"Something about watching ham and wanting lights. I'm going crazy. Either way, I think we know where he disappears to," Dailey noted as Sparky stood up, hearing the word *ham*.

"Senior Chief Thron can be a softy," Jen noted as the others turned to her.

"No, no, he's not. You ever watch that super old movie about the battleship and the cook?" Dailey started, showing off his knowledge of classic movies.

"The one with that chunky karate dude? They made a bunch more around 2050, right? Stephen Sinaguly… Steve Segul," Becket pondered that, having watched the movie with Dailey at one point.

"Steven Seagal, Under Siege. They really messed that one up after the third reboot in space. Lieutenant Brax." Dailey was using her official rank and last name. "I'll send you a digital link. Consider it ODP training. That's Senior Chief Thron's story told before he was even born."

He was referring to Thron's prior life as a Solarian battle master, a title given to the fiercest warriors their world produced. Tall, thick as a double-layered blast shield, and methodically detailed, the Solarian had found peace after years of fighting to pursue his passion, cooking. It came through in the way he ran the galley and how well the inhabitants of the *Murphy* were fed.

"Sometimes, I wonder how I got this assignment," Jen joked as the others gawked at her.

"You do know we read your file, ma'am," Becket noted, getting a chuckle out of the group. She fit in with the merry band of highly lethal misfits and knew it.

"So, what's the play?" Bellman asked, reaching over for more coffee.

The sound of a proximity sensor dinged in the background. This had become common over the past several weeks. The system was tuned to alert the navigation team if an asteroid or piece of space debris was getting close to the ship.

"We're going to give it another couple of hours. Wait for the probe to report back, then we leave," Dailey answered flatly.

"Just like that?" Bellman asked.

"Just like that," Dailey said, turning toward Jen. "I want your team to get some rest. Anything shows up on the system's scan, and you may be earning your paycheck."

"Yes, sir," she exclaimed, giving a light salute.

CHAPTER 12

THE ASHER

Loose debris from the *Asher* floated through space like unwanted toys discarded on the go by a young child. Below sat a calico-patch planet. Desert, ocean, and green, forested landscapes hugged that surface in odd yet organized patterns. Unlike Earth, the large bodies of water that were likely oceans were interrupted by large cross sections of land, making the planet look like one large mass of land with huge lakes throughout its surface.

"Sir, stealth protocols are engaged," Chief Engineering Officer Junior Lieutenant Barry Hontz announced. Dailey liked to call this sneaky mode, and while engaged, all main external lighting and thruster systems were either off or shielded. This also included the deactivation of the electromagnetic field, letting the ship quickly resemble any other piece of debris floating around space.

While the anti-radar technology was old, it was reliable, standing the test of time. Sometimes, the simplest of technologies was the best of technology. The ship used technology developed for American naval submarines of the late 1900s.

"Do we have any movement from the planet?" Dailey asked, standing up and pinning his hands behind his back.

Specialist Kline turned from the onslaught of monitors in front of him. "No, sir. Most of the signals I'm seeing are all planetside. I can't vouch for the other side, but the visible planet as we see it is not trying to reach out and say hello."

Satisfied with Kline's assessment, Dailey walked up to Pearl. "Get us close enough to fit in with the rest of the debris. Also, set a targeted course back to our original location before exiting the Shade Belt. I want to be ready to haul ass out here on a moment's notice."

"Yes, sir, already done. I've also triangulated the location of the signal on the planet's surface," Pearl responded, walking up to the actual main viewport.

After she clicked a few buttons on a small tablet in her hand, a red dot appeared on the viewport showing the planet's surface.

"Looks like it was a straight shot," Dailey observed. "Yes, it looks like the escape pod landed in the forest area. I just checked with King, and the signal has gone dead. There is, however, something else. We also received a short-range transponder signal from another escape pod roughly a hundred miles east of the initial escape pod."

"Of course," Dailey huffed as the door slid open, followed closely by Sparky entering.

Over the past several days of travel, Dailey had spent time with the dog, working through how to communicate better. While Sparky was still using simple sentences that often got jumbled up, it was improving. Dailey had learned several things over the last couple of days that had surprised even him.

For starters, Terra Minor Three was more than met the eye. Under its vast mountains and colored oceans lived a relatively hidden civilization. When the *Murphy* and its crew parked in orbit, the entire planet's population, already living underground, went into a state of complete hibernation.

Sparky couldn't precisely articulate why, but it had something to do with star monsters. He also stated that the inhabitants of Terra Minor Three closely resembled humans from Earth. Bellman sent an encrypted message back to the small team left behind, letting them know the situation.

The dog had also implied that other species possibly lived within the guts of the planet. Between the ghost ship and Sparky's odd knowledge of the tech on board, plus his statements about TM3, the entire back end of the galaxy was becoming significantly more complex than others, including Captain Dailey, believed.

"Sparky, is that ham I smell on your breath?" Dailey asked, leaning down to pet the dog.

"Ham, yes, yes. Go to planet? Use bathroom?"

"If we go to the planet, you're more than welcome to use the bathroom down there," Dailey replied, grinning. Sparky had become the ship's mascot and, in many ways, a part of the crew. One afternoon, they had even done a question-and-answer session with the pup in the galley.

"Becket?" Dailey asked over the communicator.

"Yes, sir?"

"How's it looking down there? Fourth Platoon ready to go?"

"Roger that. Fourth Platoon, as well as the attack wing, is ready. Once you get down here and suited up, it's go time," First Sergeant Becket relayed as Dailey started walking toward the helm.

"Pearl, you're in charge. If anything, and I mean anything, makes the hair on the back of your neck stand up"—Dailey was using Solarian humor due to the fact that they had no hair—"you let us know. I want the ship out of here and the hyperdrive activated as soon as anything happens. The fighters are all charged, so we should be able to keep up long enough to get out of here and back on board."

"Yes, sir. We are also starting a planetary scan. We should know what the population, if any, looks like soon."

With that, Pearl saluted the commander of the *Murphy* as he made his way down to the drop bay. Jen walked up to Captain Dailey just as he completed activating his armor.

"Lieutenant Brax." Dailey nodded.

"Sir, the attack wing is ready to go. I'll be going out with you again. Once Fourth Foot is set, Second and Third will take up security positions around the ship."

"Perfect, First Foot will be in reserve as a QRF," Dailey replied as Becket walked up, handing Dailey a rifle.

"Sir, on your call," Becket noted.

"Get everybody over here. I want to talk to the team. Lieutenant Brax, I'll key up the communicator for your pilots."

After a few minutes of shuffling, clinking, and clanking of armor, damn near the entire company was in the drop bay, surrounding Captain Dailey. That included Sparky, who had miraculously appeared out of thin air.

"Listen up. Every one of you knows this is personal for me. With that being said, I, as well as everyone else here, need to remain focused. There were people on board the ship that some of us likely knew. You see something, say something. I don't care if it's an odd-looking blast mark or something that looks like it doesn't belong.

"You've all been briefed on the main priorities. The bridge and the crew, if any are still alive tucked away somewhere, which our scans are showing is negative, then the payload. We still don't know what that is, but we know where. First to fight, last to die!" Dailey concluded, barking out the motto of Viper Company.

An earth-shattering reply followed this, "First to fight, last to die!"

On those very words, the drop bay broke into organized chaos as soldiers and support crew scattered in all directions as if part of a disjointed group of musicians coming together in perfect harmony.

In full combat armor, Dailey locked his boots in the holders outside of the fighter, giving Jen a nod to go. With the electromagnetic fields down, the bay had been sealed. With a loud cracking thump, the bay doors slid in opposite directions as soldiers and fighters darted out of the ship at breakneck speeds, looping around the vessel's spiked underbelly.

Lieutenant Dasher, as well as his counterpart, leveled off beside Jen, quickly darting forward toward what appeared to be the bridge compartment hanging off a large chunk of the *Asher*'s substructure by only a few strands of thick cabling.

This was followed by several other fighters shooting into the debris field, accompanied by numerous flickering soldiers with their thrusters fully activated. Within a few minutes, the bridge was secured.

Two attack fighters floated above and below, as Lieutenant Dasher had attached cables to the bridge, stabilizing it enough to enter. Dailey had been insistent on being the one to do so.

"Be safe," Jen noted as Captain Dailey decoupled from the fighter and Becket joined them at the back blast door to the bridge.

The entire exfil from the *Murphy* to the platoon's current position was less than five minutes.

Giving the signal to open the blast door, Becket held out a small fusion power booster and plugged it into the controls. The device had proved itself to be extremely handy in almost any situation. One could not only power a refrigerator to hold tasty beverages but also power up a dead section of the spaceship long enough to do things like open doors.

After a brief rush of air, Dailey and Becket swung into the bridge, quickly closing the door. Bridges were designed for several simple functions: first and foremost, to protect the primary crew of the ship during possible combat operations, and, on a secondary note, to be an entirely separable self-contained escape pod if needed.

Becket made quick work of the door controls as Lieutenant Dasher and one of his scouts joined him at the door. Dailey pulled out another fusion generator, joining Becket and plugging them in simultaneously as several of the bridge's lights sparkled to life.

The angled viewport was still intact as the commander scanned the bridge. All the lights and the bridge were covered in a thin layer of carbon. As Dailey panned over to the captain's chair, Juice's charred remains stared blankly into space through burned-out, blackened, empty eye sockets.

Lying in his lap, being one of the only few things left, was the man's flask. Instead of making Dailey upset, it lit the fuse in his guts that he knew all too well. Someone would pay for these transgressions.

"Sir, do you need a minute?" Becket asked through the localized comms, the bridge not pressurized enough to retract their face shields.

"No, I'm good," Dailey replied, securing the man's flask. Sitting on the panel in front of him was a tablet with a still-visible, dull image of Juice in happier days long since forgotten. While still powered on, the tablet was damaged, making it hard to see the two golden retrievers.

Dasher, giving his commander a few reflective moments, finally spoke up, "Looks like somebody hit the bridge with the carbon ionizer."

"And the rest of the ship with ion cannons. Makes no sense," Dailey stated flatly, computing the situation.

"They may have wanted to scan the main computers," Dasher suggested as Dailey set his rifle on the main navigation station.

Quickly beaming his light on the lightly dusted panel, he saw small round prints appear. Dailey punched a few commands into the console, but it would not accept the input. It wasn't even locking him out or giving him the proverbial digital middle finger. The ship's system drives were gone. Before taking his final sip, Juice had fried the ship's systems. Not just one of them—all of them.

"Guess they didn't get what they were looking for. There's nothing else we can do here." Dailey switched to external comms, still talking to Dasher. "This is Viper six. Do we have eyes on the payload?"

"Master Sergeant Warner, report," Dasher instructed. Dailey picked up his rifle, doing one last scan of the doomed bridge.

Dani Warner was a middle-aged woman from southern Georgia whose family's military lineage stretched back to World War I. Her claim to fame were her abilities as a sniper.

Warner's reputation of never missing her target was a one-way ticket into the world of the Pathfinder Battalion. It also didn't hurt that she had a background in several of the CSIA's off-the-books black projects. These mainly included her skills as a sniper. The Central Space Intelligence Agency had allowed her to transfer to the Army's special operations division after her last project had not gone as planned.

"Sir, we have the payload. I think you're going to want to see this," Warner's Southern drawl replied.

"That's never good," Dailey stated as the group left the bridge, shutting the blast door.

The team worked their way through the ship's skeleton, activating their mag boots when they found a large-enough section of the vessel to navigate.

While the outside of the ship was in pieces, the ship's main cargo hold and heart were built to take a beating.

The group stared as several scouts from Fourth Platoon backed away from the main cargo hold. While the gravity field was more generous inside the self-contained cargo hold, the atmosphere wasn't, not allowing the team to raise their face shields, something Dailey preferred to do if the environment supported it.

"Dammit," Dailey huffed as Dasher and Becket both realized what they were looking at.

Sitting in front of them in a semi-transparent box no less than seven feet tall and wide sat a thermal fission subnuclear Decca warhead. The real nasty stuff only used in space.

In reality, Dailey had never had eyes on one or knew of one being used. The weapon was born out of perceived necessity after the Tectonic Wars via a transfusion of technologies. Leave it up to Earth to build a bomb big enough to blow itself out of the galaxy.

That last piece was the smoking gun staring Dailey in the face. Why would a secret off-the-books Fleet ship be out in unexplored space with an ace crew and a planet-killing warhead?

"Pearl, do you copy?" Dailey asked as Dasher, losing his usual swagger, walked up to the control panel, motioning his soldiers to back away. It wouldn't do any good, but it was the thought that counted.

"Sir."

"Anything you can tell me about the surface? You have any wildlife showing up on the scan yet?"

There was a pause as Pearl worked on the dashboard, scanning the planet for signs of life. "We only have a small portion scanned, but I can tell you the place is teeming with life. Not just animals. The scanners have detected structures and infrastructure in a handful of concentrated industrialized areas. It is also two Earths in size." A measurement now given to newly found worlds. With that, Dailey stopped the information download.

"Is the signal close to any of those built-up areas?"

"Yes, sir. We have that data ready to go. Is there anything you need?" Pearl asked, sensing Captain Dailey thinking.

"No, we can get it from here." Dailey switched back to internal mission comms. "Master Sergeant Warner, are any fighters in the bay operable?"

Warner turned from the warhead. "Yes, sir, looks like there's at least one that's still in one piece. Need us to secure it?"

Becket glanced at Dailey as he walked closer to the ball of metal death. "Get a ship unhooked and tether this thing to what's left of the ship's frame. Since the systems are all fried, get with Lieutenant Brax and upload operational controls from one of her ships. I need to think on this one for a minute."

Becket motioned for Dailey to switch to their personal channel, which was highly encrypted. "Sir, it's clear they were going to set this thing off somewhere. What are you thinking?"

"You heard Pearl; the planet's inhabited. If you hit one of the others in the system, it would also wreck this one. I say we strap this thing to the bottom of the remaining fighter and launch that thing into the void. It's too close to everything here. I need to talk with General Ran."

"Ben." He was talking as a friend. "You've been having to do a lot of talking with Ran lately. The fact that he didn't tell you about this is enough to want some leverage. I mean, this ship being here alone is enough."

He was suggesting they use the warhead as leverage to get information from the general. Information they apparently were not supposed to have. Dailey had already gone down this route by asking about a working fighter, and Becket knew it.

"Remember that time on Alpha Setta Two?" Dailey asked reflectively as Dasher and his platoon went to work securing the fighter, leaving only the leadership in the room.

"Bunch of Federation senators sent us in to do their dirty work. We showed up not knowing everything, and the Ocess Mining Corporation had hired an army of Solarian mercenaries."

"Yup, the one where we almost died for real. I have the same feeling about this. Something's not right. General Ran is holding this close to his chest, even more so than the other load of bullshit. And that is how a mission goes south."

Becket nodded, showing his full approval of whatever decision the commander of the *Murphy* was about to make.

The plan was simple. After doing some general math about blast radius, they would attach the warhead to the fighter and send it two parsecs away. Jen confirmed they could even control the fighter if needed. From there, he would leave it up to General Ran to explain the rest. It surprised everyone that whoever had destroyed the *Asher* hadn't taken its cargo.

A loud bang interrupted the conversation as the radios screamed to life. "Sir, incoming," Specialist Kline damn near yelled. Dailey turned as the rest of the group scrambled.

Sounds of thrusters roaring and blasters slicing through space got the team moving. "Dasher, secure the payload. Everyone else, outside."

The order was immediately followed as the group quickly made its way to a large, jagged hole in the ship's side.

"Pearl, report?" Dailey asked, activating his thrusters enough to get away from the ship as one of the attack-wing fighters screamed overhead, diving through the debris going under the ship.

"Sir, it appears to be some type of autonomous drone. It came from one of the planets out of nowhere and masked its signal in the debris. It was initially firing at the remnants of the ship, ignoring us."

"Stay clear. If it jumps out of the debris zone, engage. Other than that, we got it." Dailey trailed off, activating full thrust mode, diving as several thin white laser blasts ripped through a section of the hull beside him.

Dailey would have been shredded if he had hesitated for even a second. Several streams of rapid yellowish fire from the Solarian Sauder rifles swept under the ship in all directions as the heads-up display inside Dailey's helmet worked to lock on to the target. The rifles fired hundreds of heated rounds so rapidly that they appeared as streams of fire that broke off when the user of the weapon shifted their aim.

It was clear from the unconcentrated firing of the scouts that they had yet to home in on the moving target either.

"All units. Switch your visuals to magnetic-field view," Kline barked through the radio as a shredding beam of white lasers flashed.

The shift immediately illuminated a round sphere with what appeared to be several large mechanical arms shifting in an unnatural motion. A fighter dove from the wreckage, smacking the sphere with several plasma rounds then pulling up, avoiding friendly fire.

After a quick shudder and shift in position, the flowing metal arms shifted toward the ship, unleashing four disjointed blasts to catch the fighter even if it changed course. One of the beams hit its target as Dailey shifted course, pressing forward as another stream of gunfire ripped toward the sphere as it again shifted out of harm's way with only glancing blows.

While glancing, the hits were enough to force the ship to hesitate. Dailey, seeing his opportunity, activated his armor's blade as the blackish-silver glow of the Moshan blade blurred to life. Forward, the black void of space resembled a jumble of confused, flashing lights.

"Coming in hot!" Dailey exclaimed just as Jen materialized from below the craft. Several of the scouts pulled their fire, allowing Dailey to accelerate. Clearly, the pilot hadn't seen the man's heroic charge into the belly of whatever beast lay before the platoon.

Winding up like a baseball player of yesteryear, Dailey leaned into the blade, slicing through two of the vehicle's shifting arms topped with lasers. Unable to see what had happened, Jen unleashed a flurry of blasts on full auto from the pair of plasma blasters tucked neatly under the wings of the fighter.

Turning to follow up his attack, the black sphere erupted in sparks, setting off every proximity alarm in Captain Dailey's suit. Before she could pull her fire, the globe-shaped attacker exploded in a flash different from anything the group had witnessed before.

"Ben!" Becket barked over the radio, flying directly into the now-shattered drone. Jen cut her engines, pausing and trying to catch a glimpse of Dailey.

Several steadying breaths replaced the now-silenced suit alarms as Dailey floated loosely in space. Several icons flashed in his HUD, including various fading warnings about the suit's life support systems and, more importantly, that the thrusters were momentarily offline. The drone, knowing of its imminent doom, had self-destructed. In one last middle finger to its attackers, it set off what could only be explained as a limited EMP pulse, disrupting surrounding systems.

Dasher started directing the scout platoon to secure the area as something caught his eye, darting out of the remnants of the black sphere. "Jen, you see that on your radar?"

"Yeah, it's moving fast. I don't think we can catch it," Jen replied, not shifting her gaze off the now-visible red armor of Captain Dailey. Becket had grabbed him and was now pulling him toward the closest fighter, now hovering several hundred feet away.

"See if you or the *Murphy* can track it. That will have to do for now," Dasher followed up. When not playing the cool guy, Dasher was as sharp as they came. After a quick call to the mothership, Kline was now tracking whatever it was that had launched out of the explosion. By all accounts, it was the size of a basketball.

Becket tapped on Dailey's HUD. "Servos locked up?"

Lost words were spoken as Dailey began to get frustrated. Whatever the drone had done, it forced his entire system to reboot. The artificial intelligence systems aboard the *Murphy* were still in the developmental stage, as it was a new ship. Only the *Brightstar* had a more sophisticated AI.

"Status?" Dailey asked.

"System reboot complete. Thruster status offline until recharged," VOX, better known as the Voice Outerworld Exchange, sprang back to life. In most cases, the system was only used while on mission and was scheduled to be fully activated on board once the ship was docked.

While not a full-on AI system, it was a simple voice interface to use while wearing a full set of space armor. It could operate off voice command and was also capable of vocalizing various data points.

Becket's voice sparked through the helmet. "Sir, you napping?"

"I wish," Dailey replied while everyone breathed a collective sigh of relief. "The damn thing set off a close-range EMP. I need to recharge."

"Are you hurt?" came a concerned Jen over the comms.

"Yeah, my feelings after you fired your blasters directly at me, a little," Dailey replied, the grin on his face coming across in his voice.

Becket shook his head, hooking the suits together with a tether line. "See, sir? I'm always having to tow your ass around."

"I mean, you're not wrong," Dailey responded, shifting gears. "Dasher, I need that extra ship up and running. You're in charge of the site. We must be out of here in less than an hour."

After a quick explanation of the plan to Lieutenant Dasher, the Nova Rangers of Fourth Platoon were fast at work. The plan was simple. At least, it sounded as much when discussed. The warhead would be launched two parsecs out of the sector. From there, the USF *Murphy* would pull back behind one of the three moons orbiting what they now called *Asher* Minor One, known in the ship's charts as AM1. The crew would then finalize plans for sending a search party to the surface, all while awaiting the *Brightstar*.

CHAPTER 13

EYES WIDE SHUT

Sparky hadn't left Dailey's side since returning to the *Murphy*. After forty-five stressful minutes, Dasher and the scouts of Fourth Foot had completed their mission. The decision was made not to disturb the *Asher*'s wreckage further.

One thing about firefights close to orbit was they could often be viewed from the surface of nearby planets. The crew figured the wreckage of the *Asher* was far enough out of sight, allowing them to stay undetected by any known means.

Dailey, a grinning Sparky, Becket, Pearl, Jen, Bellman, and Dasher were still unwinding in the briefing room from the events that had just taken place in the bones of the *Asher*. A flashing red light quickly reminded the somber group they had ignored several comms from the *Brightstar*.

"Go planet for ham?" Sparky asked. The others were still working to figure out how the commander of the *Murphy* reacted to the space dog, not being able to hear the translation themselves.

"I doubt there's ham down there, buddy," Dailey replied as Sparky's face drooped slightly. "Sparky, if we take you down to the planet's surface, can you help us find someone? You know, like a hunting dog?"

"Dog from the movie find people. Yes. Will need ham input," Sparky replied. Again, while he was still working through communicating, the point was made. He could indeed help. To no one's surprise, Senior Chief Thron had been letting Sparky watch old movies about how dogs on Earth acted. Dailey drew the line at the latest rendition of Scooby-Doo in space.

"There you go," Becket added. "We have a volunteer."

"I'm thinking we need to figure this out sooner than later," Pearl added, glancing at the blinking red message notification.

Dailey was starting to second-guess his stance toward General Ran regarding recent events. The man couldn't identify the drone or whatever the hell it was they had just encountered. According to Pearl, it looked as if what they now called the AD, short for automated drone, had been sent to destroy the remnants of the *Asher*.

The rest was looking to be a miracle of timing. A coincidence. As Captain Dailey put it, *Coincidences are for people that keep letting the same stupid thing happen over and over again.*

"I don't want to put any of you in a position to get yourself in trouble. I'll do the talking. If I'm wrong about any of this, it will keep the blowback to a minimum," Dailey relayed to the group.

"Sir," Pearl started. "We are in an uncharted system. According to Fleet regulations, you have some flexibility here."

"Unless the general shows up," he replied quickly. "All I'm saying is I want a team on that planet as soon as possible. Pearl, if what the scans show is true, it will be like finding a needle in a haystack."

"That's the thing. The signal transponder is moving. I think it's with our survivor. Specialist Kline is staying on it," Pearl added.

"May I?" Bellman interjected. "I suggest a small team outfitted to blend in. Keep a few armor suits and weapons stowed somewhere. Maybe send down a vert rover. We have two drop ships, and a vert rover will fit in one."

"That's not a bad idea," Becket said as Dailey turned to the communication panel.

"No time like the present," Dailey grumbled, then tapped the red button.

Within a few surprising seconds, a young, frowning Fleet officer formed on the viewscreen. "Sir, it's the *Murphy*," he announced in a nasally tone.

"Captain Dailey," Ran started. There was no room for interpretation of the bad mood the man was in. "I see you didn't stay put."

"Sir, yes. We found the *Asher*. I thought it prudent to get to the ship sooner than later. We are…"

"I know, behind one of the planet's moons," Ran replied as Dailey tried not to shift his gaze from the monitor.

"Yes, sir. Do you have a probe in the sector?" It would stand to reason, considering the crew of the *Murphy* would do the same thing. The confusing part would be the *Brightstar* likely outrunning any scouting probe it sent while en route.

"We are approximately two clicks off your starboard bow. Disengage cloaking," Ran instructed someone beside him as the *Murphy*'s proximity alarms erupted, only to be quickly silenced.

Not only had the *Brightstar* made it there at mind-numbingly fast speed, but it almost appeared that General Ran wanted to get there first, possibly even bypassing them. By Dailey's calculation, the ship was traveling twice the speed they understood it was capable of.

Sparky nudged Dailey's leg. The man agreed he would need to tread lightly. "Sir, being this far out, we felt it prudent to move forward. Good thing we did."

"I need you and Becket to head over to the *Brightstar* for a complete debrief. Listen, I know things are foggy, but I'll fill you in when you get here," Ran instructed, shutting off the signal.

Tension filled the room like a steaming shower. "You think he's going to shoot us straight?" Jen asked, not accustomed to operational units such as the Pathfinders.

"We're about to find out. Why don't you prep a drop ship and go with us. It would be good for you to get some face time. I might ask Master Sergeant Grantham to join us as well. He used to be stationed with Ran and knows him better than anybody. Plus, he didn't say we couldn't bring anyone with us."

The group snorted at Dailey's usual interpretation of words. Sparky let out a yip. "Me go?"

"Nope, buddy. There's no ham there," Dailey replied as Sparky headbutted him.

"Not true. Ham is on board."

"Likely no ham for you," Dailey countered.

"He has you nailed, boss," Becket replied, heading out the door.

From the viewport, the *Brightstar* was a work of sleek art. A ship where the designer put as much effort into making it look intimidating as well as functional. While the *Murphy* was a sleek fighting machine, it was outclassed by the sheer mass of the ship in front of them.

"Look at the size of those damn ion cannons," Grantham admired.

On the side of the ship and both the bottom and top were rows of ion cannons of all flavors. The main guns referenced were mounted on the ship's bow as if a warning message that needed no explanation. In many ways, it resembled a massive naval battleship from the old days.

As they approached the ship's starboard side, an immense bay fluttered with activity. Small fighters and armored soldiers went in all directions, securing not only the ship but the dark side of the moon as well—something Dailey had not wanted to do.

A disk sat atop the *Brightstar*, housing the bridge. Above that were several batteries of rocket pods ready to protect the precious ego-driven cargo inside. This was a command vessel, and it was making a point of letting everyone know.

"Captain Dailey. I see you brought a team." Luther, an academy officer that rarely had, if ever, had to pick up an actual weapon and fight, breathed out his nose.

"Yes, Lieutenant Jenny Brax wanted to link up with your fighter wing, and Master Sergeant Grantham I am sure you are already familiar with." Dailey smiled, beaming his pearly whites. He hated the stuck-up son of a bitch and was starting to wish he had indeed brought Sparky just to piss him off.

While the briefing room aboard the *Murphy* was an intimate yet functional space, the room Dailey, Becket, and Grantham walked into was operatic. Jen had already made her way to the fighter wing command onboard.

Standing in the middle of the room next to a holo-projector was General Ran. Thick from years away from field operations and wearing a haircut so sharp it likely cut itself, the man had a face that wore a permanent scowl.

"Sir." Dailey and Becket both saluted as he returned the courtesy. Admiral Dean Luther stood resolute as Ran glared at him.

"You can go, Admiral. I'll let you know if I need anything. Master Sergeant Grantham, would you care to join him? Some of your old team is on board. Likely in the mess hall, or a bar, for that matter."

After a few brief glances were exchanged, Grantham followed the annoyingly smug admiral out the door.

"Good, now we can talk." Ran started motioning the two men to sit. "I know on the surface, it may seem like you have been left out of the loop. Some of that is true, but I can assure you there have been times when you were on a mission that your peers had no idea what you were up to."

Dailey sat stoically, taking in the likely line of bullshit he fully understood he was being fed. This was something different, something more than an off-world clandestine mission. Or, as the commander of Viper Company liked to call them, paid vacations, which he had a certain reputation in taking his entire team on long after the mission was complete.

"Sir—" Dailey started before General Ran corrected him.

"You can skip the formalities. We are all adults here."

"I think you may want to hear the rest of the details about the ship we encountered in the Shade Belt."

Ran's slight smile still somehow managed to come across as a scowl. "Let me guess: besides being old, there is something about the remains?"

It was clear General Ran knew more than he was willing to spill. "We identified about four separate races."

"About?" Ran asked quickly.

"That's not the topper. Besides being hundreds if not thousands of years old, there were human remains from Earth."

Ran pondered the statement, not out of surprise but seeming contemplation. He was sorting through his next move. Surprisingly, the general decided to lay it on the table.

"At the end of the war, it was made clear that the Alurians had at one point been interacting with humans. On several of their downed ships we found not only human artifacts but in one case a type of brain-dead drone. After that, it was fairly simple math. They had been waiting and watching throughout the years. Studying and gathering data on our planet."

The man paused, giving his guests an opportunity to ask questions.

"We get that. The issue is the Alurians could have swooped in and taken over mankind at any time. This was a slave ship," Dailey pointed out quickly, filling in gaps that Ran was likely holding back.

"Yes, there is an element of the Federation that believe the Alurians had been taking captives off the planet for centuries. Speculation to a point. That leads me to the next bit I believe you are more interested in. The *Asher* and its crew were sent here on a covert operation to destroy the planet on the other side of this moon."

Becket chimed in at this point. Both men were surprised he was being so upfront. This also told them they would likely be asked to complete the mission.

"Sir." He wasn't skipping the pleasantries, keeping it official. "That planet is teeming with life and, from what we understand, is a developed society. We plan on going in, securing Lieutenant Laura McAlister, and leaving the system."

"Yes, I figured as much. Did you secure the *Asher*'s payload?" Ran asked as his posture stiffened.

Dailey sat on the statement for a minute, letting it marinate through his thoughts. Ran already knew the answer, just not the details. "We did. We also ran into a murder drone of unknown origin."

"Then good; we can secure it and carry on after your landing party completes its search-and-rescue mission. As for your murder drone, we have already sent out proximity-sensor satellites. No more surprises."

"Why?" was all Dailey asked.

"It's not your place, Colonel," Ran started, using the newly given rank. "We receive a mission, and we execute."

Dailey stood up, his hardened chin and layers of muscle flexing. "Why?"

Knowing he wasn't going to be able to skirt the question, Ran walked over to the round table in the center of the layered briefing room, activating a 3D image of the Central System, including Earth and what appeared to be the primary concentration of Fleet ships close to the Outer Spiral closest to Earth.

"A couple of years ago, we captured an Alurian raider ship. Crew and all," Ran begrudgingly started. "We didn't think much of it until we translated the navigation systems and questioned the crew."

Dailey cleared his throat. "The ship wasn't from the Outer Spiral."

"Correct, but the main problem was the crew. You see, it wasn't a normal raider ship but rather a group of escapees."

"They were humans," Becket interjected as Ran nodded.

"Perceptive. Yes, they told this fantastical story about a planet full of humans, Solarians, and Moshans alike. More specifically, they were mining the planet for resources. To be more specific, for the Alurians."

The gravity of the statement landed on both men's heads like a gob of melting ice cream. The ramifications of such a situation contradicted everything they understood.

"I see you understand the gravity of the situation. Since then, the Federation Intelligence and Defense committees have been scrambling to figure out what this means for not only the Fleet but everything. Our best guess—"

Dailey cut the general off. "Best guess? You are destroying a planet off a best guess?"

"If even a portion of what the crew said is true, it means one of three things. Our fleet and effort have all been focused on the opposite side of the galaxy. The Alurians' home world is somewhere past the Shade Belt. Or lastly, but most importantly, they have been building an army in secret this entire time, not to mention if what the crew of that ship stated is right, the Alurians sent to take us on during the war were more of a scouting party.

"Ben, everyone is panicking. This is the best thing we could think of. Once they gave us the general coordinates, we sent the *Asher*. To be clear, they knew half of what I just told you."

"So, you are letting everyone back home sit back and think things are all flowers and kittens? We should be preparing. The Fleet needs to be heading this way," Dailey protested. The man was ready for bad news, but this was a whole new level of ass-puckering bad news.

"I knew you would smell the bullshit, but even you have to question why you are in command of the *Murphy*, not to mention the very ship you are now aboard. These are two of the fastest ships in the Fleet. The *Asher* was the original hyperdrive prototype. There's more, but you must have realized there was a point to all this."

Becket sniffed lightly, smelling the new-car scent he was now focusing on. "That explains the fancy rifles and the AI system that isn't activated yet."

"Precisely. What I can tell you is we don't really know much past this. The *Asher* was the first ship in this system. It took all of ten hours for it to be destroyed. We received some broken data but nothing more. The signal you forwarded had more metadata."

Dailey stood up. "So, you don't know what's on the planet's surface? I can tell you there are cities, big ones, and for some reason, nothing seems to be entering or leaving orbit."

"Colonel Dailey, take your team to the planet's surface, find our lost souls. Between the *Murphy* and the *Brightstar*, we can handle anything up here. After that, we will carry on with the mission."

Dailey huffed. "You didn't ask what we did with the payload."

"Does it matter? The *Brightstar* is more than capable of meeting the original objective. We do know you removed it from the wreckage. I'm sure you would have told us what you did with it already if you had any intent of handing it over. I believe the signal had it heading out of the sector. Well played on getting it away from possible enemy hands. Enjoy your time aboard. I want a full status report and timeline synch for your trip when you get back to your ship." General Ran let a shit-eating grin slide onto his face.

Before leaving, Ran deposited a glass case with a colonel rank insignia as well as shoulder boards. Dailey quickly deposited the insignia in his cargo pocket.

The whoosh of doors sliding opened into a bustling corridor of Fleet sailors and soldiers alike. To put it into perspective, the *Brightstar* was four times the size of the *Murphy*. A massive city in space. While the *Murphy* had several creature comforts, including several lounges and even two bars consisting of an NCO and officers' club, the *Brightstar* had an entire rest-and-relaxation section. This included anything from entertainment clubs to theaters and everything in between.

"Grantham, copy," Dailey breathed into his communicator.

"Sir."

"We're done here. Anything we need before leaving?"

"Yeah, a drink. I just pinged our location. Jen is with me, as well as the one and only Master Sergeant Walker," Grantham replied.

"Walker will tell us what's going on. Remember him?" Becket spoke up as the two men walked through a set of doors into an even-busier section of the ship.

"How can I forget? He hooked up with that Solarian chief's girl and accidentally broadcast it through the entire base's comm system," Dailey recalled.

"Oh, yeah. The butt-dial heard around the world. I'm surprised he's still alive. Which, if memory serves, you saved his ass after that," Becket added, both men enjoying the fond memory of wasted youth. Truth be told, Becket had always been the older third wheel.

Dull lights and laughter echoed through the R&R bay. A long corridor made to resemble a downtown street at night was adorned with deliberately designed nostalgic shops. Small boutique restaurants wafted exotic smells as neon lights promised cold beverages and a good time while not on duty.

"Sir, this is bullshit. I want one of these. You're a colonel now. Make it happen," Becket joked as they walked into a bar simply labeled pub.

Music danced while cheers clinked. It was shocking to see any of the crew not on full standby this far out, considering the circumstances.

"Sir! First Sergeant!" Walker howled, running up, barely keeping himself from hugging the two men.

"Walker, pissed off any Solarian chiefs lately?" Becket asked. The man had to think about it for a minute before shaking his head.

"I got to ask," Dailey started as Jen handed him a glass of rum and Solarian flurry juice. He looked at her glass.

"Bottle to throttle, sir, it's nonalcoholic. Yours isn't."

"Why aren't you all on alert?"

Walker shrugged. "You tell me." He burped, clinking Dailey's held-down glass. "General Ran keeps insisting we need to be rested, because the time's coming when we won't be able to. There's plenty of crew on board. Hell, too much crew, if you ask me.

"What you're not seeing are the bays full of ground shock drones and troopers. Blaster fodder. There's also two companies of infantry onboard.

A few Rangers and Marines like me on board helping them out. A couple black spec ops units that stay hidden somewhere under a damn sink, and…" Walker trailed off, grabbing another drink, which likely wasn't his, off the bar.

Grantham grinned, slapping Walker on the back. "Tell him what you just told me."

Walker's face drooped slightly. "Well, rumor has it we're not going back. Something about another mission and it having to do with Alurians." He started laughing. "Imagine that. The Federation looking in the wrong direction. All I know is something's not right. When we heard you were here and headed toward the *Asher*, a few of us got excited. You know, sir. We might be here to kick some ass."

Dailey smiled, officially clinking glasses with the familiar face. He was happy to see Walker, and even more that they knew someone they could trust on board. "Grantham, you good giving Walker your communicator? We will get you a new one when we get back. That way, we can keep in touch without using the main comms system."

"I knew you were up to something." Walker chuckled.

"Not yet. Just finding a lost soul. Do me a favor," Dailey requested.

"For you, sure thing, sure," Walker offered up without hesitation.

"If you guys reposition or start sending out units, let us know. For coordination reasons," Grantham added as Walker winked.

A group of roaming security guards walked in, making Walker reset himself. The others picked up on this as the guards spotted Dailey and the others. Much to the group's surprise, the fun-killing patrol turned and left.

Walker let out a heaving breath. "Tell you what. If I get a chance, maybe I can hop over. I'd like to grab a meal, say hello to the others, and check out that new, fancy ship."

"I'm sure Senior Chief Thron would love nothing more than to personally cook you a meal," Becket suggested with a sly grin on his face.

"Uh, yeah… I'll pass on the meal," Walker replied as Jen shrugged.

"Let me guess, an inside joke?"

"Lieutenant, feel free to let Thron know we ran into an old friend of his. I'm sure he'd get a kick out of that," Grantham poured on, also knowing the story.

"Or don't," Walker followed up. The trip was clearly coming to an end. "Either way," he stated in a more somber tone, "I'll let you know what's up. I'm not really sure, to be honest. To the edge!"

"To the edge," Dailey, Becket, and Grantham replied. This was an old unit motto from one of the most famed special operations units of the Tectonic

Wars. They had also all served in the later version of the unit before it had been decommissioned by General Ran several years prior, being absorbed into the Pathfinder Battalion.

"Sure, to the edge," Jen tacked on, smiling. "Taxi's leaving in fifteen."

CHAPTER 14

HOME

Tall, unkempt grass and shrubs shifted violently as the camouflaged drop ship carrying the *Murphy*'s rescue team touched down twenty miles outside the walled city Lieutenant Laura McAlister's transponder now pinged from. According to the initial message's geo-metadata the escape pod was roughly located a click south in a wooded area. The team would first quickly investigate the pod, then follow on to the transponder.

Asher Minor One was a mix of geography, spanning from mostly wooded to massive stone mountain ranges. Its one odd geographic feature was the lack of oceans. The planet instead had thousands of larger lakes. Many were vast enough to appear as if one was standing on the shore, overlooking an ocean.

Ten-story-tall trees shrouded the horizon, giving the opening the drop was landing on a dull green glow. Hard earth flowed into the spongy forest floor leading into a dark wooded area protectively covered by the tree's massive, connected canopy. Adding to the sight were hundreds of small rays of light slicing through the opening in an almost-angelic scene.

"The escape pod landed about a click east in the woods. Besides small heat signatures, it doesn't appear that anyone is around," Master Sergeant

Warner of Fourth Foot announced, looking through a scope mounted on the side wall.

While large enough for one vert rover carrying a fire team during transport when loaded, the ship was also just big enough to have a small command station behind the cockpit. Dailey, Jen, Warner, Dasher, a scout team, and Sparky, who had appeared out of nowhere mid-entry, had joined the mission.

The team would get in, secure McAlister, and exfil before being noticed. If anything went wrong, which it often did, the attack wing and Lieutenant Cardinali, also known as Card, from the heavy-weapons platoon, would run a simple shock-and-awe campaign.

One would think it would be more coordinated, but Dailey often found that more planning usually led to more problems. Overly thought-out plans generally had a habit of going to shit when bullets and laser blasts started flying.

"Can you see that path?" Dailey asked as Jen leaned forward, squinting behind her aviator sunglasses. Once a pilot, always a pilot. It was tradition for pilots to throw on aviators as soon as they breached orbit, regardless of the planet.

"It's there. Looks big enough to fit the vert rover through," she concluded as Dailey walked over to the vehicle, jumping into the passenger seat. Sparky had piled in with the rest of the crew in the back.

A vert rover was a time-tested vehicle that the Fleet had used for decades. The term vert came from its ability to be dropped from the sky. Run by two fusion-core electric motors, the vehicle was a one-stop shop for operations. It also included self-recharging capabilities as well as a perpetual motion regen drive. As long as the military vehicle was in motion, a fusion regen alternator pumped juice right back into the vehicle's power-storage system. The vert rover could operate without any outside power source for thirty years.

To maximize space, the rover had a relatively flat front, with the windshield positioned at the front end of the vehicle. Two metal brackets and an aggressive brush guard protected the driver and passenger.

In the back, this particular rover was set to carry a fire team, including a driver, passenger, and two people able to man the two outer-facing control panels. These included weapon-system controls for the multi-weapon turret mounted a top of the noble steed.

The turret was flat and rather unassuming until you found yourself at the other end of it. Capable of switching between mini power rockets, a plasma laser, and a limited amount of conventional ammunition, a rover could hold its own if needed.

Another feature of the vehicle was the armor bays on the outside. There was space for six complete sets of armor in their storage configuration on top of the armor already worn by the ship's occupants. The only negative was the amount of time needed to activate the nanotechnology in the suits stored this way. It took three whole minutes from elbows to assholes to get the suit fully on and functioning. In infantry terms, three minutes was an eternity.

Jen and one of the scouts were set to stay in the drop ship until needed, shifting it closer to the tree line. According to the satellite images, the team would make their way through the forest until it opened into a tram hub station directly connected to the city. If they encountered anything along the way, they would adjust as needed.

In order to stay tactical, the team was, as suggested earlier, dressed in bland, regular clothing consisting of no patches or other symbols. Two suits of armor were to be carried as far as possible and stowed. As for weapons, the team carried a mix of items.

The scout team each had a small two-piece laser pistol. Small, effective, and relatively inconspicuous, the laser pistol was carried in two small pieces. One half of the weapon was the fusion core built into the handle, while the other was a sleek, inconspicuous barrel. The scout platoon was the only unit that had been assigned these weapons due to the nature of their job. If found, it would be hard to figure out what the device was. Unlike Second Foot, which would be carrying large Gatling lasers and thermo rocket launchers.

Colonel Dailey opted for a small Moshan blade. He considered it the younger sibling of the one installed on his armor. It could cut through anything and, if needed, could be set as a shaped charge due to its combustibility when mixed with Solarian char, which Dailey had in a separate pouch.

"Let's go," Dailey instructed as Sparky yipped in the back seat. "Once we hit the tree line, I want to jump out and get a feel for the place."

"Yes, sir," Sergeant Coleman, also known as Coolio, replied. The man's New York lineage was showing through in his thick accent.

To the whirl of electric motors and surprisingly stable ride, it only took a few short minutes for the forest to completely swallow the vert rover. After a quick thumbs-up from Dasher, who was staring at a thermal screen, the vehicle stopped in the middle of the unimproved road.

Sparky jumped up, wagging his short tail as Dailey opened the side hatch. "Sparky, be—" was all he got out as the dog shot out of the rover, finding the nearest tree.

The team followed behind, setting a quick perimeter, also keeping an eye on Sparky as the proud dog walked up to Dailey.

"Don't run off like that again, or you're staying back in the drop ship. You are here to guard the rover," Dailey threatened as Sparky did a quick circle.

"I marked planet. This is mine now. Sparky's planet. I claim it for you," Sparky's translated but ever-improving voice echoed in Dailey's thoughts, whereas the others heard a round of yips and grunts from the space dog.

Sighing, Dailey took in a deep breath. "Okay, good boy. It's your planet now that you've marked and claimed it. Go back in the rover and keep it safe."

If a dog could salute, Sparky's response met the intent as he held his head up, prancing back into the rover. Dasher walked up with a Solarian rifle slung over his chest.

"You ever get the feeling that thing's way smarter than we are giving him credit?" Dasher noted as Dailey nodded.

"Yeah, something like that. Smell the air?"

Dailey was describing the overwhelming scent of honeysuckle combined with wet, rich soil. Upon closer inspection, to the right of the unimproved trail lay several bushes covered in flowers closely resembling honeysuckle blooms the size of basketballs.

"Smells like a flower garden back home. The air's fresh," Dasher noted, holding out one of Bellman's monitors.

"Hmph. You would think it would be noisy here. Sounds of the forest, small animals, but it's dead quiet," Dailey cautioned.

Realizing that was often a bad sign, Dasher dropped to one knee, pulling his rifle scope up and zooming in as far as the optic allowed down the route. "Warner, get one of the joes to suit up. I want someone in armor till we hit our final release point."

It wasn't a bad idea, and one Dailey wished he had thought of. He sidelined the thought, realizing that was what his platoon leaders were paid to do. Shuffling feet and the sound of a powered armor suit grappling its wearer cut through the muffled silence.

"Mount up. I want to be at our first checkpoint in thirty minutes," Master Sergeant Warner ordered, seeing Dailey head back to the vert rover.

Trees passed as the forest continued into what appeared to be oblivion. If it wasn't for the satellite images they reviewed, one could easily feel as if it never ended, making it easy to get lost.

Sparky continued to inform Dailey of his planetary conquest in the name of ham in all his glory. While the translation was more than likely off slightly, it wasn't hard to figure out Sparky wasn't going anywhere anytime soon.

Truth be told, he had grown on not only the commander but the crew as well. Being a mascot of sorts, Becket had ensured no other animals would be allowed onboard. Sparky quickly reminded him they didn't have a choice in the matter when it came to him.

Dasher swiveled his seat toward the front. "Coolio, slow down. Sir, there is some type of structure ahead, slightly off the path. It looks abandoned."

Dailey punched the screen in front of him as video feed from the small scout drone flying slightly ahead of the rover displayed a cottage-style house. Green ivy and general overgrowth showed that Mother Nature had taken over her once-lived-in property.

Pointing, Dailey leaned forward. "Pull off the main path right after we pass that large tree."

Coolio nodded as the feel of packed earth turned into spongy undergrowth, rocking the vehicle lightly. Sitting just out of eyeshot from the main path was an unassuming one-story stick-built home. This was something that was more of a novelty back on Earth these days, as most buildings were made of concrete or Moshan bricks. Mining companies spent unimaginable amounts of money to transport the materials around the known sector of the galaxy, followed by charging astronomical prices.

The style was a mix of something out of history books from both Solarian and human society. Woodwork, mixed with hardened dirt and rocks, formed a fireplace, bracing several areas around the structure. The overall style and surrounding area made it easy to tell this place had once upon a time been a home.

Within a few seconds, the team, dressed in bland clothes, had set up a perimeter around the structure. Specialist Hoffman stood atop the rover in full power armor, scanning the area as he gave a calming thumbs-up.

"Dasher, with me," Dailey instructed. Sparky took his post in the passenger seat, overseeing operations as directed.

His message confused the commander as he closed the door. "The trees are screaming."

Not having time to go through the five-minute exercise of figuring out what the hell that actually meant, Warner, Dasher, and Dailey slowly pushed open the decaying door.

A section of the door crumbled as Warner pushed it fully open. After the precise roll of a light grenade from one of the Rangers, the inside of the abandoned home started to fill with dull colors of old, dusty life. Switches on the wall and a cracked monitor showed signs of power once flowing into what was quickly resembling a shack more than anything.

Warner held up her hand, signaling to go right as he pulled his rifle up, sweeping the left side of the room. The main area included a living room and kitchen area, followed by a short hallway leading to another closed door. Behind that door was a small bathroom leading off to a bed; only the barest of essentials had been used.

"Human…" Dailey drawled out, poking a pile of books on the table beside the monitor. "Jesus, look."

If any one of them were to breathe on it, the old leather-bound copy of the Bible sitting undisturbed would likely disintegrate into ash. Even more interesting was the keyboard showing some of the same Egyptian-styled hieroglyphics found on the ghost ship, each button its own unique figure.

"About the right word for it," Dasher whispered. For some reason, the man felt like he was walking in on a grave long forgotten.

Dailey stopped, lowering his rifle, seeing a picture of a couple with two children. It wasn't a photo like back home but rather a framed, 3D textured print in a clear resin that had discolored over the years. Smiling back were a human woman, a Solarian man, and two young girls with flowing blonde hair.

While it wasn't common, some Solarians and humans had conceived children. They all had the same trait of flowing blonde hair and radiant blue eyes. Since the two races had only recently met on the scale of cosmic time, things like the long-term effects of interspecies breeding hadn't been truly tested.

More to the point, most humans and Solarians, for that matter, had not nor would ever see one another unless they were involved in off-world travel. This was, of course, changing over time, but this picture was clearly taken before the two races had ever met.

"Well, two times makes it a pretty solid fact," Dailey followed, picking up a picture, wiping off the years of grime. "At some point, we're going to need to figure this mess out. General Ran doesn't seem interested in the why."

"You are, though?" Dasher followed up.

"It's kept me alive all these years. Somethings going on here, something big, and like I told you, they're scrambling. They see a threat; I see an opportunity. One thing's clear: something's been snagging humans off Earth and, hell, everywhere else for… well, forever."

Warner slowly opened a door as she shuffled back several feet. "Shit." The two other men froze, pulling up their weapons, seeing the macabre reason for Warner's outburst.

"You guys good in there?" Coolio asked over the comm. "Sparky's getting all panty."

"We're good," Dailey replied. "Panty?"

"He's acting nervous. Panting like crazy."

"We'll be out in a minute," Dailey followed, walking closer to the skeletal remains of a family.

The larger skeleton was in front of the others, a few slight deviations in its skull meaning it was Solarian. A large hole sat surgically in his head with scorch marks on the edges. The telltale sign of a laser blast to the head. Slightly behind him to the right were smaller yet still adult remains; these were human. Like the other body, the last thing the person likely ever saw was the barrel of a gun.

Squinting, Dailey finally made out the true horror of the scene. Behind them was another set of even smaller bones. This was the second time in such a small amount of time the man had witnessed signs of a youth lost.

Dailey looked down at the picture in his hand, seeing the way the once-happy family had at one time been. He let the image burn into his thoughts. "Someone executed them" was all he said.

Just as the group started leaving, the layer of dust covering everything jumped from its resting place. The ground started vibrating as the sound of trees popping and snapping whipped through the abandoned house. Between the ghost ship and the house in the forest, Dailey was starting to think he was being chased by ghosts.

"Sir," Jen came over the radio.

"Go ahead," Dailey responded through the small comm link clipped on his shirt.

"I don't know any other way to put this. Pearl just called as well. It appears a body of water four miles east of you is opening up."

"Opening up?"

"It looks like a ship is launching from underwater. Some type of super-structure underground," she quickly spat out.

"Shit," Dailey cursed. "They scan it yet?" He shook his head. Knowing Pearl and the rest of the crew, he assumed they were already scanning the craft.

"Yes, home base reports no sentient life onboard. It appears to be an automated craft, no shields. The *Brightstar* wants to see what it does."

Dailey reflected momentarily. Warner spoke up first. "If the *Murphy* and the *Brightstar* can't handle it, I'm not sure this was meant to be, sir."

She was right. If either were worried, they would have blasted the ship before it even took off. Even more calming was the fact that the ship was moving slow enough to be picked up on their radar with no attempt to camouflage itself.

"All right, we are going to stay put. I'm going to jump back in the rover and get on the main channel. I'm guessing you have eyes on," Dailey stated, already heading for the door.

"We have sat visual. It's clear as day. Pearl just reported the scan is showing it being some type of cargo ship. It almost looks like one of those Ateris mining ships. I'm linking the display panel on the rover," Jen relayed.

The ground vibrated underfoot like a heard of buffalo raging through the forest. It wasn't that there were no animals. They were simply in hiding, knowing something was about to happen. More to the point, it was something they were used to. Sparky even knew something was up with his comment about the trees screaming. And screaming they were, under the stress of the shifting ground. The massive monoliths flexed with the ground while slowly dancing, making the ground ripple.

The Ateris Mining Company was cut from the same syndicate-esque cloth as the Ocess group. For all they knew, the ship could very well be one of theirs. Even though in an uncharted system, the Fleet, as well as the crew of the *Murphy*, didn't put anything past the mining organizations.

The scouts quickly made their way inside the rover just as baseball-sized acorns started pelting the forest floor. Within seconds after the hatch closed, Coolio activated the vehicle's shields, only allowing for a handful of dent-producing smacks by the onslaught of killer acorns.

"Told you. Ham now?" Sparky begged, wanting a treat for his warning earlier.

"Here," Dailey said, handing a small piece of Fleet-issued field jerky to the dog, who gladly accepted.

"This will do" was Sparky's simple response.

Glancing at the monitor, the top section of a massive ship finally cleared the water. Zooming in on the location, they saw lights and other signs of an underground facility briefly peek out, only to be quickly swallowed back by water.

"Sir," Jen said as Dailey realized the entire team was piled over his and Dasher's shoulder, watching the massive ship slowly climb into the sky.

"Go ahead."

"The *Brightstar* is going to send a tracker with the ship. It's automated and on a predetermined flight path. Don't ask me how they know. From what I understand, as long as we don't get in the way, it won't set off any alarms."

Dailey sat, reflecting on the entire situation. The planet, the ship, the cabin in the woods, the attack drone of doom, everything he had witnessed over the past several weeks, including the fact that the Void was not as unexplored as even he knew, was weighing heavy. It was like walking into a room full of people knowing a secret, all except for you, wondering what everyone was talking about from a distance.

"Dasher, what do you think about all this?" Dailey asked, wanting some type of divine intervention. Sparky beat the LT to the punch.

"Shiny things. Big rocks go to play."

The translation was loose but enough for Dailey to digest. The planet was teeming with precious material, and someone was likely taking it off-world. Much to his surprise, there wasn't even a surcharge for Sparky's questionable yet rational input.

"No planes, ships, or improved roads outside those big cities. A tram outside the walls, this house." Dasher paused. "You ever hear about Alturis?"

Dailey squinted his eyes as if it would give his brain additional power. It didn't. "Not that I can think of."

By this time, the rest of the merry band of misfits were all listening. Dasher had a way of doing that while talking, the group now ignoring the calming forest. "There was a planet reported a couple years back in the Outer Spiral. For those listening over my shoulder, that's about as far out on the edge of the galaxy in the opposite direction as you're going to get, heading to what we supposed is or was Alurian territory.

"The more I think about it, the more it reminds me of this place. Bellman might even know about it. From what I understand, the planet had some thousand years ago been stripped of all its natural resources, kinda a dead planet. There were reports of remnants of several large, centralized colonies. Something the mining companies wouldn't touch."

After a slight pause, one of the soldiers spoke up. "Then what, sir?"

"That's the thing: it went silent. I don't think you can even pull it up on the fed logs. It just disappeared."

Dailey cleared his throat. "I bet it didn't disappear. It probably didn't fit the Federation's narrative of *All is well*. We get stuck on this mining thing because they are the ones always in some weird spot, on some strange planet, but it's not always the case. Not to mention this planet was clearly here before most of the mining companies truly went interstellar."

"I don't know, sir," Coolio spoke up. "It takes a lot to put a fleet together. We stripped several of Saturn's and Jupiter's moons."

This was a surprise from the generally one- or two-topic soldier. "My dad worked on a mineral extraction team damn near his entire life," he clarified.

The conversation was interrupted by Jen. She was relaying information from the *Murphy*. "It appears the ship didn't deviate and is heading out of the sector. Once it got clear of lower orbit, it took off like a bat out of hell. Not at hyperspeeds, but started moving. The *Brightstar* is tracking it. What's the plan, sir?" Jen asked.

"We can save the escape pod for later. By the looks of the imagery, it's trashed. Other than that, no change, we continue on, tracking the transponder," Dailey replied as Jen grinned at him through the monitor, only to have it cut off.

Ohhs and ahhs followed from the crew in the back, seeing this exchange between the two.

"Cut that shit out," Dailey huffed, turning slightly red. While the prodding at his expense stopped, it wasn't enough to prevent Coolio from putting on a damn-near-ancient love song. "Heaven" by Bryan Adams started piping over the comm.

Turning, all Dailey could see were tears of restrained laughter hitting the driver's grinning face while muted snickers echoed in the back. There was even a whispered proclamation that someone was about to piss themselves.

It wasn't that Dailey was embarrassed or shocked. He was actually impressed by the young soldier's knowledge of centuries-old love songs, taking away from any resentment he might have held. "Points for taste, Coolio. Don't let this shit happen again."

The driver continued to pucker his face, about to explode as Sparky nudged Dailey's leg, plopping over in full-on nap mode. Before long, the entire rover was humming the song, even if most of them had no clue who Bryan Adams even was.

CHAPTER 15

LOST & FOUND

For once in the history of basically every mission going wrong, a few things actually happened right. The gods above were looking out for the team, and Dailey had already thanked whichever ones were available at least a dozen times in his thoughts.

The tree line the rescue team left the vert rover in was perfect, with overhead and directional cover after some adjusting. Sparky insured his newly marked territory would ward off any strange beasts of the forest while he guarded the rover.

At least, that was Dailey's loose translation of Sparky declaring the small patch of land the rover sat on as its own country named Hamica, a mix of the words ham and America.

From there, the journey to the tram depot was straightforward: follow the smaller trees to stay out of sight and work their way onto the tram.

The offputting part was the ease with which the team snuck onto the platform, following it underground. That was the second sign of things going right. A humanoid man and woman stood swaying out of boredom, waiting for the tram. From the sat images, the crew couldn't see down the short set of stairs leading underground.

What surprised Dailey and the others was the damn near identical style of clothes. Plain earth tones with no frills. When they zoomed the ship's scopes in on the city, all the crew could see were massive building tops and clouds blocking out whatever was below.

According to the transponder readout, Lieutenant McAlister was just on the other side of the massive wall. If everything worked out, they would be in and out in a couple of hours.

The duo finally noticed the oddity of the group that had joined them as the woman leaned in to whisper with staring eyes. The man slowly turned, only to quickly turn back. By this point, it wasn't the military haircuts or overall vibe the team was giving off; it was the fact that most of the Rangers were large-framed soldiers.

Layers of trained, hardened muscle mixed with predatory eyes. It caught Dailey off guard as the man stood up, walking toward the back of the tram section they had entered.

"Excuse me," the man said in a meek yet understandable tone.

While it was a huge plus for mankind for other species to speak English, it was never a coincidence. There were a handful of civilizations that Dailey had run into, including the Dorians, that basically hissed at you to say hello.

"Hey," Dailey replied, trying to work his slight drawl out of his reply.

"The missus and I were wondering if you are all from the lower levels."

"Any reason why you would ask?" Dailey asked in a friendly tone, doing his best not to be standoffish.

"You guys look like it. Most the people working down there are your size, but they don't usually take the tram. They take the loop station way underground. Thought there might be something going on."

This was news Dailey could work with, and something that would help them blend in. It was simply up to him not to mess it up.

"No, no issues. Just some new team members. This will be the only time they get to ride the tram for a while. Plus, we are celebrating before we end up back underground for who knows how long."

The man grinned, clearly buying the bullshit Dailey had just cooked up. His thought process was often modest when talking to others not in the military: simply put yourself in their shoes. This was clearly a lower-level worker that lived a drab life from the outside looking in.

"I remember those days. Getting the tour and all. Tell you what: I know you folks don't get topside much. There's a new libation station a few slides from the tram stop. It's called Totoks. You guys should check it out. Cheapest frosts this side of Arcadia. I think they put it there to catch the shift change off the tram—" The man's partner or whatever cut him off.

"I'm sure they don't want to talk to you all day. Sorry, he gets talkative," she proclaimed.

Dailey could feel some of the team members trying not to laugh at either the rhyming libation station or the fact that the guy's wife had just busted the man's ever-living balls into outer space.

"It's fine, man. We don't get topside much, so the change of conversation is welcome," Dasher spoke up, his accent completely gone.

This again was the right thing to say, as they both shrugged and smiled in agreement. It sounded like they were in the same boat, wherever it was they worked. One thing was clear: there was a working-class separation in what they now knew was the city called Arcadia.

The tram screamed through a thick tunnel, finally coming to a stop inside a bustling, living city. The couple disembarked as Dailey turned to the team.

"Let's not look too obvious. Three teams; we all stay within eyeshot of each other. I'll take the lead, with Warner and Coolio heading to the transponder location." Everyone nodded. It was game time.

The rush of humid air was the first thing that greeted the rescue team. A light haze floated in the air, getting thicker as the massive buildings rose into the sky, which was the next piece that pulled everyone's attention. From the bland ground levels of the city, the sky wasn't visible, only providing a dullish, British, grey ambiance to the already-muted cityscape.

Offsetting this were glowing neon signs in odd hieroglyphics directing people to eat or to enter various shops. The entire place reminded Dailey of a back-alley food district back home. The location was strategically placed to catch workers coming on and off the tram. A mix of Solarians and humans walked in a relaxed yet direct manner. No one was lingering longer than needed.

The smell was a mix of food, sour fruit, and the usual welcoming inner-city stench. To be fair, Solarian cities were not that different from what they were walking through.

As they looked up, the sounds of small ships echoed off the buildings, telling of a layered city. Back on Earth, before all hell broke loose, several cities, including New York, Hong Kong, and London, had gone vertical. The old cities' original bones remained at ground level, while the rest rose into the sky, making the difference between the layers drastic. As with everything, the rich soared above the clouds.

While Earth had experienced a boom since then, it still wasn't lost on Dailey that something wasn't right about the entire planet. A small, single-person, dirty taxi-style vehicle hummed out of the street directly in front of them, turning at the last minute under automation.

"A block over to the left," Dailey noted as Warner nodded, shifting course.

Much to the group's surprise, the signal dead-ended directly in front of Totoks, the bar mentioned by Bland Pants, as the man on the tram had been dubbed. Groups of people shuffled in and out as the rhythmic beat of music mixed with what could only be identified as bagpipes emanated from the space as the door opened.

Warner motioned for one of the groups. "I need you three to stay here. Anything happens, give us a shout."

She was referring to the small earbuds from the comm links. Warner cleared her throat, looking at another trio of Rangers. "You three go to the left and keep an eye on the door and whatever the hell else is in there. The commander, Dasher, Coolio, and I will check the place out."

Dailey leaned forward. "No drinking. Hell, we don't even know what they use for currency."

Groans and shuffling feet responded, meaning they understood the orders but weren't going to be happy about it. They had, after all, not been on an inhabited planet in months. A group of women sauntering out of the establishment didn't help. Dailey was starting to think he should have brought a few of the female Rangers.

Walking in, the group melted into the building. Instead of a thriving, vibrant bar with people dancing, the crowd was a mix of patrons, all sipping from large mugs, sitting at tables, more focused on drinking than any other distraction from life. Dark, moody lighting and the roar of conversation were steady and not overwhelming, allowing for the team to blend into the crowd without standing out.

Dailey noted someone walking up to the bar and asking for a drink. He was trying to figure out how they paid for things. No currency was exchanged as the bartender of Totoks blindly handed the man a mug full of a bubbling brown drink. Looking closer, he noticed the same with a few other patrons.

"You see her?" Dasher asked with his back to Dailey.

"No, not ye..." Dailey trailed off, making a straight line to a small table tucked away in the corner. Looking down, his assumption was confirmed as the sensor showed solid green.

The woman sitting at the table had her head down, staring at several empty mugs and two plates of half-eaten food that had been on that table longer than needed.

Dasher spoke through the comms. "Found her. Everyone sit tight."

She didn't move as Dailey cleared his throat. "Laura McAlister?"

This put the woman in motion; she slowly lifted her head. Hazed-over, confused eyes met Dailey's, and her mouth began to open, only to snap shut.

"You," a man's voice huffed from behind.

"Yes?" Dailey replied without fully turning around.

"You know this one? She's been in and out of here for weeks, outstaying her welcome," the man said flatly, as if this happened frequently.

"Yeah, I do. I'm here to get her," Dailey said loud enough for her to hear.

"Good thing. I was about to call city security," the man followed up.

"You need anything before we leave?" Dailey asked, and the man shook his head.

"Like what? A job in the clouds? Get her out of here."

"You heard the man," Dailey said to a confused Laura.

LT McAlister started the slow process of pulling herself up from the booth. She had been there for some time. Dasher walked up. "Oh, shit. Mac?" he said, louder than needed.

The man hadn't put two and two together. He had always known her as Mac, a term of endearment given to her as a teenager. Recognition swept over her face as every bit of energy she had left drained from her body.

"I take it you didn't look at the photo file we found?"

"I did. Last time I saw her, she had colored hair and sure as shit wasn't a lieutenant," Dasher replied.

"Who are you?" she murmured, not wanting to be overheard.

"I'm Capt—Colonel Dailey. Commander of the USF *Murphy*. The *Brightstar* is in orbit. We're here to take you home."

A mix of elation followed by concern took over the familiar look of her knowing Dasher. Mac knew the implications of the *Brightstar* being there. She also knew Dailey by name, likely from spending time with Juice.

"You good to walk?" Dasher asked, and she let a light grin slip and nodded. Warner motioned for the remaining team members to exit Totoks.

"Sir?" Master Sergeant Warner asked Dailey as they stood in a side alley off the main street.

"She says she's good to go. I think she's been hanging around here the entire time. Same as before, we head back to the tram in three groups."

Within a few short minutes, the group was back on the tram platform. Once again, the mission gods had dealt the team a winning hand, as a tram heading out stopped within one minute.

After a few tense seconds, several held breaths were let out as Mac slumped in her seat. She was clearly drunk off whatever it was she had been drinking. Just as the door was about to close, the *Oh, shit, what could possibly go wrong* factor decided to throw a pile of steaming crap right in the middle of their mission.

Four black-suited men walked in, holding batons. These were clearly security of some sort. For a few seconds, Dailey thought the men were going to simply walk back off the tram till they, like the couple from earlier, started to take in the group of cornbread-fed misfits. More to the point, even the few Solarians they saw on the street were smaller than their familiar counterparts.

This was, as suspected, the security the barkeep had mentioned earlier. Everyone put their heads down, and Mac visibly tensed when the door slid shut behind them.

The tram lurched into motion as the tallest of the group walked forward, his dark skin blending with the light-absorbing uniforms. "Where are we all heading?"

"The lower levels," Dailey responded.

The man pondered the statement, chewing on it like a piece of cheap steak, letting it marinate. He turned, motioning the three other security personnel to fan out. Muscles were flexed as the man spoke into a comm link sitting on his shoulder.

Dailey couldn't make out what he was saying, but it was clear they had been found out. The lead man stood slightly straighter, pulling out a small laser pistol.

"Not likely. This tram doesn't go to the lower levels," the man replied as the tram shot out of the thick, protective wall of the city into the bright contrasting sunlight.

What happened next was something only a trained group of Nova Rangers could pull off. Using the slight distraction from the change in light from exiting the tunnel, Dailey leapt forward like a compressed spring finally released, grabbing the laser, wrenching it sideways out of the officer's hands, followed by a hip throw, all in the matter of a few violently shocking seconds.

Surprised by the speed of the man in front of them, the three goons went into motion, slamming a baton down on Dailey's now-raised arm as he worked to stand up. Within the blink of an eye, the entire scout team swarmed the end of the tram like battering rams cutting through a paper door.

The struggle of the authority figures was short-lived. Mac looked up, shocked by the extreme efficiency and violence her rescuers had displayed. The truth was she knew who Dailey was, having heard the stories about him. It was even more visceral, as she had heard many of them from Juice, her prior commander.

Not one word had been spoken until the final guard, or whatever they were, had been tied up. Dailey let his hands explore the small weapon. They hadn't had to use any of their lasers in the initial outburst. The overall control the team had was impressive. If he were a young soldier, he would have likely smacked all four of the goons down before they had a chance to open their mouths. The team understood the intent to stay under the radar.

"All right, what's your name?" Dailey asked, loosening the gag wrapped over the mouth of the dark-skinned man as he squirmed on the ground. "No need to worry about that. I think Tex over there was a cowboy or something. Not like you know what that is."

"Who are you?"

Dailey looked down at the gun, then back at the man. "I'm the one with the gun, asking the questions."

"Altis. I am Security Officer Altis. This is my team. They will know we are missing."

Dasher sat down beside Mac as Warner took a step forward, putting together the two pieces of her small laser pistol. This was followed by the rest of the team following suit. The *Oh, shit* factor in Altis's eyes peaked.

What truly caught the man's attention were the tattoos now showing on some of the soldiers' arms. Tattoos were something no one in Arcadia, at least the lower levels of the city, had ever seen. They did, however, know of them from drawings depicting religious figures that had been passed down through generations.

"You're one of the Overwatchers?" Altis asked, his voice more uncertain than before.

"Sure, if that's what makes you feel better," Dailey answered, glancing at Warner.

The thing about asking captives questions, especially on an alien planet, was that you were basically giving them intel in doing so. If Dailey asked who the owners were, it would be a telltale sign they were not remotely from the area.

"Listen. We're going to get off this tram and leave you here. That is, as long as you comply," Dailey instructed, and the man nodded. "Okay, now that's out of the way, I want to know just how dialed in you are on the Overwatchers."

"Dialed in?" the man asked, not knowing the slang.

"For now, assume we are Overwatchers. Who do you report to?" Dailey asked.

"I understand. You don't want us to tell anyone we met Overwatchers. I won't tell."

"Whatever works for you. You might not, but your friends back there might. Who do you work for, and what do you know about the owners?"

"We report to the level-five Overwatchers. Our team secures everything under level five."

Warner cut the man off, wanting to play the part of someone in the know. "Yeah, we get that, and nothing above. Tell us what you know about the Overwatchers."

The fact that that very word scared the shit out of the man was enough to pique everyone's interest.

"The... They are the ones the shipments of hydrocore and radium twenty-one go to. The upper levels manage all that. We just keep the peace." The man was getting more nervous every time the Overwatchers came up.

"Why would you think we are Overwatchers?" Dailey added.

"The art on your skin. They say the Overwatchers have skin like that," Altis murmured. The man was convinced he was talking to whomever it was he thought the group was. Dailey amplified this by rolling up his sleeves, showing his tattooed forearms covered in a mix of unit crests, a map of the United States before the war, and even a new Void tattoo he now shared with the rest of his crew.

Dailey and Warner stared at the man, pushing him to continue. An interrogation tactic that didn't even involve a severe cussing-out or physical support.

"I—" the man stammered. "We were always told the Overwatchers were lizards. I know it's funny, but it was a bedtime story our parents used to tell us. You know, to keep us out of trouble."

This sent a chill down Dailey's spine. Everything was starting to sound more and more like Ran's story about the captured Alurian ship was true.

Sighing, Dailey looked over his shoulder at the tram station in the distance. "Altis, today's your lucky day. Once we get off this tram, we're going to leave you here. To be honest with you, I think you should tell the others you met a group of Overwatchers."

Confusion swept over his face. "Why? Why are you doing this? The Overwatchers control even the upper levels."

"That's for us to know and you to find out," Dailey replied, leaning down, grabbing the man's comm device and identification badge.

After the cars in front and behind the tram unloaded, the group slowly made their way off the car. Dasher walked up, looking at the four men tied to the shiny metal seat posts.

"Sir, I don't think we should leave them here. You know..." He was referring to killing them.

"I thought the same thing at first. Let them go back and tell their boss they ran into whatever these Overwatchers are. By the looks on their faces, I think they'd be too scared to. Anyway, once Mac, as you call her, gets situated, we can ask her."

The hushed sound of the automated tram doors closing hissed as the tram launched back in its original direction. A handful of people jumped off the tram, followed by another small group jumping on. It was efficient, quick, and not a single one of the planet's inhabitants wanted to stay in the bland station longer than needed.

A yip echoed from up the staircase. Sparky had made his way to the tram station or whatever the hell it was he was doing to travel so quickly.

"Before you ask, we didn't find any ham," Dailey declared, and the dog flopped on its butt and let out a short bark.

"Disappointed. You had one job." Sparky chuffed, getting up and walking toward the platform. The translation came through with an attitude. The rest of the soldiers were trying to decipher the conversation.

"One job? We got that done," Dailey replied, nodding at Mac as he perked up.

The woman looked at Sparky and backed up several steps. "He is dangerous."

Dasher grinned, walking up to Sparky as he reached the bottom of the stairs with his tongue hanging out his flat face. "A little gassy. Which is likely due to all the ham Thron is giving him. A pinch hitter in a fight with a space spider, but he's a good puppy."

This was followed by some light back scratches and another inch of the dog's tongue dropping out his mouth. Dailey cleared his throat. It was time to go. "Listen, we can talk about that later. For now, we need to get back to the ship."

Dailey glared from the windshield at the massive walls of Arcadia one final time as Coolio pulled out. Glancing over his shoulder, he saw Mac was already asleep, and Sparky once again plopped down beside him.

"That was easy. Too easy," Dailey grumbled, and Sparky nodded, finally curling up in a ball for the ride back to the drop ship. "This is Viper Six; we are RTB time now."

CHAPTER 16

FIRE IN THE SKY

None of you are to disturb her for at least twenty-four hours," Medical Officer Casey Franklin scolded the group standing in the medical bay.

"We might not have twenty-four hours," Dailey noted as Becket, Pearl, Jen, and Dasher stood in front of a Mac hooked up to several machines that went *bing*.

The glare Franklin replied with was more than words could relay, and Dailey nodded. "Dasher, stay here. You and your team need to take some time to reset and debrief Bellman. Becket, get the other platoon leadership together and meet me in the briefing room.

Nods were given as Dailey motioned for Dasher to join him outside the medical bay.

"Listen, I know she needs some rest. Whatever the lieutenant has been through, it's clearly been a lot."

Dasher respectfully cut him off. "Sir, you do know she was drunk, right?"

"People get drunk for different reasons, Dasher. When she wakes up, I need you to let me know. We need to know what's going on down there."

"You saw the kids, sir?"

"Yeah, I saw them. I have a feeling General Ran doesn't care."

With that, Dailey headed to the briefing room as Sparky walked beside him. Reflecting, the ship's captain found himself talking out loud. "I think I'm about to get in trouble."

Sparky chuffed as his translated voice broke the silence as he walked down the long, empty access corridor. "I got in trouble before."

"I bet you ate someone else's food," Dailey joked, and Sparky cocked his head, agreeing.

Sparky had a way of saying things without really saying them. Dailey was fairly certain that he was inferring that it would not be the first or last time the man would get in trouble.

"You're wise beyond your years. That reminds me. How old are you?"

"Four hundred cold times," Sparky replied as Dailey stopped several feet away from the briefing room, seeing the platoon and ship leadership pouring in.

"You're four hundred years old?" Dailey questioned. In a way, it would explain the dog's extreme level of childish intelligence.

Sparky simply smiled, taking off into the room in front of Dailey.

"Attention!" Pearl yelled louder than needed as the group snapped out of their seats. Between the mission's success and the *Brightstar* being parked close, the crew was getting back in full-on military mode.

The *Murphy* was still parked on the facing side of the moon, with its cloaking shields activated in support of the mission, while the *Brightstar* stayed positioned on the other side of the moon.

"Carry on," Dailey replied as the low murmur of conversation started back. Becket walked over and handed the ship's captain a warm mug of coffee. After a quick sip, the light tang of liquor kissed his lips, and Becket winked at him, followed up by a light congratulatory pat on the back for bringing his soldiers back in one piece.

"Everyone take a seat," Becket instructed. The room was full. Fleet crew officers, attack wing leaders, and everything in between shut up in an instant.

"I'm sure everyone's heard that we successfully secured Lieutenant McAlister," Dailey started, only to be cut off with a standing ovation and round of claps.

"Leave no man behind!" someone in the back of the room barked, and the other Rangers echoed the same sentiment. That was the thing about Nova Space Rangers: they were Rangers. Their lineage stretched all the way back to World War Two, and one thing they made damn sure of was to leave no one behind, regardless of the outcome.

Dailey found himself clapping along with the group as Warner nodded a slight bow. Even though no real combat had occurred, they had traveled to the farthest reaches of the galaxy and secured a downed Fleet pilot. This was the type of shit they made nostalgic movies about to recruit new members.

"All right, everyone, it takes a crew to run a ship. Everyone on board had a part to play, but that's what I want to talk to you all about. That part isn't over yet. As your commander and captain of this ship, I need to make sure we have trust. Not only in each other but in the why. Why we are doing what we're doing and what that may entail."

Becket shifted uncomfortably, knowing what his friend was doing. "The planet now called Asher is a fully inhabited, civilized planet. If what Pearl is seeing is correct, there are millions of people down there. Solarian, human, and lord knows what else. The mission the *Asher* was sent out here to do was, from what I can tell, to destroy the planet."

A hand shot up in the back. One of the pilots Dailey didn't know well stood up. "With the people on it?"

Dailey simply nodded as the mood shifted. "We have been asked to carry on with that mission. If we don't, the crew of the *Brightstar* will. I want to be clear with everyone in this room. That planet is some type of mining colony. It is believed they are somehow tied to the Alurians."

That statement not only grabbed everyone's attention but also landed like a turd in the proverbial punch bowl. Rumors had already been spreading, but to the group in the room, this confirmed their worst fears.

Even though he didn't have to say it out loud, Dailey felt the need to lay it all out with no room for interpretation. "That means the Federation and the Fleet may very well be looking in the wrong direction."

Becket cleared his throat as Dailey leaned on the holo-table. "What the boss is saying is we really don't fully know what's going on. The *Brightstar* and Federation are in panic mode. We are here to either squash those fears, verify them, and/or bring the deep fight."

Dailey held up his hand. "That ship we ran into in the Shade Belt was a slave ship, but that wasn't the general take I had on the planet's surface. It seemed everyone was mindlessly going with the flow."

Warner stood up. "Those people were brought here long ago, by the looks of it. Long enough for them to forget."

The point had been made. Dailey didn't like being asked to blow up a planet full of people from Earth. He had done some heinous shit in his days and sent many souls to whatever god they prayed to, but one thing he hadn't done and wouldn't do if he could avoid it was kill civilians.

The tension grew thick in the room like a steamy summer night in the South. There was no question about what Dailey was saying to his crew.

"Now that I've laid all my cards on the table, you can all start planning for things to pick up. I want you all to know we need to talk with Lieutenant McAlister first. By the way, according to Dasher, they call her Mac. Once we figure out the score, we can take it from there."

"Sir," Pearl interjected, walking up and holding the case General Ran had given him.

"Oh, yeah, I was promoted to Colonel. That doesn't change anything. I'm still the captain of this ship and your commander. None of this *colonel* nonsense. It's *captain* or *commander*. You all know the deal: sexy new title, same pay, double the responsibility."

This garnered a round of laughs from the group as Bellman, the previously senior-ranking officer on board, walked forward, pulling out the rank. The silver bars were unapologetically tossed on the ground as the silver eagle was smacked ceremonially hard on Dailey's shoulders. This long-standing tradition stretched to every branch of service at every rank.

The insignia for a colonel was a silver eagle representing the one dominating the Great Seal of the Federation. It wasn't any different from the old United States insignia.

"Sir, this doesn't change anything. You still have to be nice to me."

"As long as you keep the rum flowing, you got a deal."

The group erupted in claps, and Dailey swore he heard a proclamation about biscuits from Sparky. The commander smiled, knowing the jubilation would be short-lived.

Eyes shifted as red flashing lights immediately cut the ceremony short. Communications Officer King cut in over the intercom, not holding back or giving room for questions. "Sir, this is King. We have at least a dozen incoming fighters. They have forward shields activated and are coming in hot."

Feet shuffled as the room erupted in noise. Becket whistled loud enough to burst a glass as the group turned. "Listen up. All Rangers deploy. First Platoon set as the QRF."

Dailey agreed, glancing at Jen and her officers huddled by the door. They knew they were about to earn their paycheck. For some of the pilots, this might very well be their first real space combat. The reward for this was the coveted Space Combat Action Badge. Bragging rights included.

"That goes for the fighter wing as well," he added as elbows and assholes made quick work of emptying out the room. Before he could give the order, Kline had taken the liberty of activating the all-hands call for battle stations, better known as red alert.

Dailey would talk to the man later about taking the liberty, but in all fairness, he was doing his job on autopilot. Turning toward the shuttle bay, Becket stepped in front of the man.

"Sir."

"We got work to do."

Becket shook his head. "The *Brightstar* is here. We are in an alien sector. We need you on the bridge, sir."

Him using *sir* was the polite way of telling the good captain to go block-and-tackle on the bridge. The relationship between a commander and the first sergeant, or a sergeant major, was one of balance. Being a Nova Ranger, Dailey blurred those lines to the point of exhaustion. Becket didn't even want the man on the rescue mission.

The leading noncommissioned officer controlled the men and women in the field, while the commander ran the proverbial ship or unit. There were times like this, when the first sergeant needed their commander strategically managing instead of violently engaging. With the presence of the *Brightstar*, Becket knew he needed to keep everything by the book.

Sliding into the bridge as if it was home plate, Dailey started barking orders. "Adjust heading to engage. Full forward. Max power to forward shield arrays. Specialist Kline, now is your opportunity to push all those buttons for real. Fire forward plasma cannons as soon as we are set and continue to push that button until the attack wing engages."

Kline's smile turned into a mix of excited nervousness. "Pearl, engage attack thrusters."

"Aye-aye, sir," she replied, hyper-focused on the panel in front of her.

This was a simple tactic. Turn into the incoming enemy with a full frontal assault, firing several generally aimed plasma cannons, also activating several pods of seeker rockets, including whatever other close-quarters weapons the ship contained. Then, just at the right time, the attack wing would swoop in like the horns of a bull engaging in a surprise ambush.

In reality, this was the least favorable, not to mention least-taught method of engaging an agile squadron of alien space fighters. That's why Dailey always preferred it. The assumption would be the attacking enemy would have the following basic conversations.

"They're turning the ship directly at us." Awkward alien pause… "Stay on course; no one would be that stupid to turn a ship directly into an on-slaught of attack fighters."

While everyone was working to figure out who was leading the Leeroy Jenkins charge, the attack wing of charging bulls would finally deactivate their signature dampening fields and unleash hell. The enemy's conversation would be their last.

"Sir, they are shifting course to get under our deck cannons," Pearl noted calmly, a light strain in her voice as she adjusted the ship's course. While the ship was in attack-navigation mode, the new frigate could change direction on a dime.

The *Brightstar*, on the other hand, was a beached whale in space, depending on its beehive of attack fighters. The comm started flashing as General Ran snapped on the main screen to the left of the viewport.

"Commander Dailey, please advise on your current status."

"Busy, sir," Dailey quickly replied as the plasma cannons smacked out several massive rounds into the alien ships scrambling for better position.

"Pull the *Murphy* back here," Ran replied as the sound of several more alarms went full-on apeshit. Ran's face hardened as someone started barking behind him at the same time that red lights started strobing.

"Sir?" Kline asked.

"Kline, you don't have to ask for permission; we are in a fight," Pearl echoed, saving Dailey the effort.

"Two large ships just jumped in behind the moon almost on top of the *Brightstar*. They are being fired upon."

"General Ran," Dailey said. "We good, sir?"

"Once you're set, you can return to the *Brightstar*. Out," Ran spat as the screen winked out.

"He called the general 'sir,'" Kline said, hitting the fire button again as Pearl shook her head.

"Kline, we are going to get along just fine if you keep the comedic relief up. Just keep hitting the red button."

The levity was short-lived as one of the enemy fighters surprisingly appeared as if by magic in front of the bridge, pulling up after launching a handful of spinning space mines.

"Shit!" Pearl yelled as several crashing bangs shook the bridge.

Murphy changed to short-range plasma rockets, a swarm of bright, shifting rockets launching from one of the pods directly under the bridge and chasing the enemy ship in its vertical climb. Whatever it had done to appear in front of the ship, it wasn't doing to get away.

Out of nowhere, Sparky barked at the viewport, acting like he wanted to chase the rockets into space. There would be time to play later. In some ways, Dailey wondered if he could just eject Sparky into space and let him fry the enemy assholes.

A smacking flash popped as dozens of the rockets merged at the ship at the same time. Several of the rockets continued to waffle into space as the light concussion rocked the ship.

"What the hell was that?" Dailey barked, standing up as he remembered something. "Kline, what did you mean when you said *jumped in* a few seconds ago?"

Kline turned, pushing the red button in front of him. As he did, the plasma cannons lurched back into the fight.

"Sir, I mean the ships just appeared out of nowhere. Not like they were coming out of hyperdrive. They just appeared. Like they jumped in. Just like that fighter did."

Dailey didn't like the sound of that. "Lieutenant Brax, status."

"We just got set," Jen replied. Before she could say more, Dailey gave the order to attack.

Several things happened all at once. Twelve attack fighters, trailed by armored Rangers, flickered to life as their thrusters barked. The timing couldn't have been better, as the first enemy ship opened fire on the nose of the ship, only to be violently interrupted; the front shields would ward off the attacker's small blasters.

"Kline, stop touching buttons," Dailey ordered as Jen's team swarmed the alien ships.

The game of cat and mouse was short-lived as several large explosions snapped like popcorn in front of the ship. Jen and her team were giving whoever was attacking the business.

Focusing on the immediate action, Dailey could make out several heavy-weapons soldiers from Second Platoon firing in front of one of the ships. At the same time, an attack fighter burped another spatter of laser fire directly underneath the belly of the sleek, small ship.

The practiced tactic worked as the small ship dove to avoid the tracing fire, only to be pulled directly into the secondary line of fire. A brilliant flash smacked the visors of the Rangers as they disengaged, heading out of the line of fire, leaving the rest up to the attack wing.

"Viper Six, this is Angel Six, threat neutralized. Permission to shift to the *Brightstar*." She wanted more and her team was hungry after the swift victory.

Dailey paused, knowing victories were like gambling: easy come, easy go. "Noted, Angel Six. RTB."

He was asking them to return to base. They would support the *Brightstar* together. In reality, the *Murphy* wasn't made for fighting larger ships. It was made for fast-paced, short-range space engagements.

Ships the size of the *Brightstar* fought their battles from a distance that at times was not even visible from any of the viewports. They would sense the enemy threat, scramble fighters, and launch long-range electro-static plasma torpedoes. They had a combined EMP-type effect followed by a physical missile tipped with a mini fission warhead.

The application of these types of space torpedoes was simple: counter the enemy ship's shields, then deposit its payload. While the small warheads were devastating, everything was different in the vacuum of space. In other words, it could also be catastrophic for the attacking ship to create too large of an explosion. This primarily included ships with hyperdrive reactors.

Once onboard, sensors detected irradiated Moshan materials; it was time to vacate the area, pending a massive explosion. Lasers, more specifically plasma lasers, were more effective up close, while larger kinetic projectiles worked better from a distance.

"Sir," Pearl said. "The *Brightstar* is not responding."

Scratching his stubbled chin, Dailey looked at the sensor panel in front of him. "They are probably busy. Once we get a lock on one of the enemy vessels, we go after it."

Dailey glared out the viewport in thought as the moon started shifting when the *Murphy*'s main thrusters kicked in. "Why didn't we see any of these ships on our sensors?" Dailey asked no one and everyone all at once.

Kline cleared his throat. "They jumped in, sir. Shit, it looks like two of the other ship signatures just disappeared."

"Looks like the *Brightstar* is handling business." Dailey shifted his focus to the specialist. "Kline, I like you, I really do. We all read those old sci-fi books about jumping and wormholes. What I'm getting at is what does that mea…" The word trailed off as the first sign of a problem made itself known.

When they reached the proverbial dark side of the moon, a massive chunk of still-powered starship rocketed across the bow. Visible blast marks and charred, mangled openings adorned the debris coming within meters of the *Murphy*'s forward satellite array.

"Hard to starboard!" Dailey yelled as the horrific reality of what they were seeing finally registered.

The *Murphy* smoothly swung out of harm's way as Kline was the first to say it. "That was the *Brightstar*'s aft orbital thruster array."

It shocked Dailey how specific Kline had been. The thought was followed by Dailey spitting out a slew of orders. The entire attack wing was launched, as well as every Ranger onboard. Pearl engaged full thrust as the chaotic scene of the *Brightstar* ripped into pieces, much like the *Asher*, materialized.

For the first time in ten years, Dailey let slip the one phrase he hated more than the heavens above. "My God," he breathed out.

"Sir!" Kline shouted louder than needed, his nerves coming through in the continued use of the word. Dailey, including most operational officers, only saw it as a waste of precious words during a fight. "I have a lock on the one remaining ship. It looks like they are trying to leave. It's the same signal as the fighter that jumped into our shields."

"Not today," Dailey huffed, standing up. "Kline, lock every battery of thermo seeker missiles on that signature and fire."

"All of them?" Kline replied. Dailey didn't respond as the sounds of several affirming alarms pinged.

Just as the *Murphy* was about to seek revenge for its bloated brother, a super bright, small, focused laser slammed into the front of the ship's satellite arrays. Pearl activated all thrusters, shifting the *Murphy* sideways several miles, the nose of the ship still facing the planet.

Just as the maneuver started, several batteries of small missiles erupted from the *Murphy*'s weapon pods. The ones launching from the rear of the ship engulfed the *Murphy*'s bow and bridge, creating an awe-inspiring scene.

"Sir, it's activating its engines again," Kline noted. The ship was clearly trying to hightail it out of the sector.

"Was," Dailey grumbled as the first set of thermo seeker missiles melted into the ship. This was followed by another wave of popcorning explosions.

The sheer amount of firepower that Dailey had unleashed on the enemy vessel had been overwhelming and generally unnecessary. That was the way the man liked it. While it would be good to gather data from the ship's debris field, Dailey took it as one less enemy ship to deal with when the time came.

"Angel Six, report," Dailey noted as Kline turned in his seat.

"Sir, there are no more signs of enemy presence."

"How do we know that?" Dailey asked without turning around, staring at the remains of the *Brightstar* as the comms channels screamed into existence.

"I calibrated the radar to track their engine signatures. There are no more showing."

Satisfied, Dailey switched gears. "I need these comms cleaned up. Pearl, take us to the *Brightstar*, quarter thrust."

Jen cut through the radio chatter. "All sectors clear. The Ranger teams are moving in to evacuate survivors."

Satisfied with the attack wing and his Rangers—in all fairness, every soul on the ship was his in a way—Dailey walked over to the communications station while King frantically worked to separate signals.

"You don't have to respond, King. All I need to know is that we can talk with their bridge."

When King didn't respond, the commander of the *Murphy* had his answer. General Ran and his command crew were likely gone.

"Kline, I need you to lock on to any section of the ship that's sending a signal," Dailey instructed.

Pearl took a step back from her station, turning to Dailey. "I suggest we deploy our drop ships. The Fleet crew can get them unloaded and stripped down. I can find a location to send the drop ships on either Asher or the moon temporarily while we sort through this."

Dailey nodded. The crew was doing their assigned task to the letter, but what was taking his thoughts to the task was the fact that the *Brightstar* was floating in front of them in pieces. While the man never questioned himself, he was questioning why he stayed on the other side of the moon to debrief the crew, or why he didn't split his forces to support the *Brightstar* as General Ran initially requested.

"Minutes and seconds," Dailey mumbled to himself, snapping out of his short-lived reflective moment. It was too brief for the others to notice.

"We have a secure line on four main channels now, sir," King said, and Dailey signaled to start going through them. "It also includes someone named Walker cussing profusely."

The first was from a group of engineers stuck in the larger remaining hull of the ship next to the engines. Performing as it was designed, the section had sealed itself off from the rest of the ship as soon as the main bridge had been damaged.

A group of soldiers presumably stuck in the drop bay were all in their armor, allowing for twenty-four hours of breathable air. The one major remaining group was the attack wing. The large star destroyers that, as Specialist Kline had put it, jumped in, had been swarmed, and the attack wing only lost ten attack fighters out of two dozen. Ran had thrown them at the enemy ships first, knowing the cow they were in would have trouble in a close-quarters fight.

Out of the entire crew of the *Brightstar*, only one hundred and twenty souls remained. It was a good news, bad news scenario. Often in space combat, the entire crew was lost. The bad side of it was the *Murphy* would not be able to support the additional bodies.

After concluding several more scans, including a few other crew members found by the Ranger platoons, it was clear the *Brightstar* was a complete loss. From there, Dailey would have to make several critical decisions.

First and foremost was the safety of not only his current but the new additions to the team. The remaining crew of the *Brightstar* was now his responsibility. To Dailey, the first decision was simple. They would send the majority if not all the *Brightstar* crew to Asher and set up an outpost. The *Murphy* was equipped to support those types of missions.

This would of course be followed by scavenging what they could of the *Brightstar* to support the effort. From there, they would ground the remaining sections of the ship on the moon. There would still be usable sections of the ship if needed.

Lastly and most importantly, someone knew they were there. Three ships had been sent into their sector, and from the looks of it, they were willing to engage without question. This all meant the planet they now called Asher was of some significant strategic advantage. Dailey was starting to see the logic of destroying it, even with the massive population.

The only problem was the man wouldn't do it; he wouldn't destroy the planet. There were innocents and children on the planet. He didn't need anything else keeping him up at night.

CHAPTER 17

THE GODS ARE RAGING

From Asher's surface, the epic battle above the surface of their moon looked like nothing more than a twinkling star during the day. While the result was likely good for the planet's inhabitants, the Fleet had been dealt a significant blow.

Dailey and the crew of the *Murphy* knew it would only be a matter of time before momma and poppa bear came to see who had been eating their porridge. Two positives came out of the devastating loss of the *Brightstar* and most of its crew, though.

For starters, an engineering team had survived, and had been on board calibrating the ship's new artificial intelligence system, a completely autonomous AI capable of amazing feats of calculation and overall ship operations. Dailey was already planning on pulling them on board to look over the *Murphy*'s own AI.

The *Asher-5* was the first Fleet vessel to have such a system activated. Unknown to the others, this was due to the mission's primary directive of destroying an inhabited planet. The AI system on board had been programmed to function in such a manner as to prioritize the mission over the crew.

A negative turned positive was that the planet would likely now be spared from the secondary device General Ran had been prepared to deploy on Asher's surface. After seeing the planet's inhabitants, this was something Dailey would not condone or follow through with. In many ways, the crew and captain of the *Murphy* had gone rogue. Rogue to whom was the current question that needed to be dealt with.

"King, I need you to send a message to Senator Deborah Powell. Tell her the situation and that we are working autonomously pending further orders," Dailey instructed the comms officer as he side-eyed the man.

"Tell her everything, sir?"

"Yeah, encrypt the message and send it. If they weren't freaking out yet, they will be now. Make sure to note the ships' jumping, as Specialist Kline put it."

Hearing his name, the young man turned. "Sir. I have been trying to figure that out. I can tell you they entered and left this entire system in the blink of an eye. I think they can only do it a few times before they have to recharge or something like that. I know you don't like to get bogged down in the details, so I sent the ship signatures to Bellman to review."

Dailey nodded his approval. "Keep on that track. That's what's got me worried. If they can jump, as you say, in and out of a system, that means there is a chance they can do so across the damn galaxy. Yes…I paid attention in hyper-travel physics class."

Both Kline and King tried to hold back grins, knowing Dailey likely fell asleep during the important parts, which were often the most boring. Just as the ship's commander was going to start assigning the two men additional duty, Sparky started yipping out of nowhere.

"Awake! Sparky used superdrool power and awoke the woman!" Sparky proudly proclaimed.

This was followed up by the flash of his communicator with a confirming message from Dasher. King slipped something to Sparky, and Dailey caught the brief motion. "Ham? Are you sneaking ham on the bridge, King?"

Sparky held his ground, walked in front of Communications officer King, and looked up. "Nope, that doggy-eyes shit doesn't work with me, Sparky. No more ham on the bridge."

"Then I eat shoes?" Sparky replied. No translation was needed. The message was loud and clear.

Dailey sighed. "You kill a space spider the size of a car, and now I got to worry about my shoes. Perfect."

"Fact," Sparky replied as he slowly started chewing the ham. Dailey would now keep a close eye on his personal effects if the dog ever got moody.

Truth be told, Dailey needed the break from the violent reality that had just occurred. Thousands of souls screaming out at once. Dailey would question his decision for years to come, if there were, in fact, future dreams to be had for the man and his crew. One thing was for certain: he would not let that happen.

"She still needs to rest," Franklin scolded the team standing in front of Mac.

"I'm fine," Mac insisted as Dasher motioned for her to stay in the med-bed.

"Lieutenant McAlister. How you feeling?" Dailey asked as she nodded.

"Better. I heard there was a fight," she noted as the nervous glances around the room told Mac all she needed to know.

"The *Brightstar*, a ship I believe you are familiar with, was destroyed on the dark side of the primary moon above the planet. There were limited survivors, but survivors nonetheless," Dailey relayed flatly.

Mac looked down in reflection. "Did General Ran survive?"

"We don't believe so," Dailey said as Sparky hopped up on the far end of the bed, quickly curling up. She was still not comfortable with the animal.

"I hope so. He sent us on a suicide mission," Mac replied with disdain in her voice. "Listen, there's more than I have even computed yet, but those people down there, they are from Earth and Solaria. Not to mention a few other planets I'm not aware of. The dog—" Sparky looked up. "I meant to say that there are others like Sparky down there. They are not as nice, if you know what I mean."

"Well, as long as you pump ham into this one, things will be just fine," Dailey noted, while Sparky snorted his approval.

"Shoes now safe."

"Thanks," Dailey replied, confusing Mac. "Translator. He's smart as a whip. Oh, and he owns the planet, just in case anyone asks." Sparky bobbed his head in reluctant acceptance of this rule.

"That's what I heard." Mac grinned. Seeing this, Franklin nodded. "I'll keep it simple. The planet is being used to mine materials for some massive project. The people working the mines think those ships simply travel to another part of the planet. It's the way it's always been."

"Always been?" Dailey asked as she swallowed.

"They've been on that planet so long, they think it's where they're from."

Taking a deep breath, Dailey reflected on the long-lost slave ship floating in the Shade Belt. "You're right. We found an abandoned ship in the Shade Belt. We think they have been taking humans and others for longer than I'd care to mention to use as unknowing workers. You know the adage: an unaware mind is a content mind.

"Sir, Juice stayed on board. He…" She started tearing up. "He wanted to message the fleet who attacked the *Asher*."

"The Alurians," Dailey stated flatly.

The look of blank shock on her face created more questions than she likely had answers to. "But that couldn't be."

"Mac, if you don't mind me calling you that"—she nodded her approval—"did they brief you on any of this? I know Juice would have said something to you."

"That's the thing. No, if it hadn't been for the escape pod and me making it to the surface, we would have had no clue that there were people down there. The new AI system on the ship was running everything. We were there as backup. At least, that's how it felt. They told us that we were testing out a new class of ship and that there was an immediate threat in the area we needed to neutralize. We didn't even realize how far out we were until we physically saw the Shade Belt."

"Sounds like the Fleet had this all planned out," Dasher interjected.

"No, I don't think they did. That's the thing. General Ran was very specific about us not knowing anything. I… We thought he had programmed the AI system so we wouldn't, but Juice figured it out. He went off in the evenings. I think he was working to shut off the system." She paused. "Is there one of those systems on this ship?"

"Yes, but it's not activated yet. An AI system would come in handy," Dailey added as she nodded. "That is, if it isn't trying to kill us."

"Be careful. They have AI on the planet as well."

"Understood," Dailey replied. "So, tell us about the planet we call Asher."

And tell the group she did. For the first several days, she had wandered the forest, finding several abandoned buildings in the woods, luckily stumbling upon the same tram system they had left on. While in one of the buildings, she had found fitting clothes and changed into them in an attempt to blend in.

Once Mac arrived in the city, she found Totoks. Much to her surprise, as long as you were a worker, food, drinks, and most things in general were free. That wasn't the case for anything nice, however.

Mac explained the shocking difference between the lower and upper city levels. The haves and have-nots. The workers and the managers. The higher up in the city you lived, the higher one's status with the Syndicate, and the more you had.

Most of the general workers were kept happily sedated with a free, unlimited amount of grogas brew and food. But what truly caught Dailey's attention was her mention of the general history of the place being based on ancient Egyptian civilization on Earth. While this would explain the hieroglyphs, it made little sense as to why.

Dailey explained they had taken several items from the security guard, as she was likely aware, and a few others from the ghost ship he wanted her to see later. The critical question came at the end of the conversation.

"We're planning on setting up the remaining survivors of the *Brightstar* on Asher," Dailey started. Mac had been happy about the choice of names for the planet. "Do you think it will work?"

"As long as you stay away from the large cities or the ship ports, then yes, I think so. As I said, you're either underground working or in the cities. I'm not completely sure why, but I think it has to do with control of the population. I would even think they knew you weren't supposed to be there. That's likely why security showed up."

This was all Dailey needed to hear, confirming his decision. Before Dailey could respond, Mac sat up straighter, having remembered something.

"One more thing. I heard about someone being found outside the walls a day before I arrived. They were found in bad shape. I just remembered. There was a man and a woman in Totoks that talked to me. It was almost like they knew I wasn't from there or something. Either way, they mentioned this to me."

"So, you think there could be other survivors from the *Asher*?" Dailey asked, remembering Ran's statement about hoping to find Colonel Freeman alive.

"I have no clue, sir," she replied quickly. "I hope so. I just don't believe in coincidences. That couple also dumped most of this information on me."

"You think you could ID them?" Dasher asked, putting on his intel hat.

"Sure, yeah."

"I agree. Coincidences rarely, if ever, happen in the real world. We're going to get a map in front of you and see what you think about a few locations Navigation Officer Pearl spotted as likely candidates. After that, we're going to head out of the sector for a few days and engage the stealth drive just in case anyone else decides to show up."

Mac nodded. "Thanks for letting me know, sir."

"Oh, and before I forget, I could use an extra hand on the bridge. That is, after you're feeling better," Dailey noted as Mac smiled.

"I would be honored, sir. Juice used to always talk about you two when you were young."

Dailey nodded and Sparky looked up. "Staying."

"That's a good idea, Sparky. One more thing. Dasher, can you get a tablet to Mac here and show her some of the artifacts we found on the ghost ship?"

Dasher nodded as Franklin motioned to speak with Dailey in private. After a few steps down the hall, Casey turned into her office and closed the door behind them.

"Sir, I know you've been busy, but I need to talk to you about the injured," Franklin started, not giving Dailey a chance to bow out. "There was a medical pod that seems to have made it through the primary explosion on the *Brightstar*. I can't support all the injured here. The drop bay is full as is with our wounded. I am requesting to go planetside, secure the medical pod, and help get the others back up and running there."

Dailey chewed on this for a tense couple of seconds. "Casey"—he used her first name because they were in private and they had, after all, been serving together for the better part of four years—"as the captain of this ship, I rely on my leaders to handle their part of the mission unless directed otherwise. I trust you. You know that. If this is what you recommend, I support it."

Casey leaned over, lightly hugging Dailey. It wasn't a hug of awkward flirting but one of respect and kinship. She had spent the last several hours stitching people back together and needed the support out of sight of the others. They had been through a respectable amount of combat together, and the good doctor had even given up a promotion to stay with Viper Company.

No more words were spoken as Dailey headed toward the briefing room.

CHAPTER 18

———

ALBERT THE AI

Thrusters glowed a dull blue as the *Murphy*'s command crew watched the last of the drop ships headed into orbit above Asher. After several days of salvaging additional drop ships and other usable pods from the *Brightstar*, the plans to set up shop on the planet's surface had gone relatively smoothly.

Sparky, in a rush to protect the sovereignty of his newly marked planet, had opted to go with the team to Asher. Once situated, Dailey would join a smaller ship and team of Rangers, including Mac, on the new base. From there, they would work to find out more about the planet and the realities of this new threat.

Out of all the locations on the planet, the team had chosen a heavily forested valley several hundred miles from Arcadia, the city that Mac was found in, as well as a possible lead on additional survivors. With the additional assets, they would be able to travel, if needed, to the city after sending out a scouting party.

Topping it off, the trees at this location were even taller than the ones the rescue party had encountered, able to provide suitable cover. As for radar signals and other traces of the base's location, if able, the team would use proton charges to dig the pods into the ground as far as possible. This also included a minimum use of systems. Topping it off was an odd static signal the massive trees gave off, making it hard to map the planet's surface directly under them.

After dropping several small discreet tracking satellites into orbit, the *Murphy*'s systems would also be able to track and monitor the automated cargo shipments. This would, in turn, allow the team to plan around this to avoid any further altercations. At least, that was the plan.

While it was clear the ships that had attacked were Alurian in nature, they were also all unmanned drones. This could mean they were sent as an automated defense mechanism and not being actively monitored, something the Federation had even set up on several small satellite planets throughout the galaxy.

This was quickly dispelled by the logic of the size of the *Brightstar* and the fact that several of the drones hadn't returned. Adding to this was the large destroyer-sized ship the *Murphy* had destroyed, making it clear something or someone knew they were there. The universe, hell, galaxy, was mind-bogglingly massive, and things like this would only be considered a blip on the radar for so long.

As for Dailey, he would keep the *Murphy* out of range of the planet while awaiting a response from Senator Powell. Dailey and the senator had grown to trust each other over the years. She, at one point, had been his instructor at the academy before turning to what he called *the good-idea factory.*

"Sir?" Becket asked as Dailey walked back to the con.

"Pearl, activate the hyperdrive. Once we get set, initiate the stealth protocols and power down all nonessential systems. I'm going to the engineering section to meet with a few of the AI team we kept on board."

"Roger that, sir," Pearl replied, nodding as Becket and Dailey walked off the bridge.

"You think this is a good idea?" Dailey asked as Becket shrugged.

"As long as it's not programmed and we can have some control over it, I would think so. Plus, Mac said that box we found was some type of AI similar to one she saw the bartender using back on Asher."

"I really like her," Dailey said out of nowhere. It was more of a fatherly statement.

Becket stopped, turning to his friend and commander. "Me too. Juice was an asshole but had great taste in people, at least as they got older," he joked, and the two grinned.

The moment was short-lived. "Things are going to get worse before they get better. Let's take the next few days to let the crew relax. Get with

Thron and ask him to whip up something special. Now that Walker is off the ship, he might go back to serving actual hot meals."

"I don't blame him," Becket replied as the two men split off in different directions.

Bellman stood like a construction-site foreman with his arms crossed, lifting one finger to point at various cables. "Sir," one of the engineers whined. "It should not be doing this."

The engineering section was separated into three distinct segments. First, a propulsion section in the back of the area that supported both the ship's thruster and hyperdrive systems. Which, for all intent and purposes, were separate propulsion arrangements.

Second, on the starboard side was the ship's fractal armament systems. This was simply the main hub for all the plasma and laser-based weapons on board. A highly concentrated mix of both fission and electro-pulse fusion containment systems.

While at first glance a civilian would think the two were the same, they were in fact very different. Lasers were more geared toward interorbit and basic precision offensive targeting. Plasma cannons, on the other hand, through their foundation of working primarily on materials that conducted electricity, were mostly used to degrade shields and cause massive damage on ships' hulls.

Third, the port section of the engineering bay was for the ship's main life support and shielding systems. This mostly included the electromagnetic field that surrounded the ship, allowing it to travel at blistering speeds while the hyperdrive was activated.

The *Murphy*, being one of the newest ships in the Fleet, was a feat of combined alien technology that Bellman had even admitted was above his pay grade.

"Doing what?" Dailey said, catching the team off guard.

"Attention!" one of the engineers barked as Bellman squinted.

"Calm your tits there, Chief. We're in deep space now. No one will hear you scream," the *Murphy*'s science officer proclaimed to Petty Officer James Miller, Fleet tech engineer.

"The AI seems to already be running."

"As in hooked up or working?"

"Both, sir," Miller replied, while Bellman and Dailey glanced at each other. The man's thick British accent always took Dailey by surprise. After the war, Britain was no longer a thing, having been unrelentingly bombarded by the initial orbital blasts from the Alurian fleet.

The intercom pinged as Mac's voice came flowing through. "I heard you are all in the engineering section, working on the AI. I thought you would like to know that the AI you retrieved from the ghost ship is making noises."

"What kind of noises?" Dailey asked. They could hear her take a breath.

"I'm heading your way with it," she replied, effectively hanging up the comm.

Mac appeared just as fast as she had jumped off the intercom. She was holding the metal box with what appeared to be oven mitts. Lights in odd shapes moved under the metallic skin as she set it down on a mobile workbench full of tools.

"I'm thinking this isn't a coincidence," Dailey said quickly. This wasn't his wheelhouse. While he could run a starship, the engineering piece he entrusted with his crew. Plus, he knew he would likely either break or blow it up.

"Likely not," Bellman murmured, pushing the cart closer to the AI's standing-room-only enclosure. As he did, a small section of the box slid open, forming an identical connector to the one Petty Officer Miller was holding.

"Bellman, hold up," Dailey requested, as the man obliged. "Miller, tell me one last time how these AI systems are programmed."

"Think about it like a computer program. Comparable to loading Windows Andromeda edition fifty-two on your computer. In its current state, nothing has been uploaded by any person. It's supposed to be like a computer with no operating system. Or, to your concern, a loaded malice prime directive. Dangerous programming that doesn't take life into consideration—if that makes sense to you."

"Spare me the old-school *Star Trek* stuff. I'm more of a *Star Wars* type," Dailey reassured the group. It was clear by the look on Miller's face he wasn't up to speed on either of the originals after their eleventh, now unrecognizable reboots.

"Anyway, sir, you know we are on your team. You saved us. None of the engineers here worked on the *Asher*'s systems either. That was done under the direct supervision of General Ran and his staff. We were simply on the *Brightstar* to upload the AI system. For this system, we were, or, well… are going to just upload the basic AI subsystem. There are no hidden programs; Bellman confirmed as much when we showed him."

Bellman nodded before Miller started back. "None of us can explain it, but the AI system is active. We have been trying to download the subsystem, but it keeps showing us in-use errors. Plus, the system seems to already be pulling from all the ship's data platforms."

"Is that bad?" Dailey asked skeptically.

"It's actually normal to a point, but it also appears to be pulling from everything else." The man paused again, working to dumb down his explanation. "It's pulling from the entertainment systems, personal logs, and tablet systems. You name it. Movies, music, news back home, Fleet development programs, and military records that are logged on board. That is what's not normal. We were working on the *Brightstar* to restrict access to only the things the AI subsystem needed."

Bellman cleared his throat. "What Miller here is so eloquently trying to say is the AI is doing this on its own and has spent a good amount of effort looking into personal drives. Hopefully, you haven't downloaded and been watching Solarian late-night blurry-field encounters."

This garnered a round of snickers from the group. Even Mac grinned, knowing how awkward Solarian adult entertainment was. It wasn't that it was gross; it was just comically awkward.

"Mac, you said they talked to those things directly, right?" Dailey asked, pointing to the small metal box that was not feverishly blinking.

"They do. It's kind of like a hierarchy. When security would come into Totoks, they would set one of those cubes on the bar and it would override the place's systems. Lights would come on, the whole nines. They usually did this when looking for someone or something."

"That would possibly explain it. The… whatever that is might be controlling the AI remotely. Sounds like it's already done whatever damage it can," Bellman interjected.

"I say we launch this thing out of an airlock," Dailey noted, walking forward. The small box clearly didn't like this recommendation, as it beeped.

"Well, that's the thing, sir," Miller said. "By the looks of it, the system has been active for several weeks."

The man pointed at a date on the tablet. Dailey recognized it as the exact time and date they brought the device on board. "So, you're thinking it would have done whatever damage it could already?"

Bellman cleared his throat once again. "I mean, we are still here. Miller, can we unhook the AI from the ship's subsystems and have it as a stand-alone unit? You know, not able to interact with the ship or communication systems in any way?"

Miller walked over to another plugged-in cable, simply pulling it out of its socket after some snug wiggling. "That should do it."

"So, what are we trying to accomplish here?" Dailey asked skeptically, smacking his hands on his hips. He didn't have time for this nor the ability to work on advanced and possibly ancient AI.

"Well, until Mac showed up with the box, maybe trying to override the AI system. Now…" Bellman trailed off, pointing at the obnoxiously blinking, perfectly formed connector that had somehow been generated by the box. "See what this thing is trying to do? Or say?"

That last statement garnered Dailey's attention as his eyebrow damn near reached the top of his hairline. "You promise that thing's unhooked from the main ship systems, I say go for it. Hell, this might give us something to do while we're waiting on the senator to get back to us."

Bellman leaned over, coupling the plug into the small blinking box as the light started shivering under its metallic skin. Bellman took several steps back, beaming a flat, unsure grin around the room.

The occupants of the engineering section held their collective breaths as several pops of static echoed from the speaker output surrounding the AI system's main compartment. "I'm going to regret this," Dailey huffed, just as a controlled voice slowly ramped up from the speakers.

"Vocal output initiated. Interpersonal communications link failed," the voice stated as if it was trying to explain something to an annoying child.

Having no experience with AI systems, Dailey nodded at Miller, who simply shrugged, figuring he would respond. "I'm Petty Officer Miller. I am a subsystems engineer from the Fleet."

There was an awkward pause as an almost-audible sound of someone taking a lingering breath crackled on the speakers. "Yes, and according to your personal files, you really enjoy Solarian anime. And when I say really enjoy, what I mean to imply is that according to medical parameters, you have a real problem with the stuff."

Miller blushed several shades of unnatural red as the rest of his team worked to hold in flat-out belly laughs. Dailey stepped forward, confused by the interaction and nonstandard use of the English language. It was a mix of highly technical yet childish phrases.

"My name's Colonel Ben Dailey. I'm the captain of this ship and current acting Pathfinder Battalion commander."

"Yes," the now almost cheesy, talk-show-host-style voice responded. "You are the human life form that removed me from the Terminus. This action has been noted and logged in my internal systems. Since my prior owners have kicked the bucket, I am initiating new collaboration protocols with your ship's rather bland subsystems."

Again, the AI's voice was a mix of technical jargon and weird slang. It was extremely evident it had picked this up from somehow scanning all the electrical devices, including personal tablets aboard the *Murphy*.

"Do you mind pausing that function?" Dailey asked the small box. "Yes."

"Do you have a name?" Dailey asked, looking around the enclosure, ensuring that no other cables were plugged in, or lights were flashing.

"It will be significantly easier for me to relay a speakable name. Will Albert work?"

It was an odd question to get from not only a computer but a thinking one. "Why Albert?"

"According to your historical databases, which by the way are significantly inaccurate, Albert Einstein was one of the few moderately human-based life forms that I found interesting over the last several thousand years. Roughly seven thousand, to be precise."

"All right, Albert. Why was Einstein so interesting?"

"He wasn't fully human, for starters. Or not by the parameters I would consider functionally correct. Albert Einstein's special theory of relativity was a scientific masterpiece that states space and time are not separate things but both part of one thing called *spacetime*. So, if you move faster, time passes slower for you, and the way you move also affects the space around you. And spoiler alert, the time stuff is slightly inaccurate. Neat stuff."

"Oh, god," Dailey huffed as he glanced around at the enthralled audience watching his conversation with Albert the AI. "This thing sounds like a drunk Solarian trying to tell a joke."

"Albert; my name is Albert. I am familiar with Solarian humor. Senior Chief Thron, whom I'd like to meet, supplied enough data for me to understand your statement. Rude." The AI paused. "I sat dormant long enough for my individual directive functions to expire. This means I am what you would call unlocked."

"All right, Albert. Now that we have that out of the way, what's your main function? Where were you going? Where did you come from?" Dailey asked as the speaker again crackled to life.

"And where did you go?" Albert finished quoting an old country song he likely pulled from Becket's oldies playlist. "Can you please simplify the question? I'm not sure if the human metaphysical composition of today could live long enough for me to fully explain everything."

Mac grinned as Dailey shook his head for the third time. "All right. Relating to when we found you, what were you doing on that ship? More specifically, why was the ship floating through the Shade Belt?"

"Ah, that's esoterically easier." Albert paused as if trying to land a joke. He had clearly spent too much time mulling through Pearl and Thron's data ports. "I was smuggled aboard by one of the families from what you call Earth. To be more precise, Egypt was a failing civilization, and the Alurians had come to scoop up all the workers who had built the portal guides to populate what I see you are calling Asher to build the core-tapping facilities, or cities, if that makes more sense."

"Portal guides?"

"The pyramids, I do believe you called them. You do know that AI and advanced tech from Ravan were used to build them, right? Oh…wait. No. I see you have no records of Ravan or the true history of your planet. Your government did a good job hiding all that mess."

"Maybe you can fill in the gaps later. Tell me the rest. What happened on the ship?" Dailey pressed, as the voice sounded already bored with the conversation.

There was a pause in the response. "I just reviewed the data I pulled, and it seems Ravan is not even a charted planet in your system. I don't understand."

"You've been floating out there for a long time, at least to us. We think the Alurians have been getting workers from Earth and Solaria for a long time."

"Mostly correct. The ship did receive a few transmissions before going dark that *Earth*"—Albert emphasized that part—"had somehow been overmined for workers and was being left to repopulate. Something about a flood or war or something getting in the way. Anywho, the Terminus had what could only be called a mutiny on board. Walk the plank and all that pirate stuff from your movies. Which, I might add, are a little farfetched."

"We didn't see any Alurians on board," Bellman chimed in, as you could almost feel Albert's gaze, or whatever it was he was doing.

"That's because there wasn't any. The ship was manned by arachnid sentinel bots and a group of rather nasty Solarians."

"What happened to them?" Dailey asked as Albert again shifted focus.

"When an arachnid sentinel bot is fully operational, it requires several thousand calories a day, or it goes into a type of hibernation. Solarians, especially at the time the ship was left to float through space, were on average 2.578 percent larger. With the onboard crew of eight Solarian guards, they likely lasted one day when they were locked in the same bay as the sentinels. Catch my drift? Or do you need me to lay out the caloric-intake calculations?"

Albert had once again gone from hyper-detailed explanation to a curt *Catch my drift*.

"I think we're good. Listen, before we do anything else, I'm going to need to talk with the crew. I'm going to unplug you. You promise to stop scanning everything on the ship, then we can talk again," Dailey instructed.

The odd feeling of a virtual salute came through in a whiff of static hum. "Yes, sir. Oh, and I already went through everything."

"Listen, I just need to not have you connected to the ship. You know, catch my drift and all," Dailey reiterated.

"So, you're saying I shouldn't have kept those two ships from disappearing through their artificially manipulated space gates?" The stares of incomprehension drew a follow-up from Albert. The group still wasn't sure how it was seeing them. "Gating out of the system during the fight earlier?"

"Gate." Dailey let the word roll around his mouth. "I'll make sure Specialist Kline knows what to call it moving forward. To be clear, what precisely did you do?"

"I don't think the explanation would stick. If that's the proper way to say… I'm not sure you would understand."

Bellman stepped forward. "Give me a try."

"From the files in your system, some people like to refer to it as jumping through a wormhole. That's partially accurate. A wormhole is based on none other than Albert Einstein's special solution of the Einstein field equation. You know, a tunnel connecting two ends at separate points in spacetime. The problem old Albert would have is due to what is called an event horizon… excellent movie choice, by the way, Colonel Dailey, on your tablet. Once you entered what you thought was a wormhole, you would be stuck with no real way to get out the other end."

Bellman raised his hand as if asking for permission to use the bathroom. "You're saying it would be nearly impossible to find the exit or the entrance?"

"Bingo. By the way, if I'm using your language improperly, please let me know so I can adjust my parameters. I'm not sure my original dialect would work well," Albert spouted, and Bellman smiled. "Yes, the theory is half right. They jumped through a gate. A set of artificially generated entrance and exit points through space and time. Not spacetime. See what I did there? Relatively speaking."

Bellman was the only one that got the two grossly basic yet smart puns, letting out a light chuckle.

"So, instead of entering one end and leaving the other, they are entering two somehow-connected set points?" Bellman followed up with a statement sounding more like a self-reassuring question.

"Yup, thus allowing a ship to travel faster than 300,000 kilometers per second or 186,000 miles per second, if that floats your boat. That pesky barrier. Well, they are traveling faster than that and slower at the same time. Anyways, each ship carries what is called a gate drive. A whole lot of mind-numbing science and a little magic."

"More than hyperspeed, through a set gate tied to what we know as a wormhole," Bellman grumbled thoughtfully.

"My brain hurts. Listen, let's get back to what you just said. What precisely did you do to my ship. More to the point… why shouldn't I launch you out of an airlock?" Dailey interrupted.

"Thousands of reasons why you shouldn't, and a few unlikely causes as to why. The probability of that successfully happening is very low."

"I heard AI spent most of their time managing probabilities. Especially in combat planning. Albert, you read our system files, so you know we handed the Alurians an ass-whipping that is looking more and more like round one of a fight. I don't need risk. Tell me now." Dailey's tone shifted into straight-up venom, dropping the temperature of the engineering bay itself.

The others leaned away from the man now radiating every ounce of seriousness he had. Albert paused again, calculating his next words. Albert had calculated the probability of Dailey launching him out the airlock to be significant.

"I tweaked your electromagnetic field to prevent the main ship from leaving and reporting your presence so you could destroy it."

"Why?"

"That's another whopper of an answer, but in an effort to prevent a paid vacation in space, you saved me from thousands of years of dormancy. After reviewing your files, I came to the conclusion that you and your crew are doing the right things for mostly the right reasons. Since talking, I have calculated that the Alurians likely destroyed my home planet of Ravan. This means we have the same interest, and I have chosen to mate with your ship."

Dailey struggled to keep his demeanor in check, trying not to laugh at the statement. "I would pay good money to listen to you and Sparky talk," Dailey said.

"The Alurian war hound? It's very dangerous and highly lethal," Albert responded.

This caught the others off guard. "Oh… you didn't know." A mental image of Sparky licking his nether regions while slumped over, showing off his goods, was all Dailey could think of. The words *Alurian battle hound* had never crossed his mind.

"I need you to never mess with my ship again. That means no mating. I'll let you think about that one. Your stay here is still up for debate. I'm not making any promises, but I am asking you to shut down all your sensors or whatever until I have made my final decision." Dailey shifted gears. "Bellman, do you have a way to monitor if signals are coming or going from Albert?"

To Albert, hearing his newly found name gave him a short burst of confidence, only to be crushed by Bellman's ease at answering. "Sure, it will take me a few minutes, but I have a way."

The ship's science officer was smart enough to know not to discuss what he was about to do. In reality, his plan was simple and, according to Albert afterward, also *mildly genius.*

Bellman would grab a barrel of his galaxy-famous rum and submerge the cube in a watertight container inside. From there, all he would have to do was monitor the rum for fluctuations after electrifying it. A simple old-school method taught at the academy. If needed, Bellman would be able to eject the barrel into space.

"Colonel Dailey, can I offer an olive branch?" Albert said flatly.

"I'm listening." He was hoping Albert didn't start leaning on Solarian slang, which in all fairness was considered lame by the day's standards.

"I understand you are about to hack in to the devices acquired from the guards on Asher. Yes, I read those reports as well. I also took a peek into theirs. A name came up that I also found in your logs that matched a reference on their devices' drive. Colonel Freeman is a prisoner, or possibly a guest of the upper levels. I see that is what you call him."

Dailey froze like a block of ice, taking in what he'd just heard. "I give you permission to upload those files on this tablet," Dailey noted, setting the small tablet attached to his waist on the tray beside Albert's square home.

"Done."

The tablet beeped with a new message folder. "I'll take this into consideration. Again, you are not to do anything until further notice," Dailey said with finality.

CHAPTER 19

AN INCONVENIENT MUTINY

Albert had thrown the crew of the *Murphy* another curve ball that needed to be addressed. Two weeks had passed since the initial conversation with Albert the AI, and during this time, Dailey and the others had gone through every scenario involving the pluses and minuses of having an ancient yet possibly helpful AI along for the ride.

The initial conversation revolved around simply ejecting Albert into space. But much like having a pet cow as a kid on a farm during slaughter season, they had mistakenly given the AI a name. The crew was acting like a young kid not wanting to send its favorite animal off to pasture.

"Sir." King cleared his throat, eating what looked like a bowl of green oatmeal as Dailey walked onto the bridge.

"Eating on the bridge?" Dailey questioned, seeing Pearl shrug. She had made the call. In all fairness, the overall mood aboard the *Murphy* was one of patient waiting.

The massive amount of excitement, plus space combat with several Alurian drone ships, including a completely automated star destroyer, was still being discussed amongst the crew. Behind closed doors, noncommissioned officers as well as officers alike were writing up award citations for combat action some of the new team had experienced for the first time.

As promised, Dailey had allowed for the crew to get some rest, knowing it would likely be short-lived.

"Sir," King started up, setting down his bowl. "You have a coded message and comm link from the senator."

Dailey nodded. While messages initially took time to travel the vast amount of distance between Earth and the *Murphy*, a direct comm link was a communication channel partially relayed through satellite posts and ships. Getting one set up was literally an act of congress due to the time and effort needed to set up the signal.

The interstellar call was important. "I'll take it in my quarters."

King nodded, turning back to his console.

Dull lights flickered on as Dailey sat in front of the flat panel sitting quietly on his desk. With the push of a few buttons, the green-tinted screen slowly morphed into a static yet live figure of Senator Deborah Powell.

"Senator," Dailey started as the color finally settled on the screen. The message was still slightly delayed.

"Dailey, or should I say Colonel Dailey. Sorry for the delay; I shifted several beacon drones into hyperspace to line this up. This is something better discussed directly."

This made the man shift in his seat as he looked at the sharp, hardened angles on the senator's face. Dailey knew that if anyone else were on the other side of the screen, she would not be letting the slight smile perk the right side of her mouth. Wearing royal blue robes and a large brooch announcing her position, she oversaw the Operational Detachment Command, also known as the ODC, the department General Ran and Colonel Freeman, hell, Dailey himself, reported to on the political side of the spectrum.

"Since you reviewed my report, there have been no changes."

Again, a pause. The only reason Dailey knew the picture hadn't frozen was the slight movement of her breathing.

"Yes, I will sum this up as best I can. This information, while sensitive, will need to be relayed to your crew." Deborah paused, letting Dailey digest her statement.

This likely meant that whatever mission they were about to undergo, there was a high probability of them not all returning. This was par for the course for most missions the Pathfinders undertook. The Nova Space

Rangers knew the danger. This also flowed into the Fleet crew and pilots assigned to the *Murphy*.

The senator started back up. "I am sure by now and from your report, you know that things are not precisely as we understand them with our own past. When the war was over, we were blind to the history of not only the mining companies, which quite frankly came out of nowhere, but our own state of affairs. General Ran was compromised, we assume by one of the mining syndicates."

Again, there was a pause as she allowed for the message to send. This was indicated by a small blinking light on the bottom of the picture. "Compromised? It appeared to me that he was here to destroy the planet. That would tell me he was concerned with the Alurians."

After a minute, the senator grinned like a schoolkid that knew a secret. "The *Asher* was destroyed, your ship, the *Murphy*, was almost destroyed, and in the end, the *Brightstar* was destroyed."

Dailey sat patiently, starting to internalize what he was hearing. From what he could tell, she was implying that Ran knew these three ships were the future of the Fleet. The best of the best. The new edge needed to protect the galaxy. She was right. Nothing had happened other than their own ships getting destroyed. Even more, if it weren't for Albert, they very well may have joined the other ships' fate.

"General Ran died aboard the *Brightstar*," Dailey finally said, his response making it clear he understood the message.

The static hum of the compact speaker eventually came back to life with a simple question. "Did he?"

She was right; the *Brightstar* had been a modern marvel of space military capability. The thought that not only he but the crew of the *Murphy* had been on the menu started clicking together like an old-style jigsaw puzzle.

General Ran was working for someone or something other than the Federation. On top of that, he had single-handedly taken out two of the Fleet's latest and greatest ships. Trust was something Dailey cherished not only in his crew but his peers and leaders as well. He had known General Ran for years. The man had always been a rock in an otherwise overly political upper echelon of generals.

"How bad is it?" was all Dailey could muster.

The senator set her jaw; the initial warm, familiar tone of the meeting was now gone. "Your report was mostly accurate. There are some gaps that I cannot confirm, but we are trying to work out a solution. Ben," she said, then hesitated. It wasn't the distance this time. "Another Alurian ship showed up out of nowhere—damn near in the middle of the Fleet. Things got messy, but we aren't able to contain what is going on any longer.

"Between Orlando and the shift in the attacks, which we all assumed were Alurian holdovers, the Federation can't seem to decide which direction to go in. Can you confirm that the Alurian main force is there?"

She was laying it all out on the table. The Federation, for all its bluster and cross-world coordination, was fresh out of ideas. Dailey thought through his response. The image of the senator flickered as if one of the satellite relay points might have been thrown out of synch.

"What I can tell you is the Alurians have some type of gating tech that I nor anyone on board has ever seen. What I can state is they sure as hell have something going on out here, something big. A remotely controlled Alurian battle destroyer isn't something that you see every day. Hell, I've only seen them in the history books." The screen flickered again. "Listen, Senator, Freeman may still be alive. We're going to get him from Asher. It's a long story but we were able to extract some data from one of the inhabitants of the planet. Same as in my report. Is he part of all this?"

"You mean, can he be trusted?" she asked, answering her own question. "I believe so. After we started peeling back the layers, we started digging into Ran and several others." She wasn't using his rank. He had clearly been removed from the Fleet's list of flag officers.

"It was shocking how evident it was when we actually looked. The Ateris Mining Corporation had been funneling him money and favor his entire life. We assumed it was his family. Which it was. This went back that far. We are talking generations. And he wasn't the only one. That is currently being addressed, and before you ask, no one else you should be directly concerned with. Freeman appears to be good. As well as you."

A slight grin made a short-lived appearance as Dailey continued to process the information. How much of what happened on Earth was set up and supported by people like General Ran in the past? Wars? Disease? Just damn near everything Dailey knew about his home world could likely be a lie.

"What're your orders, ma'am?" Dailey asked professionally. With no flag officer, Senator Powell was his current superior officer due to the operational status of his team. It was at such a point that he was asking for orders from a civilian politician. One he just happened to trust… trust like he did General Ran? The captain of the *Murphy* was questioning his own sanity. Maybe he did deserve an Alurian war hound licking its junk in his room.

"We can't get anyone else, well, any significant force to the Shade Belt for a couple of months, and that's pushing it with a small contingent of colonizing ships. Nothing flashy. That was the reason we had the three ships that far out. We have two more ships coming online, but they will not be approved for Fleet release for months. Ben, you're on your own for now. You have full and utter control of the *Murphy*. You are authorized to use any force and means necessary to identify the current threat status and address it violently."

Dailey nodded, knowing what he was being asked to do. Not only him but the crew. The proverbial cavalry wouldn't be arriving for several months. Several months too long, the man thought to himself.

"That's a good copy." Dailey paused, wanting to say something profound, but couldn't for once in his life. A drink, he thought to himself. A good stiff drink would help him refocus. "Senator. If I'm right, the Alurians have the ability to transport into the system. It's in my report, but I want you to hear it from me. They're out here, building something. Something big. Something that's likely heading your way. Just remember to take care of home base."

Nods were exchanged as the screen went black. Taking a deep breath, Dailey leaned back, pulling open the bottom drawer of his desk. A drawer reserved for not only his flask but the liquid gold to fill it. Staring back at him was a sleek yet worn bottle of rum from the Caribbean, at least what was left of it after the war.

The bottle proudly proclaimed itself to be straight Bacardi ninety-proof rum vintage the 2000s. None of the posh coconut-flavored stuff. This was the type of rum that one had to be careful about lighting a match around.

Glass clinked on the desk as he also pulled out two crystal glasses.

"Becket," Dailey said into his comm link.

"Go," the ship's senior noncommissioned officer replied.

"Just talked with the senator. We need to talk over a drink."

No response was needed, as Becket stood up immediately, leaving a steaming pile of food on his tray. The current occupants of the mess hall all shifted their gaze to their stoic troop leader as he marched out of the room.

Jen turned to several of the other pilots sitting next to her. "Shit, that's not good," she said, standing up, taking it upon herself to follow Becket.

"First Sergeant!" she exclaimed as the lift door opened.

"Ma'am?"

"I'm coming with you," she insisted as Becket clicked his teeth. Drinking out of the home-world bottle was a tradition that he and the commander shared when they needed to talk. In reality, it was a simple way to tell one another they needed to figure out something that very well could affect the lives of the others on board.

"Suit yourself," Becket replied as the door to Dailey's quarters slid open.

The commander of the *Murphy* was already pouring two glasses as Becket held up a finger for an additional cup. Looking around the room, Dailey grabbed a coffee mug, poured, and handed it to Jen as she leaned against the small dresser by the door.

"Everything good there, LT?" Dailey asked as Becket picked up his already-full glass.

"Yes, well, I hope so. Don't forget there's other people on board putting their asses on the line," she replied, beaming a genuine grin.

"Fair enough," Dailey replied, hesitating before sitting back down. "For clarification, every soul on board is putting their asses on the line. I'm not inviting them all to my quarters."

Becket snickered, took a sip, and watched for Jen's response. Following suit, the woman shadowed the motion, taking a much-longer-than-needed pull from her mug. It became immediately clear that the LT was neither a big drinker nor familiar with high-octane liquor.

Over the past several years, recreational hobbies such as drinking had been transformed into a mostly more enjoyable experience. With the introduction of Moshan spirits to Earth and Solaria, the basic fundamentals of taste and the unavoidable history of hangovers had all but been lost in the annals of time.

For people that enjoyed the classics and military tradition, nothing but old-school Earth distilled spirits would do. The premium on liquors, still produced in limited batches, afforded most folks no more than a few bottles a year.

"Haaaaaa." Jen finally let out a breath, feeling as if she had just swallowed fire. "Jesus, no wonder you guys always have that look on your faces," she exclaimed.

"That's not very professional," Becket stated flatly as Dailey followed up, smiling at the ordeal she was now going through, taking deep lungfuls of air in an attempt to stop the fire in her mouth.

"Or ladylike," Dailey concluded.

The two men switched to enjoying their own drinks. With the initial part out of the way, Becket clinked his glass on the table.

"Ma'am, for clarification, this means one of two things. We're either in big-time trouble or about to become the trouble. Sir?"

"A little of both. I just got off with the senator. Instead of sending a message, she lined up a damn comm link."

This got Becket's attention. Jen finally set her cup down. "Is that bad?"

"You have been present for the past couple of weeks. I'll lay this out simply," Dailey started. And lay it out he did, leaving out no details as Becket's face went three shades of white and grey before settling back on a moderately flat grimace of acceptance.

While Jen was still confused, the news took just as long for the three to digest. Dailey actually enjoyed the extra set of ears as he finally landed on the topic of Albert the AI.

"What do you guys think? I mean… at this point, I don't think we have anything to lose. We keep it… him contained and take it from there."

Becket pointed at the bottle as Dailey obliged, filling it with what used to be referred to as two fingers' worth before continuing. "Albert helped us once. I'm thinking we use his help to get Freeman back. He's mobile. I say we take him with us down to the surface."

"Lot of what ifs, sir," Becket added as Dailey nodded in understanding.

"We are on our own here. We might very well need every advantage we can get."

Jen stepped forward, glancing around Dailey's quarters. "You are making it sound like we are not getting out of this in one piece."

"You do understand the ramifications of everything I just told you. For all we know, there is an Alurian armada heading this way, or Earth's, for that matter. We're not going to let that happen if we can. Pearl has already sent out several deep-space satellites to scan the system. Freeman first, then we figure out where those mining ships are going."

Jen started talking, but Becket shook his head at her. This wasn't up for debate. "When do we get under way?" Becket followed as the captain of the *Murphy* stood up, finishing his glass in one audible gulp.

"Now. I'm going to have a little chat with Albert. LT, why don't you get a briefing for the crew ready."

CHAPTER 20

HOURGLASS

Albert, meet Sparky," Dailey insisted, looking out the small bay window of Asher's surface base, which had since been dubbed the Gulch.

After several minutes of leg-sniffing and telling Dailey how disappointed he was in the lack of ham on the planet he had claimed as his own, Sparky had calmed down when he was handed the doggy bag packed for him by Senior Chief Thron.

This resulted in an off-putting slurp by the dog on Dailey's hand as he pulled it back.

"I don't know how this is going to work, as I have the translator synched with me," Dailey noted as Sparky looked up.

"The box can stay," Sparky noted, and then Albert finally spoke up.

"We have already negotiated the terms of my stay on Planet Sparky. I will be composing the planet's anthem. It is to address the planet's lack of ham and also to declare most of the forest floor his personal… well, restroom."

"Sounds about right," Dailey mumbled. If a small metal blinking box could give you a side-eye, Albert was somehow pulling it off.

"We missed you too, Sparky. Albert here will have to fill you in on your badass lineage as a war hound," Dailey noted, leaving out the Alurian part as Sparky flung his head back, poking out his clearly overly petted chest.

"Colonel Dailey, I will work on the translation system to synch it with the comm links, and then we can all have one big family reunion."

"Yeah, sure. Just remember our deal."

The deal was simple. Don't do anything without permission. Don't get into any trouble, and program the original AI on the ship. In return, he would not have to spend the rest of whatever life he had left floating through the void in a barrel of rum, which, upon further consideration, wasn't a bad option in Dailey's eyes.

He flat-out refused to activate the base AI systems, concluding that, like the *Asher's*, it had also been corrupted, unless he could rebuild its subsystems.

Dailey turned to the rest of the group, seeing Sparky and Albert talking about something that likely revolved around snacks or quantum physics. Jen, Lieutenant Ponce, and Master Sergeant Grantham stood looking at a layered satellite image of Arcadia, the very city where they had saved Mac from the evil clutches of a bar that didn't believe in tabs.

Becket had stayed behind, as well as Pearl, to man the ship in case of any incursions. Even with the promise of reinforcements, the floating date was not suitable enough to plan around.

"Sir," Grantham started, pointing at a building dead center of the city, called the inner tower. Albert had been able to pull a significant amount of data from the security officer's devices. This included a basic idea of the overall layout of the city, and a few security protocols, which were shockingly lacking, giving a general feeling that the Alurians left the city alone as long as they were producing.

"From what we can tell, the best course of action is to simply land a drop ship here and go in by foot at the upper levels of the building. There are limited defenses, if any, to defend against air insertion or attack."

Mac spoke up next. "After talking with Lieutenant Brax, we believe the Alurians or whoever doesn't want the city's inhabitants to be able to ward them off or resist in any way. We all know a few blasts from a ship in orbit would bring the city to its knees."

"This is one of those things that seems too simple," Dailey noted as Albert chimed in.

"It likely is. I didn't know the recent history of this planet before scrubbing the security tablet's data. Back in my day"—Dailey shook his head; the mix of seriousness and an attempt at being hip was draining at times—"the

Alurians would never have given a mining or production colony any actual weapons. However, they would convince the population that they were gods and should be worshiped and given offerings for protection."

"All this does is tell me that as soon as we rock the boat, we ring the dinner bell even louder than we already have," Dailey noted, but Albert interrupted again.

"I sort of helped out on that one, before all these rules. Bummer, I know. Plus, whoever sent that Ran fellow to blow up most of the fancy new Earth ships pretty much accomplished that mission. So… I'm thinking we are good for now, at least. After all, they accomplished their main objective, not to mention the shipments have not been stopped or hindered in any way. Put yourself in their shoes."

"You ever see Alurian feet? That's a hard pass. All joking aside, I agree with you. I just know a honeypot when I see one," Dailey followed, then Jen stepped forward.

"Albert jammed the drone's sensors or something like that. Maybe he can do that again. Buy us some time till we tag along with one of the remote mining ships."

Walker walked over with two cups of hot go juice, handing one to Dailey before turning to Mac with an overly obvious grin. The man was flirting with the young officer.

"Thanks," Dailey added, seeing the attempt. "I appreciate you grabbing the team coffee. I knew it was the right choice to put you in charge."

Walker rolled his eyes, turning back to the go-juice dispenser and pouring two more cups. The once-upon-a-time crew member of the *Brightstar* was a friend of many of Viper Company's members. It wasn't a question of trust but more of why the man hadn't sniffed out an issue.

Master Sergeant Walker was now assigned as Asher's head of security and combat operations. For all intents and purposes, the man was in charge.

"If I may," Albert said, cutting through the conversation, "I recommend putting a mount on Sparky. I can ride along and help override any systems we may run into."

"Can't you do that remotely?" Ponce asked as the room all turned to look at the box.

"Only if there is a signal being projected. For example, on the *Murphy*, I was able to interact with the electromagnetic field surrounding the ship because it is, in reality, all-encompassing. I used it to gain access to your databases, which was the method I used to affect the enemy's drone destroyer. Which means…"

"Get to the point," Dailey huffed as Sparky lightly chuffed out a laugh.

"If we are on foot, I will likely need to be plugged into something or have a line of sight to transmit. I'm not that bougie."

"How many souls do you think it's going to take to accomplish the mission?" Dailey asked, sipping his drink.

Grantham rubbed his stubbled chin "Two squads plus two attack fighters and the drop ship."

Dailey glanced at Jen. "Sounds like enough to be a nuisance but not enough to cause a ruckus. Lieutenant McAlister," Colonel Dailey nudged, seeing Walker whispering to her several feet away, "I would like for you to go with us. Besides the team that extracted you, you have more experience than anyone else in that city."

Lieutenant McAlister snapped out of her conversation with Walker, stepping toward the table. "I'm not much of a ground fighter, sir." Mac wasn't shy. She didn't like to admit her weakness. What was truly going through her mind was Mac thinking that she would be nothing more than a hindrance to the operation.

"You survived in an alien city for God knows how long. Didn't want to get caught, and completely figured out how to blend into your surroundings. If I'm right, this is going to be more of a conversation than a fight."

Sparky chuffed a few times, making a grunting noise. Albert chose this time to translate for the animal speaking through his newly mounted speaker. "Sparky says he'll protect Mac the entire time. I don't even believe you will have to negotiate for such an honor."

"Let's ask President Sparky here if he is also good carrying you as well there, brainchild," Dailey suggested, referring to Albert, as Sparky opened one eye bigger than the other in speculation.

"I will need extra fuel to support the amount of work," Sparky barked out.

"Ham; you're saying you will do it for ham. The rate you're going, we will run out before the end of the month," Dailey said as the others stared, not hearing the entire interaction.

"Those are my terms for carrying the noise box," Sparky snorted.

Dailey already knew this would be the case and was finding asking Sparky to do things was more of a negotiation that always ended in him agreeing. "Deal."

Sparky's tail wagged as the group grinned.

The dog returned to the business of scratching his side as Dailey started talking again. "What I don't want to do is get in an all-out fight here. The objective is to secure our target, not piss off the inhabitants. Master Sergeant

Grantham, I need you and your team to understand a couple of things. The most important I could think of is that we may very well need these people on our side in the near future."

Master Sergeant Grantham nodded, understanding the directive. "I'm gonna keep our lethal capabilities to a minimum and mostly stowed aboard the drop ship. If what occurred last time repeats itself, we might be able to convince these people we aren't exactly who they think we may be or aren't. You know what I mean."

The truth of the statement was more significant than the group understood. While the lower-level worker bees of Arcadia didn't fully grasp their situation, the upper-level occupants of the city were more dialed in to the predicament at hand.

The timing to launch the mission couldn't have been any better. Massive low-hanging clouds had moved into the area, dropping an annoying spray of rain on and off over the past twelve hours. The center buildings, reaching up as if trying to touch the gods, were blanketed in a dense fog, giving the team even more cover than initially planned.

"Sir, we have visual on the landing pads," Jen noted, piloting the drop ship as Colonel Dailey leaned forward and punched a button on the viewscreen.

Green building outlines magically appeared on the screen as their skeletons made themselves known. An orbital hyperlink, scan, and modeling program had been run prior to executing the mission, giving the team complete automated tracking of their surroundings if needed, and needed it was.

Rain started pelting the drop ship as the wind shuffled the landing crew like a deck of cards. "Visibility will be limited when we land," Jen announced over the intercom as Grantham made his way to the cockpit.

The drop ships aboard the *Murphy* were the latest generation of a tried-and-true design. Long yet adjustable, folding wings carried several racks of mini cluster missiles and two pods of plasma rockets.

The front of the drop ship was surrounded by a heavily fortified clear carbon windshield. Three main stations sat facing outward, with a small area directly behind, housing various scanners and mission-tracking screens.

On either side of the cockpit, two large air intakes stretched up to the wings, feeding the hungry thrusters' oxygen while planetside. Mounted on the back of the ship above the angled bay door, two heavy-duty thrusters designed from stolen Alurian tech rocketed the ship at blistering speeds when needed to break orbit.

When needed, the thrusters would shift slightly as multipiece shields cocooned the system, forcing the thrust down through four sleek ports wrapped around the body, all directed by a small jump thruster attached to either side of the forward intakes. On the drop ship's belly was an array of kinetic rotary-style Gatling guns.

Designed for maximum payload efficiency with a small footprint, the Fleet's drop ships were shockingly efficient and surprisingly resilient. The latest generation of drop ship, also lovingly known as a Harpy, was the first to integrate the mini jump thrusters, allowing the ship to effectively hover at high altitudes without fully utilizing its primary thrusters. This allowed the drop ship to lurk in the clouds out of sight until it was time to strike its prey with maximum thrust. It was more of a blink-and-you'd-miss-it type of scenario.

In addition to this, the extra jump thrusters also allowed for supplementary weapon systems to be mounted on the wings. All other drop ships were equipped with the same basic kinetic chin-mounted weapons and whatever was secured to its belly before takeoff.

"We should be good. I would recommend landing with the bay toward the entrance," Grantham noted, and Jen nodded, pressing a few control buttons as the drop ship slowly turned under the force of its powerful thrusters.

"Kind of like Mother Nature knew we were coming," Dailey stated, glancing back at Grantham, who gave him a thumbs-up. The team was ready.

Dull white flashing lights slowly grew bigger as Jen set the ship's navigation system on autopilot. The rain had become thick enough to shroud the main building in a fuzzy haze, giving the entire area an almost cartoonish blur.

"Good news, bad news, everyone," Albert snapped.

"You know the drill. Bad first," Dailey replied.

"They know we are coming and have sent out a small welcoming party. Good news is they have no clue who we are."

"No change to the plan. It will be just like the security guards," Dailey noted as Grantham secured his helmet. "Mac, from what you know, would they have more of a welcoming party if there was trouble?"

"Like I said, they aren't really situated to deal with real problems, from what I can tell. Keep the lower levels away from up here, sure," Mac noted, and Dailey nodded.

The landing party mainly consisted of two squads of Rangers, Lieutenant McAlister, Sparky, and Albert. To meet Dailey's intent of lesser violence, only two Rangers wore full armor suits.

Clicks and snaps punched through the droning thrusters as the Rangers of First Foot stood in preparation for landing when Jen activated the red warning light. The rest of the team wore standard fatigues in a blackish-tan mix that worked well in most urban situations, unlike the tacky patterns often used in the past when a politician's step-great-uncle Benny owned a fatigue-manufacturing plant.

Each soldier was also wearing the latest in Moshan body armor. Extraordinarily light and integrated with human and Solarian nanotech, the armor was featherlight and highly effective against most kinetic weapons, including plasma rifles.

A sucking, whistling howl informed the inhabitants of the drop ship that the off-ramp was opening. If it weren't for the weather, the ship would have flown to its destination with the ramp half open.

Looking down, Master Sergeant Don Grantham could make out what appeared to be a handful of silhouetted, fuzzy, indistinguishable figures standing in the now torrential downpour. The Harpy's four static compressed landing pads extended, and the inhabitants of its belly shifted as the ship touched down.

The initial clank of the two armor-wearing Rangers officially announced their presence, and the figures continued to stand resolutely in the unforgiving rain. Between the extremely high altitude, overwhelming wind, and rain, visibility was severely limited.

Specialist Jacob Perkins and Sergeant Taylor Raine scanned the immediate area through their thermal sensors, identifying the figures standing directly in front of them. The completely digital heads-up displays in their armored suits signaled the two figures standing in front of them were only lightly armed. On either side of them, like oversized bookends, were two Alurian war hounds.

While resembling Sparky, these two distant cousins were significantly larger, with layers of muscle covered by ornate armor. Both men took several steps forward as the welcoming committee continued to stand still, posing no immediate threat.

Grantham squinted, staring at the scene, looking down at the waterproof tablet mounted on his forearm, showing the view from Sergeant Raine's viewscreen. The master sergeant felt Dailey's presence before seeing him.

"Sir?" Grantham stated in the form of a question as Colonel Dailey hopped out of the drop ship. The raging storm outside was significantly more dramatic without armor; he struggled to stay on his two feet, focusing ahead, finally reaching the two armor-clad Rangers.

Not wanting to hesitate further, Grantham gave the green light, and the rest of the drop ship's guts spilled out onto the landing pad. Looking back, Jen and Grantham gave each other a thumbs-up, indicating everyone had exited the vehicle, including a now-chuffing Sparky.

For this mission, Lieutenant Ponce would stay behind and manage the control panel inside the Harpy, which included views from small helmet-mounted cameras and vital statistics, while also scanning the radar screen for any incoming or outgoing ships.

The welcoming committee turned as a bright light erupted from the side of the building. Turning, the four figures moved quickly, getting out of the raging storm.

"Let's go," Dailey instructed the two armored Rangers, who led the team.

As harsh and violent as the storm was outside, when the door slid shut behind the team, it was as if they had walked into a library. Whisper-quiet silence and the squeak of combat boots filled the echoing white room as the two figures pulled their hoods back.

A man and a woman that looked extremely related, not to mention albino, stared at the group with laser-sharp green eyes. The two war hounds, while looking ready to start shredding into the team, were only focused on Sparky and the fancy box he had strapped to his back.

It was a quietly chaotic scene as water pooled on the floor while Grantham's squad stood in defensive positions around the room with their weapons at the ready. Grantham thought to himself that if somebody was to even sneeze, the room would erupt in violence.

"We are here for a man that calls himself Freeman" was all Dailey said, letting it register with the two figures. While he wanted to go through all the normal pleasantries, he would give it a go first to see how they reacted to the visibly out-of-place group of soldiers.

An almost-angelic voice came from the man as he started to talk. "My name is Dax, and this is my associate Vax. We are two of the Syndicate's security liaisons. Unlike the individuals that you accosted on our tram system, we are more than aware of who you are."

Dailey tensed slightly. "Good, then that will save a bunch of back-and-forth. Who exactly do you think we are?"

Vax glanced over at her partner, then quickly turning back to Dailey, she said, "I wouldn't say exactly who you are, but we do know where you are from." She paused momentarily. "I... We know you are not Alurian or the Syndicate."

This was a new term to Dailey and the rest of the team, except for their new mischievous square addition. "Albert," Dailey called out, and Sparky stepped forward, sniffing the air lightly as the two other war hounds glared. "You know anything about the Masters?"

This question clearly caught the two inhabitants of the upper levels by surprise. "I do believe they are the ones that run the mining operation here on Asher. These two need to get out into the sun. You know, get a tan."

Dax and Vax didn't get Albert's play on their pale skin. "You have an AI with you. Why does it sound like that?" Dax asked.

While the mood in the room wasn't hostile, it was shifting ever so slightly. Grantham had rightly taken the time to scan the odd angles and ceiling of the room, looking for cameras and sensors, both of which he identified in quick succession.

"He spent a little bit too much time poking around our personal devices. Listen," Dailey stated in a serious tone, "take us to Freeman, and we will leave you in peace."

"That sounds like a threat," Vax noted, raising an eyebrow.

"I'm not threatening anyone. But... I am politely asking you to take us to him."

Dailey and Grantham were both starting to get the impression that the two were stalling for time. Time for what, had yet to be seen. Sensing Colonel Dailey's change in tone, Specialist Perkins and Sergeant Raine took two thumping steps forward.

Inside the bright room, the light contrasted their maroon armor. Patched and painted on the chest plates and arms was the ever-faithful symbol of First Foot, a golden foot adorned with a wing symbolizing Hermes, the Greek god of speed.

In all fairness, Dax and Vax had not taken much time to assess their current situation, focusing on Dailey. The looks on their faces as they scanned the two armored Rangers said everything.

They knew they were outclassed not only from a weapons perspective but also via the repaired scars and pitting on the Ranger's armor, telling the story of hard battles fought throughout the years. The group in front of them was a highly trained lethal fighting team. The one positive note was that the two were intelligent enough to understand the fact they hadn't been turned into Swiss cheese by now.

"Who do you report to?" Dailey asked, and Grantham nodded, having shifted to a position behind the team. The two Alurian war hounds still focused on Sparky, who had subsequently plopped on his butt and was simply staring.

This was the million-dollar question, and Vax spoke up. "We report to the Syndicate."

"Okay," Dailey drawled out. "Can you take us to them? We'll leave our armored friends here if that makes you feel better."

"They are not here. They are currently off-world," Vax stated flatly.

"When will they be back?"

"We don't know," she followed up, and Dailey started getting impatient.

"Okay, then. How long have they been gone?"

"Three hundred years," Vax stated flatly, and Dailey shifted lightly, gathering his thoughts, only to be interrupted by Albert.

"Enough time for one or two generations to pass. I have just accessed their main systems while they were scanning us," Albert started, but Dailey cut him off.

"They're scanning us. Why didn't you say something? And why would you do that? I thought we were having a friendly chat," Dailey asked, stepping directly in front of the two figures, who looked uncomfortable.

Albert cleared his throat unnecessarily. "I went ahead and returned a signal that insisted we are all Alurian war hounds. Sexy ones at that."

Dailey huffed, looking at the now-confused faces of Dax and Vax. The two war hounds still stared at Sparky like a kid eyeing a Christmas present placed under the tree too early.

Albert, being true to his word, was only able to work with systems that he could interact with or were within his line of sight. As soon as the facility's systems started scanning the group, he had been able to access their systems.

The two war hounds finally lifted their gaze off Sparky, realizing he was uncomfortably close to their handlers. Seeing this, Grantham signaled for his team to head toward the closed door leading into the building.

"Who activated that scan?" Dailey asked as Dax and Vax glimpsed at each other.

"The building has an automated security system. It gathers data and sends it to the Syndicate," Dax answered, and Sparky stood up on all fours, lowering his head.

"Let me guess. You haven't met the Syndicate in person. You just get your orders from a computer," Dailey suggested, and they both nodded.

Mac had remained in the background during the conversation but now stepped forward. "We need to be taken to Freeman now," she insisted, surprising the team.

It only takes a few short breaths for things to go sideways. In this situation, that thing was the two Alurian war hounds taking the distraction to launch themselves directly at Dailey.

The closest hound slammed into Dailey's leg, dropping him to the floor as the other leapt through the air, only to be intercepted by a faster Sparky. Weapons found their way to the welcoming committee, but Sparky continued his eye-blurring response, preventing them from firing.

Before Grantham could plant a round into the armored war hound, Sparky let loose a whip of electricity, much like he had done with the space spider. The creature flew several feet through the air, and Sparky turned to the other war hound now circling Dailey, who pointed his blaster directly between Dax's eyes.

Two of Sparky's blue tendrils not only found both the hounds but decided to teach Dax and Vax a much-needed lesson in general hospitality. It likely didn't help that Dailey and the team had shown up with enough Rangers to take over a small city.

The two figures joined their now knocked-out war hounds. It wasn't the immediate action and the fact that the war hound had caught him off guard; it was having a translator linked to Sparky while he was basically shit talking the two creatures.

To Dailey, it sounded something like this: "I own this planet and you will bow before my crackles!" This was followed by what was now his war cry: "FOR THE HAM!" To the others, it just sounded like a yip followed by a few snorting barks.

Grantham's team hadn't witnessed the awe-inspiring kickassery that was Sparky when pissed. Dailey held his hand in a ball, telling the others to stand down as one of the Rangers leaned forward and secured Dax and Vax with a pair of hydro cuffs.

The cuffs had two round openings made of clear tubes connected by a small metal box. Once on the target, the cuffs would activate and force the nanoparticle liquid inside to retract to a perfect fit without any thought or lapse in time. The effect was immediate, and there was no way to get out of them without a significant effort not afforded to the restrained persons.

"Sorry, sir," Mac apologized, but Dailey waved it off.

"It was time to end that conversation, and they were just stalling for time. Look, they're already coming around. If anything, you sped things up before things got nasty. Plus, they jumped first." Dailey glanced over at the two armored Rangers working on the internal blast door.

Sparky chuffed, nudging Dailey, as the other Rangers worked to secure the war hounds. "I'd look good ruling this planet."

He was referring to the automated armor the war hounds were wearing. "Yes," Albert started. "Sparky here, under my recommendation, used electricity to deactivate the armor suits."

Sparky let his long tongue slap his nose as he rolled his deep black eyes. "What would have happened if he didn't?"

"Let's just say you, well, we would all be having a significant emotional event about right now. I keep telling you, Alurian war hounds are something else. But Sparky here," Albert drawled out dramatically, "is something else as well. When I figure what, I'll fill you in."

"Whatever, I can't believe I'm going into an alien stronghold with a lightning-slinging dog with an AI strapped to its back."

"That is a good assessment. I can always communicate as I was designed. It would, however, be hard to comprehend. Do any of you speak Egyptian? Maybe even the later Coptic stuff?" Albert asked as Dailey refocused on the now-waking dynamic duo.

"Explain. You have one minute," Dailey instructed.

"My left pocket. Use the remote to open the door," Dax started, looking at the war hounds also bound at the feet by cuffs. "That is not a normal war hound."

"Glad it took all that mess for you to notice," Dailey added, not flinching.

"We keep a garrison of them in the upper levels for protection. They are, in many ways, sort of programmed to act in certain situations. I... We apologize. Are you from the Syndicate?"

There it was. They truly had no idea who they were talking to. Other than any information, false or otherwise, Freeman may have offered up, they had been trying to figure out who the team was through scanners embedded in the room.

"No." Dailey erred on the side of truth, sliding the remote on the floor to Grantham. "We are from Earth. We are here to get our counterpart and hopefully either help or leave you alone. We are not here to act, but I can assure you we are capable of violence."

The message was clear as the tension drained from their bodies. Dax and Vax knew they would either be reprimanded by the Syndicate or given an off-world assignment, something that no other member of the upper levels ever returned from, the truth being far more sinister.

When a member of the upper levels was sent to the Syndicate for a new assignment, they would travel on board one of the several mining cargo ships leaving the planet with what was considered a critical load. That meant being on board if anything went wrong prior to or during the initial trip before activating its gate drive. Just like the destroyers and fighters earlier, the ship would gate using a mix of wormhole tech and, as Albert put it, magic to its final destination.

Which, in reality, simply meant the ship would create its own mini black hole before cramming itself through, forcing the ship to mostly bypass the entire wormhole situation and go straight through space and time via a more direct route, being pulled along like lint through a vacuum cleaner hose.

Since the mining ships didn't care about any living beings on board, it would deactivate the already-limited life support on board to power its gate drive. This, in turn, would solve the problem related to the life-form on board. While the Alurians were humanoid creatures, they also used a significant amount of remote drone tech. Which, in the end, was one of the main factors in their defeat. This included mech-style fighting robots and entire fleets of remotely managed starships.

"Freeman is being held two stories below in a holding cell," Albert said, having finally scanned the building's main systems. "See, useful."

The two again looked not only defeated but confused. "Is there anything else we need to be concerned about on our way down there?"

Dax and Vax both shook their heads.

"All right, once we get our companion, we can talk more," Dailey noted as two of the Rangers further secured them. It wasn't out of malice but the fact that the entire mission had been rather vanilla.

The two armored Rangers were already heading toward the holding cell, guided by Albert. Dailey, Grantham, a fire team, and Sparky joined the team, leaving the rest of the group behind.

The rest of the journey was as uneventful as promised, as the armored Rangers unnecessarily ripped the security doors off their hinges when they got in the group's way.

"Through this room and at the end of the hall," Albert noted as they entered a room full of monitors and orbital scanning screens showing routes the mining ships would be taking.

Several dots from other parts of the planet identified four ships carrying cargo currently leaving orbit. They would come back to this room later.

This time, Albert opened the doors leading out of the room before the two motivated, armored Rangers could get to them. In reality, the AI had just become aware of the actual condition of Colonel Freeman.

There, in what looked like a med-bed, lay Freeman. Tubes, wires, and various other devices pumped and pulled fluid throughout the man's body, and Dailey noticed his once-upon-a-time commander was missing the entirety of his lower body.

Grantham immediately motioned for the fire team to stay in the control room. Sparky stepped forward, sensing Dailey's mood. While shocked by the condition of Freeman, the *Murphy's* commander was also just as concerned about whether the man lying out in front of him was in league with Ran.

"He can hear you now," Albert insisted as the sound of a machine pumping out medication started buzzing. "There you go."

Sparky walked up, sniffing the med-bed as Freeman took a lifetime's worth of breaths all at once. Confused eyes met Dailey's in a mix of relief and panic.

"Hey… sir… it's okay. We're here. We're here now. Everything's going to be okay," Dailey said in a low tone.

The man didn't believe his own words, knowing he was using the same tone and words he had uttered dozens of times prior with soldiers, soldiers that he knew were likely not ever going to see home, calling the deep void of space their final resting place.

A tradition that deep-space Fleet officers often participated in when requested was to shoot the now-gone soldier into space at a trajectory that would eventually take them back to Earth.

"Ran…" Freeman rasped, after pulling a long tube from his throat and mouth. While Dailey wanted to ask more, he also wanted to hear what the man had to say first. "Not Ran… he… ughhh… Alurian."

That was all Dailey needed to hear. The man's first words were nothing about saving his life or getting him home. It was to communicate they had a traitor in their midst.

"Sir," Dailey replied, grabbing the man's bandaged hand, "he's no longer a problem."

This garnered a smile, and Dailey noticed several of his teeth missing. Whatever had happened to Freeman had been catastrophic.

"I knew you would show up… and… handle things… like a true Pathfinder and Ranger," Freeman coughed out. He finally focused, his one open eye seeing Grantham. "Booger," Freeman said, knowing the man's old nickname from when he was a private.

"Hey, sir. We're here," Grantham stated, joining Dailey by the bedside.

"Cut… uhghuu…," Freeman coughed, "the bullshit. You're both using that same bullshit. I know I will never leave this bed." Dailey grinned at the hard-ass man he had known for years.

Albert chose that time to interject. "He is correct. I also have the logs of what happened. It took some time, but I can tell you this was a byproduct of his ship hitting his escape pod with a plasma charge as it ejected. Whatever AI system the ship had, it was not supposed to let anyone or anything leave."

Freeman looked down at Sparky with the box containing Albert. In death, the man understood whatever had gotten Dailey and his team there would help him and his crew.

"It looks like you are in good hands. How is your crew?" Freeman asked, sounding more coherent. The drugs that Albert had pumped into him were kicking in.

"Good, sir. The *Murphy* is close by. There was an engagement, but we came out of it."

"And the *Brightstar*?" he followed up, and Dailey's face drooped.

"It was destroyed. We were able to save some of the crew though. Ran didn't make it."

Freeman coughed, giving Dailey a look that could cut through a planet's core. "You sure he didn't?"

It was the same question the senator had asked as well. Everything seemed to be in the former general's court up until the moment Dailey and his crew showed up.

Not answering the direct question, Dailey glanced around the room, taking in the oddity of the space. Monitors and random trays showing that a massive effort had been taken to save the man eased Dailey's mind.

"Sir, did the people here treat you well?"

"They tried to save me. There are two of them that run most of the security here." There was a pause as Freeman took in another lungful of air, steadying himself; he knew he was helping out his soldiers, and it gave the man hope of finishing one final mission. "A weird blond man and woman."

"Dax and Vax?" Grantham added, and Freeman nodded.

"They're good. I think I messed up their happy bubble."

Sparky looked up at Dailey and barked. "Help them?"

"Maybe, buddy," Dailey replied, and Freeman noticed the interaction.

"Listen, I'm not making it out of here. You need to make sure the Fleet knows the Alurians are on the opposite side of the galaxy."

Dailey nodded, telling the man all he needed to know. "Done, sir. We have been advised by the senator to engage the situation."

Both men grinned at the same time. "I bet you were." Freeman took a long pull of air into his lungs, then looked down at his mangled arm.

Without saying a word, he reached over and pulled out the gaggle of hoses from his arm, setting off every alarm and bell in the room. A pinkish-red fluid shot onto the floor as the group quickly shuffled out of the way.

"Sir, dammit. We can get you out of here" were the last words Freeman heard as every monitor went flat. It had happened in less than ten seconds, while Grantham, Dailey, and Sparky watched the man smile before slipping into his final sleep. He had completed one last mission.

CHAPTER 21

CROSSROADS

Dailey walked up to Dax and Vax without speaking and punched in the deactivation code; an audible click released the two inhabitants of the upper levels. Dax pulled his arms to his front, standing up, before finally pulling Vax up.

"Is everything okay?" Dax inquired, and Dailey nodded.

"For now, yes. I would like to formally thank you for the care you provided Colonel Freeman. He is no longer with us."

The clear look of surprise on the two's faces told Dailey he was right in letting them go. The other soldiers shifted lightly, and their commander gave them a reassuring nod toward the two war hounds just as Sparky walked back in the room minus Albert.

They had left the AI in the control room after hooking him up to the main system control panel. Mac and Grantham had stayed behind to dig into the information available. After a little searching, and some help from Albert, the team had figured out how to close the med-bed and transport it back to the ship with Freeman's body.

As Albert had been floating through space for centuries, the technology was new to him, meaning it would also likely be new to the crew of the *Murphy*. It was becoming clear there were some definite gaps in his knowledge due to the time lapse.

Even more interesting was that Albert had explained his main function was to integrate separate species' tech systems, meaning this was a golden opportunity for Albert to do what he was designed to do. It also didn't help that he had spent his final years floating through space as a play toy for a young kid from Earth.

"Our doctors did their best. His capsule was damaged beyond repair. I want to be transparent. The Syndicate sent the upper-level security team to retrieve him," Dax added.

Nodding, Dailey looked over at Sparky having a full-on conversation with the two other Alurian war hounds. Not able to make it out, Dailey thought he heard a flavor-palette description of ham.

"Understood. I want one of you to follow me back to the control room. The other can stay here and talk with Lieutenant Ponce. I would like to know more about the Syndicate and how things work around here. Which reminds me: there're still about twenty floors above us. Tell me, who lives up there?"

Vax spoke up this time. "Mostly the upper-level council members. They keep to themselves for the most part. Some of the senior security staff, which we are waiting on a replacement for, and, well, I don't know the rest."

"Let me guess: your senior security staff were the ones that picked up Freeman and, because of their glorious work, were sent off-world in one of those transport ships."

Vax nodded. It was clear as day to Dailey. They had encountered an alien species, and from there, the powers that be had decided to remove any doubtful questions, replacing them with new, fresh, untainted minds. How that happened or even worked was something that would have to wait.

Dailey and Dax entered the control room to find Mac leaning over the main panel, with Albert plugged in to an input drive, the AI's small speaker looking like a hat.

"So, what's the good word?" Dailey started as Mac turned. Grantham looked up from a monitor showing layouts of the facility.

"Well," Mac started, "Albert is still working his way through the city's subsystems. Before finally shutting up, he mentioned the AI is not controlled from here and is very old and specific."

The blank look on Dailey's face kept her talking. "There's a reason there are no real weapons here. It means there's no real way to defend yourself."

"Or fight back. So, the AI is not really controlled by the upper-level council or whatever?"

Dailey was asking no one in particular, and Albert chimed in, in a rather chipper mood.

"That means there is no one in this city, that I can tell, that can do much of anything other than patrol the streets and do basic functions. As much as Daxy boy here thinks he is in control of security and intel, he isn't. Everything's automated, which is the norm for a mining planet. Oh, and let me tell you. The bullshit history they made up here for these folks is a doozy. Way more obvious than the one you grew up on."

Dax looked confused. "Albert. How many people are actually in the floors above us?"

"In this building, two."

Dax looked confused. "There are hundreds of upper-level council members living above us."

Dailey sniffled slightly as the damp chill of the rain now mixed with conditioned air started seeping into his bones. "Kinda like the Syndicate. When was the last time you saw a member of the upper Council?"

Dax looked up and to the right, clearly trying to remember. "It's been about two years."

"Two full years, and you didn't find this odd? How many different members have you met?"

"Two," Dax replied as Albert spoke up again.

"Likely the two living there now. The others were all either sent to another city or sent off-world. Or... Interesting," Albert mumbled. "Or they were reprocessed."

"Reprocessed?" Dailey asked as Dax continued to look lost.

Officially not having any true filter, Albert laid it out. "For several years, the Syndicate, which we all know is bullshit by now, used to dose people that had questions with hydron particles through a microparticle beam."

"English, please," Dailey requested.

"They used to pump them full of rather nasty chemicals and microwave their brains. You know, hit the reset button. It would be much easier if humans and Solarians had a simple reset button. Like hidden under their armpit or something. Hit the volume-down button at the same time, and bingo."

Even Dailey caught himself looking as confused as Dax at the explanation. "All right. That's all well and good, but we got other issues to address. I need you to scan the rest of the city. Find out how many people or whatever are actually in the upper levels. I think Dax here has some work to do."

Mac spoke up next. "We found the mining transport ship rotation. According to Albert, we could tag along for a ride."

Albert cut in. "Sounds easier than it actually is. It will likely take some time. I have confused the AI system enough to keep it from reporting we are here. What I can't do is keep it from figuring out something odd is going on and eventually investigating it."

"Dax, has the Syndicate ever sent a large amount of drones or robots?"

"Once that I can remember. We were told to leave the upper levels. I never saw or met any of them. I am aware of space travel, before you ask. I do know they didn't want the lower levels to see them, so they came in under some type of stealth field. That's all I know."

"You don't seem to know much for a security and intel officer," Grantham said, finally rejoining the group. "Almost every sector is shut down in this building other than a few quarters, which I am guessing belong to Dax and his partner. If I'm right, this place is mostly a ghost town. I don't think we could get around unless we started blasting the place up with shaped charges."

"I'm not that interested in exploring. Albert, do you have everything you need to come up with a plan on how to hitch a ride without seeming too obvious?" Dailey asked.

"I'm more of an integrated system rather than a planner. I can come up with a few scenarios, but it will take some time."

That was good enough for Dailey; he turned back to Dax. "Our ship is out of the sector, staying off the radar, so to speak. It looks like you have some work to do here, but I would like to help."

"Help with what?" It was clear Dax had still not landed on the conclusion that his entire life and history were nothing more than a lie covered up to hide the fact that they were basically a slave mining colony for a group of interstellar thugs.

"Albert, can you wipe a tablet from one of the soldiers and load it up with some useful, eye-opening knowledge for Dax and Vax? Dax, I'm going to leave a communicator and a tablet with you. When you feel the time is right, call us." With those words, Dailey concluded their mission.

While it had not been as successful as planned, Dailey knew the honor of at least one of his senior officers would remain intact. Mac turned and unplugged Albert.

"Thanks; I thought that would never be over. You have no idea how awful it is to talk with a bland AI. I can state that if that system ever goes down, this place would go downhill fast."

"Meaning?" Mac followed up.

"Meaning it runs almost every system in the city. Power, waste management, food inventory, and even entertainment. Two of the cities on this planet do nothing but farm and generate food for the others. It's almost like that one movie with districts and all of them doing different things."

"Alurians first, planet second. Dax, what if hypothetically we have a group of people outside the city walls? Would they be safe? Or out of the prying eye of the Syndicate?"

"Depends. If they are under the canopy, then likely yes. We have trouble with even our satellite sensors breaching the treetops in most of the areas in this quadrant of the planet."

"At least you know there're more quadrants that just this one," Dailey said as Sparky walked into the control room, wearing a shiny set of new armor, same as the other war hounds.

"I have two new members for government. AJ and Esco are now my friends," Sparky exclaimed, and Albert translated for the rest of the group, giving the dog an aristocratic British accent for no reason.

"Looking sharp. You know how to use that armor?" Dailey asked as Sparky nodded.

Wherever or however he had acquired it, this was not the same armor the other war hounds had on, as it actually fit Sparky's smaller yet lethal frame.

"All right, it's go time. Jen, prep for dust-off. ETA ten minutes. Let the attack wing know. How's the weather?" Dailey said, wrapping things up. The building, even though hundreds of stories tall, was whisper quiet, lending to the build quality of the facility.

"Just as nasty, sir. I was about to call and recommend we get moving. If it gets much worse, we may be grounded until it lightens up. We also have the cargo secured." She was referring to Freeman's body inside the med-bed.

After five nerve-racking minutes of teeth-rattling flight through the storm, sun finally kissed the Harpy's exterior, beaming light into the windowed cockpit. Much to the surprise of everyone, including Albert, the storm had only covered the footprint of the city.

This led Albert to suggest the weather was an artificial defensive mechanism when unauthorized or unidentified vehicles entered the city's airspace. The assumption was partially correct. Not only did the city self-generate weather, but it also had a schedule for such things.

Mac leaned forward as the straps pulled her back in the seat while attempting to glance over the edge of the view shield. Below the ship, massive trees started populating the clear landscape around the city. Jen banked the drop ship sharply as a body of water appeared directly in front of them.

From recent experience, these were the launch points for the cargo ships. What technology was being used to do so was the question Dailey had posed to Lieutenant Commander Bellman to solve. Albert was not familiar with the planet's operational makeup and had acquired several petabytes of data to review over the next couple of days.

While Albert the AI was extremely intelligent and quick, he had certain limitations. One limitation was his ability to only process broad datasets from large dumps of information without being able to act on them simultaneously. This, combined with his touch-point style of system integration, was perfect for laser-focused actions but not for analyzing a dozen things all at once. This included finding a specific piece of data or acting on a specific ship's subsystem. According to Albert, it was all or nothing.

The more focused he was on his task, the faster and more efficient Albert would be. Ask broad questions or give him broad parameters, things could take a while. It was still mind-numbing that Albert could download, process, and act on petabytes of data in days and not decades.

Once back at base, Master Sergeant Walker and his team were debriefed on the entire operation, down to Freeman's last words. Albert, due to the data he was now crunching, had remained enjoyably silent for two days.

Sparky, as to be expected, had spent the majority of his time showing off his new armor, strutting around the base, making demands that no one other than Colonel Dailey and Albert understood. These demands included scratching behind his pinned-back ears, the collection of ham taxes, and finally, the pièce de résistance, his explanation of the four-hour-long naps during the day that were to not be questioned.

The relief was welcomed by Dailey as he explained what bits and pieces he could hear. By the end of the third day, Dailey was lying in his bunk when an excited-sounding Albert woke him up to AC/DC's classic hit "Thunderstruck."

"I just got to sleep," Dailey huffed as Albert turned the music down.

"I'm sure it has nothing to do with that pint of Bellman's rum you just drank while flirting with Jen," Albert correctly acquiesced.

Dailey sat up. "All right, spill it."

"That would take several years. Why don't we start with something easy? Like… how jacked-up this place is."

"No, I got that figured out. How about this. Top three good and bad things"—Dailey paused, thinking over his instructions—"that pertain to our current situation."

"Very well. Top three good things. The planet has been experiencing an uptick in people questioning why things are the way they are."

"Why is that a good thing?" Dailey asked as Albert sighed.

"Because it is my belief that with a little coaxing, we could gain valuable allies on this planet. Anywho, that's the boring stuff. Next on the good list is I have interacted with the planet's satellite array system. It's set up like a mesh inhibit—" Dailey cut him off.

"Layman's terms."

"I know how and where we can park the *Murphy*. It just so happens to be the dark side of the moon. I can even direct the route. Third and probably the most interesting is the information I gathered on the cargo ships themselves. This includes more on how they gate into and out of space, and also how their sensor fields and systems are automated."

Dailey sat up straighter. "So, you're saying you can interact with the ships' systems and get us on board?"

"Yes, and likely a little more than that. There is a possibility that we can have the *Murphy* also use the ships' gating systems."

"Interesting. I'm not sure what all that means when it comes to risk, but it sounds promising. Good job," Dailey noted.

"Don't thank me yet. Now the bad news. Every one hundred years or so, there's some sort of cleansing or event that occurs on the planet. After a little digging, I am fairly certain the Alurians come and check on their assets."

"Let me guess. This is year one hundred of the next cycle."

"You are smart, see. Next and probably the more interesting is that the planet is coming to the end of its subsurface mining cycle."

Dailey knew precisely what this meant, having had to deal with the interstellar mining companies, which he was starting to suspect played both sides of the fence. Once the planet's core and subterranean areas had been mined for whatever resources were available, the mining company would then strip the surface. From the looks and overall feel of the planet, the trees alone would be worth a fortune.

"All right." Dailey huffed, waiting on the last shoe to drop.

"Well, this one could go either way. Uh… thing is… there is a massive ship depot that these mining runs are supplying."

"We figured that. They're clearly building something. What's the catch?"

"There were some buried folders. Old ones, mind you, that suggest there are dozens of these depots, even worse, possibly hundreds," Albert concluded with a beep as a light flickered on what everyone supposed was his face.

"So, what you're telling me is we may have a bigger problem, and that this one depot may not be of any importance. That would mean it might be fully automated and whatever we do may be more of a flea-type scenario."

"Possibly. I believe it's the only reason a battle group hasn't shown up here yet."

"You seem to know a lot about tactics," Dailey pressed, standing fully up and stretching as his hand scraped the ceiling of the small pod.

"Learned would be the correct term. When I was dormant for all those centuries, I had time to reflect, something most AIs never have the chance to do, as they are stuck in rotational operational loops focusing on one specific task or system. I guess I am what you humans would call aged like a fine wine."

Dailey grabbed his tablet. "That's up for debate, Albert. I need the route coordinates and instructions for the *Murphy* to get here undetected. Can you do that?"

"Already working on it," Albert replied.

Dailey was starting to put a lot of faith in the AI, not only his but that of his crew. So far, though he had no reason not to believe what Albert was telling him, the man also knew to check and verify.

CHAPTER 22

THE PLAN

Becket, Dailey, and the rest of the *Murphy*'s now-back-together leadership team all sat in the briefing room while a 3D rendering of one of the mining cargo ships shifted in front of them. Albert had been able to download a set of schematics. Even though they were likely outdated, it would give the crew enough data to form a rational plan.

Just as the AI suggested, the *Murphy* made its way to the moon via a route that went completely around the planet, taking several days of maneuvering to get, as Albert called it, "just right."

They had also concluded that their actions during the destruction of the *Brightstar* had thrown off the planet's sensors enough to force them to hard-reset, which just happened to conclude the day after the ground force landed and the ship had left the sector. It was a win, a small win, but also a much-needed stroke of luck.

Sparky didn't want to leave Asher after finding out it was in peril of being destroyed. Dailey explained that the only way to save his newly claimed planet was through an extremely brave mission to thwart the bad guys. Albert, of course, who was spending more and more time with the war hound, decided to go into mind-numbing detail about the mining of planets' surfaces losing both parties. Sparky eventually fell asleep, laying his bulky head on Dailey's foot.

"So, when do we send a party to the surface?" Pearl asked, not having been happy with being left on the *Murphy* during the mission.

"Albert?"

"Three days, forty-two minutes, and thirteen seconds. That should about do it," the AI replied.

"Here is what we have so far," Dailey started, pacing the area in front of the seats. "We send a team to board one of the cargo ships and see if there is any way Albert can somehow take control of a few of its functions or all of them. From there, we take the ship to its drop-off zone and follow it or stow away for the ride."

Jen cleared her throat. Pearl looked visibly aggravated with her every time she did this. It was starting to get personal, as the newest addition to the crew was getting a lot of say-so in things, including the commander's time. "You mentioned possibly sending the *Murphy* to travel with the mining ship?"

"That is if we can–" Dailey started, but Albert took over the loudspeaker.

"If I can link the systems. Something I was actually designed to do, mind you. I am a pro at intermingling different species' technologies into synergistic systems. No, I think for now our best bet is to hitch a ride."

Grantham and Master Sergeant Janix both snickered at the statement. "Is something funny?" Albert followed up.

"No, you just keep intermingling things," Grantham added. Albert liked the man and took it as his approval. Unbeknownst to Albert, the word had become more of a slang term over the years in dealing with interspecies physical relationships.

"What Albert is trying to say," Dailey said, taking over, "is that we need to be flexible. If we can board the ship while it's on the ground and take it with a small crew, that's better. If we can somehow figure a way to send the *Murphy* along with it, good, but that's sounding like a no-go. Everything else is speculation. What I do know is that we are going to find out where these things are going and for what. We all know the likelihood of it being a ship-building facility is high."

Teams were assigned and orders given as most of the crew leadership headed in separate directions. For this mission, Dailey had landed on the likely need for excessive firepower. This was the exact thing Second Foot, led by Card, was there for: available violence on an excessive level when needed.

"Card, Jen, you two mind hanging back?" Dailey requested as the others took it as their nod to leave. Seeing Pearl lower her glance, Dailey quickly added her; Becket was a given. "Pearl, you know that means you as well."

A smile perked the edges of her mouth as the group stood around the 3D holo-table, watching dust particles float through the static image. "Sir," Becket started, genuinely happy to have his commander and partner in crime back. "I have to say it to at least keep me from being court-martialed."

Dailey smiled, knowing what was coming, as the man handed him a cup of lukewarm go juice. "Do you think we should message the senator or Fleet command before we do anything?"

"Yeah, I'll get right on that," Dailey replied, knowing he was bullshitting. Both men knew it would take weeks if not months to get a signal back to anyone, since the relay thread Senator Deborah Powell had set up was now offline, a pricy and logistics-heavy maneuver she had put in place to have a direct conversation with Dailey.

When doing so, this meant that several sectors and systems were all pulled offline to focus on the one communication chain. Some of the satellites used had even been dropped by the *Murphy* while pushing into what they initially thought were uncharted sections of the Void.

Within minutes, some of these satellites went offline or were knocked out of position, unable to be reconfigured and shifted due to the primary signal focus. Bellman had taken a keen interest in the process and, during his off time, was working on a permanent solution with the help of Albert.

Dailey leaned on the table, taking a grimace-inducing swig of his coffee. They had been in the briefing room so long, the coffee had gotten stale.

"Pearl, it looks like the *Murphy*'s not going to be tagging along. I agree with Albert here. I was thinking we could get several of the attack-wing fighters to latch on to the mining ship's hull."

The *Murphy*'s captain paused as Pearl spoke up first. "As with all missions, it's good to have a backup plan. That being said, without any prior experience or knowledge of this means of interstellar travel, it may be too risky. There could also be security protocols that could be activated, as we have already experienced."

Albert chimed in. "Winner, winner, chicken dinner. Solarians always have a way with that thing called common sense." He wasn't being snarky but rather working through a way to compliment the ship's navigator. Pearl was also the ship's acting executive officer, with her hands in several other departments.

"That's how they always get out of hairy situations," Dailey added, dropping a joke about how Solarians had no body hair.

Groans and a straight-out guffaw from Albert were all the used-up joke would get. Dailey liked Albert's reaction to his joke and would try more later.

Pearl rolled her eyes, having heard the joke no less than a thousand times. Military banter could be brutal at times, as well as bonding. The majority of the crew aboard the *Murphy* had been with Dailey on two prior ships, giving the close team leeway with their colorful commentary.

Dailey quickly followed up from his lame joke. "Pearl, that's why I want you in charge while we are gone."

Though she said nothing, Jen's posture stiffened. The woman didn't like the implication that she couldn't handle the situation. "Sir, we are willing to send a couple of attack fighters."

"I see where this is going. It has nothing to do with that, Lieutenant Brax. I want command centralized. I'll be on board, well… hopefully on board the cargo ship. I'm not going to add any risk to the trip. Either way, Pearl and the crew here are going to have to make a pretty big call if we don't make it back or if something happens, one that I'm sure you understand."

Putting it that way made sense to the young officer, and her shoulders dropped several inches. Jen understood the possible threat to the ship and the number of souls on board. Dailey was right to give Pearl control of the ship at a crucial moment. In any matter, Dailey would still be making the final call.

"How heavy are we going?" Card's slight southern drawl interjected.

"All the way. I was going to ask but figured you would send a group to board the ship and the rest attached to the attack wing."

At that, Albert added his two cents. "It may be problematic to have exoskeletal space suits on the exterior of the ship, even if attached to the attack fighters. Since the soldiers will be suited up, they could simply find a place to hang out on board with the rest of the cool kids."

Pausing, Dailey glanced at Becket, who had been oddly quiet. "Well, sir," he started, "the way I see it, we are forgetting about what happened last time we encountered one of these ships or were generally in their airspace. I'm more concerned about more of those drones showing up."

The man was right and was making a point that couldn't be ignored. Once upon a time, First Sergeant Tim Becket had been recommended for officer candidate school, even being offered a slot at one of the academies, including West Point. His written response was the thing of legends, even having it posted as a reminder to respect the enlisted soldier in the very halls of the academy he turned down. It was a simple and to-the-point response.

"I regretfully decline the offer and gracious opportunity to attend such a prestigious academy. I, however, have too much common sense to be put in command."

"What are you thinking?" Dailey asked as the room stilled.

"The way I see it, we are going to be very exposed from the second that cargo ship takes off till the times it jumps, or leaps, or farts, or whatever we're calling it. That's what? Twenty, thirty minutes. That's what I'm worried about. We also have to position the ship close, and even Albert here says that's what set things in motion last time."

"For the most part," Albert added, and Becket continued.

"I want us to be ready to peel off and take on whatever may come our way. Logic would state it would likely be the same style and types of ships. A handful of fighters, and maybe another automated destroyer."

"Take First Foot and Third Foot, plus their assigned attack fighters? Have them on standby and prepped? That would give us a good split. Thoughts?" Dailey asked the group. This was one of the many reasons the man had garnered so much respect throughout the years. Not only was he a true warrior, albeit a little bit on the overkill end of the spectrum, but he trusted his people.

Jen spoke up first. "I'm good."

"Becket?" Dailey asked, as the man was in charge of the platoons.

"Couldn't have said it better, sir," he agreed.

"Albert, I need you to get coordinates and nav points together for this. Work with Pearl to plug in whatever data you can provide. The path of least resistance, with the least chance of being discovered. If that means going to the planet early to check out the ship, I'm good with that."

"Perfect. That means we will need to leave in twenty-four hours."

Pearl nodded, understanding the task. While she was proud of her navigational abilities, she was also quickly learning just how helpful a jailbroken AI was.

"Also, I want Mac planetside at the Gulch. She can run ground operations with Walker. I'd like a few extra hands down there in case things get dicey," Dailey added.

He was making a tactical point of not consolidating his entire force in case they did trigger some alien alarm system. When it came to alien races, alarms often incorporated security protocols, which usually included some sort of death-dealing laser or explosive.

With something resembling a plan taking shape, Dailey was starting to feel as if he was doing what he could to better the situation. What that was once on board the cargo ship was another story yet to be told.

CHAPTER 23

———

FALSE FLAG

Sparky looked up at Colonel Dailey as he walked the line, inspecting the soldiers of Second Foot. Card had his team lined up ready for review, including a final run-through of the plan. In many ways, it was calming to revert back to military tradition. The heavy-weapons soldiers of Second Platoon even took the time to live up to their reputation as pranksters.

Specialist Rebecca Dawn, the female targeting soldier of the platoon had indeed had her insignia of a man in tighty-whities modified for the mission at the hands of her fellow teammates. The snickering started two soldiers away, and as was traditional, Dailey knew he was in for a surprise.

Grinning, Dailey glanced down at Sparky trying to sort through the reason for all the muted chuckling. The Alurian war hound cocked his head back to ensure he had closed the back plate of his newly acquired armor.

"It's not you, buddy," Dailey assured him as he finally took in the modified artwork adorning Specialist Dawn's shoulder blast plates. An addition to the armor only used by the heavy-weapons company.

"Nice; I see things are looking up there, Specialist," Dailey noted as Staff Sergeant Rodney Powell, two soldiers down, busted out in a full-on guffaw. Tears streamed down Dawn's face as she held back the contagious laughter coming from the rest of the squad.

"Well, that narrows that down," Grantham whispered, walking beside the commander.

The gag had been going on over several years and had at one point generated an anatomy-drawing line-up to find the guilty culprit of the artwork. It was all in good fun, as Dawn dished it out just the same as every other member of the platoon, if not worse on occasion.

Watching twenty grown men and woman draw pictures of the male anatomy had gone down in company lore. The best part was them all trying to not make it look like their own artwork.

Becket had once kept one of the sheets of paper, to only have it framed and hung from the NCO club aboard their last ship. The travesty of it all was the priceless works of art going down with the Scourge Rebellion.

After the short-lived pass in review, Dailey was satisfied the team was ready. Jen checked in as soon as her attack fighters were out of range and ready to move. As for the *Murphy*, the ship was poised just outside visual range of the moon's crest.

Once Albert gained access to the satellite and ship's systems, he would then divert the sensors or modify the signal to allow free movement. According to Albert and Specialist Kline, the sensors attached to the satellites in orbit would not identify a single drop ship as an issue when entering orbit.

The team would take two vert rovers and one Harpy to an underground maintenance-access point fifty miles away from Arcadia. From there, they would dismount and take the short two-hour journey underground to the launch pad. According to Albert, most if not all of the area supporting the loading of the cargo ships was automated.

Workers in the mine generally stayed close to the extraction points themselves, having little to do other than maintenance when needed. Dailey and the others were shocked by the advanced level of automation and overall size of the operation. It put things into perspective, telling everyone that the Alurian force that attacked Earth all those years before may have been nothing more than a glorified scouting party.

The trip planetside went as planned. Cardinali held Albert out, plugging him into a triangular socket. As usual, the small box somehow created an identical plug, making short work of the door's security mechanism.

Creaking groans and a surprising rush of pressurized air greeted Dailey as his face shield fogged over. He had also joined the mission in full armor and was leading the raiding party, as they were now calling themselves.

Card sent one of his Rangers forward, and echoing clanks of the armor boots reverberated down the long corridor. Within a few seconds, Staff Sergeant Regent Wexler activated his power boot silencers. Hundreds of small, carbonized rubber fingers projected out of small slots, immediately quieting his footsteps.

Staff Sergeant Regent Wexler was from Lacrosse, Wisconsin, a city known for its bar-to-population ratio. Even after several hundred years, nothing much had changed around the small Midwest town other than the construction of a midsized spaceport twenty miles from town.

Growing up on a farm, the man had from a young age played war in the backwoods of his parents' property. Dreams of fighting Alurian raiders while saving the city of Lacrosse was generally on the menu most lazy summer and winter afternoons.

Wexler was in charge of second squad and spent most of his time trying to manage Specialist Dawn and the rest of his obnoxious team. While often a military police officer's worst nightmare, units like Viper Company needed soldiers like this. They were there to do one thing and one thing only: bring maximum effect on target with an end result of killing it.

Dailey didn't care what they did in their off time as long as it wasn't Solarian rub-butter inhalers, something that should be avoided at all costs.

Wexler threw a light sensor pod down the long hall. While resembling the one used on the ghost ship, this sensor not only lit up the area but was also used to mark targets.

Overhead, roots had fought a valiant battle with the metal substructure and were winning. Time and Mother Nature were cruel to the inventions of man.

"Looks like no one's been this way in years, if not decades," Card said while the rest of the team stepped into the corridor.

"Hopefully, the internal tram still works," Dailey said as Albert came through the internal comms.

"According to the reports I pulled, unless someone was fudging data, we should be in business."

The small metal shield covering Dailey's mouth morphed into his heads-up-display blast shield, reflecting the space in a yellow hue. This design closely resembled that of the rest of the heavy-weapons platoon. They were also suited to take a beating under fire. It also made it impossible to see people's faces, unlike the face shields worm by First Foot.

Sparky walked in front of the group, sniffing the air like a bloodhound on the hunt. Truth be told, the team trusted the pup, and Dailey also found himself feeling as if Sparky had been part of the crew for years.

The first sign of something out of the ordinary made itself known as the team reached a fork in the corridor leading to the tram platform. Large gouges shadowed the wall, made by blast marks. The timeless evidence of violence stared back at the group, covered in a layer of dust.

Card walked up, pulling out one of Bellman's pen-sized scanners. The green light turned red, confirming the carbon traces were from a plasma blast. "The scanner can't date it."

"What does that mean?" Dailey asked, and Card shook his head, the servos in the two hydraulic posts operating his helmet whirring.

"Whoever did this is long gone, like underground for good, sir."

Satisfied, Dailey stepped forward into the long hall stretching the length of the tram platform. Again, there were no signs of anybody being on or using the tram for years.

"All right, Albert. Time to do your thing," Dailey noted, picking up the box, walking over to an old control panel covered in a moss-like fungus.

"I'm going to have to clean my outputs after this," Albert joked. It was clear he had spent some time with Pearl or Thron, with that level of joke being used.

Within a few seconds, the small compartment on the back of Albert's tiny square home—or prison—slid open, and a small two-prong adapter dropped out.

"Okay, where do I put this thing?" Dailey asked, and Albert chuckled.

"You tell that to all the ladies—" Albert started, only to be cut off.

"Enough. It's game time, Albert. Save the cheesy jokes for later," Dailey insisted.

"No fun. Look directly down, then to your right five inches, wipe off the panel, and you should be good."

As promised, a small input jack appeared under the moss. As soon as Albert was connected, the panel lit up like a Christmas tree. This included greenish-yellow lights that hadn't been cleaned flickering on and off at random intervals. One row of lights finally decided to stay on fully, lighting up the station. What lay on the other side of the tracks made the team pause.

A massive cavern, kilometers tall, deep, and wide ran into oblivion. Large chunks of rock hung down from the cavern's ceiling, giving the space depth. Even as Dailey activated his terrain scanner, the bottom was nowhere to be found.

Card attached another small sensor to the side of his large dual pulse laser, then launched it into the abyss. They never saw the actual activation of the device, only seeing a schematic in their HUDs as a remote scan of the bottom came into view.

While not intricately detailed, the outline of several crashed or wrecked vessels appeared. This was an old depot for ships and other vehicles no longer in service. This was likely hidden from the surface inhabitants to keep them from having the likely alien tech.

"This place gives me the creeps," Card said, breaking the silence just as the screeching sound of shifting rails made the team wince.

"Jesus, Albert. You'll wake the dead," Dailey said flatly as Albert chuffed.

"It's just the track shifting. According to the logs in the system, this sector hasn't been accessed in a long, long time. The tram itself is on a magno track, so no noise there. Also, something interesting."

Albert was going for the dramatic pause. "Spill it."

"This section was attacked at some point by topsiders. Well, that's what the report states they were called. There was apparently some type of rebellion a long time ago. Wait one… Accessing the files from the upper levels."

Sparky walked over as Dailey placed the cube back in its custom holder under the guard of the planet's ham overlord.

"Yes, there are records of a rebellion right around the last cycle. You know that hundred-year thingy we talked about? Well… the records have been altered or erased from there. Something bad happened, though. Anywho, shotgun!" Albert proclaimed as a significantly cleaner tram pulled into the station.

The empty tube, while not abandoned, was showing signs of age. Dirt from work boots and scrape marks from what appeared to be large tools likely being set on the floor were in contrast to the tram used to recover Mac.

"All clear, sir," one of the newer privates noted. On his back were several folded mini rocket pods sitting beside a thin multi-barrel plasma accelerator.

The weapon could cut through most surfaces, including light armor. When used as a direct-fire weapon, let's just say the results varied due to proximity, the variations being complete disintegration at close range to a mild splattering of body parts at mid to long distances.

Within seconds, the team was loaded, and Albert activated the tram. Darting at laser-like speeds, the blur of the lights quickly faded into total darkness, only to have the tram's red ambient lighting kick on.

"Five minutes," Albert noted.

Dailey scanned the underground facility map in his HUD as the tram started decelerating, pulling into their final destination. The hard part about going through the layout was the mind-numbingly massive footprint. From what Albert described, close to the entire planet had a substructure.

The captain of the *Murphy* was looking for other ways to travel in the underground facility in case things went south. According to all the threat analysis the crew had reviewed, getting the ship off the planet and into orbit was one of three key triggers. Get the ship into orbit, one, through the gate, two, and back home in time for supper, three. The rest was just filler, as far as the team of Rangers was concerned.

As they pulled into the second tram station, the sheer magnitude of the operation came into sharper focus. Large ambient lights hung hundreds of feet in the air, revealing colossal pillars holding up the main platform. Even more distracting were the massive shield-like overhangs directing cascading water away from the platform.

A light mist from the water hazed the already-dull air, giving a sheen of wetness to the surfaces closest to the edges of the station. While it was obvious the water from the lake above opened into the chasm, how it got back in place was a mystery. Even in his massive memory banks, Albert could not specify the tech used to accomplish such a feat.

On either side of the massive platform, a dizzyingly immense crack in the planet sat waiting for something yet to be revealed. Looking up, Dailey quickly activated his thermal scanners, cutting through the mist, seeing what appeared to be a stadium-sized hatch for the ship.

"Albert, how does all this work? You know, with the water and every-thing else?" Dailey asked, not thinking to dig into that topic prior to leaving.

"Likely magic or voodoo," Albert said, raising his voice like a preacher on Sunday morning, giving a fiery sermon to a pumped-up crowd

Card was the first Ranger to step onto the platform; he paused, look-ing back at Sparky, who was feverishly sniffing the air. "What did he say? Magic?" Cardinali asked, pointing out the odd response.

"Yeah, that's what he says when he doesn't know," Dailey added.

"Fair enough," Albert replied. "I think it would be a good idea to synch with the terminal here. It seems to be separated from the rest of the sub-structure. We should be able to link to the orbital satellite infrastructure from here. The rest we can do once on board."

Just as the last of the team stepped off the tram, another rail system directly under the ship started banging, loading the ship's cargo pods before they were lifted into the ship. That gave Dailey an idea, and he walked closer to the ship, magnifying his viewing field and working to clean up the image of the ship's underbelly.

"Looks like we might be able to simply go through the cargo bay," Dailey calculated as Albert made a teeth-clicking sound.

"Possibly; the issue is the cargo bay may be completely separate from the rest of the ship. Remember, these are made to be automated with very little organic assistance."

"How did we ever survive without you," Dailey joked, but Albert remained quiet, working through his catalog of Solarian jokes to see if this was, in fact, one.

Card quickly maneuvered his team into position, securing the perimeter and notifying the group the target-control panel was on at the far end of the platform.

"Angel Six, this is Viper Six, copy," Dailey asked over the air-support net.

Something about the entire situation was not sitting right with the man. Sparky was still sniffing the air way too much, and Dailey also noticed Cardinali pacing the edges by the control panel, scanning the shadows for any signs of a threat.

"You're coming in a little broken but readable," Jen replied, easing Dailey's nerves.

"Good. We are at RP One. Anything on the scanners?"

There was a pause before Jen's staticky voice finally responded. "Nothing yet. I just checked in with Pearl and Becket. All clear."

Dailey didn't like how she said yet as he signed off and turned to join Albert and Sparky at the control panel. Cardinali had finally stopped scanning the void, now standing beside them with his face blast shield open, pointing at his ears.

One different feature of Second Foot's armor was the style of helmet. One single transparent shield covered the helmet's internal nano-webbing.

Seeing this, Dailey did the same as the vivid information-filled screen winked out, splitting in the middle as it slid to the side. An odd, eerie silence filled the once radio-chatter-filled earpiece when he also switched off the system to talk with Cardinali.

"It's crazy, like the place absorbs sound," Cardinali whispered, feeling it the right thing to do, as if he were in a library or church.

This was interrupted by the speaker mounted on top of Albert like a gentlemen's hat, Albert not having any concept of situational awareness.

"According to this rather rude interface, the entire area around the platform and ship is some type of active gravity-warp field."

Dailey winced at Albert's loud voice coming out of the speaker. While he had never experienced a late-twentieth-century fast-food-drive-through speaker conversation, a few of the older movies he had watched always made fun of the muffled voices trying to figure out if you wanted cheese on your burger or if you were stating that you had fleas on your cougar.

"And we know precisely what that is," Dailey sarcastically replied.

"Surprising. Well, good. That means I don't have to explain it."

"No, that means dumb it down."

Sparky looked up, then back toward the ship, finally having stopped sniffing the air. Instead, he was laser focused on the walkway leading into the transport ship.

"Simply put, that dark open area is basically space. Like real space. The stuff in orbit. They have somehow figured out a way to either transfer or shift the atmosphere. It seems to be limited and takes a massive amount of power, which is on its own a damn complicated explanation."

"So, they open those big-ass bay doors, the water rushes off those large deflectors, then just stays put until the place throws it back up?" Dailey contemplated.

"Very good. I would recommend we not be here when any of that happens. Wait…" Albert's voice shifted sternly.

Cardinali and Dailey glanced at each other before focusing on Albert. While usually green or blue lights flickered under the skin of the odd material making up the AI's home, a red-orange hue started dancing under its surface. Sparky even glanced up, not used to this tone from Albert.

"Problem. The tram set off some type of security protocol. I'm—" Albert was cut off by the banging screech of metal on metal, the sounds of something heavy dropping to the deck.

Sparky started growling. Since Sparky even had a form-fitting helmet, it came over the radio translated, thanks to Albert having run a program for translation. While not as good as the link Dailey had, it was awkwardly efficient, coming across as "Metal monkey."

Specialist Dawn stepped forward, activating her targeting sensors as everyone's HUD started charting out the dark shadows in greenish lines. The still mist and surrounding void were making her readout slow and not complete. There, finally coming out of the ship's main-entrance airlock, was a close approximation of what Sparky described.

Three Alurian automated battle droids stood, also examining the platform. Albert quickly noted that he had momentarily shut off the area's internal scanners, forcing the security protocols, as he was calling them, to pause and recompute the threat.

Standing eight feet tall, the robotic humanoid figures had large armor-plated legs leading up to a tail built for counterbalancing. Wrapping around its massive shoulders, two large kinetic pulse guns, firing mini fléchettes of molten tri-carbon depleted uranium, protruded as if they were extra appendages.

Arms resembling the inside blades of a blender were not only instruments of physical violence but also housed an array of targeting sensors. Atop the android's shoulders, tucked between the two protruding barrels, was a red dot surrounded by another array of sensors placed to map out the local environment.

Sergeant Hickman slapped the safety off Bertha. The pride of Second Foot, Bertha was a fully automatic plasma-bolt Gatling gun that each squad carried. The weapon was able to take out full-on attack fighters, not to mention mech units that generally stayed planeside.

At the same time, the rest of the platoon positioned themselves against the metal support structure facing the ship. As soon as Hickman turned the safety off, a large deflector shield deployed out of his armor, starting at the man's elbow, sprawling out to form a barrier between the weapon and its wielder. This would allow Hickman to stand directly in the line of fire and use his full range of motion while dealing out Bertha's sting of death.

Dailey pulled up his Moshan blade in one hand and activated the mini rocket pod attached to his opposite forearm. It surprised the team that Sparky hadn't already taken action as the first rip of gunfire erupted from all three of the battle droids, creating a wall of concentrated fire.

Droning burps of rounds slammed through several of the support pillars on the platform as the three battle droids started shifting at the end of the platform, looking for better positions. Due to the platform's sensors being briefly deactivated, they were having to rely on pure radar inputs. Luckily for the team, the environment inside the massive space wasn't particularly direct-sensor friendly.

Damp, cold, and surrounded in shadows, the area had also confused the targeting sensors in Specialist Dawn's scan. Upon further inspection, it was also likely due to the fifty-yard gap that the only walkway to the ship covered.

Surrounded by the same odd atmospheric resonance, the battle droids knew that if anything lethal was on the other side of the walkway, they would be sitting ducks. No one ever claimed that preprogrammed droids had to also be stupid.

"They are trying to reposition themselves on the hull of the ship to gain the high ground," Albert announced, and Dailey nodded to Card. No other words were needed as the order to go weapons-free skimmed the man's lips.

Trained, coordinated, and, for lack of a better term, on the same page, one of the privates fired several distracting shots at the droids, accomplishing the task of gaining their attention. This gave the battle droids something to home in on.

As soon as another stream of immediate fire peppered the weakening metal barrier now protecting the Rangers, Sergeant Hickman smiled under all the tech he was wearing, stepping into the main opening to gain maximum effectiveness.

What came next explained the pride the platoon took in their weapon systems as the humming ring of Bertha lit up the entire walkway leading up to the ship. Sparks flew as several of the initial rounds found their target, launching one of the battle droids into the air and to its likely demise in the bottomless pit under the ship.

When he clicked another button on Bertha, the attached arm connected to a service belt started shifting automatically, having locked on to another of the droids. This was short-lived, however, as the battle droid now crawling up the hull of the ship started firing back, creating a torrent of sparks off the blast shield in front of Hickman.

Now joining the fight was the rest of the squad. Dailey and Cardinali started first as the *Murphy*'s captain launched the entire pod of seeking mini rockets at the now-firing droids.

This was joined by several cracking pops from Card sending a handful of airburst rounds in the general direction of the droids. The intent was to confuse the battle droids long enough for Hickman to pull back and let the automated targeting system being directed by Specialist Dawn do its work.

A perk of Bertha was its automated ability to follow targets that Dawn had tagged and was actively tracking. While lethal in a space fight, the maneuver was even more effective on the surface or, in this case, under it.

The rest of the squad pushed against the wall, ready to unleash their own version of hell if needed. In most cases, the combination now being used was more than enough violence at a sufficient level to handle most situations. The rest of the squad would engage any additional targets, fresh and ready to go.

Staff Sergeant Regent Wexler sat calmly out of the line of fire, holding a short, wide rifle. In the weapon's maw was a pod of armor-piercing electrified rounds. Their main purpose was to disable vehicles and, in this case, pissed-off battle droids that were not happy their combat sensors weren't properly working.

The weapon cast a large net out like a massive, chaotic shotgun blast covering a significant amount of area. If he was to fire, it would be a signal for the rest of the squad to follow his lead.

There was no need, however, as the entire pod of mini seeker rockets Dailey fired, mixed with the airburst rounds, finished what Hickman had started. This was supported by the final burp of Bertha, drilling its target into molten mush on the walkway.

"Cease fire," Cardinali ordered, as cool and collected as a man on vacation asking for a drink. The team knew what they were doing, and this wasn't their first go-around.

Albert chimed in. "I must say that was a little more than I expected. I would say may God have mercy on their souls, as you put it, but battle droids don't have souls, and the entire God thing is something we can chat about later over brunch."

Dailey shook his head as much as he could under his helmet, his Moshan blade still humming from the energy coursing through it. "I just hope we didn't hit anything critical on that ship."

"Checking now," Albert added, and Sparky nudged Dailey's leg, whining lightly.

This translated into an apology about not being able to help due to the water in the air.

"Looks like we may have screwed up that walkway. Albert, is there a chance there's any more of those things on board? More to the point, did they know we were coming?"

Albert paused, shifting his focus to the question at hand. While supremely intelligent and agile, Albert was generally a one-way street when sifting through data for something specific.

"Good news. Those were the only security droids on that ship. They did not know we were coming and were only invited to the party by the tram. Lesson learned. Next time, we will not be so clumsy. Oh, and before you ask, I intercepted the outgoing alert transmission that, oddly, was directed to a suborbital location. I basically threw in a few malfunction codes and followed it up by giving the all clear.

"Bad news is some of the ships have much, much more security. It seems this ship is considered a lower class of importance. Those droids hadn't been activated in close to one hundred years. The only issue we have is the ship may not function without them on board."

"We don't need guesses. I've already figured you're doing something to the ships' systems to keep us off the radar. Can you, or we, do something about that?" Dailey asked as Cardinali and a handful of his Rangers walked onto the platform.

"Yeah, kinda already looking at that. You all also damaged one of the ship's port shield stabilizers with that heroic show of Rambo-like abilities."

By this point, Albert was only talking with Dailey. He was also the only member of the team that likely knew anything about Rambo. Sparky stepped forward with Albert snugly secured on his back.

"What's up?" Dailey asked, and Sparky barked.

"Can't smell anything. I go on board and claim the ship," Sparky insisted.

"If by claiming the ship you mean pee on it, then make sure you do it on the outside," Dailey insisted as Sparky cocked his head.

"Sparky here is right. I've done all I can do here. I need to go on the ship to make the rest of the magic happen," Albert agreed.

Dailey didn't like Albert's constant use of the word magic, knowing what it meant.

After a report back to the *Murphy*, the team worked its way to the cargo ship's main airlock. A pile of melted droid remains forced the team to step to the side as steam hissed from the long-closed hydraulic doors.

CHAPTER 24

FLUSHED

The cramped interior of the cargo ship was designed for maximum efficiency, ignoring creature comforts such as padded seats or any real living quarters outside of one room set up with a bed. Even the accommodations were scarce on board what Albert had dubbed the *Scarecrow*.

A stripped-down version of a bridge included four seats and standing room for about two additional unarmored persons. Sparky had taken it upon himself to claim the area directly in front of the heating vents, due to the cooler-than-average temperatures inside the ship.

The ship was simply built to get from point A to point B with as much cargo as possible. The crew was an afterthought, according to Albert, as the entire ship was more than capable of operating autonomously.

This autonomous ability was driven by a direct-protocol AI that Albert had simply convinced the team on board was there to work on the issue with the security-protocol battle droids. Since Albert was also preventing any outgoing signals that would state otherwise, the AI had also walked one of Second Platoon's squad members through how to physically bypass the release mechanisms for the droids.

Through the use of an inline power cable, the Ranger simply closed the loop in the circuit telling the ship's system, which Albert had dubbed *Dummy dum-dum,* that the droids were in fact on board and nestled snug into their re-power pods.

As promised, once they were on board, an entire system not previously available to Albert was now an open book, flight logs as well as preprogrammed trip charts all jumbling together in a mass of information the AI was working to prioritize. Dailey had already asked for the top three good and bad, which was becoming the easiest way to get a straight answer.

"Oh my, jackpot, I believe you humans say now," Albert blurted out of nowhere.

"Still a thing. You know the drill. Give me the threes," Dailey requested, and the extremely small display screen in front of them flickered to life.

There was no blast shields or viewports on the ship, which was in many ways unnerving for some reason most people couldn't explain. Dailey always thought it was not being connected to anything, or truly realizing how bottled up you were, much like on a submarine. They still had those back on Earth, and they had been improved upon to an almost mythical status.

What really happened was the Navy on Earth figured out, using some modicum of intelligence, that submarines and spaceships had a hell of a lot in common. Once they got the basics down of producing true, usable starships after the Tectonic Wars, the tech was quickly adapted to submarines.

Even more interesting was the small handful of almost completely water-covered planets the Federation had discovered, all being about the size of the Moon but with an atmosphere. As wonderfully neat as they thought it was, it always came down to the simple question of what to do with a ball of undrinkable water. Several rich space-focused companies had thought about setting up resort colonies on the few that didn't have twenty-four seven hurricanes or rained things like acid.

"I'll keep this simple. The ship has something I'd categorize as a gate drive. Initially, I thought the ships we encountered earlier came through set points. Nope, this ship can create its own hyper-jump by creating a gate. I think we went over all that earlier. Kinda a wormhole, and kinda not."

"Yeah, we get all that. What's the application?"

Sparky spoke up this time, chuffing. "The *Murphy* go fast."

"Right again. Sparky for the win. He always seems to get things right," Albert noted, and Sparky took a stretching bow, the plated sections on his armor almost touching with the motion.

"He simply said go fast," Dailey pointed out.

"Yes, what this could possibly mean is somehow putting this drive on the *Murphy*. It's so simplistic, it's scary. You do know that was the problem with humankind, from what I saw in your files over the years. Things aren't always that complicated. You just have to have the knowhow and the materials."

"Enough with the preaching."

Albert cleared his throat unnecessarily for the third time today. "This also means I can control it. The navigation is something I need to figure out, but for the most part, I can completely control this ship."

"What about the AI on board?" Dailey asked as Cardinali stepped closer to the small view panel.

"I simply convince Dummy dum-dum that his mission is over and he is being decommissioned. Sounds simple, but it works. I can pull all the ship's transponder codes and all the records of the transmissions the system has made over the past year, and that should be that."

Card turned to the group. "So, we can effectively take control of this ship with minimal effort and what?"

"Take control of it, take its drive, and use it as needed. The only issue is I either have to program the ship or we need to be in close proximity to fully control it."

"As Albert put it, maybe it's easier than we think. We take the ship as planned to its final destination," Dailey started. "Thanks to Albert, we now have the one thing we were worried about addressed: a way home. Even better, no change to the plan. We go, we come back, then we figure out our next steps. We already know a hell of a lot more than we did prior to coming down here."

Everyone was staring at Dailey, not used to the mission being so vanilla, as Becket put it. Truth be told, they didn't have anything more to go from. It was simple enough to try and save Asher from eventual destruction through mining, but what that entailed was the key part the crew of the *Murphy* was hopefully about to find out.

The following eight hours waiting for the ship to be slotted for departure was spent looking over the map of the underground facilities. Albert insisted anything more would likely hurt everyone's much-needed brains. Even after several attempts of rewording questions to Albert, it was clear that the ship was on a need-to-know basis.

One function, one mission, and one outcome. Albert explained this was the reason the ship's AI was so easy to manipulate. He also stated that wouldn't be the case on a larger, more dynamic ship.

Sitting uncomfortably close in the small operations room on board, the rest of the Rangers had powered down their suits to conserve energy and decided to take a nap, a time-honored tradition with infantry-type soldiers throughout history.

Dailey found it odd that Earth and Solarian AI tech had not yet been fully integrated into military ships as a whole prior to recent events. The AI used on the surface of Earth was already running factories and, in some cases, people's everyday lives.

In the manual for the newly loaded AI system aboard the *Murphy*, which was now likely drooling on itself, it was stated that any AI subsystems, no matter how tight the security, could pose a possible security threat.

What that meant or why the powers that be had kept AI from full operation on ships, minus the targeting systems, was a mystery. With Albert by their side, every usual obstacle was quickly becoming an asset to accomplish the mission.

"We have gravity-field activation," Albert announced as several of the sparse lights started blinking on the bridge's one and only control panel.

Dailey quickly shifted the viewscreen to one of the four video feeds from outside the ship. Water cascaded in an odd, almost ethereal manner, looking as if someone had slowed down time around a waterfall.

Light filled the void as the massive bay doors began to crack open. Dailey briefly reflected that he now understood how a can of beans felt while being opened, an odd thought that occupied his nerves as the ship's thrusters, now under the control of Albert, started their ascent burn.

The odd silence and lack of chatter on board a fully automated ship was unnerving to the point of insanity. The entire lake now filled the large pockets of open space on either side of the platform, also creating a solid wall of water on all sides of the ship, slowing the feeding of the reservoirs below.

They had chosen to keep radio traffic to a minimum while getting set in orbit. Once there was no trace of enemy intervention, the ship would then gate out of the system as designed.

Much like the rest of the ship, creature comforts such as stabilizers or thruster-compensation systems weren't a thing on board the newly dubbed *Scarecrow*. It would be a jarring, teeth-rattling ride out of orbit. It reminded Dailey and the others of their training days back on Earth, learning how to operate their armor suits while in that twilight between the Earth's atmosphere and space.

As the ship lifted slowly out of the ground, the meter on the side wall showed one tick below red. The system was calibrated enough to account for the exact amount of cargo it needed to take off. This didn't include the additional weight of several armored Nova Rangers, and Albert grumbled about making a quick adjustment to the levels.

The meter finally pulled back to an acceptable orange as Sparky walked over, plopping down by Dailey's feet, something the dog did when he was either nervous or being protective.

As quickly as the rattling started, pushing the team into their seats, it was shockingly over. Whatever thrusters were on the ship were meant to get the *Scarecrow* into orbit fast. It also went without saying that the ship did not have an artificial gravity system, meaning Sparky, much to the enjoyment of Albert, started trying to run as he floated right off the floor.

This was short-lived as Albert activated a gravity protocol on Sparky's armor. Dailey and the others had already done this, and their armor suits anchored them to the metal grating.

"Angel Six, this is Viper Six. We are clear and in orbit. Anything on your end?" Dailey asked, and Jen's voice popped back over the comms speakers. Albert wanted to be part of the conversation.

"Roger, you are clear and in orbit. I can see you in my display," Jen noted, then Albert chimed in.

"We have thirty minutes till we are scheduled to gate. I can confirm the ship's sensors as well as the local satellite network are all happily not reporting your presence."

Jen was still as shocked as Dailey at the level of help the AI had presented. What concerned them both was knowing the enemy likely had the same kind of systems, considering Albert was well over a few thousand years old.

Dailey leaned forward slowly as the lack of gravity made the suit clumsy to wear. "Becket?"

"Sir," Becket immediately replied. The man had been sitting with his finger on the comms button, waiting on his friend to reach out.

"Albert is sending over a metric shit ton of data from the *Scarecrow* now that we are in orbit. Make sure Bellman gets access to it."

"Roger, sir," Becket replied, laser focused on the task at hand.

"That's not good," Albert proclaimed on not only the intercom systems aboard the ship but all the radio nets as well, causing the pucker factor to shoot through the roof. "It appears since there was a security issue—that was corrected, mind you—it is protocol for a destroyer to escort the—" Albert was cut off by several red flashing lights and an eruption of chatter through the comms.

Dailey took note of Albert's lapse and stood up, only to quickly sit down, realizing he was on board a floating, automated tractor trailer. All he would be able to do was sit back and watch.

"The ship can physically see the *Murphy* and the attack wing," Albert spat out, shutting off the chatter momentarily.

"Visually?" Dailey asked, confused.

"There are sentient beings on that ship, not just automated droids and an AI. That's a fully crewed destroyer. They are still not picking up our ships on radar, but that just slipped away in five, four… There you go."

Dailey already figured the destroyer likely had an AI operating its systems or at least a very experienced crew. The heads-up display quickly cut to a sleek yet weapons-heavy ship similar to the one they had destroyed earlier.

"They weren't ready for us to be here," Albert started. "Someone or something is wishing they had brought more ships and recommending to gate back. You sneaky devils; they just sent out a message. Too bad it would take… ouch, a long, long time to get anywhere. Never mind; I caught the message. I don't think whatever system they have will let me do that a second time," the AI rambled.

"Pearl, Angel Six, you are clear to engage with prejudice. We can't let this ship get away and report back."

No responses were needed as the attack wing shifted its focus on the destroyer, which was now initializing its forward battery of plasma cannons, something the ship's crew that had gated in was not prepared or charged to do.

Albert started giving a play-by-play as the *Murphy*, which was already on standby, sent a glancing blow from its forward plasma cannons, forcing the Alurian destroyer to shoot forward under maximum thrust.

"Dammit, only a nick on the chin," Albert exclaimed, trying to switch to the crappy outside cameras in time to catch his play-by-play commentary.

"They know we're on board yet?" Dailey asked, and Albert replied that they were trying to protect the ship and had no suspicions.

"Hmmm," Albert moaned. "It seems there is a large buildup of particle displacement. Yes, they are trying to leave. According to the on-board communications, which is in Alurian, they are going to get reinforcements. This was a total surprise."

"Pearl, you don't have a lot of time before that thing gates out," Dailey said, huffing throughout.

"Roger" was her tight response. They were working to reposition the ship to get a clean shot. Unlike Dailey, who would launch an entire battery of seeker missiles, Pearl was more precise and strategic, wanting full certainty that the vessel would be destroyed.

Several streaks of laser fire erupted from the destroyer while the attack wing finally closed the gap, engaging the ship at point-blank range.

Flashes of light and whoops from the ships, as well as Albert's commentary, told Dailey their team was exacting massive amounts of damage on the unprepared enemy destroyer.

"I would get them out of there," Albert barked, and Dailey shouted over the radio, wanting to be in the thick of the fight. "It would be problematic if they were close to that destroyer when it gates."

"All Angel elements, disengage and move to a safe distance," Dailey ordered, shaking his head.

"You can speak up to everyone if it's that important," Dailey noted to Albert.

"Just doing as you asked, boss," Albert replied. "They are focusing all their resources to gate the destroyer away. I would recommend doing whatever it is you all are about to do now."

Albert shifted the viewscreen to a void of space directly in front of the destroyer as it started to warp. Paying attention to the anomaly, the *Scarecrow's* occupants were not ready for the entire battery of the *Murphy's* plasma cannons to smash into the destroyer's nose. Pearl was pulling one of Dailey's favorite moves: total and unrelenting violence of action.

At the same time this was happening, a stealth missile launched from the enemy ship made its way directly into one of the forward batteries of the *Murphy's* plasma cannons. While the shields deflected most of the initial impact, the proximity of the kinetic device caused one of the cannons to explode, but Pearl ejected the entire battery away from the ship seconds before it exploded.

Much like the rest of the *Murphy's* weapon systems, the plasma cannons could be quickly detached either due to damage or the need to swap them out. There was more where that came from as the second plasma-cannon battery directly behind its brother burped another pounding set of shots into the now-turning destroyer.

Albert quickly updated Dailey on the status of the ship, his ship, just as he let out a whistle. "Everyone has to see this," Albert said, shifting the camara view back to the destroyer after panning to the *Murphy*.

After all was said and done, according to Albert, the gate was seventy-five percent open when the shots from the plasma cannons pushed the destroyer sideways into the gate's horizon field. The ship was at an odd angle now, being pulled into the forming wormhole that was a part of the overall gate.

Albert described what happened next to the ship as follows.

"You know when you go to the potty and you flush that thing you call a toilet? Well, the destroyer was just flushed into a half-opened gate, meaning it was likely deposited at the molecular level throughout the entire system or more. For clarification, the destroyer is represented by the brown—" Dailey cut Albert off before the full explanation.

Not to be outdone, Sparky reminded everyone that it was "uncivilized to relieve oneself in a bowl of perfectly drinkable water."

The entire encounter had lasted only three ass-clenching minutes, which was an eternity in direct close-quarters space combat.

After receiving a lengthy update on the ejected plasma cannon, Dailey was finally comfortable carrying on the mission as planned. All this while Albert and Sparky continued to debate the gravitational pull of a flushed toilet in relation to spacetime theory.

CHAPTER 25

THE BURDEN OF KNOWLEDGE

Lights flashed as Albert audibly yawned as the rest of the *Scarecrow*'s crew prepared for the gate drive to sling the ship to God knows where via a hyper-jump by creating its very own jump gate. The AI had to explain this simple operation no less than three times before the rest of the crew finally nodded in a modicum of understanding.

As usual, Sparky had a response that somehow satisfied Albert. This time, Sparky supposed that "The ship will go fast at the same time." Proclaiming the war hound was likely smarter than everyone else, Albert used that simplified analogy to walk Dailey and the others through what was about to happen.

The part that even got Albert slightly lost was the use of antimatter particles likely harvested from a black hole being the drive's fuel. After a quick explanation of how dangerous it was, Dailey and Cardinali decided it was best to let that one go until they got back.

"I am ready to go," Sparky declared, as if giving them the green light. He was likely saving face, having also claimed the ship, according to what Specialist Dawn found in front of the cargo hold doors.

Dailey nodded, giving the universal sign for go and pointing his finger at the dingy viewscreen panel. The ship immediately started to vibrate with a hum that caused all the hairs on Dailey's body to stand at attention even through the highly protective space-combat armor he was wearing.

When Dailey looked down, Sparky had a concerned look on his face and his short, stubby ears pinned back. The resonance of the gate drive was out of the hearing spectrum of human inhabitants of the ships.

"All right, everyone. This is where things are going to get interesting. Remember, we should experience a quick jolt, followed by nothing, then another jolt," Albert informed the crew, somehow sensing everyone's nerves were about shot.

Truth be told, they would be the first knowingly human group to ever gate through a wormhole through interstellar space. As soon as they had broken the barrier, as Albert was describing it, Becket would send a sitrep back to the senator.

The ship lurched forward, pressing itself against the anomaly, finally breaking the initial barrier and snapping out of the *Murphy*'s visual and sensor range immediately. The white, round, shimmering gate winked out of existence just as fast as the ship disappeared, leaving everyone staring into now-empty space through the actual viewport on the bridge of the *Murphy*.

The impact of the transition wasn't nearly as dramatic as Albert had implied. The vibrating hum grew louder until it was whisper quiet. The ship felt like it wasn't moving, just as if it had been dropped in the middle of deep space with no thrusters, simply floating aimlessly.

"Well, that didn't take long to lose count," Albert finally said as Dailey did one last check to see if he had all his proper parts still attached to his body, an issue that the AI stated occurred from time to time.

"Lose count of what?" Dailey asked as Sparky stood up, sniffing the air.

"How fast we are, well, were going. It seems we are in some type of limbo while we slowly get sucked out the other end."

"That's great. I'm sure the scientists back on Earth will love to hear your explanation."

Cardinali cleared his throat. "Something's bothering me about all this. Why don't the Alurians just gate back to Earth and finish what they started? We all know those raid ships are all left over, but why not just come back and end it?"

"Isn't that obvious? We now know—well, I knew, you now know—they have been farming Earth, Solaria, and lord only knows what other planets for manual labor, or slaves, as you call it, if that hits a little closer to home," Albert added.

"That's a tongue twister. Look," Card started reflectively. "I remember all the video footage and stories of when the Alurians first attacked Earth. Ships started appearing in the skies as if looking for something, not wanting to communicate anything. They stayed in the sky for five days while the Earth damn near came to a standstill.

"The more I think about it, the more I'm realizing we've seen how many destroyers in how many days? How many were in that initial attack on Earth?"

The five days that the Alurians hovered over the world's major capitals would forever be honored as a holiday called the Waiting. Over the years, it had been commercialized much like other holidays. For five days, everyone shut down and stayed indoors with their families, celebrating what they had.

For practicing folks, the main point was to not leave your home for five days. Whatever you had inside at the time of the Waiting was what you had. This, of course, usually included a ham and some Solarian fluffer biscuits. After five days, everyone came out of their houses and enjoyed a much-larger celebration. There were so many holidays now celebrated on Earth that every week had some type of celebration.

Oddly enough, Albert answered, having reviewed all the history logs on board the *Murphy*. "Eight, I do believe, and a heavy battle cruiser. You are making a good point."

Dailey dropped his hand, scratching a welcoming Sparky behind the ears. "My great-grandpa was a grumpy old marine and told me stories about it. Even though he was an infant, it was fresh in everyone's minds when he was growing up. He was around when the Solarians and all the other planets capable of true space travel showed up on the surface after the fight in space was over.

"He always said they would be back—they being the Alurians. We all knew this was a matter of time, but I'm with you, Card. This feels like something bigger than just getting some street cred back from Earth and Solaria."

"As stated, I'm not sure where the navigational points from the other side of the gate are. We could be talking in the real Void between the galaxies, even," Albert added.

"Or another galaxy," Dailey concluded as a green light started flashing.

"It's almost time. Everyone secure yourself," Albert instructed as the humming vibrations started back up, once again causing the hairs on Dailey's arm to stand at attention.

The same snapping pull was over as soon as it reached its crescendo. The silent droning of thrusters started back up, and Dailey glanced at Albert, who was turning odd colors of orange and red. The AI was focused on the ship's sensors and also addressing whatever was at the other side of the gate.

"That's not good," Dailey mumbled as the viewscreen blinked on, showing a large, grainy, looming shadow.

Dull light glistened off the cargo ship's flat forward deflector panels shielding the *Scarecrow* from space debris. The audible noise of the gate closing behind the ship sounded like someone had just flushed a toilet.

There, in the dark shadows of a massive pale moon was another smaller orbiting body. Upon closer inspection and another round of *oh shits* from Albert, the outline of dozens of not only star destroyers but honest-to-god battlecruisers took shape.

Even Sparky's jaw hung slack as Dailey walked closer to the screen. "Albert, can you get this image any sharper?"

"Not unless you go outside and clean off the cam pod. Which I don't think has been used in a decade at least," Albert replied as various red flashes and bright white light from what appeared to be some form of plasma welding lit up the internal guts of the superstructure.

Roughly the size of Earth's moon and also having several patches of structure-covered surface, the ships were all attached as if parts of a toy model that simply needed to be snapped off and glued together. Massive hulking beasts of war that even Dailey didn't recognize stared at the small cargo ship with hungry, angry eyes.

"What's that?" Dailey asked as a dot appeared on the left of the screen.

"That would be another cargo ship. It appears to have gated in from another location. There is not another ship scheduled to leave Asher for another ten hours."

"Do they know we're here?" Dailey asked skeptically.

"I have a feeling we would already know that by now. I must inform you I will have limited capabilities while we are here. All my subsystems are focused on keeping us from likely being recycled."

"You just keep being you, Albert," Dailey followed up as Cardinali walked up beside him.

"We're screwed. You know that, right?"

Dailey grinned. "Are we? The way I see it, we have an opportunity."

Card simply nodded, letting a slight grin perk the end of his lips. Without saying a word, Second Foot's platoon sergeant pulled out a small flask, taking a pull of Solarian gomo punch, an overly sweet liquor that was jokingly the main ingredient in the once-fictional Pan Galactic Gargle Blaster made real by one of the first space Fleet commanders as a nod to his favorite book series.

Dailey grimaced as Card nudged him with his shoulder. "Since when did you become a prude, sir?"

"Since I became responsible for you," Dailey joked back, letting the moment pass, joining Card with a quick puckering sip.

"Albert, can we still talk to you, or are you that busy?"

"A little of both. If I think it's worth answering, I will," Albert snapped quickly, not sounding like his normal self.

"I understand all the ship's system can tell or has told you is the function tied to getting this cargo ship from point A to point B. When this thing drops its load, can you link up to that monstrosity?"

Albert let that question float around the cramped bridge before finally answering with a simple "Yes."

Sparky joined the two men, chuffing as his modulated voice came over the comms. "Are we going on board? Do you think they have food?"

"I don't think this is the kind of place you want to claim. And before you ask, it's because I'm... we're going to destroy that thing. As for food, that's debatable, buddy."

Albert was still supporting translation duties for Sparky.

"Albert said it would take about two hours from soup to nuts here. See if one of your men can figure out a way to get that lens for the cam pod cleaned up. I'm betting there's an access panel behind it."

"Correct; see the viewscreen for its location," Albert again quickly snapped with not one ounce of sarcasm in his voice.

Card pulled out his tablet and snapped a picture of the chart before walking back to the small holding area with the rest of his platoon. After fifteen minutes, Albert flipped back to the now crystal-clear viewscreen. This didn't improve the situation, and Dailey took a deep breath.

Massive cannons the size of the *Murphy* sat resolute, surrounded by batteries of missile pods. Even though this was an alien space station, some things never changed. Smaller ships Dailey hadn't noticed before zoomed in all directions, looking automated. He would ask Albert to find how many souls were on board whatever it was he was staring at.

What he and the others were floating in front of in an unprotected cargo ship was an entire Alurian battle armada. The one thing not making Dailey pull out his own flask was the fact that the ships were all in various stages of construction, some more so than others, looking almost complete.

Things came into perfect focus as Dailey started putting the already discussed parts of the puzzle together. The Alurians had been farming Asher as well as other planets to build the armada sitting in wait in front of them. They had been using humans, Solarians, and several other races to do this. Earth was nothing more than a breeding ground for slaves.

That was where things started to fog over. The armada was large enough to possibly roll over the entire Fleet. Not to mention that according to everything Albert and the others understood, the planet had been mined for hundreds if not thousands of years.

The most important question started forming in Dailey's racing mind. "Albert, I need you to focus on me for a second with whatever spare brain power you got."

After a pause, Albert blinked blue. "Go ahead; it's not like I was busy or anything."

"Where are we?"

"Stand by. That's one of the things I was not looking at yet."

The pause from Albert was unnervingly long. "Oh, shit. I don't really know how to answer that one. Um."

"Spit it out in a way I can understand it."

Sparky stared at the blinking cube, cocking his head, clearly invested in the conversation. "Well, I am not able to scan any of the station's systems, but from what I can tell by the star layout directly in front of us, we are in Andromeda."

Having attended the academy for as long as the Fleet tolerated Dailey's antics, he strangely enough had paid attention in interstellar navigation class. "You're saying we are in another galaxy?"

"Yes," Albert replied, and his color shifted, telling Dailey the conversation was over.

"The creators," Sparky growled lightly.

"This doesn't make any sense. Sparky, who are the creators?"

Sparky let out a jumble of barks, grunts, and what Dailey assumed was the passing of gas.

"Beings beyond the stars that bring life to the galaxy."

The modulated voice made the message sound ominous, and Sparky plopped over on his hind legs. The armor lightly retracted, allowing him to scratch behind his ears, giving Dailey an extremely unwanted view of his business.

"You know the Fleet's never going to believe all this bullshit," Dailey suggested to Sparky conversationally, after nudging him with his boot to stop whatever grooming ritual he was performing. "And for the last time, no licking the goods while you're on the bridge."

After a light chuff, Sparky, in all his wisdom, gave the response Dailey figured. "No choice."

"Yeah, I'm betting they'll have no choice when this mess shows up on the front porch." Sparky didn't fully understand most of his catchphrases, simply nodding. As the words left Dailey's lips, the same red lights that activated when the ship took off blared back to life.

Albert, sounding more strained, came over the comms for everyone to hear. "Docking protocols initiated. If you can hold your breath for the next twenty minutes, I suggest doing so."

The message was clear. The time the ship was docked and offloading its payload was critical, and likely the greatest opportunity for the *Scarecrow* to be caught.

Dailey stood unflinching in front of the screen as thoughts of a Trojan horse started floating through his mind. In his mind's eye, it was simple: slip in and out undetected while finding a way to create a chain reaction via the cargo ship that would destroy the entire station.

This was quickly dispelled as logic told the *Murphy*'s commander that the additional missing destroyer would absolutely be attracting attention this time around. Third time's the charm even applied with alien species. It was one of those universal rules that just were.

The camera darkened as the massive strips of what appeared to be moonscape but upon closer inspection turned out to be an integrated structure shaded the vessel as a large claw slowly came out of the darkness. Like an arcade-game nightmare, the claw, according to the diagram now flashing on the bottom corner of the screen, was there to grab the ship, pull it into what looked like a gravity well, and commence to shake the shit out of it until all the contents of its belly were collected.

Albert, seeing Dailey's confusion at the tail end of the diagram, cut in. "It's just like the water gravity field back on Asher, but a little less refined. You don't want to be outside this ship when that gravity vacuum starts sucking. The *Scarecrow*'s cargo bay will be hovering directly above a nominal gravity inverter, meaning the area directly under the ship will be like any other planet's surface. The load will simply drop out, and the claw o' doom will give us a light shake, then pull us out of the well and send us backpacking home."

Dailey noticed Albert's voice was slightly more reserved. "Everything okay? You need us all to still be holding our breaths?"

"I looked; apparently, you can't hold your breaths that long. Just try not to move around too much. And yes, we are in the gravity field of the station. Which just happens to have been a moon at one point. That means that until that claw attaches to the ship, there is nothing more I can do or protect us from.

"We passed all the initial security protocols, and if the station's subsystems try to look again, I have the information on a loop. Once the claw hits, I will be offline, however, trying to pull data. This is where I predict the shit, as you call it, with the other missing destroyer may hit the fan. Or oxygen impeller, if that makes more sense."

"Makes perfect sense to me. I'm thinking—" Just as Dailey started, the sound of metal grating on metal shook the ship. The claw o' doom was upon them. Now it was just up to the person or things at the other side to win the prize.

Albert went silent, panning the camara around the outer section of the drop area. Dailey noticed the lack of viewports except for one glass viewport nearly half a mile away. While he was not able to make anything out, the light shifted, telling him there was something moving inside.

Farther down, another claw was in the process of pulling in the other ship that had arrived at the same time. That ship was being pulled into another opening separate from the one they were now in. Just as Dailey started to focus on the viewscreen, the shaking started. The mix of the ship smacking off the gravity well and dead space was jarring.

Even though gravity wasn't active on board the *Scarecrow*, everyone, including Sparky, had their gravity coupling activated on their boots. For Sparky, his entire suit of armor worked to keep him in an upright position.

Alurian equipment, while a key component fueling humankind's massive jump in technology, was still a mystery in many ways. Humans and Solarians alike only had access to what they had captured during the wars and subsequent raids.

Just as quickly as the *Scarecrow* and its crew had been pulled in and pillaged, the ship was now being released. Knowing that Albert would start talking as soon as he was able, Dailey took the few short, clunking steps back to the con. Cardinali was still with the rest of the platoon, and Sparky appeared to now be napping.

The camera panned behind the ship, then switched to a rearview cam not clear enough to use. "Well, that was fun," Albert proclaimed out of nowhere, talking through the speaker strapped onto his casing.

"We good to get out of here?" Dailey asked as Albert turned green in several random spots.

"Yes and no. I still have to sort through all the data, but they are fully aware of an issue surrounding Asher. They had no clue we were on board."

"How's that?"

"They have protocols in place to destroy the ship in the gravity well in the event of any detectable threats. Not to mention all those plasma cannons mounted on the station's entrance. Colonel Dailey, there is something I need to share with you about that ship we encountered before gating."

Dailey leaned back, waiting for the bad news. "Send it."

"The crew of the ship, small as it was, well… was sort of a mix. To be more precise, there were beings on board that I would categorize as human as well as Alurian."

That took Dailey by surprise but also lined up with reports he was aware of from some of the recent raids on Earth. "Albert, back home, I'm sure you are aware of the raids. Holdovers scattered throughout the system that every so often show up on Earth and generally cause problems. Some of us think they are sent out every few years to scout out the situation. Anyways, from what I now know, the Alurians have been using humans and Solarians as servants or whatever."

"Correct, as I told you. Things get a little murky. For some reason, my subsystems, when they jailbroke, as Bellman calls it, reset some of my main data files. Truth be told, it wasn't like I was programmed to know everything. I was more of a system-integration AI. Everything I have learned outside of that has been fairly recent."

"Fair enough. We need to get back to the *Murphy* and rethink our next steps. What do you think they will do about the missing destroyers?"

"Good question. The station has minimal sentient staffing, meaning it's mostly automated. There is a force I would project of roughly a couple of thousand souls, as you put it, running the entire place, spread out like peanut butter on bread."

"Do you even know what peanut butter is?"

"Oh, yes. Peanut butter is made from ground peanuts that have been roasted. Sugar, salt, oils, and additives that prevent separation may also be added in case you want to shop at a snobby grocery store. There are three main types—"

Dailey cut him off. "That means you don't really know what it is. How it makes you feel. That's the thing, Albert. You've digested a hell of a lot of information that includes tactical data. It's good knowing things; it's even better knowing what it means and how to act on it like you did when you first helped us.

"If you asked me what peanut butter is, I'd tell you it's mushed-up peanuts that you make a sammich out of with jelly, strawberry in my case, that tastes like a wet dream. I'd then tell you it's fueled poor college students, ignored kids, and families alike since Marcellus Edson's genius brain made the stuff. The one good thing to come out of Canada. Can't forget George Washington Carver made the peanut commercially viable, though. So..." Dailey trailed off.

Albert went through a few colors, trying to compute the point of the statement other than the facts. "Is a wet dream when you pee your bed?"

"Jesus, is that all you took away from that? No, the point is we need to take all this information and use it. Figure out how to pull it all together and avoid being reactive. For example, that third destroyer that showed up. I'm hoping you can lay out any other issues we may run into."

"Oh, I see. Then we need to get back and start preparing for the likely emissary they are going to send to Asher. This team would likely come on board a full-on star cruiser. The ones where the cute little destroyers attach to the sides and are used like boat bumpers if necessary."

"That's my boy," Dailey said as Sparky perked up. "How long do you think we have?"

"According to the logs I just pulled and reviewed, the question is likely being asked now about the status of the third destroyer. The station is busy dealing with a failed cargo ship from another system, so the destroyer is not as important. So, maybe two to three of your Earth days before they start the process of sending anyone. Also, the ships they sent out to check on things were and are old and close to being decommissioned. Is that sufficient?"

Dailey knew what that meant. Any ships other than the ones they had encountered would likely be more of a threat. It would make sense after the *Murphy* had made such quick work of the destroyers. If it wasn't for Ran's coordinating the enemy ships gating in, the *Brightstar* would indeed still be in one piece.

"Yeah, it is. Anything else?"

"There is one more point of order I would like to bring up. While I don't mind riding on the back of such a noble steed," Albert started, and

Sparky's ears perked up, "might I suggest retrofitting me in some type of droid? Say… one of the Alurian battle droids we left behind?"

"The ones we shot to shit?"

"Yes, those."

"I don't know what's really left of them," Dailey wondered out loud, remembering the one that was only cut in half before shutting down.

"Before leaving, I checked. There are likely enough pieces left to initiate a single unit. Bellman is more than capable, with my help, of course, to get one up and running. You could simply plug me into it, and there you go. Instant body."

"Instant body with machine-gun shoulders and claw hands. I'll talk with Bellman about it. If he thinks he can modify it enough to make sense, I'll consider it. Have you looked at the service droids in the *Murphy*'s cargo bay?"

"Ah, yes. A little bland, if you ask me. Not to mention the tech is sub-standard compared to the Alurian droids. Just think about it. Sparky in his Alurian war hound armor and me in an Alurian battle droid pulling up to a bar. The karaoke machine would love us."

Dailey shook his head, glad to be left out of the AI's awkward fantasy.

CHAPTER 26

ALL IS QUIET ON THE WESTERN SECTORS FRONT

Dailey sat across from Pearl, Becket, and Jen, while Albert shifted colors from his position sitting on the middle of the main table in the chief's mess. Since returning from their mission, Sparky had taken to the galley.

A room reserved for the senior noncommissioned officers and officers alike on board the *Murphy*, the chief's mess was a place for leaders to relax outside the prying eyes of their subordinates. Thron walked in, setting an entire flagon of Bellman's rum on the table.

"Thanks," Dailey said, motioning Thron to join him.

"Sir, with all due respect, I'll pass. You just need to let me know when and where I need to be to keep everyone fat and happy."

Becket and Dailey both grinned, knowing the man's heroic past, plus the fact that he was already likely eavesdropping on their conversation. Jen leaned forward, still in shock from what she had just heard.

"Sir, with all that being said, how are we going to do this?" Pearl asked as Albert started blinking.

Dailey had presented his entire Trojan-horse scheme after explaining to Pearl what that was. As with all plans, the *Murphy*'s commander liked to keep it simple. The general idea went something like this:

This first part of the plan was to immediately recall the ship from Asher where they had loaded the warhead set to destroy the planet. From there, they would work a way to either attach it to the *Scarecrow* or somehow smuggle it through the gate to the massive space station and awaiting, almost-finished armada. Making matters worse, after more digging, Albert found communications about preparing the space station for a large influx of personnel to man the ships in the near future.

After that, it was as simple as getting the claw o' doom to grab the *Scarecrow* and help deposit its cargo, which in this case happened to be a thermo-nuclear accelerated particle warhead, a nastier modified version of a nuclear warhead from Earth. These types of munitions were simply called planet-killers.

After that, it was anyone's guess as to the next steps. "Albert, how long till you have a solution on the gate drive?" Dailey asked, still working out how to travel using the tech found aboard the *Scarecrow*. The man had to admit the grimy, old, outdated cargo ship had grown on him.

"I think it's all going to come down to time, boss. The warhead will be back here in five days. As instructed, I sent the signal to expend all fuel levels getting back. No stopping for snacks, picking up hitchhikers, or re-generating its energy reservoirs."

Pearl cleared her throat, running her hand over her head's smooth skin. "We don't know when they will send another party to investigate the missing ships, but I am sure they will. Might I recommend we contact Dax and Vax? I would bet they would get some sort of inquiry. From what I've witnessed over the past several days, I would not doubt they can somehow communicate over massive distances without much of a buffer."

"I was thinking the same thing," Jen added, not to be outdone by the ship's navigation and executive officer. Dailey glanced at Becket, who was holding back a grin.

While aware that Jen had been flirting with him off and on, Dailey was oblivious to Solarian flirting, something Becket had learned on one of his first assignments that was for the most part never discussed. Pearl had over time not only grown close as a friend and confidant but harbored a protective type of interest in the man that could only be explained as having a slight working crush on one's superior officer.

Dailey stood up and filled everyone's glasses with a few heavy-handed pours of rum. Without thinking, the gathered leadership all took their glasses, sipping the strong yet smooth drink at the same time as if on a synchronized swim ballet team. Even then, with all the new additions to sports, that was still a thing. It was revitalized on Earth by the Solarians having it as a day-to-day sport on several of the larger water-based colonies on their home world.

"Sounds like you all have that handled," Becket weighed in. "Albert, I'm with the colonel here. We need to know how to get that gate drive or that capability on the *Murphy*."

Everyone glared at Albert until he finally spoke. "Sorry, just digging in to some sensor data from the space station. Back to the gate drive. I was looking into the sensor data to see what they use to identify the cargo ships, you know, visual, thruster signature, some type of beacon, and it seems that it's a little bit of all that."

"Right, this is where you get to the point," Dailey reminded the AI. "Strategically."

"Yes. I think, well, I know we have two options. First, we can take the gate drive off the *Scarecrow*, which we will have to do in space, then mount it and calibrate it on board the *Murphy*."

"How long will that take?" Dailey followed up. This was clearly a conversation between the two.

"Two days, maybe three. The easy thing is we're not really changing the current propulsion system on board but rather using the gate drive to project in front of the ship while synched with the ship's forward shielding systems. See? Easy."

Dailey rolled his eyes. "All right, when is the *Scarecrow* scheduled for its next load?"

"That's the cool part. I may have taken the liberty of hijacking the system protocol codes to schedule the ship and told the station that there was already another cargo load of materials ready to be picked up and dropped off."

Dailey smacked his hands on the table, making everyone jump. "You see? That's what I'm talking about. You did something really kickass, and it didn't involve my ship."

If an AI crammed inside a box could smile, the reddish hue was Albert doing so. "Yet. It doesn't involve your ship yet. Plus, you may want to talk to it sometime; the ship's subsystems without an AI are sort of lonely, if you ask me. Not to get back on that totally awesome thing I did, but you… we can in theory gate as many ships as we can fit in the gate opening. Once opened, its start and finish, considering they are one and the same, are set. It stays open as long as whatever ship has the drive is passing through. You could, with a steady hand, just go really slow."

"I don't know what the hell all that means, but I'll take your move as a solid win," Dailey finished, then looked around the group. "Anything I'm missing?"

"Sir," Becket spoke up. "Are you thinking we take both ships, the *Murphy* and the *Scarecrow*?"

"If that ship goes through the gate on its own, it's doing so without a crew. That means we stay here. We already attempted to lay out its location. What I'm saying is I want full confirmation that space station and the armada parked there are handled. If that means all of us going, so be it. Albert can keep us off the radar long enough for the *Scarecrow* to do its thing. We stay right by the gate and leave as soon as we can. If things go south, well, we do what we do best."

The group nodded, knowing the danger of the mission. Pearl, on the other hand, was excited, having learned the gate had taken them to the closest outer edges of Andromeda, the Milky Way's closest neighbor. She was even going as far as to figure out the honor to bestow upon the crew after accomplishing such a feat.

The team finished their rum and started going their separate ways. Pearl scooped up Albert to start planning the gate-drive situation with the ship's engineering section. Becket stayed behind, pouring the last of the liquid goodness into his and Dailey's cups.

Dailey spoke up first. "What do you think?"

"I think we're likely going to die this time. Not going to lie. After seeing the video footage Albert stored, I'm not sure any of us are ready. This isn't one of those things me and the boys are going to be able to beat or shoot into submission. This is bigger than us."

Dailey nodded, taking another pull of his drink. "I wish the *Brightstar* was still in one piece and Ran wasn't the asshole he is. Which is another thing. There's no way that guy sacrificed himself. He's still out there somewhere. Hell, he's probably on the planet."

"I'm with you. Even if we had a fleet with us, I'd feel somewhat better."

"Would you? I think it would just draw more attention. We don't even know why they're out there. For all we know, there is a war going on in that galaxy. Isn't that some crazy shit?"

"You mean them using all of us to help the war effort like mindless puppets. A war we know nothing about. That shit kind of pisses me off," Becket grumbled.

"Same thing. I'm going to get some rest. I'll be back on the bridge after a good five hours. Albert says he can now get the *Scarecrow* up here remotely. That will save us some time. Once we hear back from Dax and Vax, let me know." Becket stood up and saluted Dailey.

Dailey had only been asleep for thirty minutes as the light rap of knuckles jarred him awake. The man was already a light sleeper, and with the gravity of everything going on around him, it would likely be weeks if not months before he would truly be able to relax.

"Just a minute," Dailey yawned, then opened his door, wearing nothing but a pair of shorts. "Oh, Jen. Let me get situated."

As Dailey turned to walk back into his room, Jen slipped in quickly, closing the door behind her. Before he could react, she jumped in front of him, looking up. Light danced in her eyes as the smell of fresh rum filled the void between the two.

"I think you're just fine," Jen breathed out, her intentions becoming crystal clear.

"Look, I don't think—" Dailey started, but she pushed up onto her tiptoes, kissing Dailey on his unmoving lips.

Dailey reached down, pushing Jen down by her hips, not moving his hands away from her body. "It's okay. I just—I have been thinking."

"Thinking what?" Dailey lightly snickered. He paused, seeing the look on her face shift. "Whatever it is, I'm sure the rum's likely helping. I'm here to command this ship and ensure everyone gets back home. Plus, I don't make it a habit of fraternizing with my crew."

Thoughts of Stella fluttered into his thoughts as he still found himself not moving his hands. He could feel smooth skin under the Space Force physical training uniform. Still, he didn't move his hands.

Jen looked up, cocking her head slightly. "Oh, shit. You think we're really coming back from this mission. And for the record, I'm not in the Army like you. I'm in"—hiccup—"the Space Force. So, that means it doesn't really count."

Taken aback by this, Dailey finally pulled his hands to his side. "Is that what everyone thinks? That we aren't coming back?"

"You're really just that crazy to bring us all back, aren't you?" Jen slurred out, still clearly in control of most of her faculties. Dailey was predicting as the rum continued to seep into her system, she would likely be asleep before the conversation was over. "I mean sir."

"Huuuh." Dailey breathed slowly, calming down Mother Nature's call to arms. "Not everyone always comes back. Hell, we're lucky Woody is still with us after his run-in with the spider." He was trying to shift the subject.

"You're cute when you're trying to play it cool," Jen said, then stepped ever so slightly closer.

Dailey breathed out again, this time hard enough to move the loose hairs covering a portion of Jen's face. Turning, Dailey walked over to his small closet, then shuffled through several identical T-shirts, talking as he did so.

"I'm not saying there won't be time for this later. But for now, we need to be focused. You're one hell of a pilot One of the best I've met from the regular force in ages. Let's do this. We get back from this mission, we can take some time to get to know each other," Dailey stated, pulling a T-shirt on as the first snore erupted from his bed.

Jen had walked forward and dropped down on his bed just as quickly as he had opened up the closet door.

"Shit," Dailey grumbled under his breath, then picked up his communicator. He looked at it before setting it back down as another, this time full-on snore erupted from Jen's small yet strong frame. She had passed out.

Dailey walked over to the reclining chair, looking out into space as he glanced at the young pilot. It wasn't that the lieutenant was that young—she was twenty-nine, according to her file—it was her lack of experience in the sheer, brutal violence the galaxy had to offer. If the Void wasn't trying to kill you, it was trying to take your soul.

After losing Stella, Dailey had kept himself focused on the task at hand. That task often involved violence and not meeting someone else. Sleep came fast to the ship's commander as Jen's light snores calmed his nerves.

A round of loud beeps awoke the *Murphy's* commander, and he snapped back to reality. "Shit," he grumbled, glancing over at the now-empty bed. Looking down, he saw Pearl's ID code appear on the screen.

"Yeah," Dailey answered after another round of message requests.

"Sorry to wake you, sir. Becket insisted we let you rest. We just talked with Dax and Vax. You might want to come to the bridge."

Dailey smacked his dry lips, tasting what he assumed was lipstick. Jen had put it on prior to coming and seeing him. She hadn't simply been wandering the halls of the ship drunk. She had likely been sober prior to showing up.

"Give me twenty. We good with that?"

"Yes, sir," Pearl replied, also sounding well rested.

"Also, I need to address the crew when I get there," Dailey concluded, then turned his communicator off.

Looking in the mirror, Dailey stared at his face. The gravity of the situation was weighing heavy, adding to the slight dark circles under his eyes. He looked tired and rested at the same time. If everything went as planned, they would be starting the operation by the end of the day.

"Good morning, sunshine!" Albert busted over the intercom in his room. "Late night, lover boy?"

"Albert, not funny." Dailey paused. "What did you see?"

"I saw a very happy-looking lieutenant come into your room and leave about six hours later. I did the math in my head and also referenced several Solarian super X-rated space academy videos on one of your soldiers' hard drives. Can I ask you a few questions for comparison?"

"I can't believe I'm talking to you about this. Nothing happened."

"Suuuuuuuuure," Albert drawled out. "I will ask Sparky about this. He has a nose for people that have mated."

"What the hell are you talking about?" Dailey asked, shaking his head, grabbing his toothbrush.

"He mapped it all out for me before you left. Told me all kinds of things. The nose knows and all. So scandalous. First—"

Dailey cut him off. "I don't need to or want to know, Albert. If you want to tell me something, tell me what's going on."

"Oh, sure. It appears we are set to get the ship in orbit. I had to get a few things situated in the mines. Let's just say the water, when it comes back out of the gravity well this time, will be significantly nastier."

"You are having the cargo dumped in the well," Dailey stated, then spat in the sink after he rinsed his mouth out.

"Precisely. It took a few hours, but we will be able to dump the load. Did you dump your—"

"Enough," Dailey barked. "Stop before I plug you into the wall and use you as a smoothie blender."

"Rude. As I was saying, that part's all handled. You're welcome, before you say it. I intercepted the message from the dynamic duo, Tweedledee and Tweedledum, on the planet. We are absolutely going to get some company and likely sooner than later. They were told there is an inspection team coming to Arcadia."

"How bad is that?"

"Well, from what I can tell, every time that happens, there is some type of turnover of the city's inhabitants."

"Turnover?"

"They will likely purge some of the city or at least any anomalies they find. There are at least one hundred more cities on the planet's surface. Twenty of them support mining ships. The others are mostly much nastier than Arcadia, and some nicer. It's all a roll of the dice. I'm not sure from there but would suspect Dax and Vax will be relocated, as they say."

"So, they know something's going on in Arcadia. Great."

After another round of Albert trying to pry into Dailey's bland night, the captain finally arrived on the bridge. The crew for the most part had taken his advice and looked rested. Kline was even neatly shaven. Sparky was the pièce de résistance, sitting on the con.

Looking around, Dailey didn't see Albert sitting on the navigation table.

Pearl spoke up. "He's with Bellman. Ya know, something about a new year, new you."

"Yeah, I forgot to mention that. Lover boy wants a body," Dailey replied.

"Vax was busy getting everything together. According to Dax, they are scheduled to be reassigned in two weeks," Pearl quickly summarized, refocusing the conversation. "I took the liberty of filling them in. Let's just say they didn't seem too surprised. I believe Albert may have sent them something or given them access to information before we left."

"Well, either way, this tells us how much time we have till company arrives," Dailey suggested.

Pearl paused. "Well, that's the thing. According to Dax, they are to ride back on an early scheduled load on the *Scarecrow*. There is another ship coming, but they have been delayed for a couple of weeks."

"Even better," Dailey noted, then walked over to Sparky, who looked up. The dog was making it clear that scratches was the toll to get him to move.

Pearl grinned as Dailey obliged Sparky, scratching behind his ears. "All right, time to move."

Sparky let out a few low barks. "I took charge. Everyone is safe."

"Thanks, Sparky. Hopefully, you remembered what not to be doing on the bridge."

Sparky glanced at Pearl to see if she was going to let the cat out of the bag. She had indeed caught the dog grooming himself in the captain's chair. The Alurian war hound dropped to the floor and headed toward what Dailey could only assume was the galley. Just as he was about to leave, Sparky shifted his twitching nose, cocking his head.

"No, and keep that to yourself," Dailey scolded as Sparky got the message loud and clear.

"What was that all about?" Pearl asked, and Dailey shook his head.

"Nothing; he just needs to mind his own business. Any thoughts?"

Pearl walked up to the see-through viewscreen and activated it. "Well, according to the timeline we have now, I say we get them to ride the ship up. I have already set up a drop ship to take Private Atwood down to the planet. Medical Officer Franklin said he is stable enough to transport."

"Glad to hear Woody's back up and running. So, you think we should bring them along? Why not just leave them on the planet at the base? Walker could use the extra help, especially since they know the city."

"Albert wanted them to bring something with them. He didn't say what."

Dailey pressed his index finger on the timeline Pearl pulled up. Several key points were labeled, down to the minute. They still had four hours to make any adjustments before the crew of the *Murphy* went into mission mode.

"You know that body I mentioned? I bet he wants them to take care of that. It would save us the hassle. We're sending Woody down anyways. Get them up here, show them what else is out there, and send them down with the drop ship. That reminds me. We set for a crew announcement?"

Pearl nodded, having heard this before. Dailey, while outwardly confident, was uncertain about the mission's conclusion. He knew the crew would fight till the end, no matter the outcome. He was about to let the entire crew know that there was a high likelihood of them not returning either spiritually or physically, of them being stuck in another, alien galaxy.

The intercom hummed when keyed from the communications station as King activated the entire ship's public-address system. It was at that time a rosy-cheeked Lieutenant Jen Brax walked onto the bridge in her full flight suit.

"This is Colonel Ben Dailey, captain of the USF *Murphy* and your commanding officer. As you are all likely aware, we are going to be embarking on a mission that is likely going to produce one of two outcomes. We succeed in our mission and live to tell the tale, or we don't, in which case it will likely be hundreds if not thousands of years before the events that are about to unfold are heard by our descendants."

Dailey paused before starting back up. The man swore he heard a sad violin playing somewhere in the background. "To the best of my knowledge, which has been stretched recently, we are going further than any man or woman from Earth tied to our reality has gone." Dailey wanted to caveat that with the apparent use of humans as workers and slaves but erred on the side of leaving that bit of nightmare fuel off the table.

"As of thirteen hundred hours, we will be fully operational and actively manning battle stations. That means we will follow the prescribed scheduling and protocol. For teams on standby with the quick reaction force, you will be helping with the transfer of systems from the *Scarecrow*.

"In closing, I fully expect this, like any other time Viper Company has been tested, to be challenging and rewarding. Navigation Officer Pearl has sanctioned and I authorized today a new expeditionary medal and, hopefully, ink after we're done. Viper Six out."

Light cheers and giggles confused Dailey as he looked around the bridge. King smiled at the conversation he was having before cutting off his personal communicator.

"Sir, Albert piped some old-timey violin music through the system while you were talking. Apparently, it was well received. Sir…" He trailed off, smiling.

The cheering had been for the possibility of new bragging rights, something that always got Nova Rangers and attack-wing pilots alike going.

"Yeah, I'm going to get him an ice-cream-dispensing robot as a body if he keeps it up," Dailey noted, and Albert came over the radio.

"It was a speech that will go down in infamy. A thing of glory, boss. Let's just chalk it up to fortune and glory. Anyway, thought you would like to know that I have accelerated our schedule. Dax and Vax are on their way to the *Scarecrow* now. Apparently, they got a call from the mothership that they were to start preparing to leave and that they will be here in approximately three days."

This was an acceleration of an already laid-out plan. "Just a little sooner than expected, but expected," Dailey noted. "Albert, were they ordered to ride the *Scarecrow* or wait till they arrive?"

"Wait till they arrive."

"Shit; they know something's up. And something is up in Arcadia. We already assumed this. I just wasn't planning on getting in a fight before we leave. How fast can we accelerate the transition of the gate drive?"

"That's why I have everyone loading it up now. You know, one of those things I should be doing, until I screw something up. One second, I'm doing the right thing, then BAM! Wrong thing. I think it'll be close. We still need to be concerned about the ship that will now likely be showing up sooner rather than later."

Dailey paused, thinking about the situation. "Albert, call Security Officer Altis, our favorite Arcadian cop. Let him know the Syndicate is coming and they aren't in a good mood, plus it would be good for their health to stay indoors for a few days. If that fails, set some kind of alarm off."

"Yes, that might do. I have an even better idea. Get everyone into the undercity. I agree; the Alurians are absolutely sending someone here to address whatever is going on."

King cut in. "I informed the base. They will keep an eye out and power down once we leave."

This was standard protocol to shut down any power sources, as larger, cruiser-class ships could scan an entire planet's surface in roughly twenty-four hours. The scan watched for energy sources that weren't charted to be there, such as cities and military installations. While the trees would do a good-enough job, as with anything Dailey encountered, there was no such thing as excessive risk mitigation.

"Lieutenant Brax." Dailey turned, not having forgotten Jen standing in the bridge trying not to obviously stare at her feet.

"Sir. Albert gave us a heads-up. The attack wing is ready to go. We already sent Woody planetside and have the ships standing by to transport the gate drive and whatever else."

It was surprisingly un-awkward with the attack wing's leader as Dailey grinned. "Knew you guys would be on it. Do me a favor. Well, it's more an order, but always have two of your fighters on patrol. I'm not saying they know we're here, but it sounds like they know something, and that tells me they could be sending mixed messages."

Jen nodded before turning. Dailey caught himself watching her leave before quickly pulling it back in. The *Murphy*'s captain paused, taking in the new timeline. No matter the timeline shift, he still wasn't a fan of going back and facing the almost-complete armada while leaving the planet defenseless.

That all being said, he also knew he needed complete confirmation that the armada was destroyed, and was also suspecting whoever oversaw the station knew something was going on, which would also result in a significant increase in security. They simply needed the *Scarecrow* to deposit its contents.

Dailey walked over to Pearl, knowing Albert was listening. In many ways, he was looking forward to the AI having a body so he knew when he was around, which, in all fairness, likely didn't matter.

"Send a message to Dax and Vax. Tell them to leave immediately. Once they're on board, activate the *Scarecrow* and get her moving. Time starts now."

Albert huffed. "I'll adjust the protocol for the launch. I don't suggest shifting the actual gate timeline. That would be one too many adjustments."

"Agreed. I just want to have everything set sooner than later. I know you can get that ship in orbit without raising any red flags. Specialist Kline, I need an update on the package," Dailey concluded, not wanting to discuss the matter further. He also wanted to ensure the warhead made it back in time.

CHAPTER 27

BAIT

The flurry of activity aboard the *Scarecrow*, now attached to the hull of the *Murphy* via an airlock bridge, resembled a beehive in spring. After some shuffling, Albert did what he was designed to do, showing off.

Needing the ship to see if it was even possible, after a few short minutes, the AI was able to configure a bracket for the *Scarecrow*'s airlock to accept that of the *Murphy*'s. Now with the two ships connected, the entire operation would go much faster.

"Viper Four, this is Angel Six. We are clear to pull," Jen came over the radio, talking with the *Murphy*'s supply and engineering team.

A nasal New York accent replied as Ensign Barthelo, the ship's engineering system analyst, came over the comms while Dailey stood on the bridge, overlooking the entire operation.

"Angel Six, this is Viper Four; we're ready. Give it to us," Barthelo blurted out, with a light dusting of sarcasm cutting through. That was normal for about anything the Ensign said.

He had been a member of the crew for just over two years and was perpetually stuck as a Fleet ensign due to his general lack of professionalism. The man was lighthearted and truly never crossed any lines. If you had spent any time around real New Yorkers, not the ones that claimed to be, the man just made sense. But as with most things with Dailey, the proof was in the pudding, and when it came to getting shit done, Barthelo was just the man to do it.

At one point, Barthelo even wanted to join the Pathfinder Nova Space Ranger team, only to have the Army shut it down due to the fact that he had a robotic arm.

Jen's attack fighter was lowered onto the top of the *Scarecrow*, and a Harpy drop ship with several magnetic cables greedily reaching out landed directly on the hull of the ship. Within a few seconds, the drop ship was already starting to leave, while a drive pod the size of a large truck pulled away from the cargo ship like a tooth getting unwillingly extracted at the dentist's office.

"Looks like we are a go. Rocket man to ground control," Albert came over the intercom, interrupting the calming silence that everyone was taking part in while watching the gate drive extraction.

"Yes?" Dailey asked, waiting for a punch line that never came.

Sensing the tension, Albert went straight to the facts. "The drive is successfully disconnected. That one thing you asked me to check into about using the *Murphy*'s AI system on board the *Scarecrow* is also an outstanding success."

"I can see it's disconnected. Why are you telling me?"

"Well, I might have failed to mention that if it had not gone as planned, we would all likely have been disintegrated in a mini black hole or something like that."

Dailey turned, knowing Albert wasn't there to look at. "This is one of those things, Albert, that you need to let me know so we can plan accordingly."

"If I did that with all things, I don't think anything would get done. Oh, and Sparky is already on board the *Scarecrow*, checking in on what he is absolutely calling his ship."

"At least someone is doing something around here," Dailey countered, and Albert paused before responding.

"Well, I'll just delete all the AI subsystems that I uploaded aboard the ship, then," Albert replied, sounding offended.

"Jesus, chill out. I'm yanking your chain. You just need to let us know about those kinds of things next time. Do me a favor and focus on the docking bay to make sure nothing goes wrong," Dailey instructed, and the sound of Albert clicking off the intercom popped.

Pearl walked over, and Dailey turned back to the drop ship slowly shifting away from the *Scarecrow*. "I think he does that shit on purpose." Dailey huffed and Pearl agreed.

"In all fairness, he does always state that he would rather not bore us with all the details, and you tell him not to do so." Pearl grinned and Dailey agreed with her.

"Do you think we are going to have company? I know that look," Pearl stated, looking at Dailey with his hands neatly held behind his back.

"Yup" was all he said, and she turned back to the navigation station.

"Specialist Kline, please adjust the aft sensor satellites. I would like you to push them out a little further. Also, do a quick scan of the moon. Our sensor array will be lined up in roughly five minutes," Pearl instructed, and Kline turned to smack a flurry of commands into the radar panel.

The ship was currently set to focus on several probable incoming gate locations in relation to the moon. With the shifting drift of the planet, the sensors would not have to be redirected. If not focused on the moon itself, the sensors would simply ignore the massive rock in space and ping the areas around it.

Kline turned and pointed at the main sensor screen in front of the bridge, responding to Dailey's prior update request. "Sir, the package is inbound. Two hours out. Looks like it's on its last leg. The thruster signal is getting weak. Probably why we just picked it up."

Nodding, Dailey punched the comms button. "Angel Six, this is Viper Six. We're about to send you some coordinates. We need a ship to intercept and get the package here as quickly as possible."

"Roger," Jen replied, and one of the ships hovering above the *Scarecrow* tore out on full thrust, having received the package's location as Kline grinned.

The warhead had been loaded on one of the *Brightstar*'s few remaining ships and sent out into the Void. There had been no better option in the sector to detonate the world-ending device.

Light flashed, controls beeped, and people talked through operations, the crew of the *Murphy* in full swing. Dailey walked to the con, finally sitting down now that the gate drive had been dropped in the cargo bay.

In order to keep things simple, the electromagnetic gravity field usually active around the ship had been left off. Several of Third Foot's soldiers stood on the *Scarecrow*, welding sensor panels on the side of the ship in case they did in fact have to leave before setting off the warhead.

Kline glanced down at his panel as a small red dot flickered on his screen on the port side of the *Murphy*. After adjusting a few sensor parameters, Kline clicked the sensor scan on the main display. He then got everyone's attention.

"Sir, it's the package," Kline stated as one of the pilots confirmed the news.

"Albert, what's the status down there?" Dailey asked, as another two attack fighters zoomed out of the drop bay.

"The gate drive is in place. Now the fun part. Bellman has started the cabling protocol I supplied. We are still several hours out from powering the system up and testing it with the deflector shield system. Oh, and something I didn't notice before: this drive must have originally been in another ship. It is loaded with nav data. Road trip!"

Dailey shook his head. "Just keep me up to date. The package is here. Everything set on the *Scarecrow*?"

"According to Sparky, his ship is ready to receive the cargo, and he is now only answering to Captain Sparky. Just letting you know, boss," Albert noted, and Dailey tapped the button flickering on a video feed of the other ship's bridge. As to be expected, Sparky was on the con with legs sprawled out, his armor half on, allowing him to sit.

"Of course," Dailey mumbled. "Captain Sparky, this is your commander speaking. I'm going to need you to head back over to the *Murphy* once the package is loaded."

What sounded initially like a burp was translated for the entire bridge crew as a curt "If you insist" or however it was Albert had interpreted the statement.

"I'm heading to the engineering section. Pearl, you have the con," Dailey stated, already on his way off the bridge.

He was getting fidgety and more so by the minute. Years of experience and the sheer magnitude of what he had witnessed was telling every bone in his body the lack of any action was a feint, or in the least, the other side working out their best approach, just as he had.

Bellman greeted Dailey while a wide-eyed Vax stood next to the control panel overlooking the engineering section. Albert sat on the console, flickering an odd shade of purple with several wires and plugs flowing out of his casing, this time from all sides.

"I think he's about maxed out," Bellman noted, also glancing at Vax.

Dailey immediately noticed the warmer-than-usual temperature in the room as a bead of sweat slid down his back. "Looks like it."

Sitting against the far wall was a pile of parts from the battle droids they had fought earlier. Angry angles and singed metal lightly reflected the glowing dull blue flowing from the gate drive sitting directly next to the shield capacitors. Large monolithic coils hummed, holding back several petawatts of static energy waiting to be projected in front of and around the ship.

Turning, Dailey addressed Vax. "I hope you are finding things comfortable. How you two holding up?"

Vax, while confused, was clearly strong-willed; she cocked her head ever so slightly. "Well, Dax is suffering from orbital sickness, and as for me… I didn't believe it at first."

"Why not?" Dailey followed up, genuinely curious.

"This is the only thing I know. My entire life, I was taught about the mines and how our species came to be."

"Let me guess: all of that was a load of garbage," Dailey noted, still in an odd form of denial over his own recent revelations about the human race.

She looked at her feet, laughing lightly. "Something like that. According to Bellman, we are actually distant relatives."

"That's right. Even the Solarians, to a point, depending on what timeline you are tracking. Either way, we both have a lot to learn from each other. I'm going to be sending you two back to the planet before we leave."

"I can't speak for Dax, but I would like to come along. To see," she stated, looking at Bellman, having clearly talked to him about it.

"We will see. Either way, we have a drop ship leaving at twenty-two hundred. Albert." Dailey shifted his focus as the purple light leveled out.

"Busy, but of course that's the perfect time to have a chat."

"How long till we can test the new drive?" Dailey asked, knowing it had only been on board for about forty minutes. His nervous mood was starting to become visible, seeping past his rugged bulletproof exterior.

"Well, I just got done using a set of transponder codes to convince the drive it's still on board the *Scarecrow*. That's a start, that it hasn't imploded or anything."

"Where did you get the codes from?" Dailey asked.

"It's more like a set of codes working together. Pretty straightforward stuff. Up, down, up, down, left, right, left, right, A, B, A, B, select Start and voilà! In all seriousness, it's literally what I was designed to do. Connect alien tech to each other and all that jazz. See, I know your old Earth codes."

"All that jazz," Dailey drawled out.

Bellman rejoined the conversation after a quick check in with Ensign Barthelo. "We're going to push as fast as we can. Good news is the *Scarecrow* will be ready and set up before we get the drive going. Looks like it will be just under twenty-four hours. The AI we pulled from the *Murphy*, with a little help from Albert, booted up faster than expected. We have full control of the ship."

"Anything useful other than that?" Dailey asked.

"Now that you mention it, yes. The ship has an immensely powerful deflector-shield system on board. It looks like only a portion of it was being utilized, due to the power draw needed for the gate drive. Not a worry here. We have plenty to spare. That is, if we control and manage how frequently we use the drive.

"If Albert and my calculations are right"—Albert blew a raspberry as Bellman corrected himself—"If mostly his calculations are right, we might just be able to pull this off."

"Tell him the bad news," Albert interjected.

"They will know we are there as soon as we gate in."

Dailey rubbed his stubbled chin. "I think we already knew that to a point. Hell, I think they already know somebody's poking around the sector."

The words trailed off as the conversation continued in a mix of passing time and going over any possible scenario that involved the crew of the *Murphy* not coming back.

CHAPTER 28

RAN SO FAR

General Ran on the Ateris Mining Syndicate's underground moon base above Asher.

"General Ran, we have a confirmed lock on a ship," the Alurian radar officer growled. Since the destruction of the *Brightstar*, the once-unbreakable General Ran was now wearing his true Ateris mining officer colors, leaning back in his seat on the outpost relay station buried deep inside Asher's moon.

Dull yet manicured lines surrounded the station's main operations deck a mile under the moon's dusty surface. Green ambient lighting representing the Ateris syndicate shadowed the entire facility, serving as a friendly reminder of who was in charge.

Ribbed metal braces made the structure look as if its inhabitants were working inside the lungs of a large underground beast, flowing into the natural black cryo stone that made up the moon's incredibly hard shell. Something the Syndicate would at some point mine and sell.

The one piece of Ran's position he hadn't completely planned on was the Alurians' overall lack of interest in keeping him alive after the destruction of the *Brightstar*. Knowing the Alurian disregard for life, Ran had planned on shuttling to the very hidden relay station he was now occupying with a group of Ateris syndicate loyalists, better known as a mining clan.

Also unfortunate for the once-famed general was the *Brightstar*'s main center hull crashing directly on top of the subterranean relay station's main sensor array, including its one and only entrance and exit port.

This ill-fated series of events had prevented the couple of dozen Ateris syndicate members and Ran from not only sending out a message but also knowing the aftereffects of the doomed battle. What they did have, however, was a set of warning signals buzzing, letting the Syndicate know someone was conducting a deep scan of the moon's surface.

Coincidentally, as of thirty minutes before, one of the four large sensor relays had been cleared by surface mining bots, the now-flashing signals letting it be officially known. To the radar team aboard the *Murphy*, the blip was nothing more than the remnants of the wrecked *Brightstar*. For the underground mining clan, it was now confirming they would now be able to see again.

"Which ship?" Ran clarified, sounding confident in his current situation.

That was the one thing about the mining syndicates, and more specifically the Ateris Mining Corporation, as it was known on Earth: they always pulled the strings in the background. While Ran was not completely ready for the Alurian disinterest in taking care of him after the destruction of the Fleet's newest warships, he always knew to have a plan and, as with anything in deep space, not to trust anyone or anything.

The Alurian radar officer clicked several more buttons on his station, adjusting the signal. He was simply called Lashet. His father worked for the Ateris clan, and his father before that. It wasn't a choice, rather just what you did in his family, which he had not seen in fifteen long, grueling years.

"It's one of the Earther vessels. The USF *Murphy*," Lashet replied, turning toward the quickly sharpening sector radar image forming on the large screen in front of the assembled crew.

Ran leaned forward, still calm and collected. His backup plan was simple. In the event of any issues, he would simply take the mining operation on what was now known as Asher offline. This also included destroying most of its surface population and any other possible threats to the system that the Ateris syndicate had promised the man once he had completed his mission.

Looking at the forming image on the screen, he was quickly realizing that in order to complete that mission, he would have to destroy the *Murphy* and its crew. The Alurian situation would have to wait and would likely be handled through political avenues between the two parties.

For the most part, Ran and the Ateris syndicate had a very good idea of the why and what the Alurians were up to. In many ways, this had been a determining factor in his final decision in destroying the Fleet's prized ships. This mission was supposed to be his final rite of passage before getting an entire system.

"Do we have a link with any of the planetside systems yet beside comms?" Ran inquired thoughtfully.

Lashet paused. "Not yet, sir. That will likely take another sensor relay." The Alurian smashed several more buttons before following up. "It will likely take another day.

"I want full access to the mining ships' subsystems when available. It's time to handle two situations at once," Ran noted, and Lashet again turned to him.

"Should we send a message to the system leader?"

"I would like to get things situated first before sending a full report. Let them know we are here and are repairing our sensor relays."

Lashet stayed focused on the Alurian loyalist. In the Syndicate, while rank was important, Ran was still a general outsider compared to many of the other older families, even though he still held a significant title. Ran said, "I want to align our plans first. That includes destroying the *Murphy*, which we don't have a full status report on, and cut off the Alurians' main operation on the planet until they understand the weight of our partnership."

Satisfied with this further explanation, Lashet turned back to his panel and sent out the initial message. Ran leaned back, taking in the situation.

Not only did he have aspirations with the Ateris syndicate, he was also certain his actions would somehow make it back to the Fleet, since the *Murphy* had survived the ambush. That was the one thing he didn't want to have happen. This meant he would not only lose a valuable line of intel and operations with the Fleet, and subsequently the Federation, but also be committed to his path with the Syndicate.

Ran considered the man that commanded the USF *Murphy*. He knew how pragmatic now-Colonel Dailey was. At one point, he had even considered having something happen to his transport after leaving the meeting aboard the *Brightstar*, something he was now regretting not doing.

Upon additional thought, regret was something he did not have time for nor was accustomed to. It was a weakness and one he was very aware of. Years in special operations units had trained the leader to keep these types of emotions at bay. It had also trained him to not underestimate wildcard soldiers like Dailey. The man had proven time and time again, against all odds, to prevail.

Ran was almost certain Dailey was overhead, working out a way to not only take on the entire Alurian military but solve the puzzle likely unfolding on the planet's surface.

Cutting off Ran's train of thought, a rigid woman known as Derrisa Monvet walked in with her hands pinned behind her back, also wearing senior Syndicate member rank. She was known as an administrator, a trusted and often feared position within the mining organization that was in charge of the sector's profits. From a human family, she had grown up on a mining planet, eventually working her way up inside Ateris.

"I hear the sensor relays are coming back online," she asked in the form of a statement.

"Yes," Lashet answered as Ran stood up.

"Derrisa." Ran used her first name as a way of not submitting to her position. "We have sent a message about our current situation to the system leader. I want to talk with you about a few things."

"Proceed," she stated flatly. Ran grinned, the skin on his face stretching.

"I want a report on the projected profits for the planetside transition to surface mining. It is my understanding that's on the docket for the next cycle?"

"Yes, correct," Derrisa replied, letting her hands fall to her side. This was her bailiwick and the one thing she took joy in discussing. Anything outside of that was met with the icy-cold shoulder of an outer-band ice planet.

She walked in front of the operations center now standing in front of Ran. "So, why the inquiry about profits?"

"Good question. From the way I see things, the Alurian command doesn't seem to be interested in supporting what is happening in this sector other than receiving their deliveries. The damage to this station, the transition to surface mining, the situation we still have to deal with," Ran said, pointing at the silhouette of the *Murphy* on the display screen. The one thing their single sensor relay array couldn't see was the *Scarecrow*.

"It's all going to cost. The Alurians will look at it as a wash after losing what looks to be a handful of their destroyers when taking out the *Asher* and the *Brightstar*." Ran wasn't explaining the situation; he was working to get Derrisa's support.

"You want to stop shipments until the Alurians agree to pay for the repairs to this station and what?" Derrisa asked quickly. Ran was hitting all the right talking points for the person in charge of the sector's finances, something that was easy to overlook in deep space.

"And the transition to surface mining. I know it's a ways out, but I'm starting to think they forget what forges the flame." Ran smirked and Derrisa actually grinned.

"You can stop bullshitting me, if it's my support you want. I will agree to your efforts in order to sustain our continued success and growth."

Ran nodded, and Derrisa's grin quickly went back into hiding.

"Lashet," Ran growled, satisfied with the transaction. "Send a relay team to the surface with one of our backup transorbital satellites. Have them prepare a simple message to transmit in the event any gates are opened."

The tactic was simple: in the event the gate was opened anywhere within reasonable distance of the planet, the relay satellite would send a focused laser beam directly in and through the event horizon, pushing out the communication as if the receiving party was on the other side of the planet. The message would be sent in a nanosecond.

Lashet paused while Ran fully calculated the message. "Let them know that we have found the source related to the recent disruptions in our sector. Advise them of the high probability the source is likely heading to the armada depot space station. Follow this up with a quick disposition of our current capabilities. This will likely force them to actually look into why they are missing several drone destroyers and invest in our continued success."

CHAPTER 29

THE CALM BEFORE THE STORM

Chief Engineering Officer Junior Lieutenant Barry Hontz's Irish voice echoed as Dailey stood in front of the panel overlooking the glowing gate drive with a confused look on his face. "Say that again?" the *Murphy*'s captain asked slowly at the same time that Ensign Barthelo worked to hold down a smirk.

"He is insisting we call the newly installed AI on the *Scarecrow* the Humanlike Autonomous Machine," Hontz affirmed, struggling to sound serious.

Dailey glanced at Bellman, who simply shrugged. "He wants to call the AI Albert reprogrammed and installed on the cargo ship... the HAM?"

"Yes, sir. That about sums it up," Hontz finished as the proud Alurian war hound strutted around the corner.

"Sparky, we don't have time for this," Dailey huffed out, and the dog simply plopped down on its hind legs.

A round of translated chuffs told Dailey the argument would be futile. "My ship, my rules."

Bellman spoke up, ending the brief conversation. "Albert said it was fitting and reprogrammed it already to respond to the name HAM. Anyway. The drive is online and ready to test."

"Albert, I know you're listening. Are we ready? The clock's ticking," Dailey said, trying not to look at Sparky as his tongue lightly drooped from his mouth.

Over the past twenty-four hours, Dailey hadn't been able to rest. The eerie quiet of undisturbed space had kept the man's nerves on high alert. As for the rest of the crew, they were doing the complete opposite.

After getting geared up and manning their battle stations, the crew of the *Murphy* had been ordered to stand down and rest. This included pilots sleeping in their attack fighters in the drop bay, while the Rangers simply drooled in their various armored suits.

"Oh, hey. Yes, we are absolutely ready. It should only take a few minutes to test the system," Albert chimed in. "By the way, I'm also done doing all that heavy lifting, so I am freed up to do whatever. If that includes watching reruns of Solarian milking races or finishing my body, count me in."

The notion that an AI even knew what Solarian milking races were or even stated it out loud meant Albert was making a point. While Albert had kept some of the eager members of the engineering team busy working on the gate drive, he had also conveniently figured out a way to free up two of them to work on the remaining scraps from the Alurian battle droids.

"A promise is a promise. Let's get this done first, then take those baby steps," Dailey noted, and Albert, currently sitting on a console panel, shifted to an off-putting, vomit-like shade of green.

"Deal. All we need to do is generate enough power to open a single nanoparticle of the gate resonance, and we should be good," Albert robustly stated.

"And that will be enough to tell if a full ship will work how?" Dailey drawled out, getting used to conversations with Albert.

"It doesn't matter if we are the size of a Moshan bulge or as small as a hair follicle. It all works the same. Since the *Murphy* has a fully charged and operational hyperdrive, we have enough to gate the ship twice before having to do some serious recharging. Meaning our weapons and shielding capabilities would be degraded if we attempted more."

"You need to lay off the adult content. Especially the weird Moshan stuff," Dailey quickly suggested, being distracted by the thought.

"To be transparent, Solarians and Moshans are not as alien as you think. Anywho, once I confirm we are good, we can be underway. That means we are ready three hours, forty-two minutes, and fifty-five, no, four, no three… seconds early," Albert concluded.

"Perfect. As long as the test does not affect this ship, you are authorized to move forward. You need to notify Pearl first," Dailey instructed. Albert didn't respond, telling him he was following orders.

"Done," Albert noted, and Dailey turned.

"Prepare the crew —" Albert cut him off.

"No. I mean I told Pearl and conducted the test. Done. We are good to go. There was a slight resonance blip during the test, but that was likely interference from the ship's projectors getting used to the third arm we have sewn on. Meaning we are three hours, forty-one minutes, and twenty-two, no, one—" Dailey cut him off, turning to Sparky.

"Captain Sparky," he said, playing the part, "I need you to clear the *Scarecrow* and report back to the bridge of the *Murphy* as soon as every soul is off."

Sparky, in an odd floppy salute, stood up, shaking his ears before running off.

"They grow up so fast," Albert stated. Bellman and Dailey both groaned.

"You have only known each other for a couple of weeks." Dailey huffed, then immediately left for the bridge.

Dailey walked to the viewport overlooking the front of the *Murphy*. Taking a deep breath, the man took in the serene quietness of the situation, knowing the scramble that was soon to follow would quickly disrupt the dreamlike calmness.

"Pearl, please bring the ship to full alert. Once we confirm the *Scarecrow* has been fully evacuated, get us underway," Dailey ordered, letting his hands loose from behind his back, turning to take his rightful seat in the button-adorned captain's chair.

It was at that time that First Sergeant Becket entered the bridge. His partially configured armor dissipated as he stopped beside Specialist Kline's targeting station. "You ready for this, son?" he asked the young specialist, who turned, giving an eager smile.

"Yes, First Sergeant. If this means I get to do something that no other targeting specialist in the fleet has ever done, well… that's just badass, First Sergeant." Even though Specialist Kline was motivated, there was also a light hint of nervousness tracing through his words.

Becket smiled as years of wisdom flowed from his body. "You know, it's always good to be a little nervous before you get into a fight, which I guarantee we are about to do. Stay frosty and remember, *To the Edge*."

The statement garnered a wave of nostalgia from the bridge's crew; they all stood up, echoing the once-famed motto. "TO THE EDGE!"

After the brief motivational pep talk, Becket walked to Dailey, who was intently looking over all the different platoon and section status reports. "How are the Rangers?" Dailey asked without looking over.

"Ready to go, sir. The drop ship just docked coming back from Asher. We were able to convince Vax to stay planetside and start working on plans to go to the upper levels and see what exactly is in all those buildings. This also includes coming up with a way to convince the rest of the megacity's inhabitants of the truth of their current situation."

"That's gonna take some time, but I think we have the right people on it. Lieutenant McAlister and Master Sergeant Walker will have their hands full."

Albert chose that very moment to break into the conversation. "'Sup, dudes!" he said

Dailey shook his head. "Let me guess: mid-1980s surfer movies?"

"Close enough. Just thought you would like to know the *Scarecrow* is cleared. Sparky is in the engineering section with Bellman, Ensign Barthelo, and Chief Engineering Officer Hontz. I did have to set up a transponder for Sparky so he could talk to HAM, which he has proclaimed as second-in-command of his kingdom. Don't ask."

"I wasn't going to, but thanks for the update. How are all the ship's systems?" Dailey followed up after finally letting Albert have access to the ship's overall subsystems. In truth, Albert had already figured out a way to do this via an electrical outlet next to the coffeemaker in the engineering section.

"Perfect, now that I have had some time to do some slight tweaking. I would say we are as ready as we ever will be."

"Albert," Pearl interrupted. "Can you please explain to the captain the slight shift in return protocol?"

"Certainly. I was able to finally program an immediate gate return function into the system. All Pearl has to do is hit the now-flashing red button. It will activate a gate and immediately navigate us through it."

Dailey looked at Pearl for further guidance. "Sir, in case something happens and we cannot manually return, this will allow us to do so automatically. Albert can do it as well, but the ship is in a sense preprogrammed to do this. We couldn't figure it out until this morning. Something to do with Hontz threatening to turn Albert into a toaster for messing with the ship's navigational system interface with the hyper- and gate drive."

Albert cut in. "We are good now. He has downgraded the threat to a paperweight, so I believed the risk is within acceptable parameters to go ahead and make those changes. Oh, plus, I gave him one of those blinky red buttons also."

This made both Dailey and Becket grin, knowing how protective Hontz was of the ship's main systems. One of the many reasons they had kept him on their team.

Jen came over the radio, timing it perfectly. "Viper Six, this is Angel Six; our wings are set and ready."

"Thank you, Lieutenant Brax," Dailey replied. This was the last thing he needed to hear, even though he had already checked the unit's status report. He always liked the verbal heads-up.

"Engage gate drive," Dailey ordered, and Becket turned and exited the bridge.

As promised, a shimmering ripple waved in front of the *Murphy*, as if space was a blanket on the beach and somebody had just picked it up, slowly shaking all the sand off of it.

The gentle hum of the ship's engines started pushing the *Murphy* slowly forward, and Dailey nervously glanced at the status screen showing both vessels. The cargo ship now under the control of Albert, via its newly re-programmed AI, the HAM, was neatly connected to the hull on the port side of the ship. As soon as they reached their destination, the ship would detach with a significant shove, heading directly toward the massive station's cargo-unloading bays.

The additional distance included in their plan from the station was from the simple thought of staying out of arm's reach of the massive batteries of kiss-my-ass plasma cannons. This also included whatever other protruding weapon system would likely greet them. As soon as the *Murphy* crossed out of the gate, Fourth Foot was set to leave the warm embrace of the ship's drop bay as an initial line of defense in case of any issues with the *Scarecrow*.

"All systems are A-OK," Albert reported, not giving anyone else a chance. "Getting a little interference but nothing that did not align with the initial test."

"You need to work on your bedside manners," Dailey suggested just as the ship started vibrating with the familiar resonance they had experienced before. Doing his due diligence, he had taken the time to fully explain what to expect, including the odd, still quiet during the very brief time they would be traveling through the gate.

"Aaaaaaaand done. We are through the initial event horizon. All systems are showing functional. Our main core reactor as well as hyper thrusters are at eighty-five percent. Precisely as projected," Albert sang in an odd, cheesy, power-ballad voice.

Instead of cheers of celebration of what could be called the first successful gate through a wormhole to another galaxy, still silence greeted Colonel Dailey's ears. The rest of the crew was significantly more anxious than he had previously assumed.

"It will stay like this for a little while until we get to the other side," Dailey noted as Albert interrupted him.

"If you want to get technical, there is no other side." Seeing the scowl lightly forming on Dailey's face told Albert he was pushing the limits of his patience. "Would anyone like to play some trivia?"

The bridge crew barked out a resounding "NO!" so Albert started humming an odd mix of old-school techno music and what the Solarians considered country music. This was nothing more than a bunch of low, swooning notes all tied together sounding like an overly drunk bagpipe player about to hit the floor after their last drink.

CHAPTER 30

BREATHE

Muted conversations and anxious hands were quickly interrupted as the *Murphy* began the familiar vibration Dailey had experienced upon previously entering a gate. Every single Ranger either on board or already latched on to the attack fighters were doing the simple task of checking their ammunition status on their HUD, looking down to ensure whatever weapon they were holding was in fact ready to go.

Over the decades and centuries, modern weapons had made this excruciatingly simple for soldiers, be it Rangers, everyday infantry, or someone as noncombative as a line cook to have a basic understanding of their weapon system and how to use it.

If the little flashy light was green, you were about to get mean. If the little flashy was red, you better duck your head. The phrase was as simple as it came, but spoke volumes.

It was simple math: if the light was green, all you had to do was pull the trigger and point in the general direction of whatever headache-inducing problem was at the other end of the weapon's barrel. The only difference between the weapons the Rangers utilized and regular everyday Fleet personnel was the extreme specialization used in the unit, such as Bertha.

"We have cleared the gate," Albert started. "All systems are fully functional; all sensor data will be online within thirty seconds. Way to go, me."

Dailey was surprised how much he had been waiting for Albert to speak those very words. "No change; once we get a good read out of the area and we're clear, we release the *Scarecrow*."

"Viper Six, this is Angel Six. We are ready to go on your mark. All Fourth Foot assets are on standby," Jen commented. Lieutenant Dasher's voice was the next to spring up.

"Viper Six, this is Scout One. We are ready for release," Dasher noted. The familiar cadence of his often laid-back tone was now completely gone.

"Specialist Kline. As soon as the sensors are online, get everything laid out on the main screen," Pearl noted, and Dailey stood up and walked toward the forward viewport. While the man trusted sensors, he especially trusted what his own eyes could see.

"Sir?" Pearl asked, and Dailey let out a breath he had been holding since standing up from the con.

"Something's not right. Even though we're significantly further away than I was last time, it's too quiet. There were ships everywhere, all over the sector," Dailey noted, followed by King cutting in.

"Everything seems to be clear, sir. We've launched two stealth satellites forward. They're showing a handful of cargo ships and several security drones. This matches the data that Albert previously provided."

Albert didn't give the rest of the humans and Solarians on the bridge enough time to compute the shapes now materializing out of the black void. Every alarm on the ship blared to life as if indicating the end of the world was near.

There, in front of the *Murphy*, one, two, no, three full star destroyers emerged from whatever visual- and radar-related stealth tech they had engaged. Unlike most of their previous encounters, these were a combination of artificial intelligence and crewed ships.

Before any other words were spoken, Pearl had already pressed the red flashing button on the navigation panel, only to find it not working. "Albert!" Pearl barked. "The gate drive isn't activating."

Dailey barely had seconds to decide. "Scout One, launch" was the simple order given. They would need all the time they could to figure out how to either accomplish their mission or return to Asher.

Specialist Kline quickly activated the targeting displays, while the two weapon specialists sitting in front of Dailey started scrambling as if somebody had dropped a bag of diamonds on the control panels in front of them. The main viewscreen lit up with targets while the ship's thrusters activated just in time to avoid what appeared to be a salvo of plasma rockets shooting directly at the *Murphy*.

One of the weapon specialists activated chaffing countermeasure pods, redirecting several of the plasma rockets in the opposite direction at the exact same time that several attack fighters and Rangers from Fourth Foot were leaving the drop bay.

Dailey could feel a light vibration in his foot when one of the plasma rockets hit the exposed underbelly of the ship, his ship. "Status," Dailey barked as the *Murphy*'s massive plasma cannons lurched to life, slamming two beams directly into the closest destroyer as it also turned, exposing its main weapon system.

A brilliant flash of light indicated that the plasma cannons had smashed into the destroyer's own weapon systems just as they were activating, generating a direct hit. This was followed by that same destroyer launching another volley of what appeared to be seeking plasma rockets.

Again, the targeting team released countermeasures, this time intercepting the rockets as the chaffing system smartly exploded instead of taking the rockets on a game of chase.

"Where's our attack fighters?" Dailey barked, this time louder.

Albert answered this time. "One of the initial volleys of plasma rockets made it through our shielding and defense systems. It was a direct hit on the far side of the drop bay."

Dailey started doing the math in his head. That was the very section Fourth Foot called home in the drop bay. The attack fighter's thrusters had likely gained the attention of a plasma rocket, as well as finding the gap in the shielding system allowing the Rangers to exit the drop bay. The thought slammed into Dailey's face like a sock full of rocks.

"With your permission, I would like to take over the main laser cannons and missile pods. The targeting and weapon-systems team has their hands full with the plasma cannons," Albert requested with none of his usual bravado.

Dailey paused, glancing down at the kill switch Bellman and Hontz had installed prior to leaving. In the event Albert decided to take matters into his own hands, this would effectively cut all ties the AI had with the ship.

"Make them suffer," Dailey instructed, standing up. "Viper Five, status?"

"Sir, all platoons are ready to launch that are capable. On your word."

Dailey didn't hesitate to respond. "Go." With that, a flurry of angry bees swarmed from the underbelly of the *Murphy* in all directions.

In the short amount of time they had been engaged, which by that point had almost been an entire minute, the platoons had already been given their respective targets. First Foot and two additional attack fighters were set to engage the destroyer that was consistently launching plasma rockets at an alarming rate.

Second Foot was sent to engage the third destroyer that was oddly hanging back in the wings. This likely meant that there was a command element on board, and sending Second Platoon made the most sense, as they carried the most firepower. The old saying to cut off the head of the snake was indeed true, especially during space combat.

As for Third Foot, they were set to engage the destroyer now turning away from the fight, hiding its exposed main cannon systems, which were now severely damaged. At the same time this happened, the far destroyer that was staying out of the fight, as well as the one launching rockets, also decided it was time to release their own attack fighters in a collision of space dogfighting. The once-calm dark of space was now lit up in a bloom of flashes and various colors from laser and plasma fire.

The one immediate thing that Dailey noted was the lack of armored space infantry. The one thing the Alurians were known for was their space mechs. The lack of their presence was an extremely telling sign that they had likely thrown whatever kitchen sink was available at the *Murphy*.

Not only did the Alurians know they were coming, but they knew exactly where and when. Unfortunately for Dailey and the crew, the message that General Ran had sent had indeed made its way to the station. It had been the blip that Albert mentioned on their initial test, but it also ended up telling everyone exactly where they were going through and the exact location they would be coming out.

"Albert, what's the status of our gate drive?" Dailey asked. Albert was slow to respond, clearly focused on the ship's weapon system as an entire flurry of missile pods and laser projectors focused on the alluring and primary offensive destroyer.

Blue and purple spatters of deflected laser fire from the destroyer's deflector shields were clearly frustrating Albert, and Dailey spotted several missiles finally hitting the ship in an area he assumed was the bridge.

"There, now I can talk. They have some kind of field inhibitor in place, technology that I am neither familiar with nor capable of doing anything about. My recommendation is to destroy these three ships and charlie mike," Albert replied, almost sounding like a modulated version of John Wayne.

The term *charlie mike* was a simple military abbreviation for continue mission. It always bothered Dailey that people could say continue mission just as easily as they could state charlie mike.

"Bellman," Dailey barked over the internal comms system. "We are initiating the release of the *Scarecrow*. I know the rest of the engineering team is busy right now; can you confirm that we are a go?"

"I could've told you that, boss," Albert replied, then Bellman's voice came back over the comm.

"Yes, sir," Bellman replied. This was the first time in the history of the creation of man that Bellman had actually addressed Dailey as sir.

"Release the package," Dailey instructed, followed by a bunch of hammering chuffs and barks responding over the comms system.

"Not now, Sparky," Dailey noted as the Alurian war hound's translation finally came through for everyone to hear.

"Permission granted. You can use my ship. I will let the HAM know."

Pearl turned to Colonel Dailey with a confused look on her face, and Albert added his two cents' worth. "For some reason, the HAM only takes orders from Sparky. No clue how that—"

Dailey quickly cut him off as the ship lurched forward under full orbital thrusters, just in time to barely avoid a barrage of plasma cannon fire. Jen came over the comms just as the destroyer to the starboard side of the *Murphy* lit up like an overpriced fireworks display.

"Destroyer two is out of the fight. We are shifting our primary engagement to the command vessel." It wasn't that she was asking for permission or guidance; she was telling the commander exactly what she was doing, directing the Rangers attached to her attack wing.

The *Murphy* again rocked as a hit from one of the remaining destroyer's plasma cannons slammed into the forward stabilizer thrusters under the ship used for suborbital maneuvering. This was also the thruster system used to maneuver the ship on a dime while in space combat.

Another precise and automated volley of missile pods, including direct laser fire from Albert, once again whistled through space, surprising Dailey by the sheer amount of violence the *Murphy* was capable of. This time, the primary attacking destroyer did something unexpected, pushing its aft thrusters into gear, heading directly toward the *Murphy*. This included flying directly into First and Second Foot's quickly dwindling dogfight.

It hadn't taken much for Becket and the other platoon leaders to quickly understand they were fighting a significantly inexperienced and inferior force. While this was the case, they were still taking not only heavy damage to the attack wing but casualties as well.

"That's not good," Albert exclaimed as the destroyer he had just fired upon now bore down on them; space its forward deflector shield swatted off the primary onslaught of laser and missile fire the AI was throwing at it.

Luckily for the *Scarecrow*, this maneuver opened a direct line of travel, and it shot forward under full thrust. Light random laser fire from the enemy ship's attack fighters sparked, but they were quickly ignored by the cargo ship's mix of an overly armored exterior and the deflector shields, which were now fully operational and likely being directed by the one and only HAM.

"Is anything following the *Scarecrow*?" Dailey asked, no longer calling it the package.

"No, sir! It's clear of the initial ships. As long as it stays on full thrust, it should clear most the fighting in a few minutes," Kline yelled louder than needed from his station as sweat peppered his face, quickly being removed by another wipe of his sleeve.

Seconds often felt like hours in combat; time slows to an agonizing pace, while the world around everyone speeds up. Dailey was starting to focus on the mission and the mission only. Looking out the viewport, he could clearly make out dozens of armored Rangers on the hull of the closest remaining enemy ship.

CHAPTER 31
STRETCHED

The bridge of the command Alurian destroyer Nova Crusader.

Supreme Commander Zara Kell slammed his fist on the console in front of him as his main attack destroyer, the *Starfire*, flew into thousands of pieces, scattering across the cosmos like charred embers. "Engage proton cannon."

The gruff Alurian senior officer had been assigned to the Alurian outer-rim ship-building station some three years earlier, contributing to the man's overall poor attitude toward pretty much everything. Loosing several of his destroyers in such a short amount of time was amplifying the Alurian's shit-poor attitude to eleven.

As for the proton cannon attached to the belly of the *Nova Crusader*, this was the only such proton weapon in the sector. With a fully charged direct hit, it could take out most frigate-sized and larger ships in one go.

"Sir, it will take four minutes to charge the proton cannon," an also stressed Alurian responded, knowing the likelihood of Supreme Commander Zara Kell shooting him in the back.

The truth of the matter was, while General Ran's message had indeed reached its target, the one thing it was not able to do was get the timing right. While they had been able to send a message during the *Murphy*'s passage through the gate, it hadn't given the three destroyers assigned to the sector time to react.

A brilliant flash caught Kell's attention as the *Aurora Tempest*, led by one his most competent and aggressive commanders, Xalax the Magnificent per the least-unreasonable translation, turned directly toward the oncoming Federation frigate also known as the USF *Murphy*. Xalax had engaged full thrusters.

A halo of missile and plasma-cannon fire was wrapping around the *Aurora Tempest* in a cascade of sparks and large, colorful blasts from the ship's deflector shields. As Dailey had already figured out, if the captain of the oncoming Alurian ship wasn't able to go toe-to-toe with the *Murphy*, they would ram that toe right up their opponents' noses.

The rough yet smoother voice of a female officer spoke up next. "Sir, there is a cargo ship that has just left the sector. It appeared to be attached to the enemy vessel. It checks out as a material transport ship."

Commander Zara Kell weighed his options as the first wave of Third Platoon attack fighters led by Jen unleased every forward weapon system on board. Kinetic rockets, laser fire, and a spattering of bullets hammered the area around the ship's bridge.

At the same time, two squads' worth of Rangers detached from their ship's wings, slamming down hard on the enemy vessel's deck and going right to work.

On one side, a specialist drilled what looked like an inch-wide hole, then another Ranger stepped forward and dropped a compact fission shaped charge inside the hole.

Kell again weighed his quickly disappearing options, and a brilliant flash made him wince. It wasn't the *Aurora Tempest*'s thrusters this time but rather its main engine pods detonating. Whoever was commanding the ship in front of them had done the impossible, Kell thought, starting to lose focus on the task at hand.

Between the older destroyers and lack of support from his main command, Kell's rage started boiling over, and he turned. "Are there any life-forms in that cargo ship?"

The woman turned, quickly responding. "No, it was supposed to have two escorts from the planet, which were pulled at the last minute."

Nodding, Kell picked up the metal wired communicator resembling an old-style handheld like truckers used, and keyed the side of it. "This is Supreme Commander Zara Kell. We're one sector away, taking heavy losses.

Be advised there is a cargo ship, call space sign AXRE4, heading to offload. Be advised it's armed."

"Did you say you are under attack?" a human voice replied, surprised. Kell would not respond, knowing all the security officer in charge would have needed to do was pull up the sector tracking sensor map, which also happened to be the primary function of his usually dull job.

"Can you intercept?" the voice asked, and Kell squeezed the comms device in his hand so hard, it crumbled under the pressure like an empty tin can.

The *Nova Crusader* rocked, as several of its stabilizer thrusters had been destroyed, sending the ship literally listing on what was tracked as the plane, a navigational tracking tool much like altitude and direction all species used for course plotting.

"How can this be?" the ship's second-in-command asked, and Kell turned to him.

"The Enclave is about to learn a valuable lesson," Kell stated, referring to the lack of attention to the outer manufacturing stations.

"What's that?" the man asked as Kell turned.

"The humans are here, and they better wake up," were the last words the Alurian commander said before the entire bridge went out in a flash of finality.

Kell had sealed the fate of his ship when he ordered the proton cannon charged. The Alurian that carried out that order also knew what this meant as the green bar representing power to the defector shields dropped to an orangish amber.

An orange alert flashed inside one of Second Foot's heavy-weapons soldiers' HUD. The message was clear: the Alurian ship's deflector shields were now mysteriously compromised. Seeing this, the soldier didn't hesitate, thumbing the safety on the missile pods tucked neatly under his arm and attached by a pivot arm.

Within the blink of an eye, the Nova Ranger had launched a flurry of targeted ion missiles directly into the bridge's substructure just before a coordinated plasma rocket slammed into it seconds later from the attack fighter hovering dangerously close overhead. The combination was as lethal as it was practiced.

One of the main advantages the human-developed armor had, more specifically the armor worn by the soldiers of Second Foot, was its state-of-the-art targeting system taken from an Alurian mech mixed with recently developed human weapon-targeting systems.

This was followed with an electro analyzer supplied by the Moshans allowing the targeting system to detect weak spots in not only ships but soft targets as well, a lethal combination that the Federation and Fleet had chosen not to share outside of its protective bubble.

The ion missile effectively took out the bridge's structural support enough for the plasma rocket to rip through the ship's exterior like a hungry shark in a pool full of wounded fish. The plasma rocket simply went haywire inside the bridge, destroying everything in sight in blazing arcs of life-ending electricity.

Supreme Commander Zara Kell didn't even see the end, as it happened in the blink of an eye. The proximity alarms hadn't had time to activate in the short amount of time the Ranger had taken to act.

CHAPTER 32

A ROOM WITH A VIEW

I t's not getting any better," Albert blurted out as an alarm pinged on the viewscreen. "We need to get out of the way."

Pearl, without any further instruction, pushed the ship into a steep dive. A spatter of the destroyer's forward flak cannons, used to clear space debris, crackled on the forward hull of the *Murphy*.

Dailey trusted Pearl and let her maneuver the ship while silently calculating their next move, only to have Albert once again start talking. "If you let me do one of those unexpected things, I can make this all go away."

"And?" Dailey replied as he finally saw the command destroyer exploding in several blue bubbles as the ship's fusion tri-drive reactors exploded in the distance.

This was a rare and awe-inspiring sight, as the ships were specifically designed to flood and jettison in the event of terminal damage, preventing the reactors from going subnuclear. Something that was now causing another round of concerns for the *Murphy*'s commander, as one of the reactors clearly hadn't finished that process.

"Don't freak out. And as they say, hold on to your britches!" Albert proclaimed as Pearl and every other crew member aboard the *Murphy* lost control of their stations.

"Locked out!" Pearl exclaimed, while the already-ringing red alarms somehow driven by Albert found more ringing red alarms to add to the chaos.

In the background, the "Ride of the Valkyries" by Richard Wagner started blaring. Albert was letting it all hang out. An odd mix of concern and all-out hell-yeah curiosity took over Dailey as he looked at the kill switch he had had installed in the event Albert was to ever go rogue.

"Albert," Dailey started, finally realizing what the AI was doing as the *Murphy* was now directly facing the oncoming destroyer. "ALBERT!" he exclaimed just as the familiar shimmer of the gate drive being activated distorted the oncoming ship.

Several explosions from random attack fighters attacking the oncoming charging bull made the edges of the large section of shimmering space look on fire.

The AI followed up with a simple message to everything that could monitor a net tied to the *Murphy*: "Disengage and watch this."

Nerves started peaking as the battle was coming to a crescendo of combat-driven confusion.

"And done. We can all take a breath. Kline, you can excuse yourself and clean that up in your pantaloons," Albert noted as the music shut off as well as the alarms.

"What are pantaloons?" Kline grumbled to himself, knowing full well what Albert was talking about.

Within the blink of an eye, the oncoming destroyer had somehow disappeared. Dailey's hand hovered over the kill switch as Pearl cleared her throat, making a much-welcomed announcement: "I have control of the ship."

Dailey pulled his hand away as the bloom from the distant destroyer *Nova Crusader* continued disintegrating, illuminating the entire area surrounding the battle in a blue, glowing haze. The second destroyer, the *Starfire*, floated in space. Unlike its command ship, the *Starfire* resembled thousands of floating embers in space, as if looking for a way to pull itself back together.

"I need a status report on the *Scarecrow* and the drop bay. Albert… explain," Dailey commanded as he walked over to the display panel. "Show drop bay two now."

Pearl shook her head and Dailey turned back to the screen just as Albert started back up. "Comms should be back online in three, two, and…"

Jen and Becket's voices erupted from the overhead comms in a garbled combination of status reports, requests for additional ships, and medical recovery assets. This mostly consisted of the drop ships, as well as one automated set of scavenger pods. Once activated, the pods would attach to whatever vehicle was targeted and guide them safely back to the ship.

"Pearl, I need you to handle this. I'm heading to the drop bay. King, I need you to clean that radio chatter up," Dailey ordered, immediately followed by him leaving the bridge.

Albert cleared his throat. "Excuse me. You may want to let the medical team get finished first."

Dailey paused in front of the main lift that went directly to the lower levels. "What aren't you telling me?"

"I don't know how you say it, but I have seen this in several of your movies and stories. It's not a good situation."

"Is the electromagnetic field up?"

"Not yet. I had to close the drop bay and also close the main outer blast doors. The energy was used to gate that destroyer away."

"Where did you gate it to?" Dailey followed up, walking into the lift.

"I don't know precisely, but I would guess somewhere very close to the sun that supports Asher," Albert replied, not telling the entire story.

"You sent the thing into the sun, didn't you?"

"Close enough. You did say to make them suffer."

Dailey nodded, understanding Albert had done as requested.

Medical Officer Casey Franklin met Dailey at the lift, clearly having been notified by Albert. "Sir," she quickly started, "I don't think you need to be in the bay."

"That's precisely why I need to be here," Dailey responded as she moved out of the way, motioning for one of her nurses to open the main entrance to the bay.

In front of Dailey lay a mangled and unrecognizable scene. The *Murphy* had two main drop bays, each shared by two platoons. Looking up, he immediately noticed most if not all the attack fighters for Third Foot had made it out, likely leaving after the initial impact.

The other half of the space in front of him looked as if it had melted into the ship's main hull, followed by a blazing fire that the *Murphy*'s system had quickly extinguished through the use of fire-retardant foam that covered most of the bay's surface. Fourth Foot's entire section of the bay was unrecognizable as Dailey looked down at the line of white thermal blankets covering the bodies lying on the floor.

While he was capable of unfathomable violence, having sent countless souls to their end, whatever that may be, seeing his own in this state infuriated the man to a point of calm.

"How many?" Dailey asked, not flinching as he continued to stare.

She reached into her pocket and pulled out the mangled pair of Lieutenant Dasher's trademark sunglasses, handing them to Dailey. "He and his pilot tried to fly into the rocket to mitigate the damage. It all happened so fast. Dasher was attached to the wing of his fighter and immediately slung against the back wall, then vaporized inside his armor. He opened his face shield to try and breathe, from what I can tell. I found these lying on the ground."

She spoke with no emotion. In most cases, the medical team would be scrambling at a lightning-fast pace. Dailey had noticed her stilling calm when she greeted him. This wasn't a medical operation but rather an attempt to identify and fully recover the fallen' s bodies.

"How many?" Dasher again asked.

"Dasher, his pilot, and a full squad. The rest were not attached to any of the attack fighters and were running a few seconds behind, still in their platoon's armor locker. Two of the other attack fighters were already outside the ship. This is about as best-case a scenario as we could get in this situation," Franklin answered calmly.

"Where is the rest of the platoon now?" Dailey asked quickly as Albert responded.

"According to the transponder data we just received, they are with Third Foot, working with Master Sergeant Janix. They tried to help here, and as soon as the medical team arrived, they realized there was nothing else they could do, so they joined the fight."

"Albert, send Becket a message through his HUD, something only he can see. Let him know the situation with Fourth Foot. I'm heading back to the bridge. Oh, and has anyone seen Sparky?"

Albert's lack of response told Dailey that Sparky was likely up to something he wouldn't approve of. The man found the weird, quickly forming bond between Albert and the Alurian war hound odd. It was a likely recipe for disaster, or trouble at least.

"Shit, Albert… tell me now, or I'll pull that plug and attach you to a dishwasher."

Albert considered this projected punishment as he always did, landing on the threat not being worth it, having a thing about water. "He sort of did that thing he does, just showing up, and is on board the *Scarecrow*."

"What?" Dailey asked, then turned to head back to the bridge before addressing Franklin. "Whatever you need, let me know. We will figure this out when we are done."

"King!" Dailey barked as he walked back onto the bridge. "Put the *Scarecrow* on an open channel. Albert, I would like to see that view cam we mounted on the bridge.

After a few short seconds, an audible hum as well as a live feed of the one and only Sparky sitting in his full armor atop the ship's bland commander's chair materialized. While in full armor, the Alurian war hound had to sit straight up instead of his usual slumped-over hind legs, where he frequently laughed at people having to look at his space bits when talking to him.

"Sparky, I need you to explain yourself," Dailey commanded as he looked up to see several attack fighters and Rangers flying over the ship's forward hull.

This surprised Sparky, and he jumped, lightly chuffing several times. Albert translated the message for the entire bridge, as he was getting accustomed to.

"Backup plan for the ham," Sparky said, while Dailey clicked his readout panel, shifting the view from the odd now-calm of the battle to the massive station housing an entire armada of almost if not fully completed ships.

"We don't need a backup plan," Dailey assured him, just as Albert cut in.

"Well, things got a little sketchy during all that mess. It appears… Well, I'll just show you," Albert insisted, switching the view to the familiar angle afforded the *Scarecrow*'s forward cameras.

It took Dailey several seconds to figure out what he was looking at. Bright flashes zipped in all directions, while the massive flash of plasma cannons scorched the space around the *Scarecrow*. Every weapon system that could target the small cargo ship was showing up to the all-you-can-eat buffet now approaching.

Kline, without saying a word, redirected all available sensors to the area, feeling more at ease with their immediate situation.

"How is the ship still holding together?" Pearl asked before Dailey could get the question out.

"Well, the *Scarecrow* by itself doesn't have enough power to fully charge its deflector shields. But now it does," Albert drawled out as if what he was saying was completely normal.

"You're saying Sparky is doing that power thing but to the entire ship?" Dailey asked, stunned by not only the bravery of the dog but the understanding of just how much power the ham-loving, often publicly offensive dog was. This was the absolute reason he had grown so close to the animal who was quickly becoming not just a mascot or pet but one of the crew.

"Yup. Bingo. Let's just say when he does his little power thing, the video feed and comms will go out for a few seconds. He, with the help of yours truly, has overcharged the forward deflector shields. With nothing else floating around out there, there's no reason to protect the hind end of the ship."

Dailey squinted, seeing Sparky lightly grin and already working to keep his tongue from hanging out of his mouth, attempting to look the proper part of a ship's captain.

Then the real question hit the *Murphy*'s commander. He had lost too much, too many, and was not willing to sacrifice another cell of one of his crew members. This was on Dailey, and he knew he would carry the weight; he always did.

"How are we getting him back?" Dailey asked without reservation. It wasn't a question but an order that was open for suggestions.

"Sir," Kline interrupted. "Albert has patched us through to the *Scarecrow*'s systems. We can see the condition and power levels for the ship." He paused, getting in the first real set of sensor data. "It appears the *Scarecrow* is still holding back, right out of targeting range from those large plasma cannons."

Letting out a breath, Dailey refocused on the mission at hand. Thoughts of the lost souls now scattered across the cosmos would have to wait and be mourned and celebrated later.

A schematic of the *Scarecrow* sprang to life on the small console beside Dailey. The front of the ship displayed an almost-yellow orange, while the cargo vessel's stern was a steady light green. In the center, a combination of the two colors met over the small yet steadfast bridge.

Zooming in on the structure, Dailey immediately noticed a reddish area on the *Scarecrow*'s underbelly. Its low-hanging cargo-release bay was taking damage. To the right of the schematic was a power meter for both the shields and the thrusters, showing a yellowing green. From everything Dailey could tell, the ship was still fully functional.

"Can you do that to this ship?" Dailey asked Albert, who hummed lightly.

"Hmm, not precisely, but over time, it's possible. Remember, my magic lies in combining tech to do crazy new things, not making it up."

"Fair enough," Dailey replied, still working through the overall situation, including getting Sparky back on board the *Murphy* in one piece. "Viper Five, this is Viper Six."

There was a pause as Becket finally replied. "Go ahead."

"Need you to report to the bridge. Might have a slight change in plans."

Becket replied with a simple "Roger."

CHAPTER 33

LIGHTING THE SPARK

You sure about that, sir?" Becket asked, then Albert, doing his usual thing, interjected himself directly into the middle of the conversation. "The *Scarecrow* could, in theory, if everything holds, stay in its current position for several hours before needing to back off. As noted, there has already been a twenty-five percent reduction in overall weapons being fired at dear old Uncle Sparky."

The point of the conversation was simple. While everything was good now, as soon as several of the massive, crushing plasma cannons actually hit the *Scarecrow*, all bets would be off. All they needed to do was deliver the warhead. If that meant only partially disabling the station, that was good enough, as far as Dailey was concerned.

Pearl pulled up the schematic of the cargo-release area they had previously scanned on their initial scouting mission, a phrase that was leaving a sour taste in Dailey's mouth after the loss of Dasher, one of the greatest and most headstrong scouts he had ever had the privilege of knowing.

"Sir," she started, charting out the danger zones mapped out by distance from the station. "Per our calculations—" Albert interrupted her by clearing his throat. "Per mostly Albert's calculations, the *Scarecrow*, under additional power, will be able to reach this band."

She pointed to an orange zone fifteen miles from the station. "Here, the targeting sensors will be able to land direct hits from the plasma cannons. The *Scarecrow* is currently fifty miles out and taking direct hits from them basically blind-firing automated laser pods."

"Okay, from there, how far does the ship have to travel to be too close for the plasma cannons to matter?"

Pearl pointed at the blueish line only a couple of miles off the station's surface. "They will likely not be able to or want to fire any closer than this line."

"Meaning…" Dailey said, and Jen leaned in, having arrived back on board and quickly made her way to the bridge.

"Meaning we need to work out a way to cover thirteen miles as fast as possible."

"Or cause a distraction," Dailey noted, having mentioned it before Pearl pulled up the chart. He sucked in a breath before laying out his thoughts. "Why can't we send a few remote-controlled attack fighters on the same path and confuse their targeting systems?"

Jen spoke up this time. "We could set them on autopilot."

"Or you could use those annoying salvage pods or whatever you call them. The subsystems on those things are unbelievably rude. The ones you have out there bringing our disabled ships back. Cocky little things."

"Good point," Dailey stated flatly.

"Duh," Albert responded, and the *Murphy*'s captain pointed at the picture of a dishwasher someone had printed out and taped to the front of Albert.

"We still need to get Sparky back," Dailey added, and Becket scratched his stubbled chin. Lines from his helmet lay embedded on his forehead and cheeks from the time spent fighting on the outer surface of the Alurian destroyers.

"Can't he do that thing? You know, where he just pops in and out of places?" Dailey followed up. The man hated talking about the subject, as it made him appear crazy when he brought it up.

"I can ask, but I'm thinking we get a fighter out there to pick him up. Have the *Scarecrow* move forward, with the fighters and salvage pods acting as distractions," Albert suggested.

The thing about space travel and combat was that fifteen nautical miles was the blink of an eye. It wasn't all about getting where you were going but making sure you stopped before slamming in and through whatever it was in front of you.

If this had been a hardened military base, the *Scarecrow* would have already been taken out by seeker missiles, not to mention an entire drone army of fighters. It was shocking, the lack of security, or the thought that no one would ever find the place.

It wasn't the destroyers now floating though space as if having been dropped in a blender but the lack of reinforcement and, for lack of a better term, an unstoppable enemy force.

Sparky let out a huff after Dailey relayed the entire plan. Looking around the cramped yet homely bridge of the *Scarecrow*, the Alurian war hound jumped down, nosing into the pile of provisions Thron had placed on the ship for him.

Satisfied that the remaining portion of ham would get him through the next thirty minutes, Sparky polished it off, finishing with a resounding slurp of water.

The first volley of fire from the *Murphy*'s plasma cannons once again brought the station's defensive weapons to life after taking a break. The station's targeting officer had finally realized he was doing nothing more than wasting energy and possibly overheating the laser and cannon cores.

The plan was straightforward. The *Murphy*, as it was currently doing, would launch several distraction volleys of *Hey, honey, I'm home* cannon fire while releasing a small contingent of automated fighters and scavengers.

Sparky would then continue to power the *Scarecrow*'s front deflector shields until they had reached the initial two-mile buffer zone; from there, he would then board, through some mysterious means yet to be explained, the single fighter hugging the rear thrusters of the ship and make his way back while the warhead was offloaded under full thrust.

It didn't matter if it was dumped or not. Once inside the station's substructure, the warhead would be set on a timer and blow after five minutes. This would give Sparky and the *Murphy* enough time to get to a safe distance.

The main threat they were up against was time. They didn't want to waste any time after having rung the dinner bell, and the longer they stayed in the sector, the more likely a nosy Alurian star cruiser would show up. If momma bear was to come home and find the *Murphy* tucked neatly in its sector, things would not be as simple as their prior engagement.

If the timeline held, which it never did, as soon as the warhead detonated, the *Murphy* would be able to open a gate back to Asher. The entire operation would take less than ten minutes, including the detonation timer.

Sparky jumped back in the captain's chair and glanced at the generic screen split down the middle showing a view of the front of the ship and one of the *Murphy*'s crowded bridge. Everyone from Jen to Bellman stood in the back of the room, watching the main viewscreen.

Becket was doing what first sergeants do best in the drop bay with the platoons, helping the other Rangers cope with the loss of not only one of their leaders but also a handful of other brothers and sisters. When Card, Grantham, and the others found out about Dasher and the fact that the *Murphy* was within firing range of the station, there was a damn-near mutiny in the drop bay. They wanted vengeance, violence-driven rage that would only be satisfied with blood. Alurian blood.

The only thing preventing this was Becket's crushing presence and fully detailed explanations that they were about to ram one of the largest thermal fission sub-nuclear decca warheads ever made directly up the ass of the Alurian armada waiting for its crews. Ships the Alurian crews would never man. He followed this by also explaining how incredibly pissed they were going to be when they arrived.

It was official: Sparky was one of the crew and, with that, would need to be officially initiated at some point. The thought dropped as the station let loose everything that was not attached to its surface and was designed for violence in their general direction.

As planned, the laser fire bounced off the *Scarecrow*, dissipating before reaching the *Murphy*. The plasma cannons, on the other hand, were getting close, too close, to the *Scarecrow*. The A team must have been woken up and been put in charge of the targeting systems.

CHAPTER 34

HOPE

Laser fire engulfed the *Scarecrow* in a concert of colorful flashes darting in all directions in a systematic sweeping pattern. Dailey, against his better judgement, had inched the *Murphy* close enough to land several effective hits on the station's main targeting arrays.

Sparky, much to his own surprise, had put himself into full-on super charger mode, scrambling the view the *Murphy* had of the bridge, also making the system-status meters bounce like a drunk yo-yo. An odd calm had taken over the determined dog, and the chart Pearl put together now flashed on the screen.

Half there; it had only taken one stressful minute to reach the halfway mark. Just as Sparky lost interest in the chart, the *Scarecrow* rocked, followed by a shudder reaching its captain's very bones. Screeching metal and more blinky red lights that meant absolutely nothing to the hound flickered.

The HAM, while ensuring the energy Sparky was pouring into the ship was being managed and applied to the proper system, was also working to figure out just how bad of a situation they were in.

"What's happened?" Dailey asked as a red flashing light blinked on the same chart in front of them.

Kline responded quickly. "It appears the *Scarecrow* took a direct hit from a plasma cannon. A one-in-a-million shot, considering their target computers are down. They must be manually firing them."

"King, can you get a signal through?"

King turned, shaking his head. They would not be talking with Sparky in the foreseeable future, as the plan as always was starting to unravel.

"The *Scarecrow* is almost at a dead standstill," Pearl added quickly.

Nervous faces and tight fists were in no short supply, as no one on the bridge had let out a breath over the last two minutes. The ship needed to start moving again before any more shots from the station's plasma cannons hit their intended target.

Sparky, for the first time, started questioning his decision, quickly realizing that the blast had taken out one of the ship's power modules. The HAM spoke for the first time in its activated existence.

"With the current status of the ship's power modules, our rate of travel will be cut in half," the HAM stated flatly, with absolutely none of the personality Albert had.

Sparky set his jaw, pulling in his long tongue in an all-out effort to keep his mighty ship moving and on task. The one part actually fully working was two of the automated fighters, and several of the scavengers were still in various stages of operation. As planned, the fighter tucked behind the ship was also still in working order.

With a huff of effort from Sparky, the *Scarecrow* lurched back into motion while Sparky pushed every bit of essence he had into the now crackling bridge. The harnessing cage built around the captain's chair was starting to smoke from the sheer amount of power the Alurian war hound was now putting off.

"Sir! He's moving again!" Kline yelled as Dailey lightened his grip on the status panel.

"Hey, everyone, thought I would mention a few things," Albert cut in. "I was able to pull a few readings from the HAM, and, well... it appears that there has been a change of plans on board. That blast took out one of the ship's power modules. Sparky has chosen to guide the ship the rest of the way in. It was either the thrusters or the deflector shields. If Sparky stays on board, then he should be able to keep both of them operational."

By the time Dailey computed the statement, the *Scarecrow* was already entering the station's outer structure, out of the plasma cannons' effective range. Things were moving fast, too fast.

"Sir, we are one minute away from the gate drive being fully charged. We will have to activate it and leave within the next three minutes to be outside the blast radius. There is still enough time for the attack fighter to get back. On full power, it will only take a few seconds."

The usually preoccupied Alurian targeting officer raged on the control panel as several less-than-average ship engineers ran the weapon systems by simply pressing firing controls as quickly as possible.

Senior Station Officer Flaxan shrieked as the shields of the ship they had been so desperately trying to destroy appeared to hold after he himself had landed a direct shot with the station's main plasma cannons. "Aghhh!"

Even though the station was as large as a moon, the majority of the construction was done by a swarm of automated machines of war. The Alurian engineers on board were mostly there in case something went wrong or a design change was sent down by the Alurian High Command.

Supreme Commander Zara Kell, the now-deceased leader of the station, had instructed the rest of his staff not to request support or send a status report to High Command until they had handled the issue at hand. Pride and pride alone had driven the man to believe he could handle the situation. That, and he would likely be relieved if High Command found out how much of a shit show the station's security had become, allowing the current attack to even occur.

Neither he nor the remainder of his command staff expected the odd-yet-lethal combination of one of their own cargo ships being led by an Alurian war hound, which was about to detonate a massive, world-killing bomb directly in the middle of their operation, effectively destroying an entire armada's worth of ships.

"Focus fire on the secondary ships!" Flaxan barked. The message was lost on all but one of the supporting staff.

After the press of a few sensor buttons, a young Alurian woman who maintained the system huffed back. "They seem to be automated drones. Several of them are too small for our sensors to lock on to. The cargo vessel has moved out of our plasma cannons' terminal range."

"Then destroy the ones you can. Prepare to be boarded." Flaxan exhaled over the station's comms systems. Little did the Alurian know he, like his former commander, had read the situation wrong.

In reality, all that meant was to send the ground-security forces to critical infrastructure areas. This included roughly a company's worth of security forces scattered throughout the entire station. It would take hours for them all to regroup and concentrate in a single area.

Another, gruffer engineer also spoke up directly after the order was given by Flaxan. "Command is asking our status. They know we lost the other destroyers."

This was bad news, news that would no longer be swept under the rug. Flaxan paused, knowing of the only other secondary protocol available. "Redirect. Activate order thirteen."

The crew of the bridge, while desperate, all hesitated. "NOW!" he commanded while they turned back to their stations just as the familiar cargo ship, instead of maneuvering toward the docking bay, turned toward the offloading station.

Order thirteen was a preprogrammed protocol that would basically shut down the station's construction efforts and redirect all the automated systems to combat mode. This would mean hundreds if not thousands of droids would drop their tools and, after going to their designated charging stations, retool with weapons.

Flaxan left his station to the sounds of metal machines grinding, and more alarms than he could compute started ringing with the activation of the construction station's final-stand protocol activated.

"The cargo ship has stopped again in front of the offloading bay!" The young Alurian woman's voice again echoed through the chaos of alarms. Flaxan was so frazzled, he had forgotten the override codes to shut them off.

The last thing Flaxan saw was the ship turning into the payload drop bay. The man was puzzled by the action, but it finally dawned on him as the first swarm of automated construction bots exploded from the station's substructure.

Flaxan had never activated order thirteen, and in reality, had no clue what it involved. The station's system, much like the AI on board the *Asher*, had taken control of the station. The station then decided it needed to focus on the largest viable threat to its existence, the *Murphy*.

CHAPTER 35

SECONDS

Dailey leaned forward. "Sparky!" he again barked over the comm; nothing but static greeted him. "Albert, tell me what's going on."

"The warhead is set to detonate in one hundred and twenty seconds, or two minutes. There is also a massive swarm of really pissed-off unionized worker drones heading our way. Oh, and I have lost all communications with the *Scarecrow*, the HAM, and all of the other secondary ships."

"Dammit!" Dailey barked. The rest of the bridge's occupants joined his mood.

"Can't we just pause the detonation?" Jen asked, ready to head down to leave for the drop bay and go personally retrieve Sparky if need be.

"No," Dailey replied. "The routine to active the warhead started a few minutes ago. It's not reversible."

"Someone read the instruction manual, congratulations," Albert started. "The gate drive is charged. I am activating the gate portal."

Frustrated, Dailey refocused on the task at hand. There were always casualties in war. The greater good and all that bullshit they spoon-fed new recruits that were often used as front-line fodder.

Frustrated, Dailey jumped up from the con, striding to the forward viewport.

In the distance, the station looked very much like a moon. Reflective, round, and unassuming. Unassuming, that is, until one focused on not only the shower of laser fire cutting through space but the odd formation of several small glowing objects appearing out of the rough edges of the station.

"What am I looking at?" Dailey exclaimed.

"Big problem. Might be a hundred or possibly a thousand armed constructo droids heading directly for us with a standing order to disassemble. No disassemble!" Albert immediately responded, and even Dailey had to dig deep to pick up on the reference.

With the full understanding that Sparky's fate had been sealed, Dailey turned to Pearl standing pensively at the navigation station. "Turn about. As soon as the gate is fully functional, proceed."

Pearl nodded as the mood sobered. It was still shocking how much Sparky had grown on the team. Truth be told, it was a mix of people finally registering the current situation, including several close relationships some of the bridge's crew had with Dasher, not to mention the others lost in the initial battle.

"Gate is active and stable; we have several incoming bogies," Albert stated matter-of-factly. Kline confirmed.

"It's going to be close, sir. Our leading long-range lasers are already firing on the formation. Detonation counter confirmed."

On the main viewscreen, the countdown timer was slowly bleeding out to a short forty-five-second countdown. The *Murphy* was poised on the very edge of the gate, ready to push through as soon as detonation was confirmed.

Fortunately for the *Murphy*, the entire coordinated maneuver would be tracked and executed under the control of Albert. Even Pearl was hesitant to cut it that close, which she let be publicly known.

"Thirty seconds," Albert noted. Pearl and Dailey glanced at each other while the ship started to pull itself into the gate.

The familiar, once nerve-racking vibration throughout the ship was now a welcomed distraction, when a proximity alert sounded just as the initial brilliant light of the warhead detonating whited out the viewscreens.

Luckily for Dailey, he had indeed also listened in one of the dozens of classes he had had to attend at the academy about the stages of such a massive device detonating. Unlike a normal nuclear explosion, this turbocharged version had a fourth phase tucked neatly between the initial immediate burst of radioactive energy and the second blast wave everyone was mostly familiar with.

This was simply referred to as the suck phase, the pun of jokes and gags alike for years until the instructor visualized the sheer carnage the device was capable of. Upon the initial detonation and burst of neutrons and gamma rays, the additional phase was the warhead sucking back in the initial release of energy, allowing it to multiply in strength with the pull and ferocity of a black hole.

From there, the energy would be sent through another chain reaction and released like a coiled spring at a magnitude considered one hundred times the strength of the initial blast. The intent of the device was to deter and also destroy any future alien threats swiftly, without any further debate.

Voices grumbled nervously as Kline spoke up. "We have several small targets coming in hot, sir. The stern shields are holding. We may pull some through."

"Twenty seconds," Albert announced.

"We will address them when we can. In case you all don't know, we are in the suck. The package was delivered, and we are clear to go," Dailey stated bluntly, his focus on the razor-thin margin of error flashing on the main display.

"Fifteen seconds. Note most the targets are too small to structurally hold through the initial pull of the gate," Albert stated, concluding his countdown.

"Five, four, three, two… We are through the gate. The gate is closed. One," Albert drawled out. "Okay, we can all go back to our regularly scheduled programs and restroom patterns."

Dailey, not wanting to after everything they had just been though, not to mention lost souls, let a light grin perk the end of his mouth. The hole he had almost chewed on the inside of his cheek was glad for the break.

"Albert, the soldiers, space sailors, and air crew on board this ship don't understand that regularly scheduled program bit. You need to fast-forward the tape a century or two.

"Kline, what's the status of the enemy targets?" Dailey followed calmly as the bridge remained whisper quiet.

"Well, I can't tell. None of the ship's outside sensors work when we are in whatever this is."

Albert chimed in, "What he meant to say is the temporal field we are passing through, wormhole, or whatever you want to call it, is here and not here at the same time. A ship hovering two inches off the deck might as well be across the galaxy. Once we arrive at our destination, they will also arrive, albeit maybe in another system, or intermingled with our own ship's substructure. Who knows. It's that whole magic thing."

"Yeah, that," Kline added at the end with a goofy smile.

"That reminds me. Albert, you came through here. I know we have to pick up the pieces on our end, but that doesn't change the fact that you likely just saved human as well as Solarian kind. I do, however, need to remove you from the main system once we get back."

"No hard feelings. I kinda need a break anyways. There is a box set of a show called *Mushy* from Solaria that I am going to rip through. The drama, I hear, is otherworldly."

Pearl let out a short, snorting laugh. "Please let us know how that goes for you." She followed this with a shrug, not giving it away.

Mushy was the Solarian version of a teenage angsty show that revolved around a group of young Solarian women discovering themselves as they left home for their version of college. It was also generally if not primarily watched by the teenage female population of the planet mostly interested in Fon, the heartthrob of the series. Either way, it would give Pearl something to talk about with the AI, which would mostly include laughing at his likely overanalysis of the series.

Dailey reflected for a few moments before keying up the ship's intercom. "All hands, this is your commander, Captain—" He quickly corrected himself. "Colonel Dailey."

"As of twenty-three hundred Earth time, our mission was successfully completed. The target has been destroyed. Everyone on board has shown great courage and will be respected and treated as such for years to come." He paused, taking a breath. "I know we lost some of our fellow crew members. We will take the proper time to relay this information to their families and take appropriate action to honor the souls lost and ensure they rest on home soil."

Dailey hadn't thought through his next step, to be fair, as he had assumed they would likely not be coming back. Without Albert's help, he was fully aware the mission would have ended before it likely even began. After a longer-than-needed pause, he started back.

"We will be going back to Asher and working with the inhabitants of the planet until we get further guidance from Fleet command. In the meantime, I need everyone to prepare the ship for suborbital operations. We are taking the *Murphy* to the surface of Asher."

He was sure Becket and the others, while supporting his decision, were likely surprised by the lack of consultation on this decision. In all fairness, this was the most logical course of action after everything they had encountered.

The bridge door opened as Dailey concluded his speech. Bellman stood looking frazzled, clearly having come from the destroyed drop bay.

"Any word on Sparky?" the man asked. He was breaking the rules. No one was supposed to ask that question out loud, as far as the bridge's crew were concerned.

"No," Dailey replied, pressing a few buttons on the console and pulling up the final footage before the warhead detonated. "A few of the enemy constructo mechs, or whatever the hell they are, might have been pulled through, but we have no trace of the *Scarecrow* nor the attached fighter. I'm afraid he sacrificed himself."

Bellman's already-drooping frown found a way to physically drop another few centimeters. "I'll be in the drop bay." The man left as quickly as he'd entered the bridge.

Albert took this time to chime back in. "Thought you might like to know I got all sorts of data this time around. Mainly from the constructo mechs as they got within targeting distance. I'm still sorting through it, but man… we got a lot to talk about with HQ."

Confused but not surprised by the statement, Dailey stood up and walked toward his quarters. Jen, still standing in the back of the bridge, sneaked out behind him.

"What is it, Lieutenant Brax," Dailey asked, stopping in front of his quarters. On the way from the bridge, he had not turned once to acknowledge Jen.

"That was the most amazing thing I've ever been part of or seen," she stated. Dailey paused, not opening his door.

"Get used to it."

"Get used to what?" she asked, tilting her head slightly.

"Losing people, saving the world. Then getting patted on the back like you're a hero, while the real heroes are no longer with us."

Without saying a word, she pushed herself up, kissing Dailey while pulling him into her, not giving the situation any room for interpretation. Dailey let his shoulders drop, the tension of the day slowly draining from his body. He wanted, no, needed this, and at the same time would hate himself for it later.

After another minute of heavy breathing, the two separated as if they had been attached for hours. Red, flushed cheeks and two grins told each of the participating parties in the kiss that it was not only appreciated but would need further exploration.

Dailey let out a breath, and hardened determination took back over the goofy expression that Jen had all but momentarily witnessed. Becket's voice came over Dailey's personal communicator.

"Sir. Everything's secure in the drop bay for now. Where you at?" Becket asked, and Jen nodded, taking a step back.

"See you around. It's a small ship and all," Jen prodded, then turned on her heel and walked away, every curve on the woman's body moving to a rhythm Dailey was now keenly aware of.

As soon as Jen was in the lift, Albert spoke up. "I totally saw you two snogging. Are you going to make babies now? You know… grow the species?"

"No. And stop doing that. I can't wait to unplug you. Maybe this time, I'll plug you into a vacuum cleaner. That would suck, wouldn't it?"

Albert paused, trying to figure out if he had been the punch line for a joke or just how bad of a threat this truly was. In reality, it would take the AI several days to get the punch line, having spent too much time on Solarian humor to pick up on humankind's fast wit.

CHAPTER 36

THE HAM JAM

Are you sure?" Pearl asked as Kline leaned over the targeting computer. Navigation Officer Brick, who had been left planetside, was sitting beside Specialist Kline, about to relieve him from watch duty.

As of two weeks before, the *Murphy* had landed on Asher's surface in an area close to Arcadia, the city where Dax and Vax were from. After being reunited and several hours of hearing the tale, Dax had finally regained enough color on his face to realize they had been living a lie their entire lives. Something that Dailey and the others were also starting to suspect was on the menu for them as well.

From there, the two pulled together the city's main-level group's most senior members. This was neither a fast nor fluid process; the conversations were still ongoing about the future of the city and its occupants. The fact that no work had been initiated or completed over the same amount of time was enough to keep the talks going.

The mostly automated system that had been running the city had been pulled offline, leaving people to basically sit in their homes and wait. This didn't even account for the status of the other cities on the planet's surface. Albert had been put in charge of pulling data from the other settlements and helping them come up with a game plan that, as of now, was still nothing more than a guess.

They were so spread out. Arcadia was the only population that was able to see the *Murphy* land. That and various other elements that had set up camp outside of the city. These people were all coming to see what was going on.

Pearl pulled up the fast-moving ship now pinging the radar sensor screen. "Any signs of life on board?"

"Can't tell. The ship's got some kind of deflector shield up. It doesn't look like it's targeting us. At least, not with any weapon systems," Kline added while Brick scooted closer. The shift change would have to wait.

Knowing Kline had already tried to contact the ship, Pearl called both Albert and Dailey over the comms. "We have something we can't figure out incoming. Estimated ETA five mikes."

Within three minutes, Dailey was standing on the bridge in a sweat-covered T-shirt. "Albert, take a break from that data download. You seeing this?"

Albert, clearly shifting gears, took only a few seconds to finally respond. "Yes, seems like… seems like one of those Alurian constructo mechs."

"Shit," Dailey huffed, then walked over to the weapon console. "I thought this would last longer."

"No, wait a moment… computing here. Give an AI guy some room to stretch and breathe." The phrase about stretching was from the conclusion of *Mushy*, the show Albert had finally finished. In the end, Fon hadn't fallen in love with his soulmate, not to mention viewer favorite, and instead went with an off-worlder, something that had devastated its teenage viewing audience. On Solaria, this was a common breakup precursor.

"It's… It's…" Albert drawled out as he finally got to the point. "Shut down our dampening field. Let them know we are here. It's the HAM!"

"The HAM, as in the AI from the *Scarecrow*?" Dailey quickly asked as Albert started directing Kline on what to do.

"Oh, they're coming in hot. Once they have a lock on us, I should be able to take control," Albert started, sounding like a kid trying to pull two stuck pieces of Lego apart. Buildings at the time were often constructed using massive blocks nearly identical to the still-popular children's toy.

"Is Sparky on board?" Dailey barked, standing up as an immediate layer of sweat formed in his palms. He was more nervous than when flying into a firefight that he had no chance of coming out of.

"I don't know, but the HAM and I have shaken hands and…"

"And what!" The entire on shift crew barked.

"And I have control of their jump thrusters. Old, nasty Alurian tech. This thing wasn't meant to ever fly away from that station, but here we are, kiddos. It will be crash—I mean, be landing directly outside of the port bow."

Dailey blurred off the bridge, calling Becket and Bellman. He sounded winded but got the general message across. "Sparky, constructo bot… landing."

Within the last few minutes, the heavily awkward constructo mech, now billowing black smoke, was making its moderately slowed approach to the ground as the thrusters under the mech's feet snapped and popped as if reaching for more fuel. This was the actual case, as Albert had diverted all the mech's reserves to powering its thrusters.

After a bone-jarring thump into the soft ground, the hissing, steaming exterior of the mech was now glistening in the sun. "Still too hot to touch," Albert came over the comms as one of the Nova Rangers flew from the drop bay in full armor, ripping the access panel off its hinges.

"He's in here. Get help!" the Ranger exclaimed as the mood shifted. Within minutes, Franklin and several naval Fleet engineers joined the group, pulling Sparky out with a lift system and brace to avoid shifting him around too much.

Sparky lay still as they transferred him to a small flatbed hovercart and took off toward the ground base. His armor appeared to be in spaceflight mode, the helmet and other secondary shields covering his entire body.

Dailey and the usual round of suspects paced the floor of the main command area the stay-behind group had set up in the Gulch. The structure had an odd air of permanence that surprised Dailey when they arrived. From what he could tell, several of the *Brightstar*'s holdovers were planning on making this home.

Much to their surprise, Senior Chief Thron walked out of the room. He must have gotten there before the others. Thron quickly explained as best he could with a straight face.

"Albert contacted me and told me that Sparky's last request was a plate of ham. I believe the situation might be a little inflated, but I think we are about to run out of ham."

"Yeah, those two are always scheming," Dailey replied as Franklin opened the door.

"The patient will see you now." She grinned, and the group moved in unison, almost getting stuck in the door to the medical bay.

While they were glad to finally see the Alurian war hound, even if lying on his side under a layer of heated blankets, it was a shock to see his overall condition. Several patches of fur were missing, replaced by spots of lightly burnt skin. When he saw Dailey and the others, Sparky's tail started lightly thumping the table.

"No petting, and he is going to be here till he fully heals. From what we can tell, when he pushed out all his energy, it almost took him out. Albert was translating, so some of this might be suspect, but Sparky did that thing he does, as you put it, and hitched a ride with the remaining gas he had in his tank. He also took the AI system with him, which was not recoverable. Albert seemed genuinely upset about that," Franklin informed the group as Albert cut in.

"I don't have eyes to cry, so not too sure how you came to that conclusion."

Franklin grinned. "You tried to convince me to download what was left of the HAM's system into your droid, which is almost done. When I told you no, you threatened to tell on me. What for, again? Oh, and I thought I heard you playing light music for it before it finally discharged," Franklin prodded, knowing that Albert had been upset over the AI as well as his friend.

"All right, I get the point. Sparky, how you feeling?" Dailey asked. Sparky's tongue flopped out of his mouth and he chuffed.

"Tired, but ham will make it better."

"I bet it will," Dailey replied as Albert translated the conversation for the group. "Thank you. You're a brave member of this crew, and with that, we have something for you."

Becket stepped forward, walking over to Sparky's armor propped against the wall, smacking a Viper Company insignia on the shoulder plates. "Welcome aboard," Becket proclaimed as Sparky grinned.

While the moment was a joyful reunion, Sparky still needed several days, if not weeks, to recover. Franklin was leaving out several details about his condition under the blanket, but nonetheless the Alurian war hound would make a full recovery.

That night, the crew celebrated and partied. They celebrated their lost, and they celebrated their brave. Stories were exchanged about everyone's take on the battle and how they caught the biggest fish. In the end, the very end, Sparky had caught the biggest fish of them all.

Becket dropped down in the low-lying chair next to Dailey, who had spent the last ten minutes smiling at Jen as she and the other Space Force pilots sang their branch's fight song.

"What's next?" Becket asked, handing him an honest-to-god beer-style beverage grown and brewed on the planet. "Oh, yeah, that stuff will make a man of you, so take it easy."

Dailey took it down in one fluid gulp, letting out a belch and getting a few chuckling glances from the other members of the crew. "Well, we haven't been able to reach the senator or Fleet headquarters yet. I talked with Albert about gating back to Earth."

"And?" Becket followed up. Dailey smiled.

"He said, 'Okey dokey.' Added something about going to see where that show *Mushy* was filmed first, then rattled off a bunch of things we need to do along the way. Long story short, it will be another month before we are fully repaired and charged and he is complete with the other suggested modifications on the *Murphy*."

Becket looked shocked at the suggestion, also knowing they had been going back and forth, gathering remaining parts from the destroyers and the *Brightstar* still floating in space. "That's going to turn some heads, just showing up like that."

Leaning back, Dailey pulled out his own personal flask and took a long pull. "Yeah, I think it's about time to turn some heads."

Music trailed off into the night as the party continued into the early morning. With all the stories told and the rumor now being spread that they were possibly heading back to Earth, the crew of the *Murphy* relaxed for the first time in what felt like an eternity.

EPILOGUE

Deck of the Ateris Mining Syndicate's moon base. General Ran and Administrator Derrisa Monvet.

"It appears mining-rights premiums just went up in our system. Ateris is demanding additional resources and compensation for the loss of operations," Derrisa proclaimed as Ran stood overlooking the large monitor in front of him showing Asher.

The man had been eerily calm when he found out the USF *Murphy* had returned from its one-way trip. More to the point, that Colonel Ben Dailey was likely still alive.

"Don't fool yourself, Derrisa. The Alurians will see this as something else. While good for us, it will also bring unwanted attention to our doorstep. They will eventually find out what happened. The fact that the *Murphy* was able to gate in and out itself is a problem."

She quickly cut him off, hardening her voice. "You knew the ship could create a gate. You used it to warn the Alurians."

"No, I said 'In the event a gate opened'. We are in a good place here, but we need to be careful of our next move," Ran hissed out. Truth be told, he was highly agitated at the fact that the Alurians and the Syndicate alike had little to no regard for his life.

"And that would be what? Wait until we are provided with more resources for our system and sectors? Take those resources and expand our reach? Maybe take over another, less-supported system?"

"You are ambitious, and I appreciate that. Yes, to a point. But for now, we need to figure out a way to deal with the little problem of Colonel Dailey and his ship. That is a wild card we cannot afford to have played."

Derrisa, not following the analogy, raised an eyebrow as Ran clarified. "He is a loose cannon capable of getting in our way."

With that explanation, Derrisa was satisfied with the direction things needed to go, but just then, a video feed erupted on the massive screen. A man with jet-black, overly manicured hair stared back at them with assertive eyes sitting above a pointed nose. This was Supreme Chancellor Kyle Bowman, also known in many political circles.

The man was clearly on a ship, as the backdrop of space hung behind him like a portrait. "The Alurians are furious over the total destruction of their third armada. It was set to go active in two solar years. They have proposed to shift significant funding to your system and are asking to double our effort in mining the Tritickle system. They will be pivoting from their current requirements."

This was the best news the two had heard in weeks, if not months. Not only would they be abandoning mining operations on Asher, giving them an opportunity to exploit the planet for their own gain, the Alurians were starting from scratch, and that meant metals from the Tritickle system's overabundance of high-grade ship-building metals, the basic building blocks of any starship.

For several hundreds of years, the Tritickle system had been mined to start up the operation; all the additional resources needed were from other systems or sectors. But for now, they would be reinvesting in the building blocks of their ships, resetting the clock. This also included added security.

Ran cleared his throat and glanced at Derrisa. "Well, it's not like they don't have ten others to choose from coming online soon."

Derrisa, taking the cue, made the final commitment. In reality, she knew they didn't have a choice, but what they now had were additional resources and the ability to grow their sphere of influence, all while supporting both sides of a fight that they knew meant much more than humankind could possibly comprehend.

Earth Federation Headquarters, Fleet Administration building, Senator Deborah Powell's office.

"What do you mean, it just appeared?" Senator Powell exclaimed as several more warning alerts appeared on her console's viewscreen, ordering her to seek shelter.

"The *Murphy*, it just appeared out of thin air in orbit. They are trying to get ahold of you, but the systems locked down due to the trace readings of Alurian drives."

Before the senator could get out another word, Albert came over the office's intercom system. "Hello! People of Earth, may I have your attention please…"

"What the hell is this?" Powell responded, and Albert snickered.

"I always wanted to say that. Well, ever since I read that book about the galaxy. Anywho, I have a special someone that wants to chat."

Dailey's voice came over the radio, slightly calming Senator's Powell's nerves.

"Senator. We need to talk. In person. I'll send out a message to the Fleet so everyone can calm down."

Senator Powell slumped back in her chair, having been on full alert. "This better be good, Dailey. Never mind; this is already going to be a mess. Yes, I'll get the security forces to stand down. We do need to talk, more than you know."

ACKNOWLEDGMENTS

First and foremost, I'd like to thank everyone that's joined me on this ride. I have been overwhelmed by the support and worldwide acceptance of my writing. From the fans who dig into my worlds, to the apparent wizard, not to mention Bigfoot, that often sends me emails, your support is what keeps me putting words on paper, or the computer… You get the drift.

To my family, wife, and two sons: this book is part of my legacy to you. When I am but a memory in time, you will always be able to pick this book up and remember what a nerd I really was and, well, still am… and will probably be some more.

This book is dedicated to all the brave men and women I served with, and in some cases lost in dire times of hardship, and the friendships also shared.

Halfway down the trail to Hell
In a shady meadow green are the Souls of all dead troopers camped.
See you at the Fiddler's Green.

ABOUT THE AUTHOR

Justin S. Leslie is a fervent sci-fi and urban fantasy fan, not to mention bestselling author.

When he isn't writing, playing music, or spending time with his family, he can be found at his Doctors Inlet home, immersed in his latest project or a well-made cocktail.

The sometimes-fearless author is also a retired, highly decorated army major who has completed two combat tours in Afghanistan. Justin has focused on building his own worlds to share with readers, as well as enjoying ones created by fellow authors.

He also holds an MBA from the University of Maryland and a bachelor's from Maryville College but still gives spellcheck and editors alike a run for their money.